PRAISE FOR
WILDERNESS OF TIGERS, A NOVEL OF SAIGON

"Author Colonel Bruce Arnold writes in a swift moving film-worthy style, highlighted by dialogue of Elmore Leonard quality. This is the Vietnam War as it really was, with all the hardship, deaths, intrigue, danger and romance laid out with page-turning authenticity. Bruce is at his best in pointing out the perverse military/political contradictions of the conflict. From personal experience, he illuminates fighting-man's pervasive loyalty to the foot soldier mired in jungle in sharp contrast to the mindless betrayal from above that extended directly to the Oval Office. This authoritative novel comes at exactly the right moment, when the United States seems to be waking up to the fact that the Americans who fought the war in Vietnam were heroes who deserved adulation rather than reproach. Get it, and then watch the inevitable movie into which it will be made."

—Walter Boyne author of
The Wild Blue and *Silver Wings*

"For everyone eager to explore the dark heart of the Vietnam War as it happened in the streets of Saigon, take a break from dry accounts of battle statistics and dive into the belly of the beast. *Wilderness of Tigers* takes you into the steamy world of emotions and intrigue that drives all human behavior and, when driven by war, who really behaves well?"

—Christina Olds author of
Fighter Pilot: The Memoirs of Legendary Ace Robin Olds

Col. W. Bruce Arnold, USAF created *Wilderness of Tigers* after serving in Vietnam 1967–68 as the chief of DARPA's Research and Development Field Unit Vietnam, based in Saigon. Bruce Arnold was a 1943 West Point Graduate and served in World War II, the Korean Occupation as well as the Vietnam War. After a singular military career ranging from riding as a trooper in George Patton's horse cavalry to ballistic missiles, Col. Arnold enjoyed a rich, full life, that included starting a winery in Sonoma, California with his son Robert and wife Barbara. He passed away in 1992.

This photo was taken in Saigon in 1968.

Robert Bruce Arnold owns and operates a winery in Sonoma, California. Like his father, Bruce Arnold, Robert grew up as a military brat in many places coast-to-coast and overseas. His background includes starting a successful system house in the early desktop computer industry, educational filmmaking, and radio. He worked on Capital Hill on both the House and Senate sides and, for a summer, there as an elevator operator. Robert holds degrees in archaeology, and in journalism.

This photo was taken in Maryland in 1968.

WILDERNESS OF TIGERS

A NOVEL OF SAIGON

W. Bruce Arnold
with Robert Bruce Arnold

Chandelle
The Spirit of Flight

PUBLISHING

Published by Chandelle Publishing
Chandelle of Sonoma Inc.
PO Box 2167, Glen Ellen, California 95442, USA

However, Saigon was a real place. For now, it hides behind the modern mask of Ho Chi Minh City. And the Vietnam War was very, very real ...

Wilderness of Tigers, A Novel of Saigon
A Chandelle Book, published by arrangement with the authors

For information contact: Chandelle Publishing
a division of Chandelle of Sonoma Inc.,
PO Box 2167, Glen Ellen, California 95442, USA
www.wilderness-of-tigers.com

ISBN: 978-0-9911987-1-9 – Print Edition
ISBN: 978-0-9911987-0-2 – Electronic Edition

Book design by Maureen Cutajar
www.gopublished.com

CHANDELLE SPIRIT OF FLIGHT LOGO
is a registered trademark of Chandelle of Sonoma Inc.

For Pop:
One long journey is over and another now begins.
Thanks for being the best Dad ever.
I love you, Rob

"And for those who did survive
And came back home alive ..."
The Last Full Measure of Devotion
Lyrics by Alan "Buz" Cohan

For all of them it was a
Wilderness of Tigers

AUTHOR'S NOTE

The time and place of this story, Saigon 1967-1968, is fast fading into distant history.

For that reason, I have added several maps, a list of characters, places, organizations, and things, as well as other material to aid the reader.

Warning: This book is not for sensitive readers. It contains rough language, explicit sex, strong violence, and the attitudes of a time before political correctness.

This story is about people in a time of war, in a faraway place, now long ago.

CONTENTS

PEOPLE – ORGANIZATIONS – PLACES – THINGS & TERMS xi

MAP OF VIETNAM 1967-1968 xvi

DETAIL MAP OF SAIGON 1967-1968 xvii

PROLOGUE – APRIL 1967 1

CHAPTER I – MAY 1967 13

CHAPTER II – JUNE 39

CHAPTER III – JULY 91

CHAPTER IV – AUGUST 173

CHAPTER V – SEPTEMBER 199

CHAPTER VI – OCTOBER 221

CHAPTER VII – NOVEMBER 269

CHAPTER VIII – DECEMBER 291

CHAPTER IX – JANUARY 1968 333

CHAPTER X – FEBRUARY 373

CHAPTER XI – MARCH 409

CHAPTER XII – APRIL 425

CHAPTER XIII – MAY 441

EPILOGUE 477

AFTERWORD 491

APPENDIX ONE 495

APPENDIX TWO 497

APPENDIX THREE 501

PEOPLE – ORGANIZATIONS – PLACES – THINGS & TERMS

PEOPLE
THE AMERICANS

BLACKSTONE, Staff Sergeant tour escort at Trong Thoi
MARK BUCKLEY, Lieutenant Colonel (LTC), US Army
PETER CHARLES, Friend and associate of Brandy Masters
POLI DE SALLE, Professor of political science
CYRUS NED GREEN, US Army deserter and painter, a.k.a. "Ned" or "Cy"
JANET HOLDEN, PhD, Anthropology, wife of Ted Holden
TED HOLDEN, PhD, Anthropology, husband of Janet Holden
BRANDY MASTERS, free-lance entertainer
UNCLE JOE MASTERS, US senator and Brandy's uncle
MEAD, Master Sergeant, US Army
DAVE MURPHY, Seaman, US Navy, friend of Red Neddo
RED NEDDO, Sergeant First Class, US Army, friend of Dave Murphy
NEWELL OSBORN, Deputy Ambassador for Revolutionary Development
BILL SCOTT, Major (MAJ), US Army, an assistant to Ambassador Osborne
JIM TEAGUE, US Advisor, Chau Doc Province
REVEREND FRED WHITE, missionary located at Ban Me Thuot
SALLY WHITE, Fred White's wife
WESTY, General William Westmoreland, commander of MACV
BUNKER, US Ambassador to GVN, Elsworth Bunker

THE VIETNAMESE

ÔNG – "gentleman" or "sir," a sign of respect
CÔ – "miss," a title of respect for a young woman

AHN, assistant to Duat

BA THOA, madam of "The 92"

BU, professor, Saigon University, and father of Mai Lei

DUAT, Chinese-Vietnamese, a Hoa, descendant of Chinese Mandarins, ruler of the Saigon black market and underground

HIEU, cyclo operator, Tu Do Street, Saigon

HO, Major, Army of Republic of Vietnam (ARVN), commander of Vietnamese forces at Trong Thoi

HUE, artist, brother of Kam

KAM, sister of Hue, art kiosk operator, Saigon

MADAME KY, wife of South Vietnam's elected vice president, Nguyen Kao Ky

MAI LEI, daughter of Bu

NGUYEN, cyclo operator, Tu Do Street, Saigon

OOOGG, female house servant, Saigon

PHUC, van driver, streets of Saigon

QUI, a Saigon fence for black-market goods, friend of Hue

LUU, prostitute, friend of Ned Green

SOO, male house servant, black marketer, Saigon

THI, French-Vietnamese ex-actress, an agent of Duat

TRA, Brig. General, North Vietnamese (NVA) Army, leader of the Spring Offensive

TRAI, small boat operator, Mekong

TRAN OU, Brig. General, North Vietnamese Army, field commander of TET Offensive

THE KOREANS

KIM, Corporal, Korean Army, Colonel Uhm's driver

UHM, Colonel, Korean Army, Kim's boss

THE ORGANIZATIONS

THE BIG RED ONE — First Infantry Division, the US Army's most famous infantry division in many wars

SIXTY-NINTH SPECIAL ACTION GROUP (VC) — a terrorist organization operating in Saigon. Key members are Sam, Wok, and Tam.

716TH MILITARY POLICE BATTALION (US) – responsible for security of Saigon, Tan Son Nhut and Cholon

ARVN – Army of the Republic of Vietnam (South)

CHIEU-HOI – South Vietnam government's initiative to encourage Viet Cong defectors

CORDS – Civil Operations and Revolutionary Development Support, the US "Hearts and Minds" civil-military effort

GVN – Government of (South) Vietnam

HOA – ethnic Chinese minority living in Vietnam, controls 75% of the Saigon economy plus most of the black market

JUSPAO – Joint United States Public Affairs Office, provides information operations in SVN and public diplomacy

MACV – Military Assistance Command, Vietnam, US forces joint HQ, "Pentagon East"

NLF – National Liberation Front–South Vietnamese Communists. Political face of the VC, often used synonymously.

NVA – North Vietnamese Army

RESCUE PARTY – Organized to rescue Ted Holden. Members are Buckley, Ho, Nam, Bin, and Troc.

USAID – US Agency for International Development, administers US civilian foreign aid

VC – Viet Cong, guerilla forces in South Vietnam. Often synonymous with the NLF.

THE PLACES

"THE 92" – Saigon brothel said to be "the best"

BAN ME THUOT – Capital of province of same name. Site of Rev. White's missionary school

BAO TRE – Location of a secret underground VC headquarters complex

BUON HO – Locale of Janet Holden's original project

BUON SUT MGRA – Locale of Janet Holden's work with Rev. White

CAMBODIA – Neighboring country to Vietnam

CHOLON – Area of Saigon on the west bank of the Saigon River, heavily Chinese influenced, center of illegal drug and black-market activity, and a haven for US deserters

CON THO – Capital of the Mekong Delta area

TRONG THOI – Special Forces camp in the Delta under joint command of LTC Buckley and Major Ho

XA BUI – Name of Duat's organizational headquarters in Saigon

HAI PHONG – Main port in North Vietnam

THE HANGOUT – Saigon billet used by some MACV officers

HANOI – Capital of North Vietnam (NVN)

HUNG VU 'O' ONG – House of prostitution in Saigon, known as "The 92"

MEKONG DELTA – Large expanse of marsh and farm land at the eastern end of the Mekong River in SVN

NVN – North Vietnam

PX – Post Exchange–the US Military's general goods store

SAIGON – Capital of South Vietnam (SVN)

SVN – South Vietnam

VUNG TAU – Town in South Vietnam, popular R&R spot on the coast

THINGS & TERMS

.45 – US Colt automatic pistol, model 1911A, standard US sidearm

ANTI-INFILTRATION FLARES – Flares with parachutes that allow slow descent and provide illumination to spot enemy infiltrators

AK-47 – Russian-designed assault rifle, used by Communist forces worldwide

BA MUI BA, VN beer sometimes called "tiger piss," translates as the number thirty-three

BOO KOO – Slang for the French *beaucoup*, meaning "many"

BÁC SĨ – Vietnamese for doctor or medic

CAR-15 – Assault rifle with collapsible stock similar to an M-16, popular with US Special Forces and MACV officers

CHẢ GIÒ – Popular traditional Vietnamese dish: crispy minced pork roll

CYCLO – Bicycle-driven three-wheeled public transport

DUSTOFF – Code name for a medevac helicopter mission

GUNSHIP – Modified UH-1 or other helicopter with additional fire-power

F-100 FIGHTER – US Air Force jet fighter, widely used in VN for close air support

H.E. – High explosive. A standard aircraft delivered bomb.

HUEY – UH-1 helicopter, iconic transport of the US Army in VN

MEDEVAC – Any US transportation method used to remove wounded from battle

M-16 – Colt-manufactured assault rifle, standard US Army issue

MPC – Military payment certificate, US Military scrip, used in lieu of US currency in SVN at PXs and other operations

NAPALM – Aerial-dropped weapon of jellied gasoline

NUMBER ONE – Asian slang for "the best" (US influenced)

NUMBER TEN – Asian slang for "the worst" (US influenced)

P – Piastres–SVN money

R&R – American military slang for "rest and relaxation" leave

SALEM – American brand of menthol-flavored cigarettes, widely popular in Vietnam

SPOOKY – AC-47 special USAF version of World War II-era C-47 transported with side-mounted rapid-fire mini-guns for close support, nicknamed "Spooky" or "Puff the Magic Dragon," capable of tremendous firepower, based on the 1930s Douglas DC-3

TET – The major Vietnamese holiday

TRI-LAMBRETTA – Motor-driven tricycle transport

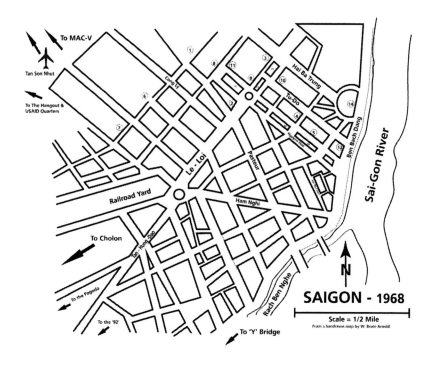

Map Legend

1 Cathedral
2 Hotel Rex
3 Thi's New Flat "Number 516"
4 Hue's Flat and Studio
5 Hotel Catinat
6 Palace
7 Circle Hipplque
8 City Hall
9 Hotel Continental
10 Hotel Caravelle
11 Air Vietnam Office
12 Hotel Majestic
13 Marine Statue
14 Tran Hung Dao Statue
15 Opera House
16 Park

Prologue

APRIL 1967

The first mortar round struck the north wall of the fort a few minutes after midnight. The delicate, dark silence was abruptly shattered into brilliant shards of light, like a thrown wine glass finding a black stone wall.

Mark Buckley barely had time to pull on his trousers, boots, and flak jacket before the second round struck. For a large man, he moved quickly, grabbing his helmet and then dashing from his room into the hall. The flash of the explosion illuminated his way. He turned left into the courtyard and, ahead, could see the trapdoor entrance to the underground command post in the floor. Mead, Buckley's First Sergeant, was waiting and holding it open for him. More rounds struck as Buckley jumped through and the hatch slammed behind him.

"Not bad, Colonel, considering the hour," noted the sergeant.

"Yeah, I'm getting better. Any position reports?" Mark asked as he sat down to lace up his jungle boots.

"Two and Four so far," replied Mead. "Think this is the big one?"

The thud of the mortar shells increased in tempo, their sharp sound muffled by the walls of the underground room.

Mark completed lacing his boots before he answered.

"Yeah, probably. This is the big one before the monsoon."

He walked across the small room and looked at the operations board which was, in actuality, a large-scale map of the fort and surrounding

1

terrain. The fort, known as Trong Thoi, was originally built by the French for their war. It consisted of a series of connected earthen-work positions, laid out roughly in a rectangular shape on a small peninsula in the Mekong River. The French had selected this position, about eight kilometers from the Cambodian border, to control river traffic entering and passing through South Vietnam.

The Americans found it ideal as well.

The twenty-foot-high north wall faced a swampy area, while the south and west walls rose thirty feet from the river's edge. These walls were taller and thicker in order to accommodate the barracks and offices built into their base. Only the eastern wall was rooted directly in the ground. Here, a large gate opened upon 800 yards of bare terrain. Beyond lay the fishing village of Trong Thoi, from which the fort took its name. Long insignificant, the town was now swollen with the shack accommodations of the families of the Vietnamese soldiers that manned the fort.

Mark's eyes, following the map, quickly covered the four main gun positions located at the corners of the walls, and the secondary positions, located above the gate in the east wall and above the sally port that penetrated the south wall for entrance from the river.

A young US Special Forces soldier, wearing earphones, marked on the acetate-covered map with a black grease pencil the approximate locations where the mortar shells were hitting. Another soldier checked off the gun positions on another chart as each commander contacted the command center with his report.

"Notice the pattern?" asked Mead, who had followed Mark to the map and was standing beside him.

"Yeah, the north wall's sure catching it."

"Think it's prep for an assault?"

"Yes, but not on that wall. It's a feint. We gotta watch the east through the town—or even the river side."

The soldier on the phones was busy taking reports from the firing positions. By this time, each one reported minor action—except position Three, which reported a much heavier attack with several casualties on the north wall. Across the map from Mark, a radio operator was reporting the status of the attack to the US Special Forces Headquarters at Can Tho.

"Notify all positions that I'm heading for position One to talk with Parker," Mark informed Mead as he adjusted his helmet. "Then I'll speak with Major Ho about the town. We probably will need air support before the night is over. So dial 'em up."

Mark mounted the ladder and vanished into the darkness, out of the range of the small, low-hanging lights. As he pushed open the trapdoor, the room filled for a moment with the thumping sounds of the mortar barrage. Then, with a deep thud, the heavy door shut and Buckley and the noise of battle were gone.

Outside, Mark lost no time in crossing the open courtyard into the safety of the sally port. He moved toward the outside end of this dark tunnel and, after giving the countersign to a Vietnamese soldier, paused at the edge of the opening that gave him a view to the south, away from the immediate battle.

Some twenty feet below him stretched the Mekong. He looked to his left and right along the quiet waters with only a brief glance at the large, square float moored below the sally port. This acted as both heliport and dock for the fort.

"Good *ebenning*," said an almost invisible Vietnamese soldier who grinned at Mark from the shadows.

"Good evening," Mark replied.

"Good *ebenning*," said another Vietnamese voice in the darkness, this time from an invisible position across from the sally port.

"Good evening," Mark responded to this other unseen guard as he continued on his way. "See you later," he added as he found the entrance to the passage that led upward above the port to the top of the south wall.

As he climbed the ladder, he looked up above him.

The trapdoor opened. His men were alert and expecting him.

"Howdy, sir. All okay here in One," Major Bob Parker, Buckley's executive officer, shouted above the noise of battle.

Mark didn't answer. Instead, he turned and looked out across the parade ground to the north wall.

"Your comms in good shape?" he asked.

"Yes, sir. Been monitoring telephone and radio. Four just asked for a flare. Said some of their tip mines had blown ..."

3

Suddenly the harsh light of a magnesium flare illuminated the field outside the fort, and almost immediately, machine gun fire erupted from position Four.

"Well they must have something out there," Mark commented as he took advantage of the light to look around position One.

In seconds, the flare was out and darkness returned, but not before Mark had satisfied himself that all was in order at One. Half-dug-in and half-sandbagged, this position was a smaller version of the underground command post. All the necessary communications equipment was there to allow Mark to direct his forces when the battle developed. At that point Parker, as second in command, would move to the main CP and take over there.

Mark took the telephone and called position Four.

"Four, this is Top Dog. What you got out there?"

"Sir, looks like a sapper squad. We got some of them. The others took off. Gimme another flare—I think there are more of them, maybe a platoon or so in the brush at the north edge of the swamp."

From his vantage point on the highest wall of the fort, Mark waited for the second flare. Then he would be able to look across the far walls to the village and the swamp. The sudden glaring light brought a crescendo of small-arms fire mingled with the deeper, more emphatic sound of the .50 caliber machine guns located at Four and Five.

Mark then saw several VC at the edge of the swamp, as reported earlier, but the flare revealed a larger group of the enemy near the north edge of the village.

"There's a hell of a lot of the bastards hugging the swamp edge on the north side of town," a voice from Four reported through the phone, confirming Mark's observation.

The flare died. When blackness returned, the enemy stepped up his mortar bombardment, and Mark lost no time making his decision. He told his R/T operator to switch to the command channel and then took the radio earphones and mike.

"Hello Foxy, hello Foxy, this is Top Dog One."

"Go ahead, Top Dog One, this is Foxy," the answer crackled back.

4

"Foxy, this is Top Dog One. We've really got it this time. Looks like a battalion, maybe more. Better send us a 'Spooky' ASAP. Over."

"This is Foxy. Roger on Spooky. Will see what's available. Several out already. Full dance card. Over."

"This is Top Dog One. It's going to be rough here in an hour. Will keep you posted—but get me that Spooky. Now. Out."

Mark turned to Major Parker and his voice displayed his concern.

"Bob, keep this thing going—and keep a watch on the river. They're trying to get us a Spooky but seems we're last on the list. Hell's going to break loose at the main gate in about twenty minutes. I gotta get to Ho like right now. Call him and tell him I'm comin'."

Mark did not wait for Parker's reply but turned and started down the tunnel that took him back to the sally port and into the small courtyard. This time he crossed the open area and entered the hallway, guided by flashes of light in the doorway that led to the porch and the fort's central parade ground.

As he swung out and turned right into the porch, the sound of battle returned in a loud crescendo. But this time he heard the muffled voices of the Vietnamese families crowded in the bunkers under the porch. He hoped that they all had made it into the fort because it was possible he might have to direct fire from the 'Spooky' AC-47 into the town if the turn of battle required it.

Mark raced along the porch toward the east wall. In the intermittent flashes of light, he could see a grim-faced ARVN soldier holding the door open for him.

"Di theo toi!" (Follow me!), the soldier told Mark.

The Vietnamese led Mark up an inside stairway to position Five, located on the top of the east wall by the main gate.

In seconds, he was in the middle of Major Ho's command post. Half-dug into the top of the wall and augmented by sandbags at the sides and front, it was almost an exact copy of Major Parker's position One.

"Ha, Colonel Mark, this one biggest one! *Beaucoup* VC!" exclaimed Major Ho with enthusiasm that bordered on joy.

"You know it, Ho," Mark replied. "All your people in?"

"All in—but if not, too bad. Go hide river bank."

The two were speaking directly in each other's ears, trying to be heard over the noise. Mark explained that he expected the main thrust of the attack to be through the town against the east wall, or if that failed, from the river against the south wall. He also relayed that headquarters was tying to scare up a 'Spooky.' His thinking was that the attack would develop quickly in order for the enemy to take advantage of as much darkness as possible.

Mark looked at his watch: 0145.

Four hours to daylight ...

"Ho, it might be necessary to fire into the village if Spooky spots the VC in there."

"Yes. Yes. My people know," said Ho stoically.

In a flash of light, Mark spotted sadness in Ho's eyes.

"We will try to spare as much as possible."

Mark patted the young ARVN officer on the arm and then turned and descended the stairs, quickly making his way back to the main CP.

"How's it out there, Colonel?" asked Mead.

"A lot worse real soon. Guess you heard me ask for air ..."

Mark made his way over to the operations board. While he studied the situation, he overheard two soldiers talking.

"... an' it's this old C-47 Gooneybird, see; but it's loaded up with three mini guns and a shit load of ammo and flares. We tell her where to fire and she pours all that lead down like three guys pissin' on an ant hill."

"That's a pretty fair description," Mark interrupted, as he turned to the soldier who had asked the question. "Your first combat, Rinehart?"

"Yes, sir," the young soldier replied, rising to his feet.

"As you were, stay down. Well, don't worry. It's going to be a bit rough, but with our guys fighting like they always do and Spooky on the way to help, we're going to make it okay."

Mark hoped he sounded convincing. He knew the outcome of this battle depended on a tired, thirty-year-old airplane that might not ever arrive. A quick pat on the young man's arm, then he turned and moved to the status board.

More wounded were now listed.

Busy night for the medics ...

Mark looked around the command post. All seemed to be in order and operating well. It was time for him to take over topside. He signaled Sergeant Mead.

"Tell Major Parker that the colonel will be coming topside, now," Mead said to the telephone operator as he grabbed his helmet and followed Buckley up the ladder.

As they crossed the courtyard and started up the inside ladder to position One, Mead thought about his men, the fort, and the coming battle. But most of his thoughts were about LTC Mark Buckley. In all his twenty-five years of service, Mead had never worked for an officer quite like this man, and he felt lucky to be working with him now. The sergeant knew that every man had a boiling point, but to Mead's knowledge, Buckley had never reached his, even though the provocations on this assignment had been many and great. But most of all, this big, sometimes clumsy half-colonel had the ability to produce confidence among his people.

Tonight, Mead was sure, they would win this battle because Buckley never lost—and they were Buckley's men.

The trapdoor above them opened and instantly the light and sounds of battle burst upon them as they made their way to position One.

Mark quickly shouted some last instructions to Parker about the wounded, over the noise, then clapped him on the shoulder and sent him on his way to the underground command post.

After the major departed, Mark checked his watch.

It's 0215. It has to start soon if they really meant to take the ... have to come from the east ... through the village.

Mark looked in that direction, then he turned and checked the river below him.

Quiet down there ...

Next, he scanned along the top of the wall to his right and left, well aware that Ho's men were there in the dark, restless, waiting, anticipating their part in the action to come.

Something's changed.

Mark realized that the mortar attack had stopped. The heavy

thumps of exploding projectiles gave way to the sharp staccato of rifle and machine gun fire.

"This is it, Mead. Keep in contact with Four and Five—and I want continuous illumination."

Mark could now see an enemy force of considerable size running toward the east wall. His men in position Four and Ho's ARVNs in position Five were laying deadly fire down on them. The fact that the mortars had stopped was a good indicator that other VC had already crossed the open area and were within danger-close area of their own shells.

"Trouble over at Four," Mead shouted to Mark. "Halstead wounded and Sergeant Manheim killed."

"Dammit to hell. Manheim ... how is Halstead?"

"Evacuated to the aid station. Gut wound."

"Who's in command at Four?" Mark shouted back.

There was a long pause before Mead got the answer, "Corporal Green, sir."

"Green? Well he's a good man. Give me the phone."

"Four, this is Top Dog One. How you doin'?"

"Okay, Colonel, but we sure are catchin' it here."

"How about some help?"

"What kind you offerin'?" Green asked.

"Don't worry," Mark replied. "I'm not sending anyone to take over, but I am going to send a couple of squads down from Three to give you a hand. You're doing good and you're still in charge."

"Thanks, Colonel. We'll be watchin' for the two squads."

"Okay. Now remember, those mortars are going to start again just as soon as they think all their close-in guys are dead or have fallen back."

Mark returned the phone to Sergeant Mead.

For a moment, Mark Buckley indulged in a dangerous practice. He allowed himself to think of Sergeant Manheim—one of the best non-commissioned officers he had ever served with.

This goddamned mess. This stupid fucking mess—and to think Manheim gave his life for this ...

"They're on their way, sir," Mead yelled in Mark's ear.

"Yeah? Oh. Okay ... thanks."

"Hope Green does okay. He's been pretty pissed off lately," added Mead.

Mark thought of the big, black corporal now in command at Four. He had always liked Green and felt he would show them a lot if he ever got the chance.

"Well, this is his moment, Sergeant. I'll bet he can't remember what he's been pissed off about right about now!"

There was sudden, sharp machine gun fire to Mark's immediate right. He wheeled toward the sound.

"What the hell is going on over at Six?" he yelled.

He checked out the position and then looked over the Mekong for a possible target.

"Six reports a hell of a lot of small sampans crossing the river and comin' this way," Mead shouted.

Mark's eye caught some shadowy images in the darkness just outside the range of the flares.

"Get a flare up over the water. Now!"

It seemed like hours while they waited the few minutes for the bright light. Then, suddenly, the river side of the fort was starkly illuminated and the sight brought a gasp from the throats of the defenders.

Three distinct waves of boats were rapidly approaching the near bank of the river. The first group was almost at the bank below them and the others were following in good order at about fifty-yard intervals.

"Shit!"

If I've figured this bastard ass-backward ...

All hell broke loose around Mark as the soldiers on each side of him along the whole length of the south wall found their targets among the boats.

"Where's the main thrust, Colonel?"

Mead's question sounded at first naïve to Mark, and then he realized that Mead was only a bit more confused then he was.

9

He paused for a second to let his brain clear.

Think ... think ...

Rapidly he reviewed the situation. There were only three waves, but spaced to make them seem like an infinite number coming out of the darkness.

"Another flare over the south wall! And keep the south side illuminated as much as possible."

The new flare revealed what Mark suspected. There were only three waves, but they were big. He estimated seventy boats, total. Now several were destroyed and others in trouble. His men on the wall had taken a toll.

But it was obvious that many would make it to the river bank below the south wall.

"Send a squad from the west wall to reinforce the sally port. All we need is a bunch of VC running around below us blowing up the place."

Mark glanced across the parade ground to where the main attack was developing with all its power and fury; but a heavy pall of white acrid smoke, undisturbed by the still, damp night air, had settled over the fort and the surrounding battlefield, making it difficult for Mark to see.

"Get reports from Four and Five," Mark ordered.

"The enemy's on the wall below the gate and east of Four fighting hand-to-hand," said Mead, hoping his voice did not betray his concerns.

"Jesus, what a time for a Spooky! Call Can Tho and tell 'em we may not be here tomorrow if they don't get some help down here."

Below the south wall on the river bank, the VC that had landed formed into squads, and were now attacking the sally port. The steep, almost vertical path they were required to take, combined with Mark's now-reinforced force, made their task seem almost hopeless.

But in the darkness, targets were not easy to define, and Mark's forces did not have complete advantage. For a time, it looked like the issue was in doubt; but finally, Ho's men firmly controlled the vital entryway.

"Colonel, they got one! I'm tuning in on FM. His call sign is 'Fancy Three'!"

Mark, equally excited, shouted his instructions back to Mead.

"As soon as you get him, tell him every minute counts, then tell him you are putting me on with him. Now, give me the phone. I've gotta talk to all positions."

In seconds, all posts had reported in, and Mark quickly told them of the imminent arrival of the gunship.

"It will be necessary for him to fire directly on the wall between positions Four and Five, so pull your people back from their east wall positions on my command. Ho, I want you to put out a red smoke flare on the wall for an aiming point. Ned Green, hold Four as long as you can, but if you have to give up tell your people to fall back along the wall to Three."

"Colonel, I've got Fancy Three," interrupted Mead as he thrust the radio handset in front of Mark's face.

Mark closed off phone contact with his people and then talked to the C-47.

"Fancy Three, this is Top Dog."

"Top Dog. This is Fancy Three. I am approaching your position from the west and will be directly over Trong Thoi in five minutes."

"This is Top Dog, Fancy Three. Don't waste time on a pass. As soon as you can make out the walls of the fort, start your turn. Your first target should be the area between the town and the east wall. The rest you will see when you start your flares.

"On your second pass, you will see red smoke on the east wall. Use it as an aiming point. Fire directly on the wall in the space between the red smoke and the northeast gun position. Do you read? Over."

"On the wall? Did you say *ON the wall*, Top Dog? Please say again."

"Hell yes, Fancy Three. Affirmative. I said *on* the east wall, *on* the east wall between the red smoke and the gun position at the northeast corner. Over."

"Jesus ... Top Dog, you've had a rough night. But sit back, watch the show, and let Fancy Three take over."

Mark smiled as he saw the first flare leave the AC-47. The air-dropped flares were brighter and lasted longer than the ground-fired ones his men were using. The swaying, brilliant lights revealed several enemy units advancing on the east wall, and many of them gaining the

11

top. Almost instantly, long bright strands of tracer rounds left the slowing, circling aircraft and hit their marks among the advancing VC.

As "Spooky" swung past the east wall, Mark instructed Major Ho to set off the red smoke, then at the last minute, he told Ned Green and his men to fall back along the north wall to Three. In moments, Fancy Three made his second attack on the east side of the fort, this time firing on the wall itself, north of the red smoke, clearly seen in the bright light of the flares.

"Fancy Three, this is Top Dog."

"This is Fancy Three. How'm I doin'?"

"Fancy Three, you do outstanding work for an Air Force type. This time get at the base of the south wall, right at the water's edge."

"Roger, Top Dog. I see the target. Tell your guys to duck."

Again, the stream of brilliant tracers loped down to their targets and after the airplane had lumbered past, Mark was convinced the last of the enemy that had come by boats had been eliminated.

Throughout the remaining darkness, "Spooky" circled the fort, attacking targets as Mark called them out. By the time dawn broke, the remnants of the VC force had withdrawn and all was quiet at Trong Thoi except the droning radial engines of the AC-47.

A light early morning breeze drew away the smoke, like a curtain pulled back, revealing a scene of destruction, horror, and death. Mark looked up and noticed the red-gold eastern sky was fading to daylight.

"Top Dog, this is Fancy Three."

"Go ahead, Fancy Three."

"Can I go home now? Over."

"Fancy Three. This is Top Dog. Affirmative. Head for the barn. And thanks for the help. Tell your boss you just earned a three-day pass."

"This is Fancy Three. Any time, Top Dog. Just give us a ring."

Mark put down the handset.

"Come on, Mead. Let's check the men."

As they descended the ladder, both men, on their own, silently gave a little prayer of thanks.

Chapter I

MAY 1967

A fitful night breeze wandered across the Mekong.

    It wandered over the high mud walls of the Special Forces camp and into the old fort's barracks windows. Then, exhausted, it stirred slightly and died without the slightest effect in that close, rank-smelling room, or on the restless men who slept there.

Ned Green lay on his sweat-drenched bunk and thought of tomorrow and Saigon and Luu. His tall, muscular, naked black body glistened in the dim red light of bulbs marking the exits of the building. He was far from sleep.

I'm goin'! He's giving me the courier trip to Saigon. Can't believe it. Been near four months. Four months since I been outta this damn hellhole. I never want to be around for another attack like that last one ...

He twisted his body in the narrow bunk noticing only briefly the bright red glitter of the light and the sweat.

They say I'm bitter. Man, they're so right: black 'n bitter, that's me. Ain't had no real break since the Buck give me corporal's stripes near three damn months ago. I'd like to tell 'em why I'm bitter. I'd like ta tell 'em how I was yanked outta school to come over here and fight their shit war. I'd maybe be making my own livin' in commercial art by now. Might be doin' pretty good. Might even left Chicago for New York and be in the big time. But you can't tell these mothers about art school 'n drawin'. They'd laugh. They can't believe this nigger could do sump'n like that. All he can do is fight their shit war.

13

Ned's thoughts slowly returned to Saigon and the little Chinese girl he had met there.

Wonder how many 'co bo' ol' Luu has by now? Don't make no difference, once I'm there. I'll run them mothers off when I get to Saigon—When I get to Saigon—When I get to Saigon, I'll be the only one. Right. The only one.

A new breeze somehow found its way into the dark barracks. Ned felt its caress as he finally fell asleep.

Ψ   Ψ   Ψ

The morning broke clear and cool, and the camp was up early to take advantage of the best hours of the day. LTC Mark Buckley, commander of the American forces, had already checked in at his command post and walked the walls with Sergeant Mead before breakfast. He was now at his desk waiting for Corporal Ned Green to report. Like most regular officers now in-country who had served in Vietnam before, Mark was somewhat less than enthusiastic about the way the war was going and the way politicians were directing it from 10,000 miles away. For a moment, he reflected on his two tours in Vietnam, and compared this war with the Korean mess he had been unfortunate enough to be involved in fifteen years before.

It's the communications; they're too damn good. Communications and transportation allow Johnson and McNamara to control every squad in combat like a pawn on a chessboard. In the old days officers had to be leaders—real leaders, no matter how low ranking they were, and no matter how small their command. They made the decisions—not some colonel in a chopper, screaming at them through a radio.

He thought of the young lieutenant colonels—stateside hotshots—who had never fired a round in anger, now brought over as battalion commanders. After a few months, by the time they got to know their job, they'd be passed off to a cushy assignment in Saigon while another "virgin" was brought in to learn to run the battalion.

The guys who really suffer are the poor draftees. God, how'd ya like to be a draftee finishing the last year of your hitch in Vietnam? By some stroke of luck, you'd kept your ass in one piece for the first four months while you learned how to fight. Then they'd bring in some new, unblooded kid and say, "Here's your new commander, boys. Follow him, he's your leader. He doesn't know how to run a battalion in combat, but you can teach him—don't mind the casualties. Just so he gets the experience!"

He leaned his tall, strongly built frame back in his creaking camp chair and looked around his spacious, but austere, office while his thoughts returned to his own assignment.

Well, one thing about this old fort, Trong Thoi: all the officers and NCOs in this place know which end of a rifle the bullet comes out.

Situated on the southern edge of that vast, swampy Viet Cong collecting zone known as the "Plain of Reeds," Trong Thoi was one of the key defense points of the Delta. It was an old fort built by the French before World War II. It was good sized and well engineered. Situated on the Mekong River about twelve miles from the Cambodian border, from a distance it looked like a huge blob of mud and grass. With a lot of guts and sweat, the garrison of twenty-eight Americans and two hundred Vietnamese had made it a pretty livable place, considering the location, the weather, and the war. Mark was proud of the fort, its important mission, and—most of all—the people he commanded to carry out that mission. He stretched, yawned, and looked at his watch while his mind slid away from Trong Thoi to the war. He wondered how long Congress was going to allow this carnage, this sacrifice of young Americans to continue.

You just don't fight wars like this, standing like a wall and letting the enemy beat themselves against you. You sure don't, if you expect to win ... and those bastards in the Pentagon know it ... but that one smartass that's always looking for the goddamn light at the end of the tunnel has convinced everyone back there that his computers are the only way to fight this one.

Only thing is, his computers aren't getting knocked off, real people are. I'd like to take one of those computers and jam it up his ass.

And then there's the damn press. Film crews. Instant experts sticking microphones in your face. Making smartass comments. Have to be nice to them. Keep them from getting dead. And then they jump a chopper in time to get back to Saigon for a cold drink and ...

A knock on the door brought his attention back to his own problems at Trong Thoi.

"Come in," he shouted.

The door opened and Ned Green entered and reported, a big grin spread across his face.

Mark returned the salute. "Well, Ned, first time I've seen you smile for a long time."

"First time outta this place in a long time, Colonel," Green answered.

Mark looked the corporal over with an experienced eye. Green was one of the best men he had. He was a tall, powerful man who towered over the other Americans, including himself by several inches. He had hard, cold eyes that missed nothing and forgave no one. He obviously didn't like soldiering, but what draftee did? Still, he played the game and was always well turned out—a good soldier. Whether he liked it or not.

"I know. Ninety-six days, to be exact. Am I right?"

"Yessir, you sure are. But how did you know?"

"My business to know these things. But you earned this trip, Ned. You did a great bit of business during the last attack, taking over when Hallstead was wounded.

"But about this report you're taking into the head shed," Mark continued. "Remember to ask if there is a reply. If they say no, you will have to return on the chopper this afternoon. If they say yes, tell them you will check with them in two days to see if it is ready. Got that? And don't worry—the way I've written this report, they gotta reply. It's my guess you'll get at least five days in the big city. It'll take them that long to write a good answer.

"That chopper's due in ten minutes. Here's the report. It's classified SECRET, so be sure to get a receipt because some HQ commando will insist we have one. And Ned—have a good time, but don't get messed up, understand? Good corporals are hard to find around here!"

Green took the report and saluted. As he left, he said, "Don't worry, Colonel. Everything's going to be okay—okay—okay."

Mark Buckley went to the window of his office. He watched the chopper come in low over the muddy river and land on the float below the main wall of the camp. The crew delivered two sacks of mail to his eagerly waiting men. Ned Green scrambled aboard and waved to his less fortunate comrades. Then he looked up at his colonel and gave an exaggerated salute. Mark smiled and responded with a similar gesture. He was happy that Ned had this trip. He deserved the break. Later, on another day, he would remember this moment well.

Ψ   Ψ   Ψ

Brandy Masters was a so-so singer.

But she was blond. Built and acted like a girl with a capital G, and that was the best you could hope for in the "boonies." Besides, she was an entertainer, friendly, and developed an easy rapport with her audience.

It was that little wiggle she gave her ass, Mark decided as he watched her murder *Thrill Me*.

He looked around at the soldiers in the audience.

I must be getting old. Not one of these guys has noticed what she's doing to that song. But if that's what the guys want to spend their dough on, it's okay by me.

Official USO shows, which were at no cost to the forces, almost never made it to places such as Trong Thoi. The last one that showed up was a terrified accordion player who played for twenty minutes and then ran for the chopper.

By saving the Exchange Service dividend money, which was prorated among the units, and by Mark adding some funds of their own, the camp had collected enough money to hire a real "round-eye" show (which is what they had voted for). It would be an unofficial act, making a living of sorts in the backwaters of South Vietnam. To Mark's official visit to IV Corps Special Forces HQ had also been added the unofficial duty of scouting any entertainment that might be playing in Can Tho, the largest city in the Delta.

As he watched Brandy Masters, he decided that most of the commercial acts which supplemented the USO shows would never make it stateside. But what the hell, if they satisfied the troops, they were doing their job. Hell, he'd be satisfied if he were in the market for a blonde with a big chest.

And this is one great-looking blonde with a big chest.

Mark finished his drink and started backstage while the troops were still yelling for another encore. The heat was oppressive in the open-air cafe, and every man had sweated through his fatigues. Swarms of white insects flew about the floodlights that shone down from two high poles on either side of the stage.

Suddenly the lights went out, and the troops emitted anguished groans and a selection of curses as they shuffled out in the thick, damp darkness.

Sitting at the makeup table in the improvised dressing room, Brandy Masters flicked her long golden hair to one side in an unconscious gesture and made a quick female appraisal of Mark Buckley in the poorly lighted mirror.

Exceptionally good material. Hmmmm.

She turned and faced him directly. In so doing, her short silk Asian-style dressing gown parted, showing a generous portion of shapely, creamy white thigh.

Mark took in the whole picture. *Nice body, beautiful face, those gorgeous blue eyes were dynamite. And, by God, the lashes were real.*

Brandy's long, straight blond hair, lately brushed, glistened as it fell below her shoulders.

But that white skin ... the creamy white, white skin, and plenty of it showing. Steady, boy. Hold it.

He quickly yanked his thoughts back to his mission.

"You see, Miss Masters, our mail and logistics chopper gets into the camp Mondays, Wednesdays, and Fridays. If you could come in on a Monday, you could give shows at camp Monday and Tuesday evenings, and during the day, you could visit some of the outposts. Then you could leave on the Wednesday chopper. It's an isolated area, but things have been pretty quiet since the rainy season started, and I would take every possible precaution for your safety."

Brandy Masters was quite aware of the effect she had made.

They're so easy.

She smiled slowly in a sort of taunting way. Her eyes narrowed and flashed, her lips parted just a bit, and she did not answer immediately, but paused for a number of heart beats.

18

What a bitch she is! She'll wreck that camp in fifteen minutes if we don't watch her like a hawk.

"Colonel Buckley ... Do you mind if I call you Mark?"

Mark noticed a small, warm purr in her voice that hadn't been there before.

"Not at all, ma'am, I'd be honored."

"Well, Mark—I love that name. So—well, so solid, so honest. Isn't it a Bible name? Of course, Matthew, Mark, Luke and James ..."

"... and John. The Gospels," Mark finished.

"Yes, silly of me to forget ..."

"If you please, Miss Masters," Mark started to get impatient.

But her presence was overpowering him. Now the scent of female perspiration and perfume was becoming an additional hazard.

"We don't normally go so far off the beaten path," said Brandy in her best business manner. "However, in this case I think we can manage it. Besides, I like you and hope to get to know you better."

Observing Mark's expression, she quickly added, "True friendship is something which I hold in high esteem, Colonel Buckley."

"Me, too," Mark replied, and decided now to refocus the conversation. "And I'm happy for my men that you will come to the camp. When do you think you can make it?"

"It will have to be the first week in June. We're booked in Vung Tau for the remainder of May. See, Peter ... you know, Peter Charles, the guitar player. He acts as booking agent. And ... well, I have to get dressed. I promised Captain Parsons I would have dinner with him, but how about a late drink with me at my billet?"

"Sorry, Miss Masters. I wouldn't wish to cut in on the captain's evening for anything. Thanks again for promising to come to Trong Thoi. I'll find Mr. Charles to firm up the date. Now, if you'll excuse me ..."

Brandy watched Mark leave the room. Then she turned and looked at herself in the mirror, and smiled at what she saw.

"Anything for the troops," she murmured. "Especially if the troops are anything like this Mark Buckley."

19

Ψ   Ψ   Ψ

Peter Charles was always careful about disturbing Brandy too early in the morning.

But, on this morning he had come to her hotel room and found her alone, having breakfast on the deep porch that encircled the second floor of the old French colonial hotel. He wondered how long the captain had been gone. The day was already hot and still. From the porch, the endless green rice paddies and connecting waterways of the flat delta land extended to the horizon. Nothing seemed to move except one white egret, lazily wheeling above a slowly moving sampan.

Peter, in all his thirty years of show business, had never before been associated with anyone quite like Brandy Masters. Sitting opposite her at the tiny porch table, he watched her absently devour a bit of hard French roll. He had time to reflect that she was a dame who had it made without doing much of anything—but for some reason she was continually doing everything in her power to ruin her own chances at happiness.

Although trying to give the opposite impression, Brandy was watching Peter closely. She was thinking of their once wild affair. As she swallowed the last of the coffee, she let her eyes rove his thin, emaciated body, his expressive hands with long thin fingers, and his scruffy head of very long, dark hair.

Guitar players … Why did I ever decide to screw this guy? Well usually, any screw is better than no screw. Thank God it didn't go on very long. Three months? Hard to remember much about it. Then I found that little Marine. Now he …

She picked up another piece of roll, and then tossed it back on the table. Peter's once handsome looks had disappeared long before he teamed up with Brandy, but the great black eyes in his thin, dark face could express a quiet sadness that some women found enchanting. At that moment, he directed such a look at her hands, avoiding her eyes.

"Honey …" Peter said, as he reached across the table to take a roll.

Brandy, now long immune to that look, had lit a cigarette and was using the smoke to screen any hint of excited interest in Mark Buckley that Peter might detect in her face.

20

"Look," Peter continued, "have I ever told you wrong? That camp deal is 'number ten' and you know it. We've been through a lot together, and I know you better than anyone else in the world. And that includes your uncle. You can get into a lot of real trouble with this one, baby. What I mean, well, like real trouble. You know—the kind that even those high-ranking relatives of yours can't get you out of."

He was now looking into her eyes. Brandy was impressed. Peter never looked directly at you when he spoke unless he was completely certain or absolutely serious about something. She turned and watched a sampan disappear behind a distant turn in the channel. The war seemed very far away.

But then on the other side of the hotel, a long convoy of heavy "deuce-and-a-half trucks" approached. The distant noise slowly increased until it engulfed the hotel and shattered the lazy green stillness of the morning.

Her mind returned to Peter and his warning.

She thought of her "high-ranking relatives"; actually only one, her uncle Joe. He was a United States senator and she loved him very much. Also, she was his favorite niece, a nice position to be in, and he had helped her immensely. After her parents had both died, he had become her guardian. But if Uncle Joe only knew what she was up to over here, that help might not continue.

Peter broke into her thoughts. "I know your uncle helped you get the USO job that brought you here two years ago, and I know he worked your resignation last year in Saigon and got us permission to stay around. But baby, this trouble is for real. I'm speaking of the kind of trouble that even a congressman can't fix."

"Senator."

"Okay, senator."

"What date did you settle on?" Brandy moved on, changing the subject.

Peter sighed. "Monday, the fifth. Return on Wednesday, the seventh. Keeps us on schedule for Saigon."

Brandy rose from her chair; this was Peter's signal to leave.

"That's fine, Peter. I knew you would see things my way."

She walked into her room, the ceiling fan barely ruffling her long blond hair as she passed under it to the door.

"I wish you wouldn't worry about my little bits of fun all the time, Peter."

"God, Brandy, it's not your morals, it's you I'm worrying about … the way you're acting. You might get … well, knowing you, you might end up dead—or something!"

Brandy laughed.

"My God, Peter. You're being so dramatic."

She pushed him out of the room, her laugh following him down the hall. He did not look back.

Ψ   Ψ   Ψ

In Saigon, daybreak came complete with a monsoon thunderstorm that did little to cool the air, but raised the humidity.

By noon, the storm had moved away from the city and the sun was alone in the sky. The streets glistened brightly and the gutters were busy with residual water. For an hour or two, Saigon had a shiny new brightness that belied the squalor and decay.

Corporal Chung Kim finished wiping red mud from his black Ford sedan parked by the Rex Hotel. As he lit a cigarette, he guessed that his boss, Colonel Uhm, would be taking another long lunch hour. He always did after a hard night and from all indications, it had been just that.

I wonder why Colonel Uhm didn't stay with the pretty girl over on Cong Ha Street. If he would just settle down, everyone would be happier and I would get more sleep.

Kim walked down the line of cars to talk to a couple of American soldiers who were also drivers. He was proud of his English and used it whenever he had a chance. He had gotten to know the two soldiers during their mutually endless waits in front of various headquarters, embassies, and billets—and some rather fancy cafes.

"Hi, GI, what's new?" he asked as he offered Salem cigarettes to the men.

22

"Howdy, Gook, how's it going?" joked one red-haired GI.

Kim knew these two drivers very well and enjoyed the back and forth.

"You keep calling us gooks and we all pull out of South Korea come down here. Then you Yankees have to go up there and defend that place all alone!" he bantered back.

Kim, like most Koreans, liked Vietnam duty. The climate was good, the girls were pretty and receptive, and the privileges were many and worthwhile, especially the PX. There you could purchase hundreds of items that were available only to the very rich back home. The fact that most of these items ended up on the black market was not a bother to Kim, not at all. That was the Asian way. He couldn't understand why the Americans kept getting so upset about it.

"Oh, we don't want all you guys to come down here. It's hard enough for us to get into the PX as it is. Any more gooks in there would make us do all our buying on the black market."

Kim started to reply, but was interrupted by the other soldier.

"Where'd you learn your English, Kim? You speak number one!"

"Hell, GI, I'm number ten, but I speak every day to *boo koo* Americans. It not so good, but it sure helps.

"But since you ask me, I tell you how I learn English. You see, when Korean War broke out I was small boy, only six. Pretty soon, boom, boom. No Mama, no Papa. GIs found me.

"Four years I was orderly to a number one US captain. Then I became unit mess boy and mascot. Then in '54 many GIs go home. They took me to orphanage set up by GIs. I spoke number one English but number ten Korean, so I acted as interpreter for orphanage. I was sent to learn to read and write more English, but I learn not so good. When I left orphanage, I went to get good job with Americans, but I lose one job for not reading and writing well. So I say 'What the hell,' I join the army and be Korean GI."

"Better hold off on the rest of your life story. Here comes your boss."

"Wow, you know it, GI," replied Kim as he trotted back to his car just in time to salute and open the door for Colonel Uhm.

The colonel, who spoke only Korean, was glad to have this driver. Kim's English assisted him in meeting many Vietnamese girls. Things always worked well early in the evening when Kim was there to make the introductions. It was always after Kim had discreetly withdrawn that Uhm got into trouble. Uhm was too vain to think that Kim's seemingly great success with women was the result of the very apparent difference in the physical makeup of the two men.

Kim, like many South Koreans, towered over Vietnamese men by six inches or more, was well built, and over six feet tall. His green fatigue uniform was always immaculate and beautifully pressed. In short, he was a neat, clean, good-looking soldier. But there was something else about the big Korean. Something more than the fine features and high cheekbones, that made him very popular with the Saigon girls. There was a hint of laughter in his eyes that seemed to say, "I'm living life to the hilt."

Uhm, on the other hand, was short and chubby. The high life of Saigon had added several pounds, which Uhm passed off as lately added robust strength. No matter how well his uniform was washed and pressed, he somehow managed to look as if he had slept in it.

The colonel barked, "Back to headquarters, but careful when you go down Le-Loi. That Buddhist demonstration might still be going on."

Uhm settled down into the soft back seat. He was in no mood to communicate with anyone. The phone call that summoned him to headquarters had interrupted a much-needed rest.

Kim slowly guided the Ford through the impossible Saigon traffic. As he proceeded west down Le-Loi he was stopped by a police cordon. Colonel Uhm sat up quickly. He saw the police and anxiously looked behind to see if they could reverse and get around the barricade. Too late. Already cars were stacked solidly behind them.

"Get out and ask those 'white mice' what the problem is. Tell them I'm late for an important meeting."

Kim left the sedan to do as he was ordered, but the source of the trouble had already become obvious. Advancing upon them from the left and traveling north was a sea of saffron-robed monks. They almost filled the street as they passed on their way to the palace. All traffic sounds had stopped. The only noise was an unorganized, low-pitched chant, sung at random by an occasional monk and then echoed by his brethren.

Kim returned to his seat in the car.

"It is a demonstration, sir. The Buddhists have many factions. Lately they have done away with their old charter of control that bound them together, and this group will not agree on the new charter. Some people think the VC control one, maybe two of the groups."

"They look formidable."

"They are men of God, sir. The people hold them above the war."

"The VC don't."

Uhm glared at the marching men with malevolence. They might each be concealing a weapon under those robes and they were making him late for his appointment. He unconsciously reached down and patted his own American .45.

Ψ   Ψ   Ψ

Ned Green was also delayed by the marching monks.

He was sitting in the back of a Tri-Lambretta along with six Vietnamese. He wore civilian clothes. He was ten days AWOL–and very frightened. The civilian shirt and trousers he was wearing were already drenched with sweat, and the six Vietnamese in the vehicle, who invariably found the smell of all Americans repugnant, were looking at him with anxious eyes.

Ned had followed his colonel's orders, up to a point. He had delivered the report and, as Mark had predicted, was told to "wait out" for the reply.

Then Ned Green had gone his own way.

No air was moving in Saigon that afternoon. The sun was baking the passengers in the hundreds of vehicles now crowded eight abreast and bumper to bumper. Numerous Hondas, Izukis, and other small motorcycles threaded through the traffic lines, anxious to get to the front. The traditional cyclo drivers looked with disdain at the exhaust-belching "cyclo MVs" which, with the other gas-driven vehicles, were filling the street with a thick pall of exhaust smoke. Before long, the people were muttering to themselves, coughing, and honking their horns.

Ned couldn't stand the crowded, smelly vehicle any longer. He worked his way out between the other passengers and started walking between the cars to lose himself on the crowded sidewalk. He made his way away from the procession and down a side street to the relatively open area of Nguyen Hue. Slowly he pushed his way into the less crowded center of the street. At last he could breathe again.

Gotta watch it. Way I look, I'm a dead giveaway for the MPs. Goddamn monks. They really fixed me. Would have made it back to Luu's if it hadn't been for them.

He carefully avoided the USO by crossing to the Catinat Hotel and proceeded east toward the river. He tried to walk purposefully and directly, in case he was being watched by the MPs. At the same time, he was turning to watch for a taxi. It would take the last of his piastres, but he had no option. He couldn't stay out on the street like this. Presently he saw a cab parked behind a large truck and walked over to it, only to find the driver asleep behind the wheel. Ned shook his arm.

"How much to Cholon?"

"Where Cholon? Cholon big place."

"Near PX."

The driver, with a sly look replied, "Four hundred P."

"Robber—you number ten. I get 'Com Coc.' He put you in Phu Quoc!"

"Okay. How much you pay?"

"Fifty P, and that's tops."

"You pay one hundred P and I get you number one girl."

Ned got in and slammed the door. "I no need number one girl. I already have. 'San boy.' You go—but stay away from Pasteur. Today Pasteur number ten street."

With a grumble, the driver started the little blue Renault and swung out into the traffic. Ned all but filled the back seat of the tiny cab. He was deep in thought as he hunched down to avoid hitting the roof.

Well, I suppose I made a big-assed mistake going AWOL but son of a bitch, why should I go back to that slimy camp and fight for the Man so as when I go home he can piss all over me. No, I've had enough. I'll sit the rest of this one out. Here's one black-assed soldier who's really got it made in Saigon, Vietnam. That Luu's got a pad there that's really not too bad. With a little money, I could really fix it up. When I get into the black market better, I'll have plenty of dough and maybe even marry Luu if that's what she wants. I know one thing—I ain't goin' back to take no AWOL rap, and I ain't goin' back in the army to fight for a better Vietnam for anyone. I like it just the way it is.

After a while, these thoughts gave way to feelings of concern.

That Luu, she don't like the idea of my ration card runnin' out. Gotta get a new one somewhere. Gotta get out tonight and roll a drunk GI. Gotta get some P and maybe some green. Big wad of green'd make Luu sit up and take notice. Drunk GIs are easy to roll. Wish I coulda made contact today with that big black-market guy. I gotta get to be somebody in this town. Well, be part of this town.

Luu watched the cab roll up to her building from her fifth-story balcony. When she saw Ned, she scowled and got up from the broken wicker chair and walked into her tiny room. She had been drying her freshly washed hair on the balcony and was naked to the waist. She glanced at her distorted image in the cheap mirror on the wall. Her skin was a dull gold and her small, firm breasts pointed up proudly and unassisted. She grasped them in her hands. By slowly moving in front of the mirror, she found the place where the distortion of her reflected image made her breasts seem larger. She stopped there for a moment and smiled. Then she remembered Ned. Quickly she picked up the ice-blue, high-necked Chinese blouse and put it on. She had just finished the last button when Ned came in and removed his sweat-drenched shirt. He dropped it to the floor and went to Luu. Quickly but tenderly, he held her and kissed her.

She laughed and pushed him away. "Look at Luu blouse now! All wet! Oh, Ned, you number ten!"

"Number one, baby. Remember what you said?"

Luu lit a cigarette and retreated to one of the two wooden stools by a small round table. Her mood seemed to change as she scowled and spoke quietly.

"Ned Cheap Charlie! No more ration card, no more cigarettes, no more whiskey. No more money. Ned leave. Luu get more GIs here. Get more cigarettes, get more money. Ned no come here while Luu have other."

Her words were like whiplashes to Ned, who could not stand to hear her talk of having other soldiers in her flat. He had warned her many times before not to talk of it or even think of it. This time was too much for him. He had had enough. Enraged, he leaped to his feet and in two strides crossed the room. He slapped her hard on the side of the head.

With a cry of surprise and pain, Luu hit the floor. She lay very still as she stared at him with wide, terrified eyes.

"You think I'm goin' to move outta here so you can screw all the GIs in this city for a couple of lousy bucks and a carton of Salems?"

He looked at her opened blouse. A glint of golden skin caught his eye. Without thinking, he reached down and ripped the blouse open, then carefully, almost tenderly, removed it.

Luu knew men. This was no time to resist. She hated him now, but she knew he would have his way and she had no intention of trying to stop him. That would be foolish and dangerous.

Ned gazed at the golden breasts now quivering with fear. Quickly he reached down and picked her up. She was like a doll in his large, powerful, black arms. He carried her to the bed and laid her crossways upon it. He kicked off his shoes and removed his trousers and under-shorts. Then he reached down and slowly pulled off her black satin trousers and small underpants.

Luu shut her eyes. She was determined to remain passive. Too well trained as a prostitute to show her true feelings, she now wanted Ned to experience the least possible enjoyment from this act. With little ease, he guided his hard, swollen member into her. She could not stifle a gasp as she felt him enter her body.

So big. So ... Oh ...

Ned began a slow rhythm, but almost immediately he increased his tempo and in no time, he was completely out of control. She tried to remain passive as he wildly thrust deeper into her, but it was impossi-ble for her not to respond. Her resolve vanished and she threw her arms and legs about his undulating body. She thrilled as she felt his power engulf her. Moist lips covered her tiny mouth. His tongue forced its way between her teeth. She was completely part of him ...

Ψ   Ψ   Ψ

Poli De Salle, PhD, was nervous, hot, and uncomfortable.

He sat at the small table on the un-air-conditioned veranda and crossed his legs for the sixteenth time. The sweat dripped down his back, making dark lines on his white stateside suit. In the Western world, he might have been taken for a Creole planter with his dark complexion, his high, thin, slightly hooked nose, and dark hair and eyebrows. He looked down at his long, thin legs, noticed the added wrinkles in his trousers, and immediately uncrossed them.

Obviously, I've picked the wrong night. God, if there were a way to call the whole thing off, I'd do it, but Janet would be on her way by this time ... She's always on time. This club, the Cercle Hippique, is the perfect place for our meeting—not fancy, no loud music. It's civilized, understated, quiet, and businesslike. We can talk in relative privacy—only how did I know I'd pick the most miserable evening of the year.

De Salle knew that he would be nervous, because everything depended on Janet now. He couldn't afford to botch this meeting. He had arranged to arrive early so that he could get a couple of drinks to settle him down, but they merely added to the rivers of sweat.

As he sipped his gin and tonic, he looked through the large open arches across the wide veranda, outside to the riding oval where Vietnamese grooms were exercising three beautiful chestnut horses. In the center of the oval was a group of jumps. Two were bar jumps, two were of brush, and one was of wood painted to resemble a brick wall.

A young Eurasian girl was guiding her horse over this series of obstacles. She was dressed in a typical European riding habit of brown jacket, jodhpurs, and boots. Her black hair was in two long braids, which fell to her waist. In her right hand, she held a long braided quirt of black leather.

Poli watched the girl. Although she was very attractive, what intrigued him most was the determination and strength she displayed in handling the large white hunter. Four times, she negotiated the course,

29

and four times the hunter performed perfectly on the first four jumps. However, each time the horse took the last jump, his right hind leg nicked the top bar, which fell off its resting pegs and into the grass.

In disgust, the girl would halt the horse while a groom replaced the bar, then she would start the course over again. After a while the girl began to lose her patience. Her exasperation at first was not visible to those on the veranda, but the horse sensed it and responded in a nervous, uneven gait, breaking his stride as she urged him back to the jump. Each time he repeated his mistake the girl's temper became more evident, and the horse became more nervous. Finally, large areas of sweat appeared on the big hunter and foam flecked his mouth as he fought the bit. Again, the pretty girl halted her mount at the start of the course. Carefully she drew a small handkerchief from her sleeve and patted her brow and neck. Then, just as carefully, she raised the quirt and brought it down full force on the flanks of the anxious animal.

The hunter responded instantly. He fought the bit in an effort to give his head freedom. Failing this, he reared, turned, and charged through the first jump, knocking down the bars with his broad chest and powerful front legs. Poli rose to his feet to watch the girl and horse fight it out, but most of the club members, having seen similar situations many times, merely sipped their drinks and glanced indifferently at the struggle.

As he watched, Poli heard two men at a neighboring table speaking in French. He turned to see that they were Eurasians, half-Vietnamese. Both were small, slight in build, and somewhat effete in their speech and manner.

Poli was instantly jealous of their apparent immunity to the ravages of the humidity. Not a trace of sweat, not a wrinkle on their white linen suits.

"Marie seems more vindictive than usual today. Poor Prince, he's fighting her hard," the younger man observed.

"Didn't you know? We've lost our Marie. She has decided to take her father's name and is now calling herself Dao Thi."

"Really?"

"Yes, she must have acquired a strong sense of Vietnamese patriotism lately."

"But how can you call it patriotism when she hates the Americans so? Premier Ky says we must love the Americans with all our souls if we are to be good South Vietnamese."

"That's why it's so much easier to be French. We are expected to despise everything American!"

"Yes. Of course. Have a Salem?"

Both smiled as they lit their cigarettes, blowing long plumes of smoke into the languid fan moving slowly above them, then turned again to Thi and her struggle with the white hunter.

A groom ran quickly to the first jump to replace the bars. By this time, the horse was progressing sideways to the next jump. Thi was using her spurs cruelly, but it made no difference to Prince. With wild eyes, he turned in place and knocked down the barrier of the brush jump. As he spun around, the girl was almost unseated. There were snickers from the crowd on the veranda.

Poli decided that this girl was not popular at the club. The ridicule was not to be taken lightly. Her long quirt was brought down time and again on the haunches of the horse, now bathed in lather and sweat in the still, muggy twilight. Suddenly Thi turned her wrath on the crowd. With no warning, she brought down her quirt on the shoulders of a groom standing nearby. Then, by sheer willpower, she managed to guide the terror-stricken horse out of the debris of the jump and brought him, now plunging, now dancing, in front of the veranda.

Then, standing in her stirrups, she yelled something clearly rude in Vietnamese at the spectators, and galloped off to the stable area.

Wonder what she said ... better act like I understand.

He affected a small, wry smile and a barely noticeable shake of his head.

But Poli was now intrigued by the entire performance. He momentarily forgot his meeting. He took the opportunity to pose a question to the two men in his own adequate, but somewhat academic French. Like malicious old crones, the two Eurasians warmed to the invitation.

"Who is she? Ah, Monsieur, in a way she is the spirit of our country—fierce, proud, misguided. She is Miss Marie Le Blum or Cô Dao Thi, I should now say. Her mother was a rich widow, the product of

31

France. Her father, Vietnamese … sometime poet, sometime scholar, sometime, ah … financier, but full-time lover!"

"The girl is—well, very attractive," Poli ventured.

"Very, and also well educated. First, University of Hue; then two years at the Sorbonne. Then … well. Papa ran off with the money; then Mama died and Dao Thi found herself very much alone, very pretty, but very poor."

The older man then took up the story. "What could she do? Get married, of course! But who? He must be French—and he must be rich. She spent her last cash on a trip back to Paris to pursue a few hopefuls she had met in her more affluent university days, but competition was too keen there and—well, she didn't land any of her wealthy fish. Ran into some sort of trouble with the *La Sûreté Nationale*. Never spoke about it since her return."

"But why would she return to Vietnam?" asked Poli.

"Why indeed? A job in Vietnamese films as an actress. One of our best directors met her in Paris and offered her a chance to star in his pictures. He called her *Solange*."

"But she starred only in his bed!"

"Come, Henri, that's not fair. There was the war, the wound, the convalescence, and the breaking up with the director!"

"That's true. Ever since the shelling by the Americans in 1964, her career went downhill. They say she dropped the director—or vice versa."

"She was a lousy actress—but *belle poitrine!*"

"But be careful, Monsieur. She hates Americans. She blames them for the wound and all her troubles."

Poli wondered what wound they were talking about. From where he sat, the girl looked lovely. He glanced up just as Janet Holden entered. He immediately excused himself and rose to meet her, noticing with satisfaction her open and friendly smile.

"Janet, darling," he greeted her, as he held out both arms. It had been ten years. His eyes searched for changes in her.

Still very attractive. That ginger hair. Amazing creamy white skin. But … more self-assured. How old would she be now … late thirties? Still keeps that great figure, but hard to see it under that sensible dress. The red curls still there, but cut above the shoulders, and those green eyes! I'd forgotten—but they're a bit sad, now. Probably because of Ted's disappearance. Let's see, been missing for six months. They say it was the VC, but what would they want with America's so-called greatest anthropologist? Could they use him against us? If so, they should have taken both of them … she's just as good as her husband. Maybe they just killed him …

She smiled as she allowed him to take both her hands in his, and proffered her cheek.

"Poli, you old dear! Whatever are you doing in Saigon?"

Poli De Salle wasn't ready to play his hand completely. It wasn't his nature, nor was it his desire to do so. But he needed Janet's support, and needed it badly. She was to be his entree into Saigon's official circles—both American and Vietnamese. She was known and admired for her own contributions to Ted's work, but best of all for his purposes, she was pitied because of Ted's disappearance. If she would go to bat for him, she could open any official door in South Vietnam and solve his immediate problem. He snapped his fingers for the waiter before answering Janet's question.

After they ordered drinks and were alone again, Poli leaned forward and said, "There is so much to be done here, Janet. You know there is. That's why you are here. That's why Ted came over. But, there are so few of us—and so much to do! We can't just sit back there in the States in our ivory towers and let this horror go on. After all, we are social scientists, and it isn't right for us merely to write it up as history for new textbooks.

"You have been a great help to these people, Janet. You and Ted both have really set the social science community on its ear, back home. You are doing something for them. Everyone is reading your stuff. That last article of Ted's in *Foreign Affairs* really brought me here."

"But Poli, that was published over a year ago!"

"I know, but it has taken me that long to get untangled at home. After all, I'm a tenured senior professor. I had to leave my work in good hands. And then—my God, Janet, it has taken me months to get clearance for this place!

"I think I can help these people too. I think my background and experience can have a direct impact on their future. I feel that—well,

33

perhaps working with you ... after all, Janet, you can't carry out that study by yourself now that Ted ..."

"Please, Poli," Janet broke in. She wasn't going to let Poli carry on this conversation about Ted any further.

"I don't mean that I could ever think of taking Ted's place, Janet, but I could be a great help. As your colleague, I could be in charge of your data-gathering teams."

"Poli, dear. This is anthropology—your field is political science. And besides, we aren't using the interview system on this. We are participant observers. Knowing you, well, it seems to me that your best approach would be with USAID or JUSPAO. Remember, the elections are coming up, and you would be a natural as an advisor or consultant to one of the political study groups. It's really fascinating, being here at the birth of a democracy."

Poli had no intention of getting that close to the delivery room. He knew that the period of the coming elections was going to be an extremely dangerous time, and he didn't like inconvenience, let alone personal danger of any kind. As an American authority on political science, his own academic area was the United States. He felt insecure elsewhere. His perception, his keen-mindedness, and his phenomenal memory had helped establish his position at home. He looked into his glass.

Vietnam is ten thousand miles away from my place of business. These dirty little people aren't capable of sustaining any democratic process. The elections are going to be a failure, in spite of our presence. I don't want any part of them. God, how I wish I weren't here! But I am, dammit, and I have to scramble about to get a safe vantage point from which I can observe this absurd, stupid operetta.

Janet sensed his internal struggle and wondered if she would ever know the real reason why this vain, insecure, often unhappy man had come to Vietnam. Both she and her husband had admired his early work, but in the last eight years or so, Poli had started accepting special jobs outside of his academic field. As an advisor or consultant, he was apparently available to accept assignments in any scientific discipline, so long as it was at a high enough level to allow him to work above and outside any real details of the problem.

"I think you're right, Janet," said Poli, smiling.

34

He offered her a cigarette.

"If I could help someone like Newell Osborne ... do you think he could use me?"

Janet knew that Poli was aware of her friendship with Newell, and was relieved. If she could satisfy Poli with merely an introduction to Newell, she would be getting off easily. At first, she was taken aback by her thought. Then suddenly the realization reached her that she did not trust Poli, and that she really never had in all the long years she and Ted had known him.

"Poli, why don't you plan on joining me next Thursday? Newell has invited me to lunch in his office. We are to talk about our—my project. Of course I couldn't bring you without Newell's permission, so I'll get in touch with him first thing in the morning."

Poli was pleased. He hadn't expected such immediate assistance. He smiled, thanked Janet, and turned to summon the waiter again.

As he looked up, he found himself staring at Thi standing in the doorway between the dining room and entrance hall. She had changed from her severe riding habit to a beautiful dark green *ao dai,* the traditional Vietnamese women's clothing. Occasionally, she glanced at her watch and moved to the main club entrance. When doing this she moved out of Poli's field of vision. Then in a few minutes, she again returned to her position in the doorway. Each time she appeared, most of the men on the veranda turned to watch her. The rain that had started with nightfall drummed pleasantly on the metal roof of the club. Janet looked up to see the object of Poli's attention.

"What a gorgeous girl! Who is she, Poli? A friend of yours?"

Poli answered slowly, without taking his eyes off the girl, "No, she isn't a friend, but we have ... ah, mutual acquaintances. Perhaps during supper I will tell you about her."

At that moment, a large Mercedes sedan pulled up under the porte-cochere of the Cercle Hippique, and a young Vietnamese man in an immaculate white suit emerged and spoke to Thi. She favored him with a dazzling smile as she followed him to the car.

They spoke not a word as the chauffeur drove them out into the rainy night. The car headed toward Cholon, the Chinese quarter of

Saigon. Thi gazed at many familiar landmarks through the dark and the rain.

"Wonder where he lives?" Thi asked herself. She would not dare to ask her escort. She must be patient. Suddenly the car slowed and stopped in front of her own apartment building.

"What is this, some sort of joke?" protested Thi as she looked at the man seated next to her.

"I am sorry, Mademoiselle," replied the man in the white suit. "We received word just as I left to pick you up. The master cannot see you this evening. There has been ... ah, a change in plans. He directed me to take you to your lodgings. I am to return early in the morning. Be ready. I shall be here at six."

"Six? You must be ..."

Thi caught herself in time and did not complete the sentence.

The young man smiled as he pushed open the car door. "Six," he said with finality. "Be waiting!"

Thi ran quickly through the rain to her door. When she reached shelter, she turned to smile but the car had already driven away. There was a power failure and the building was in darkness. Cursing in French, she made her way clumsily up four blacked-out flights of stairs to her apartment.

"God, it's hot," she said aloud as she stripped off her damp clothing and shook out her long black hair.

Naked, she fell onto her bed. In the distance, she could hear the American artillery conducting "H and I" fire.

"More action across the river," she said aloud. Several anti-personnel flares were descending by parachute over the dark city. The swaying light spilled in the open front of her flat and illuminated her still body. The thud of artillery fire continued.

What a complete failure. That damned horse. Now, no contact. Has he changed his mind?

She felt defeated, alone, impotent. As she lay there, her frustration and fatigue slowly changed to anger, and her face became ugly and horrid in the swaying, changing light and darkness. She reached up under her hair to her cheek and felt the scar. As she traced the familiar outline with delicate fingers, she clenched her other fist and beat upon the bed in rhythm with the booming cannon.

"Those fucking Americans," she muttered in French. "Those *merde*-eating, swine-fucking bastards! Someday they will pay for this!"

Tears of bottomless hatred rolled down her face, wetting the satin-covered pillow. She cried for a long time before she fell asleep.

Chapter II

JUNE

T he helicopter landed Brandy Masters and Peter Charles at Trong Thoi in mid-afternoon.

As the pilot circled the fort, the men of the garrison left their work and lined the walls to catch a glimpse of their "round-eye girl."

Privately, each man already considered Brandy his personal property. She was his to live with, his to see, to smell, to touch, to talk to, to watch, and to protect for the forty-eight hours she was there. After she left, she would be the subject of his sexual fantasies and dreams for several months to come.

Mark Buckley knew and thought about these basic feelings that soldiers had when away from their own kind of women and shuddered.

She's the only round-eye among all these horny GIs. She belongs to all of them, but also to each of them exclusively. We've got a powder keg here and she's the fuse. I've got to talk to her. She'd better watch her ass or she'll set off the biggest explosion of this war.

He ran forward, fighting the downwash of the rotors, and guided Brandy from the chopper and up the crude steps cut into the sloping walls. Shyly the men attempted a hesitant, tentative cheer. At first, their efforts almost died away, but as the girl approached the sally port, the thin, embarrassed sound developed into a deep-throated, spontaneous roar. At the entrance, two small Vietnamese children were pushed forward by their mothers. They shyly offered her some wilted

39

wildflowers. These she accepted with a bright smile, then turned to wave at the men along the wall. The day was bright and sunny. A moderate breeze whipped Brandy's long blond hair and pressed her thin white blouse against her body.

Mark hesitated for some time to let the men appreciate the full effect of a wind-blown Brandy, her eyes hidden behind large, round violet-colored sunglasses. He looked at the happy faces and then at the chopper. The last of its cargo was almost unloaded; it would lift off shortly.

She's already been worth the price we paid for her—and we'd be money ahead if I could put her back on the chopper right now.

He looked back at Peter, who was standing a bit behind Brandy, his eyes averted.

"What do you think of our fort?" he asked, attempting to make Peter feel welcome.

"Well, it's ... it's great," answered Peter a little lamely.

"That was an unfair question, I guess, because it's not much to look at, and won't ever win any architectural prizes, but we've successfully sustained two major attacks—the worst one just last month. That's why it's looking better to us all the time."

Mark could see that this turn of conversation was not alleviating Peter's uneasiness. It seemed best to drop the subject. Leaving Peter, he turned to lead Brandy through the entrance into the courtyard. Several of the men followed and were now crowding about the girl in an effort to hear her say a few words or just be close to her.

"All right, back to work," laughed Mark. "You all know Miss Masters' schedule and will have a chance to meet her during her stay with us. Let's get the lookouts back on their posts, First Sergeant. The VC may decide they want to engage Miss Masters for an extended stay!"

Brandy glanced up at Mark and grinned. He led her across the small courtyard and into the hall that led through the buildings to the porch and central parade ground. Brandy smiled to herself as she noticed the stares of the men in the orderly room on her left as Mark held the opposite door open for her.

She found herself in Mark's office.

The two entertainers took seats on a makeshift couch while the few other officers of the fort and Sergeant Mead took places about the room, responding eagerly when Mark made the introductions. Presently a petite Vietnamese girl entered with a tray of soft drinks. Brandy looked at the girl with interest. She was pretty. Then, clinically, she looked at Mark.

Nope, he's not getting any action from that little gal.

"Boy, real ice!" she exclaimed as she took the glass. "It isn't so bad in the 'boonies' after all."

As they laughed, Mark broke in, "The men drew numbers to see who would be assigned as your escort. Who won, Mead?"

The first sergeant eyed Brandy with a smile and answered, "Sergeant Bob Blackstone is the lucky guy, sir. Shall I get him?"

"No, not yet," Mark replied pleasantly. Then his face clouded and certain harshness appeared in his voice. "In fact, I want all of you to clear out while I tell Miss Masters and Mr. Charles the name of the game around here. I'll let you know when to bring Blackstone around. It'll be about fifteen minutes."

The men left after telling Brandy what an honor it was to have her at the fort, but she hardly heard their voices. Mark's harsh tone had made both her and Peter feel uneasy and out of place.

"I had a hard time getting permission for you to come up here, Miss Masters. This camp is not exactly the safest area in the Delta. The Vietnamese garrison has not been completely pro-American for too long. Now, don't get me wrong. They don't necessarily have to like us. We just require that they hate the VC more. Anyway, we've made great progress with them in the past six months, especially since the last attack. We feel for the first time that we have a really close-knit, loyal team and we don't want anything to destroy that situation.

"But perhaps the greatest danger is the presence of a single American girl here in an isolated garrison. It's a natural feeling, I think, after a man has chipped in his own dough to hire an entertainer, that she ... well, belongs to him personally. What I'm trying to say is—when men are in the total majority, isolated for long periods, their basic feelings take over. They are inclined to be jealous, and are easily provoked if a single female should show preference to one of them. My advice to you is to be friendly with everyone, and don't refuse any legitimate offer. Of course, I'm referring to requests for a dance in our dayroom, having pictures taken, and so forth ..."

"Legitimate offers?" asked Brandy with just the hint of a leer and challenge in her eyes.

Mark did not smile. His dark eyes went stony cold. He was silent for a long heartbeat.

Then with a voice that was textbook serious, he replied, "You're a big girl, Miss Masters, and you know perfectly well what I mean. I wasn't born last week, and neither were you. My men have been warned, briefed, even threatened. There will be very few out-of-line propositions from them. I'm counting on you to refuse the few that you do receive. On the other hand, if the propositions come from you, I cannot vouch for any of the men's behavior. That is all."

"Colonel Buckley, I don't like your insinuations," snapped Brandy.

Her eyes were flashing in anger. She jumped to her feet and strode over to the window, then turned and approached Mark.

"What makes you think you can judge me? What makes you think that you are so goddamn holy? So goddamn better than the rest of us?"

"Quiet down, Miss Masters—and sit down," responded Mark quietly.

"Your morals are no concern of mine at any other point in time except the next forty-eight hours which constitutes your stay at Trong Thoi. I'm merely telling you here and now that bad conduct on your part while at this post may very well destroy the futures of some of the people here. I know it would destroy the future chances of entertainment groups coming here. I'm just making you aware of your responsibilities as a woman while you are our guest. I expect you to live up to those responsibilities. Have I made myself clear?"

Brandy was visibly shaking now. Never before had she had a man talk to her in this manner. She went back to her place and sat down. She was furious and embarrassed. She was also intrigued. Suddenly all of this made her want Mark Buckley more than ever. Much more than the usual way she felt about powerful, out-of-reach men.

I know just how to show him who's who. He has no idea. None.

Quickly she drew out a cigarette. Peter leaned over and lit it for her. His hand was shaking too.

He leaned close to her and whispered quietly, "Don't blow it, baby."

As if to indicate the termination of the lecture, Mark went to the door and called for Sergeant Blackstone. Presently a short, stocky staff sergeant in immaculate fatigues and shiny combat boots entered and reported. Mark introduced him to Brandy and Peter.

"Sergeant Blackstone will escort you about the camp to all meals."

His manner had become cordial and pleasant again.

Taking her cue from Mark, Brandy changed the tone also.

"Tell me, Sergeant, who does your laundry?" she asked with an amused smile.

"Oh, one of the ... the local girls," answered Bob Blackstone. He blushed visibly and looked at the floor.

Mark scowled and said quietly, "I would stick to less personal subjects if I were you, Miss Masters."

My, we are touchy around here.

Brandy decided to keep her pleasant tone.

"I hope you complimented her on the beautiful job she did on those fatigues," she added with a laugh.

Mark, relieved by her remark, was glad he had an opportunity to end the discussion on a light note.

"Well, let's get your schedule out, Sergeant. As I remember, our guests are in for a tour right after lunch. Let's show them their quarters and let them wash up a bit. Miss Masters, I've turned over my quarters to you. Right here—right off my office. We did this to give you some privacy, and it also gives you access to the only private bath in the camp, such as it is."

"Oh, you didn't have to do that," said Brandy turning on the charm.

She was genuinely touched with this hospitality. She rose and went to the door and surveyed the spartan surroundings of Mark's room. An army cot with mosquito netting, a footlocker, and a low chest of drawers comprised all of the furniture.

"How very thoughtful of you to do this."

"Peter will be moving in with First Sergeant Mead, and I have taken

43

over Lieutenant Southern's bunk. He is in Can Tho for a couple of days. Now, if you will excuse me ..."

They all rose to leave Mark's office. Brandy said she would be ready in ten minutes, and disappeared into Mark's quarters. Now alone, Mark went to his desk and started through the papers from his in-basket.

Brandy closed the door behind her and stood in the center of Mark's room. She couldn't believe that anyone could live in such a barren, imper-sonal atmosphere. There wasn't one picture on the wall, one personal item lying about. She went to the footlocker. It was unlocked. Quietly she lifted the lid. In the top tray were neatly stacked socks, handkerchiefs, a small box of insignia, medals, and other military ornaments.

"What a disappointment," she thought as she stared at the tray.

She felt guilty for prying and wasn't brave enough to raise the tray to see the contents underneath. As she was about to close the locker she noticed a picture tacked to the inside of the lid. It was a large color photograph of a very attractive woman with a small boy, five or six years of age. The woman was smiling; the boy looked very serious.

He's the image of Mark.

Brandy slowly closed the lid. Suddenly she felt alone in the world and unwanted. She did not like that feeling.

She moved to the window and looked across the porch onto the open center court of the fort. There was a flagpole with a crossbar on it. From one side flew the Stars and Stripes, from the other the red-and-yellow flag of South Vietnam. Directly below her, a bored group of Vietnamese soldiers was receiving instruction in .50 caliber machine gun maintenance. Surrounding the court were single-story buildings built into the mud wall. In the distance, beyond the far wall, the mud-dy Mekong flowed silently through the green lowlands of the Delta.

Her attention now turned to several Vietnamese women in the cen-ter of the court, drawing water from a well and pouring it into a rag-tag collection of containers. Some of them were washing naked little children as they gossiped and laughed. One spotted her and pointed to the window. Brandy waved and the women smiled and waved back, then turned away and with their hands over their faces dissolved in torrents of giggles. For just a moment, Brandy wished she were with them, happy among the war's horrors because they had a man to love and his children to raise.

To her right, Brandy noticed a break in the wall where two large wooden doors formed a gate. The doors were open, but it was clear they could be secured when necessary. A profusion of barbed wire was everywhere about the gate and atop the wooden doors. Through the entrance, she could see a small town, composed of little shacks made of mud, bamboo, cardboard, tin, and whatever else the inhabitants could find. She knew that this miserable little village supported the families of the Vietnamese soldiers who had followed them to the field and made a place to live as close to the camp as possible.

Brandy looked at the crooked, muddy streets of the town, the piles of trash and garbage, the poverty, filth, and squalor, and shuddered. Then she noticed something common to all the people of the village. They all seemed to be happy—or at least not unhappy.

Perhaps that's the secret; perhaps if you care for someone enough, you don't care how or where you live, so long as you are near him. What man could be worth all that?

There was a knock on the door.

Was this the sergeant? Where did the time go?

She would have to forgo the wash-up. She took one last look at the townspeople before turning to the door.

Could I ever love some man that much? Children?

As Mark entered the mess hall for the evening meal, he thought with satisfaction about the progress of the day.

Lunch really went well and, from all reports, so did the tour of the fort. The mess hall seems especially clean this evening and wow! Look at the special slick-up the men have given themselves. Hair carefully combed, all fatigues clean and pressed.

He watched Sergeant Bob Blackstone escort Brandy and Peter to a special table, where a select group of diners awaited them. He briefly caught Brandy's eye and smiled at her as he took his place at a table on the other side of the hall.

I wonder if I've misjudged Brandy and been too harsh with her since her arrival. She sure has a familiar, friendly personality that lets her make friends easily. Very easy on the eyes, that's for sure. I know she has promised several of the men a dance in the dayroom after the show. I'd like to attend, but I'd sure be out of place. I'd better remember to tell Sergean Mead to let the dance last till ten minutes before eleven o'clock curfew.

The men filed out of the mess hall and Brandy and Peter left to change for the show. Part of Brandy's act was the use of several costume changes to match each group of songs she sang. With each costume change, the songs became more intimate and suggestive.

To accommodate the performers, the men had constructed a stage in front of their quarters. There was a small portion curtained off at the rear of the stage, with room enough for Brandy to make her quick changes. They had even set up a lighting system with a few footlights. The afternoon breeze had died down and a thick, oppressive humidity settled on the community. In the twilight, a few bats darted about the lights, making a supper of the insects collecting there.

The fort's entire garrison, except those on guard duty, began to assemble in front of the small stage. To this group was added the dependents of the Vietnamese soldiers. The women, in the Asian manner, were shy and tended to linger in female groups to the rear and one side of the crowd. Most of them carried naked infants on their hips. Little children uninhibited in their nudity ran through the crowd, fighting, yelling, and teasing the soldiers.

Mark had arranged for his officers to entertain the officers of the Vietnamese garrison during Brandy's performance. Seated on the wide porch in front of the orderly room, they sipped Vietnamese beer poured over ice, which was a favorite drink for Vietnamese and Americans alike. The porch extended from Mark's office past the orderly room, and on to the mess hall and barracks in a wide semi-circle about the parade ground. Being raised two steps above ground, it gave the officers an unencumbered view of the stage.

The Vietnamese officers were all eagerly awaiting this glamorous change in their usual routine, but Major Ho, the Vietnamese troop commander, was especially intrigued with Brandy. He had seen her from a distance during her tour and was eager to meet her.

At this point, Brandy and Peter, accompanied by Sergeant Blackstone, made their way along the porch from the orderly room. Peter, dressed in a Spanish costume, was carrying his guitar while Brandy, in a long skin-tight gown of silver sequins, carried a small tambourine. All talk stopped as the pair approached the officers on their way to the stage.

Mark drew Brandy and Peter over and introduced them to the Vietnamese officers. Major Ho was completely charmed and Brandy was quick to exploit her position.

"Mark, we usually start with Peter coming out on stage alone and playing a couple of songs. In this way, we get the electrical hookup for the mike and his guitar adjusted. May I stay here while he does this? I could make my first entrance along the porch to the stage."

"Number one idea," interrupted Major Ho. His English was surprisingly good, and he used it at every opportunity.

"Fine," said Mark with a smile. "Will you have time for a beer while Peter starts the act?"

He offered her his glass.

"Love some. Here, Peter, have a sip and then off you go. I can't keep the boys waiting."

As Peter played his opening numbers, Major Ho stood as close as possible to Brandy. She was aware of his interest and used every opportunity to brush against him as they stood in the crowd of officers.

Little bastard wants me. Just like all of them.

"After your performance tonight, will you come to my house for small late refreshment?" asked Ho quietly.

Brandy found Ho exotic and exciting. She somehow felt that if she accepted the invitation Mark would also have to attend and perhaps pay more attention to her.

"Why, yes, I'd love to," she replied.

"I think Miss Masters has forgotten about the dance she is to attend this evening," interrupted Mark. "And I think every dance is taken."

Brandy was furious. Her eyes blazed as she turned on Mark.

"That was no official commitment," she said.

"It was to those men, and you are going to keep it."

His voice was quiet and even, but Brandy felt the finality of the words. On the parade ground, the soldiers were getting restless. Their patience was short. After each of Peter's songs, the cries of "Bring on the blonde" became more distinct and demanding. "Bring on bronde," imitated the Vietnamese.

"Your audience is calling, Brandy," said Mark.

His voice reflected a mock sweetness, but Brandy knew it was an order for her to go.

"Please excuse me," she said, pressing through the people on the porch to make her way to the stage.

Later, after the show, as Mark sat at his desk finishing the last of the administrative papers, he reviewed the events of the evening. The show had been a resounding success, in spite of the girl's limited talent, and now she was in the mess room dancing with the men to the record player. Peter had joined a poker game in the NCO quarters. He looked at his watch—almost ten forty-five, and Sergeant Blackstone would be bringing her back any minute.

There was the sound of steps on the porch. Mark heard Brandy invite Blackstone into her room. He smiled when he heard the sergeant reply nervously that it was a great thought, but that the old man was probably still working in his office and would see them. The sergeant then tried some hasty goodbyes, but there was a long silence. Mark smiled, knowing that Blackstone was getting a kiss out of this.

Finally, there were hasty footsteps retreating and Brandy called "Good night, Bobby."

Seconds later the door opened and Brandy stepped into the office.

"Well, if it isn't my good fairy—always around to keep me out of trouble," commented Brandy bitterly.

"Poor choice of words, Miss Masters," smiled Mark.

"What do you do, post yourself around to see that the little lads stay pure? Don't worry, I won't corrupt your little Boy Scouts!"

It was obvious to Mark that a few beers had come Brandy's way.

"That's right. I'm not going to let you," Mark replied with a smile. "Now take a cold shower and go to bed. We're going to cut the generator in ten minutes."

Things weren't going Brandy's way at all. She knew she would have to change her tactics if she were to get anywhere with Mark.

"Mark," she said as she walked to the couch and sat down, "Can't we at least be civil to each other? Could it hurt you to come over here and have a cigarette with me and just talk?"

"I'll go you one better. I'll get you a coke," replied Mark. He rose from his desk and left the room briefly. In a moment, he returned with two cokes in glasses. "Real *nook dau*, ice, again, Brandy," he said, mocking her earlier remark.

"How about putting some real rum in it?"

"Will you settle for real whiskey? I'll have to get it out of my ... your room."

He crossed to the room and flicked on the light. The change occasioned by Brandy's belongings and the smell of her perfume was a staggering surprise. He lifted the tray of the footlocker, picked up the bottle, and returned to the office. Silently he mixed the drinks and joined her on the couch. He was relaxed and pleasant.

Brandy took a long look at him through her cigarette smoke.

This guy actually has some charm.

Every man she met was a sporting challenge to her. She thought that Mark was going to be difficult. But, he was obviously interested.

Could he really have been sincere this afternoon? Or was he just being "army" about the whole thing?

They talked about her show and the great morale boost it had been for the men. As they talked, Brandy's mind raced onward. She had learned something about the woman and boy in the picture while dancing in the dayroom with the soldiers. Nonetheless, it was inconceivable to her that this very virile man would walk out of this room tonight and go to sleep alone when she was right there in front of him.

Suddenly Mark got up.

"It's been pleasant, Brandy, but this place is going to be in pitch blackness in about three minutes. You'll find a candle and matches on that table by the bed. I'll also leave you this flashlight. I'd better be ..."

"Mark, please." She felt her need for him taking over. Her skills automatically kicked in. Her body language softened.

"Why don't you stay here with me tonight?" She rose and wrapped

49

her arms about him; the significant curves of her body met his firm, tall frame in a clear statement.

Mark gently extricated himself and quietly said, "We went through all that. Now go to bed."

Brandy now played what she considered her trump card: sincerity.

With all the quiet earnestness she could muster, she said, "I know that you have no ties at home. I know you're not being true to someone back there. I'm sorry about the ... the accident that happened four years ago. Why don't you ..."

Mark couldn't believe his ears. All inside of him became white heat. He fought to control his temper, but it was no use. In seconds, he was in a complete rage.

Who is this silly bitch who thinks she can pry into my life and bring back all those memories? For what? For her?

In a blur of motion, he struck at her with one heavy open palm. Brandy somehow managed to shield her face from part of the effects of the blow but she staggered to the couch blinded by one gigantic sunburst of light.

Instantly Mark regained his composure. Inwardly he was shaking from the residue of his rage and then, the enormity of his act.

"I'm sorry, Miss Masters. Are you all right?"

"Yes. Yes. I think so ... yes ... okay."

"Good night."

Mark turned and left the office. She heard his footsteps down the porch as the camp was plunged into darkness.

Ψ   Ψ   Ψ

Naked, Mark lay on the cot in the heavy, damp darkness. The still, thick air was like a blanket about him.

I suppose I'm the world's biggest idiot. Probably should have screwed the hell out of her ... but it would have been around the camp inside of ten minutes. Everyone would have known it and then ... hell. She's probably terrific. Just look at those tits, and what a great little ass ... but she sure as hell isn't worth a mutiny.

He turned in the soggy bed and fought with the mosquito net. Then his anger returned as he thought of Brandy's reference to Jane and Bill, and their death in the car accident.

My fault. My own damned fault.

He wondered how long it would be before he could accept the accident as a fact and go on from there ... when sleep finally came, he was drenched in sweat.

In Mark's bed, Brandy was also restlessly pursuing sleep. At first, the sheet felt cool against the heat of her nude body, but it soon became sticky with sweat as she tossed about. The side of her face was still hot from the force of his blow. Inwardly she burned with a strange combination of resentment and shame, which slowly became a desire to hurt Mark, to humiliate him in some way. She rolled over and lit a cigarette. Her body glistened in the brief flash of the match. She lay back, silently inhaling the smoke.

Suddenly she became aware of a slight noise outside the open window.

"Miss Masters ... ah ... Brandy?"

"Yes, yes—who is it?" she whispered anxiously. She rose from the bed, fumbled for her thin, short silk robe and walked to the window.

In the pale light of the quarter moon, Brandy recognized the face of one of the soldiers she had danced with that evening. In the shadows, she could make out other forms.

"There're four of us and we're wondering if you would like to walk into town? Major Ho is throwing a party. He thought you might like to come."

Of course! That cagey little Major Ho.

She had almost forgotten his offer earlier in the evening.

"How do I get out? The guards ..."

"No sweat, baby. The guy on the gate is my friend. He don't worry about round-eyes goin' out, but only about slant-eyes comin' in!"

"Wait a sec," responded Brandy. Dropping her robe, she slowly slid her way into a short cotton dress and shoes, skipping any underwear. She tossed her long blond hair and smiled wickedly to herself for providing a moonlit show for the GI, still at the window.

Hope he didn't faint out there.

She laughed aloud. Then, after running a comb through her hair, she went to the window and sat on the ledge.

Strong arms grabbed and lowered her to the ground. She felt hands on her breasts and inner thighs. She laughed.

"Easy, boys! Don't be in any hurry. Let's get out of here."

The group hustled her to the gate that was just open enough to let them pass. Strong arms were always on her: directing her, steering her, lifting her, guiding her. Her heart raced and her body trembled in anticipation. Where was she going? She didn't know. She didn't care. Whatever happened was what she wanted. She thought of Mark and knew positively that this was the way to get even with that idiot.

The town was dark, with only an occasional light spilling through a window or door to waste itself on the quiet, deserted muddy street. Suddenly the group turned off the main thoroughfare into a small alley. Brandy had some recollection of a sign that read "Butterfly Bar." Someone knocked on the door. It opened quickly and there was light. There was Major Ho.

Inside the large, rather gloomy room, Brandy could hear the sound of a small record player turned low. She accepted a large glass of whiskey. She hadn't half finished it before she found herself dancing with Major Ho. Brandy had several more drinks. Gradually more men appeared, and she danced with them all.

It was hot and very close in the Butterfly Bar. She realized that everyone seemed to be pawing her. At first, intrigued, she grabbed their hands and held them on her body. Finally, there was too much whiskey, there were too many hands, and she no longer tried to assist the men. She let them fondle her, paw her, kiss her as they wished. Time passed. She was dancing with a young soldier when Major Ho gently pulled the young man away from her and guided her through a curtain to a back room. It might have been a kitchen, but Brandy didn't really care. The only light came from the room behind her and a flickering flame from a cooking fire over in the far corner.

In the center of the room was a large table. He led her to it, motioning that they were to use it.

Major Ho had planned well. He had been working for this moment ever since he had met her on the porch. His own people, who had joined the group in the front room, were there to assure him privacy. Consequently, he was prepared to take all the time necessary to satisfy himself completely with this woman.

It worked out more easily than he could have imagined.

Brandy's tiny bit of caution had long ago been engulfed by her desires, flamed with drink. Her only thought now was to be taken by Major Ho as soon as possible. Quickly, she kicked off her shoes, slid out of her dress and lay naked, back upon the table. She waited impatiently as she watched Ho prepare himself.

Major Ho was a very methodical man. Carefully he folded his trousers and laid them on the sink. In similar fashion, he disposed of his shirt and shorts. As he advanced to the table, he thought to himself,

A blond Western girl! Just like all the motion pictures. So large and round.

At the table, he found Brandy eagerly waiting for him. He was conscious of the sweet smell of Brandy's perfume as he stood at the table's edge, pulled her legs around his waist and quickly penetrated her. She had been well ready for him. He held her hips in his tight grasp. In the dim light of the dying fire of the cookstove, he glimpsed her body.

What large breasts she had. How big she was, compared to his own women. As he thrust again and again, he leaned over and buried his head in her chest. He stood upright again and as he looked down at her breasts moving in lazy half circles below him, thrust deeper and deeper into her. Her large, upright, white mounds with cherry-pink nipples were hypnotic in the half light. As he watched, her nipples grew erect and huge. He had never seen anything like them. He moved his hand from Brandy's hip and took her left, very erect nipple between his thumb and first finger. He pulled and twisted it.

Brandy let out a loud moan of pleasure. He increased the pressure and she became louder. He applied more pressure. A scream of pleasure erupted between Brandy's moans. He paced his thrusts.

"Fuck me, oh God, just hurry up and fuck me," Brandy moaned.

But Ho was a good soldier, which meant he was also a realist and an opportunist. He was well aware that this chance might never pass his way again. Consequently, he was making the most of the situation. He had to control his actions and movements to produce for him maximum pleasure before reaching orgasm. Her firm breasts with nipples quivering in the center commanded his attention. He looked down and watched himself move in and out of the mound of blond hair at his loins. He was going to savor every moment of this for the rest of his life.

Brandy, on the other hand, quickly reached the very heights of passion and desire and was soon well beyond any semblance of restraint as she came for the first time.

Then again. And again.

Her hips rocked, matching her internal pulsing contractions. The longer Ho delayed, the wilder she became. The men in the outer room, where a growing number of Americans and Vietnamese drank, smoked, sweated, listened, and waited, heard her thrashing and her moans and screams of ecstasy.

"Fuck me you little bastard, fuck me!" she screamed, "Deeper, oh God. Faster. No. No. Make me. Make me. Yes!"

By the time Ho reached the climax he had patiently waited for, several Vietnamese and Americans, overcome with curiosity and desire, had crowded inside the door to the kitchen. They watched Ho's slim, muscular behind moving with precision in and out, between the creamy white thighs extended from the table's edge.

Brandy by this time had her ankles around the major's waist. Her body thrashed against him. Looking around Ho, they could see her long blond hair moving back and forth on the shaking table. The creaking and pounding sound of the wooden legs echoed loudly.

She screamed again. Her legs gripped Ho even tighter. The crowd could see Brandy lift her hips off the table and, in the air, gyrate madly against the major's body.

"Fuck me. Fuck me!" Brandy screamed as loud as she could.

Then with a low shout, Ho climaxed. He paused for a moment looking down at Brandy who was still quivering before him on the table. Her large breasts came to a stop and she was breathing hard. There was now, just visible to Ho in the dim light, a soft rosy blush that started between her breasts and continued up her neck to her cheeks. Her closed eyelids were darker. Her red lips curled in selfish delight.

"So," Major Ho said coldly.

The men pushed apart the plastic ribbon screen and watched in stoic silence as Ho dismounted, dressed, and left through the back door without looking back.

Brandy did not move. She hadn't been ready to stop. She had to have more. She knew others would come. They always did. She closed her eyes and waited.

This is what she always wanted and, since she had been a sixteen-year-old cheerleader back in Texas, had gotten whenever she chose. But this was so much better than that first night with the five starters of the varsity basketball team in the school locker room.

She became aware of several people about the table and opened her eyes. In the dim flickering light, she saw naked men.

She recognized the first one as the big American who had helped her off the window ledge. She smiled and opened her legs and arms to receive him.

"So, you want to fuck me? Think you can handle me, soldier boy?" she murmured.

He did.

As men returned from the Butterfly Bar, the word spread fast through the barracks. The men off duty quietly left the fort and raced for town. This was a situation often dreamed about, but never experienced by most of the garrison, and they were not about to let it go by.

"What tits. Great ass! She moves it like a washing machine," was the word.

It was nearly ninety minutes later that Brandy, now more sober, realized she was no longer enjoying her experience. There seemed to be a large number of men in the room. She could see the red glow of lit cigarettes all around. A cloud of smoke filled the air.

Sometimes she had looked for Mark, but he was never there. Brandy's loins now ached and she was bathed in sweat. The air in the small room was foul with the smell of sweating men.

Then she was lying face down, her legs were hanging off the table's edge, and her feet just touched the floor. She then became aware that there were no longer any Americans in the room.

Behind her, she felt a man thrusting against her and then strongly climax. Brandy heard a shout of something in Vietnamese, then a sharp slap on her behind, and finally she felt him back away. There was much laughing in the room.

The sting of the spank sobered her to the fact that she was alone with these foreigners. She became frightened. She was not even close to being in control. Brandy always controlled men. When would this end? How would she get back? Where were her clothes? Would they ever let her up?

Strong hands suddenly took her by the hips and flipped her over. A stocky Vietnamese loomed above her. Rivulets of sweat rolled down his body and dripped on her. He grinned, spat on the floor, and looked down at her blond body. He spread her limp legs apart, stepped up, and then started to enter her. Brandy felt his large erection. Then she smelled an overwhelming odor of garlic. Brandy opened her eyes, looked up, and saw dark eager menace in the eyes of the stranger looking down at her.

Suddenly she panicked.

"Get off of me! Leave me alone! Stop it, oh God, stop it. Let me up, you filthy creep!"

This soldier, late to this party, couldn't understand the rejection after she had accepted so many others. Since it was a matter of pride and face with him, he had no intention of stopping, but pressed his body against her even more forcefully and into her more deeply. His hands were firmly on her hips as he began to move in and out with force. He looked down in fascination at her huge, up-thrusting breasts, with the rosy pink nipples still so large and erect, shuddering with each of his thrusts, below him.

Brandy, now overcome with anger and fright, reached up and raked the soldier deeply, from face to waist, with her long, sharp, painted fingernails. With an oath, the soldier struck her across the face. He quickened his pace. Then, enraged because she continued to struggle, he grabbed her about the neck with one of his hands and started beating her head against the table even as he continued to thrust against her in a faster and more violent motion.

Brandy was pinned in her place. Blood from his long scratches dripped onto her body and mingled with her sweat. He was going to have his pleasure in spite of her struggles. For one brief moment, she realized in panic that she was not in control. She was not using some man for her own pleasure. It was not on her terms.

She was being raped.

She screamed, this time in a high-pitched sound of panic and terror. This only made the soldier's excitement quicken. He felt pressure from deep down begin to build within him. This was stronger than he had ever felt before. He sensed himself become even larger and stiffer and went deeper. Much deeper. He was close now.

Suddenly there was a blinding light and the men around her melted into the dark margins of the room. Brandy was aware that Lieutenant Colonel Mark Buckley had entered the room. Then she passed out and knew no more.

Ψ   Ψ   Ψ

Mark tossed the flashlight to Sergeant Mead, and then pulled the sweaty soldier off of Brandy and threw him across the room. The naked, angry man started to rise and come after Mark.

Mead put his other hand on the .45 pistol on his belt and that ended the matter right there for Brandy's would-be lover who then staggered out of the room with his trousers at his ankles, muttering curses in Vietnamese.

Mark looked down on the very sweaty, very bloody, and quite unconscious girl. He cursed himself for bringing her to Trong Thoi.

Without a word, he picked her up. Her dress was long gone. A souvenir for someone. Pushing through the silent crowd of Vietnamese, he carried her, nude, through the streets of the town, escorted only by Sergeant Mead, who walked ahead lighting their way with the powerful flashlight.

Mark took her to his quarters and called for the camp medic. When he arrived, he and Mark, trying to avoid getting bloodstains on their fatigues, placed Brandy in the stall shower and turned on the water. Mark sighed with relief when he discovered that the large smears of blood on Brandy's chest and stomach were clearly not hers. The medic checked her head and pronounced nothing serious beyond some small abrasions and bruising and probably a headache to come.

As the water splashed against her body, Brandy stirred and half awakened, half-sober. She groaned and looked wildly about until her eyes focused on Mark. At first, not knowing where she was, she assumed he also had joined the line of men.

"I knew you would come," she whispered. "Knew you wanted me. Bet I wore your ass out."

Grim-faced, Mark pushed her head under the shower spray. Only then did she gain full comprehension of what had happened.

"Okay, get out of there, dry yourself, and go to bed," Mark rasped. He turned to the medic. "Leave her. She's all right!"

Brandy heard the two leave, and then leaned against the wall, her head down, her wet blond hair hanging straight, covering her breasts. Drops of water ran down her body to the floor. She watched them run down her body and disappear down the drain.

The two men, slightly wet from the spray of the shower, crossed to the orderly room in silence. Mark turned to Sergeant Mead, who was waiting there for them, and said, "What a total clusterfuck! Post a full-time guard on that door. She goes nowhere, no one goes in, and she talks to no one. Then come see me."

Ψ   Ψ   Ψ

Saigon at dawn, after a long night's rain, has a fragile freshness that ends with the sun's rapid rise from the horizon.

At this early hour, the quiet wet streets seem clean and the cool air somehow gently cloaks the sweetly putrid odors that become more prevalent as the day progresses. To the east, across the Saigon River, when the sun breaches the flat green sea of rice, a few distant palm trees are silhouetted against a vivid red sky that quickly changes to gold, then saffron. It is at this moment that the new light first touches the very tops of the tallest buildings of the city and bathes them in a fleeting beauty that disappears as the sun rises above the flat marshy fields.

Thi, riding through the dark streets to her six o'clock appointment, watched the beggars in the doorways stir and prepare for the day. If she had bothered to look up at the skyline as the Mercedes turned on-to Nguyen Hue, she would have noticed a complex of pagoda-like structures, saffron in color, nearly matching the sunrise, with jade-green tile roofs, perched upon the top of the twenty-story Catinat Ho-tel. Only at this passing moment of the morning, when highlighted by the colors of Saigon's sunrise, did the buildings stand out so vividly.

She was unaware that this golden, pagoda-like place would soon become the hub of her existence. For at this moment, Thi was entering Xa Bui, the office and residence of Thua Duat, a Chinese.

At the same moment in Xa Bui, Duat was strolling in the small, but exquisite, garden that grew under two well-pruned tulip trees. Duat had designed his penthouse quarters with great care. The northern end of the area housed his living quarters, the southern end his offices. In between the two was the garden, complete with beds of rare flowers, trees, a small fish pond, and a quiet waterfall. Here, up some twenty stories above the noise, the filth, and the danger of Saigon, life was tranquil, calm. Life was cool and peaceful. A man could let his brain address the business of the day unencumbered by the wild, raucous environment of the streets.

Duat rarely left Xa Bui. He habitually dressed in the classic old-style Mandarin costume associated with his ancestors, rarely seen in Saigon for decades. This bright, fresh morning he wore a light blue brocade coat over a white ankle-length gown. The matching blue bro-cade hat and slippers completed his attire. He knew that his dress would only sharpen the antipathy his Vietnamese servants and associ-ates felt toward Chinese after a history of ruthless domination which in his time took the form not of occupation, but of nearly total finan-cial and black market control of Saigon and much of South Vietnam.

Duat was native-born Hoa, Chinese-Vietnamese. In addition, he was a very rare Hoa: the blood of the old Mandarin elite ran in his veins. Most Hoa in Saigon were Cantonese and deferred to and respected Duat.

That his non-Hoa minions could not react to him and his appearance out of well-placed fear and terror was fine by Duat and brought him minor and gratifying amusement.

He looked at his reflection in the still waters of the pool. A lotus blossom was blooming in the water. He was able to lose himself completely in this small setting of designed beauty.

Then, he was aware of another reflection in the pool. Slowly he looked up. A servant had approached and was now standing with eyes downcast, holding before him a silver tray. On the tray was a note. As Duat picked up the note with his long, well-manicured fingers, the servant made a slight bow and vanished into the house. Duat read, then folded the note, turned, and strolled to the red-lacquered railing at the edge of the roof. From this position, he could see the giant dark coil of the Saigon River, which embraced the city on two sides. He smiled with satisfaction as he slipped the note easily into the pocket of his robe. His eyes drifted along the near bank of the river where the great ships were docked. He scanned one after another.

Which one is she? Ah, yes, of course. There she was at the foot of Ha Ba Trung—very close to the German hospital ship, the Helgoland. That was amusing. Such a large shipment of heroin.

He looked at several other ships and identified them as vessels in which he had some interest. He looked at his fine Cartier Tank watch. It was time to go in and greet his visitor.

Thi had been delivered to the regular entrance of the Catinat Hotel and, following instructions, had gone immediately to the ladies' room on the ground floor. There she was met by a cleaning woman, who escorted her into what outwardly resembled a closet. The back row of mops and brooms, however, cleverly concealed another door, which was an entrance to a small elevator. After closing the outer door, the cleaning woman sent her up alone in the elevator.

When the lift stopped and the door opened, Thi was met by a white-uniformed servant who ushered her into a spacious, pavilion-like parlor. The room was completely open on both sides, but its ends connected to other rooms that composed the living quarters. The right side opened into the garden, while the left side opened onto a balcony that overlooked part of the city of Saigon. Sliding glass doors could enclose the room in inclement weather, but this morning the doors were thrown open wide, and a light cool breeze stirred the floor-to-ceiling curtains and the fresh flowers that filled a bowl on a table in the center of the room.

Beyond the table, seated in a grouping of rattan furniture, was Duat. He was smiling as he watched Thi contemplate the expensive decor of the room. Had he misjudged? Had he been mistaken about her? He would not know for some time to come. It would be interesting to find out.

"It is a pleasure to meet such a charming girl on such a beautiful morning. Please come here and sit near me. We are going to have breakfast."

As Thi approached Duat, he rose and held out his hand in Western fashion. She took it briefly with a light pressure, but she never raised her eyes. Duat was pleased that she knew the Western ways, but showed deference to the traditional customs.

"Sit down, Cô Thi," ordered Duat, as he resumed his seat.

Only then did she slide into the chair he indicated. Despite Duat being Chinese, whom Thi—like most Vietnamese—felt a strong cultural distaste for, mixed with unrecognized envy, she was thrilled. She knew that, at last, she was in the presence of the man who probably ruled Saigon, and possibly all of South Vietnam. Her heart raced. She hoped she would be accepted. It never occurred to her that to come this far and not be accepted would mean instant death. That would become clear only after she knew Duat better.

As they ate their breakfast of mango, fish, rice, and tea, Duat talked at length. He had scheduled this period of their relationship as one of learning for Thi. His agents had already told him that she was sometimes emotional, but intelligent, quick to learn, vindictive, and ruthless. He casually filled in parts of his background in order to let her quick mind put the pieces together to produce the proper picture of power and strength that he desired her to have. Consequently, by the time the breakfast was over, she knew that he was a direct descendant of Mandarins far back into the mists of ancient Chinese history. As such, he despised any society or political ideology other than the ancient Mandarin culture and government. In this respect, he had only contempt for French colonialism, Communism, American democracy, and even the National Liberation Front, his so-called current masters.

In Duat's mind, this was only a business alliance that suited him. A point of view he did not share openly with others. Definitely not with the NLF or VC. He had no interest in their ideology or wider goals.

Thi surmised from Duat's musing and inferences that his wealth came from legal importing as well as smuggling drugs and manipulating the sale of rice, through control of the "Rice Barons" of Cholon and Can Tho. His power came from bribery, blackmail, and violence. She also concluded that his personal strength came from a cruel, impersonal cunning, and that he imposed discipline and enforcement on his business network with a subtle covertness of action.

"But, my dear, you have hardly touched your food," he said with mock surprise. It was a signal that the meal had ended.

"Oh, but I'm really not hungry, sir."

He rose from his place. She immediately rose also, still looking down. He was pleased.

Some hidden demon in this one? Perhaps. No matter. She knows and understands. She accepts.

Silently, with no wasted motion, he started for the garden.

"Come with me," he murmured.

She followed without a word.

Duat proceeded across the garden, then turned to the red railing. The sun was higher now, and the day was hot and clear. Below, the incessant traffic of cyclos, cars, trucks, and Tri-Lambrettas was already choking the streets. Duat called Thi to his side and pointed out the ships along the riverbank that were part of his enterprises.

Then, with a sigh, he said, "But it is time for me to say 'good night.' I avoid the worst part of the day by sleeping through it. My rising time is just before sunset."

Suddenly he clapped his hands twice. A servant approached and bowed.

Duat said, "Get me Ông Ahn."

The servant disappeared into the office building and soon a Vietnamese, dressed in a Western business suit, was making a little bow to Duat.

"Cô Thi is ready for you now," said Duat.

Then, without a word of farewell, he turned and left Thi and Ahn beside the rail.

"Follow me, Cô Thi," commanded Ahn. As he headed for the office, he added, "I will be your contact for everything. In the future you will only see Ông Duat when he summons you."

Ψ   Ψ   Ψ

Newell Osborne sat at his desk and reviewed his daily schedule.

The United States Deputy Ambassador for Revolutionary Development was a thin, energetic man. Hand-picked by the White House for this assignment, Osborne was determined to be successful in it. In a sense, he was the US leader of the civilian side of the war, as General William Westmoreland was the leader of the military side. Newell was concerned with the civilian population in all aspects and conditions resulting from the conflict: refugees, pacification, hamlet security, and rehabilitation were just some of his worries.

He was a very busy man.

Newell checked the calendar and noted with satisfaction that he was lunching with Janet Holden—and a Dr. De Salle. He slowly passed his right hand through the rough-cut, dark gold hair atop his head.

"Who is he?" he wondered aloud.

Unconsciously he plucked at one of the small collar buttons of his white dress shirt. Then he turned and pressed a signal switch on the desk. Major Bill Scott entered the office and stood with relaxed ease at the side of Newell's large desk.

"Who the hell is Dr. De Salle?" asked Newell, without looking up at Bill, his army staff officer.

"You mentioned the other day that Dr. Holden was bringing a friend. This guy's a well-known political scientist."

"Oh, that's right," sighed Newell with a smile. "I had forgotten he was coming. In fact, you kidded me about my quiet tête-à-tête with Janet going to hell!"

"Well, we wouldn't blame you, sir," responded Bill. "She certainly is an attractive lady. If I were ten years older … "

"If I were ten years younger," Newell broke in. They both laughed as Scott turned and left the room.

At precisely 1200 hours, Janet and Poli De Salle entered the reception room of Newell Osborne's office. Bill escorted them into Newell's room and Janet introduced Poli to Newell.

On the opposite side of the room was a brown leather couch, a coffee table, and two leather chairs. Newell came from behind his desk and led the visitors there.

When everyone was seated, Newell laughed and said, "You must congratulate me, Janet. Did you know that the VC have again picked me as the most dangerous American in Vietnam?"

Janet laughed too, and replied, "Well, you are always looking for indicators of progress. You couldn't ask for a better one than that!"

"What exactly does this phrase mean, this 'Most Dangerous American'?" Poli asked.

"Well," replied Newell, "it means that the VC would like to exterminate me, as my programs seem to be threatening the success of their own."

Shivers played relay races up Poli's back.

How can they joke about something like that?

He tried to smile to cover his fear.

Janet, thoughtful for a moment, finally said, "To be serious, Newell, your three big programs—Refugees, Hamlet Evaluation, and Revolutionary Development—seem to be, at last, going well. They are all working at one level or another and apparently the enemy thinks they are going to be successful to the point where you have become a threat …"

"With a lot of luck and the help of some wonderful people like you, we've managed to notice some progress lately. However, one great challenge is just coming on the horizon."

"The election?"

"Exactly. That's a real milestone! A really free national election. The first time in the country's history. But, I guess you're here to observe the election, Dr. De Salle?"

"Yes, of course. But I think the team you already have will do very well. This time I thought I might ..."

"Oh, then you plan to stay for some time?" Newell broke in. "I think it's great that someone of your background can work it into his schedule to come over and give a hand."

Janet hoped that it were true Poli's motives were so noble. Perhaps they were. One of Newell's secretaries entered, pushing a large teacart. Janet was happy with the diversion and the welcome change of subject.

"Ah, our lunch," exclaimed Newell. "I wish I could have taken you out to a nice restaurant, but it takes time to do such things, and frankly I can't afford those two-hour lunches. This way we can eat and talk about your project, too."

"With all your other programs, I'm certainly flattered that you have this time to give my project," said Janet.

Newell looked at her and smiled.

Her project is just as important, in its way, as any of our larger ones. She knows this, but is smart enough to see all sides of the big picture and realize it's really made up of small projects like hers. Wish everyone around here could understand that. Unfortunately, their egos get in the way and they come to think that their little efforts are the only way to win the war. Janet's a real thoroughbred—but this De Salle. What's he all about? Not all that sure about him.

"Come on, let's eat."

$$\Psi \quad \Psi \quad \Psi$$

At Trong Thoi it was also lunchtime.

Brandy Masters sat in Mark's room. It was awfully hot, and she was alone. A prisoner with a guard outside the door wasn't her idea of great fun. She wondered how long she would be detained.

The night before, wet from the shower and sore from her time at the Butterfly Bar, she had stumbled onto the hard army cot and fallen asleep. In the morning, her first feelings were of shame and embarrassment. Afraid to get up, she lay on the cot listening to the sounds of the camp outside her window. The commands of the non-commissioned officers mingled with the excited shouts of children and the chatting of the women seemed to indicate that life was going on unchanged by the events of the night before. Yet something was astir. She could feel it in the mood of the Vietnamese words she heard even though she could not understand their meaning.

At last, she pulled herself from the cot and picked up her mirror. Her neck was sore, and red marks were visible where that soldier had choked her. She slipped on tight Capri pants and a blouse and went to the door. To her horror, she saw the guard posted there and retreated hastily into her room. The soldier, embarrassed, kept his eyes on the floor and didn't speak.

Suddenly Brandy's apprehension turned to anger.

What makes this goddamned tin soldier think he can do this to me and get away with it? He can't treat me like one of his grunts. I'll have my uncle cashier him before next payday.

She went to the door and tried to pass the guard.

"I'm sorry, ma'am," the guard said with an embarrassed grin. "My orders are to let no one in or out. Please go back into the room."

Must be the only man here that I didn't … right. Mark would have gone and found one for guard duty.

Brandy retreated, but demanded to see Peter. The guard, greatly relieved, called to the orderly room. Some time passed before Peter arrived, carrying a large tray of fried eggs, bacon, toast, and coffee. He brought the food into the room and had barely lowered the tray before Brandy was in his arms, sobbing like a baby.

Peter, whose love for Brandy had never really died, comforted her as best he could. Tears were in his eyes as he hugged and caressed her.

"Baby, oh, my baby. Why did you do it? What made you go out there? Who took you out of the compound?"

"Oh, Peter," Brandy sobbed. "Am I in real deep trouble? I mean, who has to know about last night outside of this godforsaken camp—I mean, officially?"

"Well, you might have gotten away with it if it hadn't been for ..."

"For what, Peter? For God's sake, tell me."

"Well, one of the Vietnamese soldiers later got killed in a fight. I guess it's a direct result of your ... your performance in the bar."

"What do you mean?"

"There was this fight among the Vietnamese after ... after you left. I heard that one was choking you, and Colonel Buckley ... pulled this ... off you and ... oh my God. Brandy, how could you ever have gotten into this mess?"

Peter put his face in his hands and sank to the cot.

"Who was killed? Who was killed?" demanded Brandy.

"Well," sobbed Peter, struggling to go on, "This man who ... who was pulled off you was angry and when another man accused him of breaking up the ... the whole party, there was a fight. One was stabbed. He died. There's going to be an investigation."

Brandy sat down beside Peter. She remembered the smell of garlic and the sweat, and shivered. She felt frightened. Abandoned. Small. For a long time they sat in silence. Then Peter put his arm around the girl.

"No matter what, you've got me, baby ..."

Ψ   Ψ   Ψ

The Army moves quickly when the reputation of the service is involved, and such was the case in the affair at Trong Thoi. Decisions, orders, actions, were accomplished with remarkable rapidity.

As a result, Mark was relieved of command while Brandy found herself in official custody in Saigon.

Following the example of the United States Army, the ARVN quickly held a pretrial investigation into the circumstances relating to the murder of the Vietnamese soldier.

For two days, Brandy was questioned closely by a board of attentive but very unsympathetic ARVN officers, who seemed more interested in the details of her personal sex life before the incident than any relationship she may have had with the dead soldier. There was much in

Vietnamese that she could not follow. The looks, stares, and laughs she understood.

It wasn't until the conclusion of the investigation the following week that Brandy realized the ARVN had, from the first, considered her little more than a common prostitute—a commodity to be used and reused for the convenience of the troops, and then cast aside when no longer needed. They had compiled a dossier of her time in Vietnam and a list of lovers.

Consequently, the board branded her a woman of loose morals and recommended she be declared *persona non grata* in their country. To this, the Vietnamese government agreed at high levels.

The US Embassy was so advised, and requested that she be deported as soon as possible. It was an afterthought that the board found her not guilty of direct responsibility in the murder of the Vietnamese soldier.

Alone in her detention billet, Brandy mulled over her situation.

To leave Vietnam now would brand me a whore in two continents, a whore of the worst sort. One that digs a mass clientele.

"Ready, men! Line up by the numbers. Next man up!" she said aloud in mock military tone.

My best chance is to stay here in some respectable job while this goddamned war rattles on and buries the whole incident beneath some new series of events. Then when I do go home, there's a chance the whole incident will have been forgotten.

Then there's Mark. God, how I'd like to see him broken and stripped of that super-holy, self-righteous attitude of his, that regular army veneer he's built around himself. Maybe underneath there's another guy—a real Mark. Somehow I know he's there, the soft, sweet, gentle, loving guy that needs and wants my love just as I want and need his. God! With a man like that, I could be the woman Senator Joe Masters thinks I am ...

She laughed at her own outrageously naïve, schoolgirl-and-pulp-romance-novel daydream.

Mark, hard-assed or soft, can't help me now. Wherever he is, I'm sure he has his own problems. What I need is Joe Masters, and I need him like yesterday.

She looked at her watch. It was less than an hour before Peter's daily visit. She sat down on her bed with pen and paper and composed a rather vague, cryptic telegram.

Dear Uncle Joe: Because our army wishes to cover its blunders and poor judgment, I have been chosen as their scapegoat and told to leave Vietnam. I am innocent of any wrongdoing. As your niece, I cannot disgrace our family name by running in the face of cheap lies and deceit. I plan to stand and fight. I need your help.

Please come immediately.
Your Little Princess

An hour later Peter was sitting on Brandy's bed with the draft before him. A thin wisp of smoke from the cigarette dangling from his lips rose to join the layers of stale, damp air that formed above them. Brandy, standing by the open French doors that offered access to a narrow balcony, watched the crowded mixture of humanity in the street below. None of them paused or remarked on the two beggar women sitting with their rented babies lying naked in their laps. The rich tapestry of Saigon had long since become normal to them both.

From her position four floors above them, Brandy could almost distinguish the festering, pus-filled sores that the women rubbed with filth to resemble leprosy.

In a year or two those little arms and legs will be deliberately broken and twisted so that they will mend misshapen. Then the kids will be sent out on their own to beg in the streets. God, there's enough horror over here without the war—and this is just one example.

"Show me a reason why a child should suffer and I'll believe there is a God," she whispered.

"What'd you say, Brandy?"

"Nothing, Peter, just trying to remember what some Russian once wrote. But tell me what you think of my cable."

"It's ... it's just what you need to get your uncle over here. I'll send it right away. When do you think His Nibs will appear?"

"I hope in four or five days, Peter. Depends on what's going on in the Senate."

She noticed his uneasiness and knew he was having difficulty bringing himself to tell her something.

There was silence for a long minute before Peter finally stamped out his cigarette in the ashtray beside him, and with great deliberation said, "Brandy, I was wondering how you felt about my leaving you ..."

She laughed; somewhat surprised that it had been such a difficult thing for him to say. "Peter, I don't own you. You can go anywhere you wish, any time you wish."

"Oh, I know that," he replied. "But, well, since we teamed up I've always sort of ... looked after you and tried to advise you."

"And you were always around to pick up the pieces when I told you to 'stick' your advice and I did as I damned well pleased," Brandy said with a softness Peter hadn't heard for a long time.

She left the window and went over to him. Taking both his hands in hers, she looked into his eyes. This time they were steady.

"With your uncle coming, you'll be in good hands and, well, our act is *fini*," he continued.

She was coming to realize for the first time how much he had worried over her, and how indifferent she had become to his attempts to love her, to help and to protect her. Tears welled in her eyes as she squeezed his hands.

"Oh, Peter, Peter, how I've hurt you," she whispered as she moved closer to gently entwine her arms about his frail body.

Peter lowered his head and stood quietly. What he didn't want was pity, which was all Brandy was expressing, whether she was aware of it or not. Still, the sweaty feminine scent of her brought back stirrings from long ago.

Could we go back? Back to those first months, that first year? God, if only we could!

Impulsively he lifted his arms to embrace her, but the moment was over. She dropped her arms and backed away, then turned and wiped her eyes.

"My brother has a small house band in Vegas. He needs another guitar."

"That's great, Peter," she said with forced enthusiasm.

"I'll go now, and I'll send that cable. And, well, we've got fifty-four bucks in the B&P fund. Remember the agreement: all extra earnings split right down the middle!"

She tried to match his forced, sad little smile, but it was impossible.

That first year! How could I forget our special fund. Anything over and above our "salaries" was to go into it for a special weekend at Vung Tau. The best air-conditioned room in the best hotel, the two of us, just lying on the beach or in the room making love ... that was long ago, before we knew the score about ourselves, about this place, about the war. Before we knew we were losers, before we knew that all the soldiers over here were losers too. Oh God, will it end this way for everyone over here? Will the last round-eyes that are left just turn to the slant-eyes as they are leaving and say, "Here's your share—twenty-seven bucks—so long!"?

Peter placed Brandy's share of their money on the bed, then turned to face her for what he hoped would be the last time.

"Take my part for the cable, Peter." Her words were rushing, desperate.

She scooped up the piastres and held them out with a nervous hand.

"No, this is on me, baby," he said quietly as he opened the door.

"Peter! Peter," she cried, suddenly afraid to let him go.

He paused only a moment, knowing he would have to face her again and wondering if he had the strength to pull it off without making a damned fool of himself. He turned to see her still standing with outstretched hand. His great dark eyes watered.

God, she's beautiful! Even without makeup, standing there like an awkward statue. Even like this—sweating it out in this hotel room she's still the loveliest woman I've ever seen. But there's no place for me in her life now. I've gotta get out of here before I really mess things up.

He took a deep breath and looked her squarely in the face. His voice was just above a whisper.

"Baby, no matter what happens from now on, just remember that once there was a guy, a scrawny no-good guy named Peter, who loved you very much." He quickly closed the door before the tears came.

She heard his footsteps going down the empty hall. The money fluttered to the floor. She turned and fell onto the bed. Her tears mingled with her sweat, and disappeared into the moldy pillow.

Ψ   Ψ   Ψ

The Pan Am DC-8 stretch jet was in final approach at Tan Son Nhut and Southern Democrat Joe Masters, a four-term US senator, was fighting the usual case of jet lag.

He tried to remember how many trips he had made previously to Vietnam.

Six, no, seven times, for heaven's sake.

He abandoned the effort to adjust his huge, flabby bulk in the seat for the two hundredth time. Whatever trip this was, it was the first time he had made it on a commercial airliner without staff or military escort.

God, how wonderfully free I've been on this trip. I can sleep when I want, snore if I want, drink when I want, belch if I want—even fart when I want without one of those goddamned flunkies looking at me cross-eyed.

I shouldn't have made this trip. Missing a couple of real important votes. Of course, I paired with Jim, but come election time it's not the same.

But I'll pick up that crazy kid and be back before they know I'm gone. Wonder what happened over here to get her in this trouble? Hope it's not like that mess she got into with those idiot Frenchies over in Paris. She's a good gal, trying to do her part as she sees it. Suppose I'll have to get nasty with the Army again if they been mean to the Princess.

He reached in his pocket for the crumpled "Personal and Confidential" wire he had received from the American Embassy, and couldn't suppress a smile.

Smart guy, that Bunker. He knows the Princess is my ward and he's not about to let this get out without telling me first. Only thing is, he doesn't really say much. Doesn't want to chance a leak. Knew I'd come on the run—he's got to treat me right. What's that he calls me? Yeah—Senate's most effective hawk! And he's right, too.

The chirping squeal of the tires as the big airliner touched down brought Joe Masters back to reality. By the time the plane had taxied to a stop in front of the terminal, he had put on his tie and tucked his shirttail back in the trousers of his seersucker suit. The senator allowed the other two first-class passengers to precede him down the steps just to confuse his welcoming party. Then he put on his white panama hat and his election smile and paused in the doorway.

Well, let's see—a Two Star, two chickens, one major, a sergeant and a photographer. That's about right for third-ranking members of the Armed Services Committee. Bet that sergeant could do a better job than all the rest put together! Wonder what happened to all the real officers that used to be around when I was at CMTC Camp in Maryland. Well, that was two wars ago ...

The senator turned on the Southern charm and exaggerated drawl he was well known for back in Washington and in his state.

"How are ya, General? Glad to see ya again," exclaimed Joe as he stepped to the tarmac and shook the general's hand.

"Welcome back, Senator," the general replied. He stood like a bandbox soldier in his spotless boots and newly starched fatigues.

"Now, General, before you get to tellin' me 'bout the great schedule ya have for me, let me just say all I want to do today is to visit with my niece, Miss Brandy Masters—have an early supper with her, and then get some shuteye. Think ya can arrange that?"

"Well, yes sir. No problem there. In fact, Miss Masters is waiting for you at the Caravelle. General Westmoreland sends his greetings, sir, and hopes you can have supper with him one evening while you are here—and of course he is at your disposal whenever you would like to see him."

"Of course," the senator agreed.

"General Westmoreland also realizes that—well—under the circumstances, he understands perfectly your desire to see your niece, and he wants you to know that he stands ready to offer you whatever assistance he can. He asked me to give you his private number which can reach him any time, day or night."

While the general was passing this information, Joe Masters studied each one of the welcoming party. To a man, they suddenly became very interested in their combat boots. None of them returned the senator's gaze.

From what this Two Star says and the way they're all interested in their feet, I take it the Princess is in pretty bad trouble. Well, she'll tell me, and tell me true. I'm not going to waste any more of my time around here.

"That's mighty fine of Westy—mighty considerate. Please tell him I intend to be as little trouble as possible. You boys got a war to fight, an' ya don't need the US Senate to get in your way.

"Say, Sarge, that pretty gal in that airplane wants ta see ya. She's got about three pieces of hand luggage of mine ta hand ya. And here— somewhere I got some stubs for the hold baggage. Ah, here they are. Can ya kindly oblige? Now, which way is that sedan ya got for me? I want to get to the Caravelle and see the Princess."

Forty minutes later Senator Masters entered the glass doors of the Caravelle Hotel and walked up the steps to the lobby. Before his eyes made the transition from the white sunlight to the cool darkness, Brandy was in his arms.

"Uncle Joe! My own dear Uncle Joe! I knew you would come and help me," she cried as she hugged and kissed him on both cheeks.

The senator hugged her close to his soft, damp body.

"Now, Princess, ya knew I'd come a'runnin' just as soon as I knew ya needed help."

He felt Brandy's tears on his cheek and pulled away slightly.

"But what's this? Tears? How, Princess, nothin' could be that bad that could cause you ta cry. Let's go up to the suite and ya can tell me all 'bout it. An' don't you worry, Princess; whatever happened, your Uncle Joe can fix it."

Moments later, Brandy, enjoying the luxury of the senator's air-conditioned suite, stood at the large picture window and gazed south across the river to the sea of rice that extended to the horizon. She had rehearsed her story to perfection. Now as she waited for her uncle to "get a drink and get comfortable," she thought again about Trong Thoi and Mark Buckley.

God, all the guys I had that night—and how they all wanted me. They always do.

She shook off the old, familiar, hot excitement.

But the only one I really wanted, I couldn't have ...

Tears of anger, sorrow, and frustration welled up in her eyes. For a moment, she thought she was going to break down completely.

Stop it, Brandy! You're tough. You've seen damn near every form of sorrow imaginable in this goddamned country. Cry for the dead kids, if you like, for the young girls in agony, or the suffering old women, but forget about yourself. You haven't qualified for tears yet ...

"What's the matter, Princess? You crying again?"

She turned and forced a smile as she confronted her uncle. The rumpled seersucker coat and limp tie had been abandoned, the damp shirt was open at the neck, and the tails hung out of his trousers.

"Here, take my handkerchief, come over and set down and let's talk."

Quickly she dashed away the tears and tried to suppress a sudden guilty feeling.

"Don't worry, Uncle, I'll be okay. I'll be just fine."

Brandy's version of her evening at Trong Thoi was concerned primarily with Mark Buckley's inadequate briefing on her position at the camp and lack of instructions to guide her while she was on her own.

"Some of the boys suggested we go dancing in the little town outside the fort after my show. Colonel Buckley didn't say anything about going out with them. They were all nice fellows. Since he had asked me to dance with them in the dayroom, I knew it was all right.

"We went to a little native dance hall where I had a drink or two. I danced a long time with all the different men. The sticky heat got to me, I suppose, and I fainted. When I awoke, I found myself on a table in a dark room and a man, a Vietnamese soldier, was trying to ... to have sex with me. Well, you can imagine how I fought. That's when Colonel Buckley came in and found me. He carried me back to my quarters and put me under guard. Later I found out that some other Vietnamese soldiers killed that pervert. And Uncle, the Army thinks it was all my fault! Don't that beat all?"

Senator Masters listened in amazement to Brandy's story. He couldn't believe that such a horrible thing had happened to his niece.

"Princess," he said, "you spoke of a Vietnamese soldier. Did he–did he actually ... or were you able to fight him off until the captain came?"

"Lieutenant colonel. Lieutenant Colonel Mark Buckley," she said slowly and clearly, as she considered how to answer the question.

If she told of the rape, he might really tear into the Army and the ARVN, which would result in a very detailed and gory counter-attack by the military. Besides, he would never let her stay in Vietnam if he thought this had happened.

"You know what a fighter I am when the chips are down, Uncle. I managed to kick and scratch until the colonel came."

"Thank God," the senator said softly. "My poor little Princess. No wonder you've been crying. It's a wonder you're able even to talk rationally about it. That's a terrible, terrible … thing to have happened to a young girl, and that soldier sure got what he deserved. Weren't you under the protection of the Army, this Colonel Buckley? I think it's fine that he rescued you, but what kind of an officer is he to let you get into that situation? The Army was supposed to be in charge. The Army must be held responsible. That's all there is to it. That Colonel Buckley is not fit to command if he can't protect a non-combatant better than that. Don't ya worry, Princess, they can't blame a thing like that on you. A fine thing! An attempted rape and a murder and they're trying to blame it all on the victim!"

Brandy could see that her uncle was working himself up into a state of exquisite agitation. His face was flushed and his breath was coming in desperate short puffs. She would have to work fast. Burying a smile in a veil of false anguish, she pressed on.

"Oh, Uncle, I'm in so much trouble I don't think that even you can clear me completely. You see, it's not just the US Army; it's the South Vietnamese too. Our Army controls them, and they've done and declared me *persona non grata* because of what our Army has told them about me."

"Don't worry, Princess, I'll have ya out of this hellhole in two days. You'll come right back with me to the States, and this whole nightmare'll be over."

"But, Uncle," she cried. "Can't you see that's impossible? By leaving now, I'm only admitting that the Army is right. I'll be branded as just a little spoiled girl who came over here to play among the horrors of this war. I was bad and caused trouble, and my powerful uncle came and snatched me home to escape my punishment.

"You see, you and I know I'm innocent, so I welcome your help in having the unjust charges against me dropped, but beyond that it's up to me to prove to them that they're wrong—that I am a good person—that I can do a job here to help in our country's time of need."

Taken completely by surprise, Joe Masters could only gape in wonder as Brandy finished her story.

"Ya mean ya don't want to go home–after all that?"

"Of course I want to take the easy way out. Of course I want to leave this horrid place. But certainly you don't want me branded a ... a bad person. If I had a respectable job in Saigon–maybe with the embassy or USAID–for a while. I can type, I can file, I can be useful here– and you could keep track of me. Please, Uncle Joe!"

For a moment, Joe Masters remembered her as a little girl begging for a puppy. He gave in then, and remembered how happy it had made her. He gave in again and she reacted accordingly.

"Oh, Uncle, Uncle, you sweet dear loving Uncle Joe!" she squealed as she covered his face and head with kisses.

"But ya gotta write me once a week and ya gotta promise ya won't go near soldiers or Vietnamese. Just stay with the US civilians and mind your own business," Joe said between her kisses.

This whole damn trip was worth this moment–just to see her smile again.

Two days later, from his seat in another stretched DC-8, Joe Masters waved goodbye to Brandy. She was radiant, standing there with the young Foreign Service officer who would help her move into the apartment in the newly completed American billet.

He turned and smiled to the stewardess.

"See down there, Miss?" he said eagerly. "That's my niece. She's–she works for USAID!"

The smart-looking Pan Am stewardess looked over his shoulder to see blond-haired Brandy, smiling and waving, as the breeze gently played with the skirt of her off-white linen suit.

"She's pretty as a picture, Senator. You must be very proud."

"Pretty as a princess, you mean. That's what I call her–Princess," he said. "That's her favorite outfit. I bought it for her myself and sent it over last Christmas.

"Goodbye, Princess!" the senator called, even though he knew Brandy couldn't possibly hear him. He saw her waving until the plane turned onto the runway. It was to be his last memory of her. Later he would wish he had hugged her one last time. But mostly he would wish that he had taken her home.

Despite Senator Masters' damning of Mark Buckley in defense of

Brandy, the US military did not intend to lose one of their most experienced combat officers in wartime. However, since the senator had turned in anger to the highest military levels, bureaucratic expediency made it imperative that Mark be relieved of duty as subsector commander. He was reassigned to staff duty in Saigon.

"You may think it's being kicked upstairs, Mark," said the Special Forces colonel, "and in a sense it is. But it's a full colonel's billet and it's a good job. Ambassador Osborne has been looking for someone to represent him personally on Revolutionary Development matters. There's no one presently in the country that is better qualified than you."

"But sir," said Mark, stubborn to the end, "I volunteered for field duty."

"Just a minute, Mark. Sometimes we have to run a 360-degree war. We have to fight the Viet Cong in Vietnam and the US Congress at home. It's the same war," the colonel replied sternly.

"Yes, sir," responded Mark. The issue was closed.

Ψ Ψ Ψ

Ned Green was running flat out.

He knew if he made it to the next alley, he would be safe.

"Damn that bitch to hell," he murmured as he stretched out to make the turn into the safety of the shadows.

"Why did she call the MPs? Maybe she didn't. Maybe some other Viet or maybe her girl friend ..."

He and Luu had been getting along pretty well, but he remembered her friend saying she wasn't pulling in enough customers while he was around.

"Bet that friend of hers did it," he muttered as he sprinted for the alley ahead.

He turned the corner and dodged into a dark doorway, breathing heavily, trying to get his wind back.

They can't get down this alley in the jeep ... Well, one thing, I can't ever go back to Luu, and all my stuff is there. They have it by now. All I got is the clothes on my back.

78

He leaned against the wall to rest, trying desperately to breathe quietly.

Suddenly a powerful spotlight shone down the narrow alley, casting deep shadows as it moved to penetrate the dark corners. The jeep didn't try to enter, but stayed on the main street. Ned, in complete darkness, could see the white light crawl up the walls only two feet from him.

Oh, shit. They're going to get out and search. I'm SOL.

As he tried to shrink farther back into the shadows, he suddenly became aware of someone with him in the doorway.

"Quiet," said the stranger. "Here, I open door, you step inside, but no noise."

Ned heard the door scrape open, and then he felt hands against his body. They grabbed his arms and half led, half pushed him farther into the darkness. There was a smell of oriental cooking as the door closed behind him. He was in utter darkness.

Outside Ned could hear voices. "Hi, big MP. You number one soldier. You got match?"

"Hell no, I ain't got no match. Whatcha doin' out after curfew? Oughtta turn you over to the white mice."

"Oh no, number one MP. Only GI curfew. Vietnamese curfew in one hour. This my house. You want come in? I have sister. Five hundred P!"

"We're lookin' for an American. Not in uniform. Unnerstan'? Black man. You know?"

"Oh yes, me know. AWOL, ha ha! He no see tonight. Maybe yesterday. Maybe next week."

There was a pause, a period of dead silence. Ned was shivering in the hot darkness, wondering if they would come in and search. Suddenly a gruff voice broke the silence.

"Come on, Frank. Let's get the hell outta here. He musta gone on down the street," said another voice.

Ned heard the two soldiers depart. He was sweating through his shirt and trousers. Suddenly the door opened. He heard a laugh and a Zippo lighter lit up the bright eyes and delicate features of a young Vietnamese man as he lit a cigarette.

"Salem?" he asked, and offered one to Ned. "They gone now. They number ten."

Ned left the closeness of the room. His new friend shut the door behind him.

"Yeah, I'll take one of those," said Ned, much relieved.

"Whatsa matta, GI? You have no girl? You have no place to stay? You AWOL?"

"Yes," replied Ned as he inhaled the smoke.

"Then, GI, you come with me. I give you food. I give you bed. Nice, clean. Everything nice."

"Where is it? Here?" asked Ned, although he was in no position to argue or barter.

"No, this bad joint. Bad men here take all GI money. Hit, stab, bad."

"That's okay. I have no money," Ned laughed. "All used up on girl-friend."

"Okay. I have money, I have food, I have whiskey. I have everything."

They were walking out of the alley.

As they came to the street, the Vietnamese pushed Ned against the wall. "Stay here," he said, "while I get good cyclo."

He was able to flag one of the noisy vehicles and soon they were racing down Tran Hung Dao toward the northeast. In minutes, they were on Le-Loi, passing the colossal marine statue. They turned right down Tu Do Street, then abruptly into an alley and stopped.

"Get out. Get in doorway. I pay."

The two men quietly climbed a dark stairway. Ned decided they had gone up five floors when the Vietnamese guided him to a door. He took out a key and opened it, then pushed Ned inside. Suddenly the lights came on; they were in a large, but modestly furnished living room. There was a round table with a lamp, two plastic-covered easy chairs, and two straight-backed wooden chairs. To the right, French doors opened upon a narrow balcony overlooking Tu Do Street. On the left was a bedroom. Through the open door, Ned could see a young girl sleeping.

The Vietnamese put his finger to his lips and they passed quietly toward the back of the room to a large door leading onto a terrace.

The left border of the terrace was bounded by a bathroom and kitchen. From the terrace, along the kitchen wall, was a narrow set of stairs. Ned could see they led up to what appeared to be a large room above the kitchen.

"Stay here," whispered the man. "I go back. Turn out lights."

In the darkness, Ned could hear his new friend talking to the girl. He wondered if he could trust this Vietnamese. Then he remembered he had no choice. He had run out of places to go.

"Follow me," the Vietnamese whispered when he returned. "I tell my sister I bring GI home. GI my good friend."

He led Ned up stairs to the large room.

"This my part of house. I work here. I sleep here. You stay with me." He flicked on the lights.

Ned saw a large room with windows on two sides, a large bed dominating the closed end of the room. The opposite end seemed to be an art studio. Finished and unfinished canvases were scattered about that end of the room.

Feeling uneasy at first, Ned passed beyond the artwork and disappeared through a door that led to a dark terrace. Only when he was sure that there were no other entrances to the studio did he return to the art.

The work was good. Ned whistled as he walked over to the easel.

"This your work? Say ... you're some artist."

He turned his attention to the various paintings. Immediately he was completely absorbed. The fact that he was a hunted man had entirely left his thoughts.

"Well. Allow me to make acquaintance," the Vietnamese said self-consciously.

"I am Tre Hue. I am artist. I live here with my sister, Tre Kam. This place my father's. He business man. He send me school where I make art. When I am young boy of fifteen years, my painting win prize. I go Paris for study one year. I want stay Paris, but I must come back. My father die. I try keep business, but I lose. I sell. I keep house. Now I paint. Sell very good. GI buy *beaucoup* my pictures."

"They are good," commented Ned. "I was in art school in Chicago before I got drafted. I do some of this too."

"Ah, you are painter, GI? You first one GI painter I find. You stay here with Hue. Make pictures. What your name?"

"Cyrus Green, but everyone calls me Ned. That's my middle name."

"What I call you?"

"Well, why not Cy?"

"But you still wet. Here, give me clothes. It's okay, no one here."

Ned looked about. He felt strange undressing before Hue. Hue turned, went to a cupboard and handed Ned a large piece of cotton cloth.

"Here, you dry."

Ned removed his wet shirt and trousers, then sat on a bench and removed his shoes and socks. When he stood up, he noticed Hue's stare.

"You beautiful."

"Never been called that before."

"Black and beautiful. I make sketch."

Embarrassed, Ned began to dry his upper body. Then he took off his shorts and quickly covered himself with the large cloth.

Hue turned and disrobed, except for a similar towel, which he tied about his body. In the corner of the room was a cold-water faucet and a large sink.

"Come. We wash."

Ned followed the artist to the sink and they both washed in the cold water. Unembarrassed now, they dried themselves.

"It late now. We sleep."

They climbed into the bed and pulled a light sheet over them. Ned, exhausted, fell quickly into a deep sleep. He didn't even feel Hue's arm go about him.

Later, sometime before dawn, Ned partially awoke and felt Luu caressing his body.

"I love you, I love you," Luu seemed to say.

"I love you too, baby," Ned mumbled. He rolled over into Luu's waiting arms. It was only then that he came fully awake. With a start, he raised his body and looked down at the figure below him.

Night infiltration flares outside, floating high in the sky, were lighting the room with an uneven, soft glow. In the dim light Ned could distinguish Hue, eyes filled with passion and longing.

"You no stop. Please, you no stop."

"You're not Luu, I forgot. I was asleep," Ned said.

He rolled off Hue and faced away from him. Soon he felt Hue's arms about him and his body pressed close to him. Hue murmured in Vietnamese as he began caressing Cy's chest and hips. Fully awake now, Cy realized how it was going to be.

In exchange for security and a place to live, he was expected to do his part. For an instant, his thoughts flashed back to his boyhood in Chicago, and the nights he had spent with his cousin Franklin. That was a long time ago, before he had learned to appreciate girls.

Well, if I did it with Franklin, I guess I can do it with this Hue.

He turned and faced the ardent young Vietnamese, then slowly gathered him into his arms and pulled the small body to him. Hue became completely feminine and yielding. It was easier than Cy had expected. Without much trouble, he could imagine Hue as a woman.

He used him as one.

Ψ   Ψ   Ψ

There was a very small bell ringing somewhere far away.

Cy decided to open his eyes.

"It must be about seven in the morning," he thought.

The early sun was streaming in the open windows. He looked at the small, naked body curled up against him. Hue stirred and opened his eyes. He smiled at Cy and gave the big man a hug before he jumped up and went to the top of the stairs. Cy could see him leaning over the railing and talking to his sister on the terrace below. Soon he returned and sat on the edge of the bed.

"Sister to bring food. She be surprised see you."

"Cy better put on some clothes," he replied.

He jumped out of bed and headed for his trousers, still soggy from last night's rain.

"Here. You wear these."

Hue was holding out a pair of black satin trousers, part of the classic Vietnamese outfit. For a Vietnamese, they were cut large and loose, with a stretchable elastic band about the waist. But when he put them on, Cy filled them out with little slack to spare. The length of the trousers came to just below his knees. Cy laughed with Hue at the sight.

"Better than wet trousers, I guess."

The bell rang again and drew Cy's attention. He saw it now, a small brass temple bell, to which was attached a long string extending to the terrace below.

"We sit down. That my sister with food. She not know you black GI. I tell her last night you GI."

Cy glanced at the doorway as Hue said, "This my sister, Cô Kam."

The girl almost dropped the tray as she sucked in a startled breath. A quick exchange of Vietnamese, however, seemed to make everything all right. Now she was laughing at Cy in the quiet, embarrassed manner of the Vietnamese. She hurried over to the table and carefully placed the tray there. Then she turned with hands over her face and skittered to the doorway, where again she turned and laughed through her hands once more before disappearing down the steps.

Cy grinned as he watched her.

Funny. If that had been some damned honkey bastard, I would have been mad as hell. These people can laugh at me and I don't feel bad at all.

"Hope sister not make you mad. She still small girl, she only sixteen."

"No, she's okay. I think she's very pretty."

"She sell pictures. We make *beaucoup* moneys. She have kiosk on street. Every day she take new pictures there. Then lock up tight at night. No one can get. Here, you see new ones she take, tomorrow."

They walked to a group of paintings leaning against the wall. Cy looked at them in a critical manner, his thoughts going back to his instructor in school. The paintings were all sunsets. Most were delta scenes, but a few were marine scenes with junks and sampans against the evening sky.

"GI all like much color. In Vietnam, we have much color sunset and sunrise. Which you like best, Cy?"

Cy immediately went to a marine scene. It was less colorful, but the composition was excellent and the perspective was good.

"Why you like it best?" asked Hue.

"Well, it tells me a lot, man. You see the dark headland in the center ground, with the village lights and the lights of the cabin of the boat in the foreground. Well, you wonder is the ship coming into the harbor or going out? What is she carrying? She a smuggler or what? That her home port or not? That cabin. It looks warm and inviting, but the land looks dark and scary-like. You never get tired of that picture. It's good."

"Ah. You GI, but you artist, too."

"Like I told you, man, I studied art too. I won a couple of prizes myself."

"You stay here, Cy. You paint with me."

Cy thought for a moment.

There are some real possibilities here. This wouldn't be bad as a permanent arrangement, but there would have to be some changes. Like a switch in bed partners, for one thing. That is a priority.

"Well, let's get some of that breakfast and we can talk it over," he said, heading for the table.

Ψ Ψ Ψ

Thi sat in the front row of chairs in the largest room of the office complex at Xa Bui.

Behind her, she could hear people filling up the room. Occasionally she could catch them out of the corner of her eye, entering in ones and twos, dressed in all modes of dress. She was tasked to assume the clothes and looks of a woman street laborer, and to use an assumed name: Chuan. She wondered why. Were not all these people working for Duat?

Ahn came in from a side door and pretended not to notice her. At Ahn's entrance, everyone got up and Thi followed their example. Ahn motioned and they all took their seats.

"Our leader sends you greetings. He is pleased with your work and congratulates you. At the same time, he warns you of the difficulties ahead. He asked me to tell you of our plans for disrupting the elections.

It is possible to negate the elections and discredit the Americans by our activity."

Ahn walked to the back wall, where there was a large blackboard. Picking up a piece of red chalk, he wrote in large letters: TERROR.

Then below it, he wrote:

1) Shelling the city from without.

2) Individual killings from within

3) Claymore bombing of US and GVN public places

"This is our general plan," he said, as he pointed to the words. "Each of you will have a part in our program. You will be given instructions today as to when to report for specific details of your part."

Ahn turned again to the board and wrote: VONG CA CHUA.

"This is the sign and countersign for the week. Everyone learn it. It will not be written again."

He then erased the words.

"Now, all pay attention. These are the schedules for your reporting time back here. Give your name for identification."

A little old lady passed among the rows of people. She stopped before Thi.

"Chuan," she whispered to the girl.

Thi was handed a small typewritten piece of paper that said:

CHUAN
Remain after this meeting
for special instructions.

When the old woman had completed her task, Ahn again spoke.

"That will be all for now. Leave in the designated order."

Everyone rose and gave Ahn a slight bow. Thi watched them file out of the room.

"Come with me, Chuan," directed Ahn as he left the room.

Thi quietly followed Ahn into the garden. There they waited. Thi hoped it was to see Duat again. He had not been present during the long meetings when Ahn had given her training in her duties. She liked her nickname Chuan (Dragonfly), especially since Ahn had told her that Duat had picked it himself. She now noticed a large green and blue dragonfly motionless in the air above a red lotus blossom in the garden pond. The setting sun reflected red and gold in the still water.

She noticed Duat approaching from the living quarters, leading five persons. She could see that they were all young men.

When Duat appeared, Thi placed her hands together and bowed over them to Duat. She remained with head down, awaiting his acknowledgement.

"Good evening, Cô Chuan," he said, his voice low.

"Good evening, Ông Duat," replied Thi, her voice barely audible.

He introduced her to the five men. She raised her head and spoke to them. She quickly sized each one up. They were all lean, wiry, and seemed men of purpose. She wondered what she would be doing with them, what her relationship with them would be. They all followed Duat back to the office room. As they took seats in the front row of chairs, Thi saw that the blackboard had been erased, and in the place of "TERROR" was a neatly drawn diagram of downtown Saigon.

Duat took a seat behind the desk, while Ahn stood to one side of the drawing on the blackboard. Quietly Duat explained that the five men were the key members of the Viet Cong Sixty-Ninth Special Action Group, which had been operating around the Saigon area since 1964.

Thi's thoughts immediately flew back to the famous My Canh floating restaurant massacre of June 1965.

Wasn't it 125 persons? Yes, mostly Americans met death that day!

In spite of her affected shyness, she turned and stared at the famous men. Of course, she wouldn't recognize them. They were so quiet, so unaffected–they were real heroes. She noticed their leader, Sam. She felt extremely attracted to him. Thi hoped she could work directly with him, to prove to him her own bravery and courage. Then she would become important, the star.

Abruptly her mind snapped back to the present. Duat was mentioning her. She saw that Ahn was pointing to the diagram on the board. She oriented herself with Nguyen Hue and its intersection with Le-Loi.

"Chuan will take over an apartment on the top floor here."

Ahn pointed to the corner of Tu Do and Lam-Son, across from the Continental Hotel.

"She will have access to the roof and can cross to the square over-looking the park in front of the City Hall. From there, she can observe the Rex Hotel, which houses all the highest-ranking American officers, and the JUSPAO office, where all the US propaganda is created, and even the McCarthy Hotel, where most of the rescue workers will come from.

"We would like to put her in an apartment directly across from the Rex, but the local police control all of that housing. Of course, we could "buy in," but after the explosion she would be suspect, at best. The entrance to the building where Chuan will reside is next to the sweet shop on the corner.

"Go directly to flat No. 516 on the fifth floor. She will be using the name, Cô Dao Thi. It is printed on a small card pinned to the door. The leaders of the Sixty-ninth will use Chuan's flat for a headquarters while planning this exercise. Make your own arrangements with her so that she is present at all your meetings. For appearances, she will be teaching you French and English. That is your reason for being there."

Duat rose from his seat and smiled as he turned toward the members of the Sixty-Ninth Special Action Group.

"We are honored to have you with us, comrades. Good luck with your plans."

Everyone rose as Duat turned and left the room. A servant brought tea and soon Ahn, Thi, and the five men were grouped about the desk, talking about the coming terror activities.

Thi was thrilled that she was to use her real name at the apartment.

These men will speak my name! My deeds will shine out!

Of course, no one in the Sixty-ninth would know it was her real name, but that didn't make any difference.

After the tea, the men left and Thi was alone with Ahn.

He became very serious. "There are several more things that you should know."

"First, you, as a member of the inner circle, have certain privileges regarding your travel to and from our headquarters. You came in the secret entrance to the private elevator. Many others you might see up here do not have this privilege.

"How do they get in? They are escorted here and, well, they aren't exactly sure where they are. Most of the people you will find here are led through one of three tunnels that end below the hotel. Each start at three different places in Saigon. In time, you will be told where these entrances are located. It is important that you do not divulge the entrance that you use to anyone you may meet here.

"Second, you must use the new No. 516 flat immediately and make it your residence. The back room of the flat is for your use alone. Its existence must not be divulged to anyone who is not one of us. You will notice that you have a living room, bedroom, bath, kitchen, and workroom. You make your living teaching English and French and in dressmaking. Your file states that while in Paris you showed an interest and some skill in this occupation. We expect you to entertain your regular friends at this flat, and later on we will designate others whom we will want you to meet and get to know ... ah, rather well.

"However, to allay any suspicion, you must say that the No. 516 flat actually belongs to your aunt. She has gone to Hue and has lent it to you. Keep your old place in Cholon just as it is, and be sure to visit it at least once a week, but tell your friends that you are spending most of your time at the new residence."

Thi nodded her understanding, but her interest was in the new flat.

"Where is the—the back room? Is it hard to find?"

"This is not Western cinema. There is no secret panel or spring. Behind the tapestry in the bedroom is a regular door. It opens into the back room. You will make full use of the items you find in there. You will be guided by special instructions. Here is the key, and here is some money.

"Go there now and make it your home. Don't move in any of your own things. The place is completely appointed in exactly the manner in which we wish you to live. Bring in nothing that, if found, could be traced directly to you. Go there directly now and remove that disguise. From now until further word from me, wear the Cô Thi clothes you find in the bedroom closet. Remember, your meeting with the Sixty-ninth is tomorrow morning at 10:00. Be ready. Go now. Do not fail."

Thi was pleased and flattered. The tradecraft was an annoyance and secondary in her mind. What was important was that she was a member of Duat's inner circle. She was accepted and she was trusted. She would be working with the most professional group of terrorists in Saigon. She was on her way to the top. Quickly she got up to go. She bowed slightly to Ahn and turned toward the door.

Chapter III

JULY

M ark Buckley stood very tall and straight and tried to cover the effects of the hangover he was suffering.

The old and new commanders of Trong Thoi, standing side by side, watched the troops pass in review. The party, hosted by Major Ho and given in his honor the night before, had been spectacular. The affair had lasted into the small hours of the morning.

The river of rice wine, beer, and whiskey, which flowed between the courses of duck, puppy, and fish, had affected all the men at the camp. They all suffered as they went through the routine of this change-of-command ceremony.

Mark had been popular with Americans and Vietnamese alike. Additionally, they all thought he had been unjustly relieved, and most of them felt personal guilt because they had been involved in the sordid affair. To them the injustice was the fact that Mark, one of the few who had not been involved, was the only one to suffer censure.

Major Ho looked up at Mark's stern face.

How emotional, these Americans.

He knew that Mark hated to leave and was fighting hard not to reveal his feelings. He liked Mark. They had worked well together. There had been progress. Mark knew his country, and knew and trusted his people. In turn, Ho's people had trusted Mark, and would do far more for Mark than any other American with whom they had served.

Ho wondered about Mark's replacement. That officer had visited once and then left. He had come back for this ceremony and would leave, not returning for another week. No one could really replace Mark. He only hoped the new man would not betray all that had been built in the way of trust and respect.

The parade ended, and all the officers gathered around for one last handshake. The chopper was due in about two hours. Mark excused himself to do some more last-minute packing. Many of the Vietnamese had given him small gifts, and an extra box had to be worked up to hold them all.

While he was in his quarters, some of the officers and men came by singly or in twos and threes to say a personal word of farewell. The cold beer in his refrigerator was a welcome balm to the many hangovers.

Finally, the time came to leave, and Mark walked slowly down the steps of the mud wall to the landing float below. Suddenly the sound of clapping reached his ears. He turned and looked up to see the walls lined with American and Vietnamese soldiers. A bugle sounded. Instantly the clapping stopped and the men snapped to rigid attention. Another sound of the bugle and the men came to a salute.

Realizing this special honor, Mark, stern-faced, snapped to attention and returned the salute. Then he turned and boarded the chopper. In seconds, he was gone. The fort was a little scar by the muddy river. It was to be seven months before he would see Trong Thoi again, and the circumstances would be very different.

But now he had another job to face in an entirely new environment—one not of his choosing. One he did not like.

Ψ Ψ Ψ

The sun was setting as the chopper crossed the Plain of Reeds and approached Saigon.

A rainstorm had left the city glistening in the twilight, and the river coiled about the city like a golden python tight around a circus performer. Mark gazed down on Saigon and thought of his previous visits. Memories of her dusty, smoke-filled streets, her decaying houses, her large trees, now dying, all produced a picture of sadness and despair. The twilight, like a cosmetic, was masking an old woman's blemishes.

Saigon was an old woman. A used and reused old whore that had felt the weight of the Chinese, the Japanese, the French and, lately, the Americans. She was tired, she was diseased, but she knew her role. She would accommodate her masters as best she could. The lights now were coming on. The old woman was dressing for the evening, but her baubles could not mask the decay.

The chopper touched down and Mark, after thanking the pilot, grabbed his bag and walked to the operations building.

"Hi, Colonel Buckley, I'm Bill Scott."

Major Scott saluted and held out his hand.

"Glad to meet you, Bill."

Mark noted the large, West Point ring on the major's hand. They fell in step as Bill tried to take Mark's bag and Mark successfully deprived him of this honor.

"I have put you in 'the Hangout' with me until we can get you regular quarters. Hope you don't mind, but Saigon is busting at the seams."

"Why, that's great," replied Mark. "Hope I haven't put you out."

"Hell no, we have this villa. Not too classy. Four of us live there, but Hank is at Vung Tau with the R.D. school, and Freddy is in the Delta. He may stay there. If you want to ... that is, if it suits you ..."

"Well, we'll see. I kinda like to be alone ... Maybe it would ..."

"I just thought I would suggest it as a possibility. Anyway, you are welcome until you want to leave."

"Can't beat that."

They approached a jeep.

"Let you drive around Saigon by yourself?" asked Mark as they got in the vehicle.

"Sure. The city's safe. Just gotta watch the 2300 hours curfew."

Bill drove the jeep through the dark city to one of the residential areas. He stopped at the gate of a large house and honked the horn. A Vietnamese guard, recognizing the major, allowed the vehicle entrance. Soon they were in the house and Mark was well ensconced in Freddy's room.

"Bathroom's down the hall. Come on downstairs when you are cleaned up, and we'll have a drink and some supper," Bill suggested, as he started downstairs.

It wasn't long before Mark came down and joined Bill in the living room.

"Mighty nice quarters for field grade," remarked Mark as he came into the living room.

Bill mixed the drinks. "Best-kept secret in Saigon."

After some reflection, he added, "Well, you see, Ambassador Osborne gets a lot of official entertaining to do. Sometimes it falls off on us, and we have to have a place to do it."

"How did you get into this racket, anyway?" asked Mark. "You're an Academy graduate. Why aren't you out in the boonies with the rest of the pros?"

"Along the way I did some graduate work at Stanford in political science. I specialized in Far Eastern Affairs. I asked for a unit assignment and thought I had it made with the Big Red One, but when I reached Long Binh, my orders were changed. Oh, there was a minor tug-of-war over me, but no one fights for very long with Ambassador Osborne."

Mark half laughed, half snorted. "Oh, I thought maybe you got crossways with a senator's niece like I did."

He swallowed a long quaff from his glass.

"Colonel Buckley, we all know what happened down there and believe me, we all feel badly about it. For years, I have followed your career, and I know that you aren't the kind of guy that would knowingly allow something like that to happen. I was a student at Bragg when you came through after your first tour. You've been a ... well, some kind of hero to most of us in that class ever since you gave those briefings on Operation Nui Ho. I know you won't be too happy working with us in the pacification area, but I'm honored to be working with you, sir."

"Call me Mark."

"I'll try, but it's not going to be easy."

"Oh come on now, Bill. Remember that old saying: 'Rank among lieutenants is like virtue among whores'? Well, the same thing applies to field grade too."

"I also know another one—'Familiarity breeds contempt,'" added Bill. "And I don't want to run the chance of finding your clay feet."

"Don't worry, friend Bill, I'm not very good at fancy footwork. You'll find them all right."

They both laughed. "No matter what you do, sir ... ah ... Mark, I could never find clay feet on you."

They drank in silence for a while, each keeping his own thoughts. Mark was reviewing the sordid and unbelievable circumstances which resulted in his arrival in the villa. He couldn't keep the bitterness from his mind.

That bitch! That dirty, double-dealing rotten whore! Wonder where she landed? Probably writing a book about her exploits in the war zone. Whatever she's doing, she'll end up on top. Well, maybe not on top. After all, the bottom is the top in her business!

He smiled as he stared vacantly at the large Vietnamese lacquer mural on the wall opposite.

"What happened to the girl? You know, the flower of Trong Thoi, one Brandy Masters?" he asked.

"Didn't you know? She's here in Saigon. Her uncle made State give her a job. She's in USAID."

"My God! Here in town?"

"Yep. And from what I hear, she's a good girl now—at least in public," Bill laughed nervously.

"Do you know her? Have you seen her?"

"Oh, no. We travel in different circles."

"Well, I hope I never see her again." Mark got up and mixed himself another drink.

Bill thought for a long moment about what he was going to say next.

"Look ... er, Mark," said Bill uneasily, "it's probably a bad idea to keep thinking about her and what happened. If you do, you'll just become bitter to the point where it could affect your job and even your career."

"Am I on trial or something? Oh, I know! After all, in spite of what they say officially here, the fact remains that I was relieved of a combat command and put on staff duty."

95

"But sir ... Mark," Bill broke in, "you are a special guy over here. Your reputation was made during your last tour. Gosh, it was Westy himself who interceded and suggested strongly that Osborne take you."

A look of stunned surprise crossed Mark's face.

Damn. Well ...

A Vietnamese servant appeared and announced dinner. Both men headed to the dining room. Bill could still sense the mounting bitterness from the brittle sound of Mark's voice as the discussion continued through supper.

"As for any reputation over here, be it mine or Brandy Masters'," continued Mark, "the fact is that this place has a memory only one year long. Every twelve months the old players leave and the new ones arrive. The slate is washed clean. This is the month for normal rotation. In two or three months, Brandy and I both get a new start. Aren't we both lucky?"

"I wish you wouldn't keep mentioning your name in the same breath as that ... that slut."

"Why not? Maybe we are all whores. Maybe I'm one because I sold my honor by not demanding a court-martial. That was my right. Maybe the Army is one for not telling the good senator to go screw himself and stay out of the Army's business. Maybe the senator is one for protecting Brandy in the first place. Maybe this whole place is nothing but one big goddamn whorehouse where, instead of selling our bodies, we are all selling our souls."

"Oh come on, Mark. I know you must be disappointed, but you should be glad that you survived that situation and can go on now and do some good."

"Some good. Some good. That's the point. We all sell out so one guy who was in a spot to do a lot of good can now do good. My place is where I was, not here in this lousy city, where only a small part of my capabilities will be used. I don't have a master's in social studies—I have a master's degree in combat, period!"

Bill now saw the depth of Mark's bitterness. Perhaps it was a risk to bring him into Osborne's office. However, he could not believe that

Mark Buckley, the hero of the battle of Dak Pam, was in reality so small a creature that he could not take this setback in his stride. He figured that Mark had held all these feelings bottled inside and had not given his emotions a chance to boil over. If this was the case, he had better give them a chance now, before he started working for Newell Osborne. Bill decided what action he would take.

Tonight he would get Mark Buckley drunk ... so drunk that he would wring out every emotion in his being.

"You know, you don't start work till Wednesday," Bill remarked casually.

"What the hell, this is only Sunday."

"Yes, I know; but I thought you would need a few days to settle down. Find a place to live, if you didn't want to stay here—get your laundry done, you know."

"It's one hell of a war we Saigon commandos fight."

"Well, you may as well make good use of all the time off. Once Osborne gets hold of you, it's high tempo all the way."

They finished their coffee and moved into the living room.

"Drink?" asked Bill.

"No, thanks."

"Oh, come on. I don't want to drink alone. Besides, we have to continue our discussion. I don't believe that you are fit only for field soldiering."

Ψ   Ψ   Ψ

Thi rushed up the stairs to her new flat.

She loved her new surroundings and each time she returned she found pleasure in wandering through all the rooms. As she opened the door, Thi quickly forgot her latest long session with Ahn and she dropped the case that he had given her onto the floor. It was to play a part in her duties tomorrow, but for now, her only interest was her delightful new home.

The living room of No. 516 was exquisite. It was furnished in new rattan and the drapes were a double-faced green silk. Her bedroom was lovely in old Chinese teak. Embroidered silk tapestry almost covered the whole wall behind the large double bed with its massive posts. She idly wondered if she had been chosen to be Ông Duat's mistress, and this other business was a cover so Ahn would not suspect. The thought of her being at his side and sharing his intimate thoughts and plans thrilled her.

What will I wear? Mandarin dress as well?

Today she gave the workroom a closer look. She was impressed with the complete supply of dressmaking materials. There were bolts of beautiful cloth and a file of patterns. On a low table in front of a well-used couch were the latest French and American fashion magazines. In the center of the room was a dressmaker's form, half-draped with exquisite red-orange brocade.

But it was the secret room that she found the most intriguing. She couldn't stay away from it. She hurried to the bedroom and swept away the left edge of the tapestry that covered the hidden access door.

She pushed it open. On the wall to her right was a series of switches, which she had discovered as she groped for the light. Finally, she found the right one and the room lit up. There were no windows, but along the far wall was a series of built-in closets. Inside were many types of costume, male and female, new and old, clean and dirty.

On the left wall was a complete makeup center, with a bulb-circled mirror and vanity. There were also shelves with wigs of every color and hairstyle, and drawers of shoes, some smart and chic, others used, dirty, run over. Mirrors covered the opposite wall.

She tried many of the other switches and found that one was a ventilation system. The others controlled ceiling lights to various colors and intensity. Under these lights, makeup could be brought to a perfection that would defy detection.

Thi noticed the pull-down stairway that led to a trapdoor in the ceiling. Ahn had told her about the access to the roof and here it was. She held off a deep urge to pull down the stairs and explore the roof.

Instead, she sat down at the vanity in front of the mirror. Her eyes saw the small note pinned to a pincushion and, for the tenth time since she had moved in, reread it:

This room is for you alone. Allow no one else the use of it, unless instructed by message such as this one. Until further notice, only you and members of the Sixty-Ninth Special Action Group will use the room. From time to time, you will be directed to assume disguise for some of your duties. At other times, you will be expected to use your own discretion in this respect. Use your free time practicing makeup. Perfection is required. Destroy this message after reading.

Thi had, up to this point, skipped over the final instruction.

After a final look at the costumes, she returned to the bedroom, where she tried on several of the beautiful dresses and *ao dais* she found there. She stood before the mirror, marveling at the wonderful fit of the clothes. It was a long time before she wearied of this. She finally looked at her watch; it was 10:30 in the evening. No wonder she was tired. She must go to bed.

She caressed the note's paper between her fingers, feeling the coarseness of the cheap paper. She so wanted to keep this note as a souvenir. To take it out and to read it over and over. The pleasure she felt drowned out any thoughts of the security procedures that Ahn had spent many hours boring her with.

Then she thought of Duat. She felt suddenly cold for a moment at the idea of his reaction to her failure to carry out any of his instructions to the letter. Hastily, she found matches and burned the note in an ashtray.

She had nothing to do until tomorrow at nine when the action group's men would arrive and then ... oh yes, at two. There had been two visits before, starting shortly after she had taken up residence.

The attaché case!

She had forgotten about it.

"Guard it with your life," Ahn had ordered.

She raced to the living room. It was still there. She rushed over and picked it up.

"Come on, my little one, you are my bed partner tonight." She laughed, and hugged the cold leather to her warm body and returned to the bedroom.

The morning noises reached her before the rising sun, because the people of Saigon get up early to beat the heat. The staccato of the cyclos and the motorbikes awoke Thi with a rudeness that she had never quite gotten used to; she was annoyed and angry as she first opened her eyes.

When she realized that she was in her new flat, her humor turned. She smiled and slowly pulled the silk coverlet off her naked body and walked slowly to the mirror, all the while gazing at her own reflection. Her eyes moved from her ankles upward over her thighs, flat stomach, and well-formed breasts to her face, ringed with long, tousled black hair. Then her eyes rested on the scar on her cheek, now uncovered by her black tresses. Instantly she moved close to the mirror, examining the scar in detail. She scowled and cursed softly at the deep red gash, but her lips held a half smile. When she noticed the reflection of her whole face, the smile, like a fugitive caught unaware, instantly disappeared.

She turned so that the scar was not visible in the reflection, and examined again her nude body. Suddenly she laughed, turned, and walked to the living room. In less than two hours, the men of the Sixty-Ninth Special Action unit would be there and she could not linger long. She wanted to bathe and dress with care.

Promptly at nine, the men arrived. It thrilled Thi to see them.

She greeted the men in an orange silk *ao dai* with the low-cut neckline introduced by Madame Nhu. Although Thi was merely in a supporting role, she become obsessed each time they met that they would make her as something more important than a helper. Perhaps even the center of the operation. In her mind, she saw herself leading them into battle with all eyes looking at her in wonder and envy.

The men, however, were all business. In the prior meetings, they had never shown a single sign of pleasure in her looks and today was no different. The one called "Sam" instantly took charge. He removed the ash trays and a vase of flowers from the coffee table in the living room, and spread out a large blank piece of paper.

On it, he started a scale drawing of the area in front of the Rex Hotel. In the center of the paper he drew a long, thin rectangle which he marked "park." At the right end of the park, he drew the City Hall, and at the left end, a circle. This was the traffic circle. Thi recognized the fountain in the center. North of the park, Sam drew the Rex Hotel and indicated the cinema. South of the park, he drew a block of buildings and labeled the Air Vietnam office on the right end and a restaurant on the left end. He then added Le-Loi Street running perpendicular to the park, and across this street, beyond the traffic circle, an ice cream parlor called "North Pole."

The drawing complete, Sam sat back and lit a cigarette, while the others had time to study the drawing and get their bearings.

Sam slowly exhaled smoke. "We have been out walking over the target area."

Thi noticed that the exact target was located less than a block from her new flat. Later, she would come to understand that for security reasons Sam did continue the drawing to include her location. At this meeting, she remained silent, stifling a strong urge to speak out. Her fragile ego mixed with ardor for revenge made her eager to be top billed as the center of the plan despite operational security concerns.

Sam was measuring off distances from the Rex to the Air Vietnam office and to the restaurant and the North Pole.

"This is the best location for one of the big ones," Thi said, indicating the Air Vietnam office.

"Yes, there, and the restaurant here," Sam agreed. "Our people tell us that most of the Americans and Korean officers eat lunch here at the hotel. Today and tomorrow, we will observe to see what the most popular time is. We want to catch the most possible."

Sam then turned to Thi. "We are going to use Tam's old trick of exploding another claymore, about five minutes after the first two go off. It really worked well at the My Canh two years ago."

"Very good!" she agreed enthusiastically. "Don't forget that JUSPAO is also there. That should account for at least thirty more casualties."

"What is the JUSPAO?" asked Hok. He was the explosives expert but his curiosity extended beyond his technical area.

"Joint United States Public Affairs Office," replied Thi, trying not to sound too officious.

"Well, we will place the last bomb over here on a flower stall across the traffic circle. It will catch all the rescuers."

"I think it should go over here at the North Pole. It's a more direct line."

"Depends upon the traffic. Let's see. It's about 11:45 now. I think we should go up on the roof and get a bird's eye view of the whole scene. Come, bring this map."

"I will lead the way," declared Thi. "Please follow me, comrades."

She enters the scene from the left.

Ψ   Ψ   Ψ

It was Cy that stepped back from the canvas and looked at it with a critical eye, not Ned Green.

It was his first use of oils since he had left art school years ago, and he was pleased with the result. Having found out in school that pictorial expression of his impressions was always best if done quickly, he seldom changed a canvas once the impression in his mind was duplicated.

The army corporal, Ned, had been put aside for the artist, Cy. Yes, there was the fear of the MPs finding him, but being AWOL had become just another layer of his life in Saigon. He was painting again. That's what mattered.

It was hot in the studio. He turned and sat on a bench, fanning himself with a newspaper. His dark skin glistened and drops of perspiration rolled down his chest and back to be absorbed in the white terrycloth shorts Kam had made for him.

He had found that clothing was not necessary or desirable in this calm, quiet, and happy hideaway. The heat was such that he was uncomfortable in anything more. Kam herself often went about her work downstairs wearing nothing from the waist up and only a long cloth wraparound below the waist. Cy often watched her as she crossed the terrace. When she came upstairs, however, she always had some garment covering the upper part of her body.

He looked toward the door in anticipation of her arrival, although he knew that she always rang the bell before she came up.

This little honey Cô really turns me on. I haven't even touched her since I arrived that night three weeks ago. It's her shyness that has things going so slowly between us. Of course, she knows about me and Hue. That's obvious. To just go and grab her and screw her, would really rip it with Hue and I'd find myself out on my ass, or worse, in the Long Binh stockade.

This would be a very unfriendly city if I were on my own. Besides, I like this setup. I'm getting some painting done, the chow is good, and the booze is getting better now that I've convinced Hue that a little whiskey makes me a better bed partner.

Now if Kam chased me around, that would be different. There's plenty of time for me to be alone with her, with Hue always out running around with his artist friends. But I know that any hanky-panky between me and Kam would have to start off being her idea. I only hope my feelings don't take over and decide not to wait!

Jesus, it's hot—an' I'm gettin' hot thinking of that Kam. These shorts sure don't leave no room for a hard-on. Wonder how long I can wait for her to move first.

The little bell rang.

"She's comin'," he whispered. "Maybe ..."

Soon Kam appeared with a *Ba Mui Ba*, some bread, fruit, and a can of C-ration cheese. She was wearing a knee-length Western-style dress with an oval-cut neckline and no sleeves. She smiled at him as she set the tray down on the table. Then she turned to look at the picture he had been working on.

"Ah, number one!" she declared, emphasizing the "one."

He watched her tilt her head a little to one side, as if to try to puzzle out the meaning of the painting. He also noticed that under the thin cotton of the dress, she wore no bra. Her legs were very pretty. He went toward her and stood looking at the picture, mindful of the pain and the bulge in the front of his shorts. The girl missed nothing. She looked down and laughed, then pretended anger.

"You number ten man," she said with a pout. "You no like girl. You like only boy!"

"That ain't true, baby. That ain't true. Here, let me show you."

He reached for her waist. Kam laughed, dodged his arms, and ran

103

to the stairs. She turned again, pointed at his crotch and laughed. Then she disappeared. Cy laughed too as he watched her leave.

Then he called to her, "Come back here if you think I'm number ten man!"

Only her laugh came up from the lower floor.

Cy walked to the table, grabbed the beer she had brought, and swallowed two big gulps. Then he took the bottle back to the picture, but his thoughts were not there. Suddenly he took the picture off the easel and replaced it with an empty canvas. With a blunt piece of charcoal, he started sketching in broad lines. He became so absorbed in his work that thoughts of anything other than Kam were not within his conscious memory.

His unit, the Delta, the troubles in Detroit he had been reading about, and his black power friends there, had all vanished as if they never existed. Cy's impression of Kam's effect on him was the paramount thought in his mind. He worked until late afternoon, using raw, basic reds, blues, and yellows, along with more subtle tones of olive and umber. He was so absorbed in his picture that he was unaware of the fading light. Even Hue's presence beside him went unnoticed for some time.

"Say ... number one! You work very good! This your best. Very strong. Very ... ah ... you number one!" exclaimed Hue, never taking his eyes off the painting.

Suddenly Cy was tired. He was covered with sweat. He could not recall ever in his life concentrating so completely on anything. He went back to the bench, sat down, and rested his eyes by covering his face with his hands and propping his elbows on his knees. For a moment, the painting was impressed upon his vision. He closed his eyes. He did not want to open them again until the vision was completely gone.

Seeing him at the bench, Hue came over and sat very close to him, patting his sweat-covered back.

"You good artist. Maybe you sell pictures. You make money same-same Hue. I let my friends see. They tell me best what to do, yes, that good idea!"

"What's a good idea?"

"Tomorrow night my friends come see your pictures. You have show!"

"Up here? To see me? Now, wait a minute. How do you know one won't rat on me? Bring the MPs up here?"

"Never happen, Cy. You see, I know these men long time. I know all about them. They all do some bad things. You know? Dodge draft, do black market, drugs; all men in some way bad. I know all things of them. They know all bad things of me. I tell them, 'You tell about me, I tell about you!' You see, we all good friends and don't give away friendship!"

"They know about me being up here?"

Hue nodded.

"How long they know?"

"After two days you here. They no tell, I kid you not!"

"Well, I'll be screwed!"

"They come up see my sketches of you. They come up see your pictures. We have party. No other people, only my number one friends."

Hue turned and went to the stack of papers resting on a shelf. They were his new work, charcoal sketches of Cy. He carefully arranged the drawings on the floor. The charcoal work was excellent and Cy had been impressed with each one as Hue had finished it. Now looking at them one after another, he saw the quality of this man's work and felt the impact of the group of pictures. It was like getting to know himself better as he looked at each one.

As they walked from sketch to sketch, Cy saw himself in what seemed to be every possible pose. Some were large studies of his head, some were torso studies, others of the whole body. There was no getting around it—the man had real talent.

Hue smiled. "One pose we not do, Cy. How about you make one pose today so Hue have one more picture for friends to see?"

"Right now? Boy, I'm tired! I did that whole painting since lunch."

"This one easy, Cy. Here, you lie down on bench. You rest. You even go sleep!"

Cy laughed. "Okay, but don't bother me now. I'm really tired."

Hue moved the bench to get the best of the failing afternoon light

105

and spread a towel on it. Next, he led Cy to the bench and posed him flat on his back with both feet on the floor, on either side of the bench. Then he turned Cy's upper body so that he faced the room, with his head resting on his folded arms.

"You go sleep. Hue sketch."

Cy closed his eyes, but he could not sleep. His thoughts jumped from one subject to the next. First, it was the surprise of Hue's friends knowing about his living there, and the possibility of arrest because of them. Next, he thought about Trong Thoi and Colonel Buckley. He had seldom thought about his outfit in the Delta, and wondered if that offensive north into the Plain of Reeds had ever come off. He was glad he wasn't there–wasn't fighting.

He thought of home and his art school friends in Detroit. He recalled their bitter letters, their talk of riots, the coming of a real black revolution, the real hatred of the honkey bastards, and a review of the wrongs he and his black friends had suffered. Yes, he could never fight over here again. To risk his ass for the Man was stupid.

Then there was Kam downstairs. Every thought of her made his insides twist with longing. He wondered when he would be able to make love to her. He knew it would have to happen soon–on her invitation or not. He couldn't wait much longer. He would have to take the chance.

The following day Hue spent most of the afternoon cleaning up the studio and the upper terrace for guests.

Cy was glad to help. This was a welcome diversion from his normal routine. The paints and easels were put away in cupboards and Hue's sketches hung like clean laundry on a string along one wall. Cy did not want to display his two paintings, but Hue insisted that they were very good and the guests would appreciate them.

There was also a lot of preparation going on downstairs, and Cy was anxious to see what Kam was doing in the way of refreshments. Finally, about four p.m., she appeared with beer, ice, and two bottles of whiskey. These she placed on a long table that she had previously brought up from the kitchen. He had helped her push it onto the terrace. Next, she brought up a large plate of fried squid, fish, and Chả giò. The food was placed on the table where Cy had his meals. An additional trip produced plates of various sizes, chopsticks, and a bottle of nuoc mam, the ever-present fish sauce.

Cy went to wash up before the guests arrived. When he finished, he noticed that Kam had also produced the shirt, trousers, shoes, and socks he had been wearing the night of his arrival. The clothes were washed and pressed and the shoes were beautifully shined.

Some of Kam's old shyness returned when Cy complimented her, and she giggled and hid her face in her hands.

The guests began arriving about five-thirty, and by six, all were present. Hue made a point of introducing each one to Cy, who was obviously the center of attention.

Wonder what Hue has told 'em about me.

Cy poured a drink.

Wonder if they are all fruits like Hue? Probably are.

Each guest in turn admired Cy's paintings and tried to express his thoughts to Cy in broken English. Kam was the only woman present, and her presence was allowed merely because she was required as a servant. She wore a dark red *ao dai*, with white silk trousers. Her hair was brushed straight back and held with a wide band of red silk over her forehead. Black wooden slippers with high heels gave her a well-dressed look that Cy had not noticed in her before. His desire for her once more filled his thoughts, and he wondered if things would work out for him that night.

"Why you no bring Salem? Why you no bring Coca-Cola?"

Cy looked down on a very small young man, whose name sounded like Tang.

"I sure would like to get to a PX," Cy replied, "but my ration card's long run out and I only have my old ID."

"Who know you not good GI if you have good ration card, new ID card?" Tang snapped back.

"Where'm I going to get those?"

"I get for you. We make deal, okay? I get cards, you buy me ..."

"Wait a minute. Easy now. We better get Hue over here."

Hue responded to Cy's signal and joined the conversation. He was against the idea of Cy roaming about Saigon on a bogus pass and ID card. He knew it would only be a matter of time before the MPs would pick up Cy.

Still, he had long realized that it would be impossible to keep Cy cooped up on the top floor of the flat forever. From experience, Hue knew his relationships were at best temporary in nature, but he was a long way from tiring of Cy and had no desire to end it any time soon.

"We think of some idea," he said by way of pacifying both men, "but not now. Let's get back to painting. I think everyone like buy painting and agree you number one artist. I get more paints for you make ten painting, then we see how they sell."

To sell paintings! An old dream returned; only this time it seemed as if it really might come true. The aspirations of his art school days flashed again through his mind.

"In that case, I better sign my work," said Cy as he went to the cupboard and brought out some vermilion and a small paintbrush. He had never done this in oils before, but long ago, he had placed his special signature on his sketches and drawings. Carefully applying the paint to the brush, he went to each painting and printed the Greek letter Ψ, "Psi," in the lower right corner.

Course you have to know that Psi rhymes with Cy ... even most honkies don't know that ...

Ψ Ψ Ψ

Corporal Kim couldn't believe his good fortune.

His boss, Colonel Uhm, was on an inspection trip to the Korean Tiger Division near Plei Ku, but before leaving, he had actually signed a three-day pass for his driver. Of course, Kim was to use his time wisely and to good advantage–for Uhm. He was to line up some new girls for the colonel. This, of course, was never spoken about directly, but Kim knew his boss well.

In any event, he had borrowed enough Military Payment Certificates from Colonel Uhm to purchase a small radio and Seiko Japanese watches in the PX. These he promptly sold in the black market and now, fortified with a pocketful of piastres, he was making the rounds of several second-rate bars new to him. He wished he had enough money to hit some of the really number one places where the Americans hung out, but that took a lot of piastres, and if he was going to live it up for three days and in the meantime line up a couple of girls for Uhm, he would have to be careful about spending.

Buying that Saigon tea for them was expensive stuff.

He walked idly down Tu Do Street, stopping now and then to talk with some of the bar girls who were clustered about the doors of their places of business. They were waiting for the afternoon siesta to end and the evening rush to start. They all knew the big, good-looking soldier by sight. It was easy to talk to him as Kim's cocktail bar English was much better than theirs.

Kim didn't enter any of the bars. He merely stood outside and casually looked over the girls, keeping in mind the names of the ones that really interested him. He planned to be back later, after he had picked out six or seven around town.

Near the Astor Hotel, he decided to cut over to Nguyen Hue to catch some of the action in the area near the river. As he threaded his way between the people on the narrow side street, he suddenly came upon an art exhibit. The pictures were propped up against the buildings and about the kiosk that was the sales office during the day and a place to store unsold pictures at night.

"Hey, you very big Korean GI. Why you no buy nice picture?"

Kim looked into the door of the kiosk and saw an attractive Vietnamese girl leaning against a stack of paintings.

"You have painting of pretty girl here I might buy?" he replied.

"We have some here. Look at these."

Kam came out of the kiosk and started to lead Kim to the pictures displayed on the far side of the little stand. She pointed out three paintings Hue had done of her, each in different mood and in different colors. All were lovely and Kim liked them, but he wasn't about to buy a picture. In the first place, he didn't have money to waste on a painting of a girl he didn't know. In the second place, he had no place to hang a painting if he owned one.

"Nice paintings, but why such ugly girl? She number ten!"

Kam was quick to realize the joke and she laughed shyly. Then looking up at the big Korean, she noticed his nametag on the right pocket of his fatigue jacket.

"Kim! Your name very much same-same my name. My name Kam."

"Cô Kam. That's pretty name," Kim answered. "Who painted your picture? Husband?"

"No. Me number ten girl. Have no husband."

"Boy friend paint picture?"

"No. Have no boy friend, no husband, only brother. He paint."

"Where you live? Maybe I come around tell brother no paint number ten sister if he want to sell pictures."

Without thinking, Kam quickly answered, "Up there. You see top of building there with vine on porch."

Then she remembered Cy and knew he and her brother would be angry if Kim ever showed up.

"But you no come up see brother. He be angry," she added hastily.

"Maybe I come visit his sister."

"Oh, no. You no come. His sister number ten."

"Maybe not number ten. Maybe only number six and half."

They both laughed. Then Kim thought of his mission. "I go now—maybe I come back see you. Okay?"

"Okay. You come back see number six-and-half girl!"

She watched him as he disappeared in the crowd. He was nice. She hoped he did come to see her. She could keep him downstairs. He must not find out about Cy.

The afternoon dissolved into a humid thundershower as Kim ducked into a small Chinese restaurant for a quick supper. He was happy with his reconnaissance. When the rain stopped, he would make contact with the prettiest girls. For a while, he sat at the small table and watched the crowds of people trudging through the rain. One girl in particular interested him. She was tall, willowy, and beautifully dressed. Obviously, she was going to work and was trying to shield the orange-red *ao dai* she was wearing and an attaché case she was carrying with a cheap blue raincoat and a black umbrella.

Thi paused in the shelter of the overhang of the restaurant and anxiously looked at her watch. She didn't notice Kim, although he was sitting on the other side of the window, just feet away from her.

My God, this water. I can't pose as a bar girl dripping wet. Yet I'll be late if I try to stay dry by waiting here. Lucky it's only around the corner. But since the rain isn't going to quit I'd better make a run for it.

Before leaving, she once again went over her instructions. They were very detailed, but she had found them easy to memorize. She was to meet a man.

Wonder what the contact will look like?

Her instructions mentioned that he was under surveillance and might have to elude his followers in order to make the pick-up. Nervously she reviewed in her mind the contact "conversation" word for word. She had memorized both his remarks and hers, like a movie script. It had been easy for her. Once more, she looked at her watch as she hurried off into the rain. The case was heavy. Five million piastres! How heavy all that money was!

At precisely 4:30, Thi entered the back door of the Queen Bee Bar and quickly removed her wet raincoat. In the gloom of the unlighted hall, she saw a small, chubby Vietnamese woman dressed in a short American-style silk cocktail dress and high-heeled shoes. She had to be Madame Tun. The description in her instructions had described her in detail. The dress Madame Tun was wearing was bright blue and a size too small, but the plump lady was totally oblivious to this. She merely thought a tight dress made her sexier.

Thi remembered her first line, which was actually a countersign: "I am Cô Thi. The gardener sent me."

"Here, my dear. Let me take those wet things. Now let's see. Turn slowly. Stop there. Yes, yes, I suppose you will do. Can't see what men like about you stringy ones, but you sell the drinks. Look, I'm hanging up your coat here. Now come with me."

Thi, carrying the attaché case, followed Madame Tun down a dark hall. She could hear music getting louder. The older woman opened a door and the sound and colored lights of the bar spilled down upon them as they entered the main room.

Standing at the bar were three other bar girls. They quickly and expertly took in Thi's complete appearance from head to toe. Madame Tun introduced her in a professional manner, totally impersonal and dispassionate, as Thi stood respectfully, a pace behind.

"This is the girl I was telling you about. She is here for a special job. Leave her alone. She will be gone by 5:15."

Thi nodded a hello as she stared at the floor.

"She bring along her lunch?" sneered one of the girls, noticing the case.

Madame Tun's withering glare was the only answer. Thi followed her toward the front of the bar. The other girls giggled, but Thi was oblivious to this by-play. She was looking for the ordered special spot, which was to be her station. Madame Tun, by moving one of the girls to a table, was able to station Thi at the proper place at the bar.

"You are on your own, child," she murmured as she left Thi.

Thi put the case on the floor and wedged it between the bar and her leg. The feel of its solid bulk gave her a sense of security as she surveyed the room and glanced, again, at her watch.

It was 4:46 when a young US soldier in dirty fatigues came up and in very poor Vietnamese, asked her name. She immediately knew from his words that he was not the one. Therefore, she had to get rid of him to keep the coast clear for her contact.

"I am sorry; I cannot speak to someone who smells as bad as you." Thi dismissed him with a laugh that did not really hide her apprehension.

The soldier, hurt and embarrassed, turned and approached one of the other girls. Thi relaxed. Her fears dissolved instantly when she realized how easily she had got rid of the American.

It was raining again. Business would be poor until after the shower. Thi was happy about this. It would be easier to recognize the man who walked in at five.

Through the open door, she could see a man waiting outside. Why did he not come in instead of standing out in the rain? Perhaps he was her contact. Perhaps he was waiting for the appointed time.

Kim was standing in front of the Queen Bee waiting for the rain to stop. He had tried to follow the pretty girl he had seen outside the restaurant, but by the time he had paid his check, she was gone. He wanted to go into the Queen Bee. This was one of those expensive places that mostly catered to Americans. Should he go in and drop a thousand piastres or so?

He looked at his watch. It was 4:55.

If it's still raining at five, then I will go in.

Meanwhile, three blocks west on Pasteur Street, a well-dressed Vietnamese was urging his cab driver to go faster through the rain. He was already late for his appointment. Suddenly a squad of Special Security Police, who were following instructions to take the man into custody, forced the cab to the side of the street.

A large number of Vietnamese, ignoring the rain, crowded about to watch the action. In the confusion, the man was able to pull a small pistol from his pocket. With a quick movement, he managed to foil the police by blowing a neat hole in the front of his own head. The other side was not so neat.

The onlookers then dispersed quickly and the incident was soon forgotten. The baffled policemen took the corpse to the police station.

He would not be keeping his appointment.

Kim looked at his big PX watch—exactly five o'clock and the rain was still pouring down. He turned and entered the bar. Thi looked up from her watch and saw one of the most handsome men she had ever seen approaching her through the door. Inwardly all was turmoil, but outwardly she was calm, almost aloof. He was Korean, but she had been told to expect any sort of contact. The correct words were all that mattered.

Kim, happy to find the girl he had seen in the rain, smiled as he came to stand by her at the bar.

"Aren't you a little late?" asked Thi, following her script.

"Oh, I guess so," replied Kim, a little puzzled by her question. Then as an afterthought, he smiled and added, "But maybe my watch stop." He looked at it and shook it a few times.

Thi was angry.

He shouldn't stray so far from the script, no matter how good an actor he is. All he had to say was, "Oh, my watch stopped." But if he isn't going to follow the rules, I certainly am.

"When did it stop?" she asked coolly.

Kim decided to try a joke. "Maybe an hour ago–but that was last Tuesday, I think."

That too is an improvisation! What's he trying to do anyway? No one has come in since he entered; he must be the man!

Again, she followed the script. She laughed, uneasily. Kim also laughed at his bad joke.

Well, that's better. He did that on cue.

"You buy me tea?"

Kim looked out the door. The rain had stopped.

A very interesting girl by her looks, but this is a strange conversation. She won't do for the colonel, because he likes his women shorter and with a little more weight. But for me ... I will come back. She's number one!

"You buy me tea?" This time she seemed more anxious.

I wonder if the prices are high? This is a pretty classy place. And it's always one tea turns to two tea, three tea, four tea ... I can't run up a big bill.

"Would like to, but well, it's getting pretty late. I'll come again–tomorrow." He checked his watch. "I didn't realize it was so late," he added lamely.

Why wouldn't he stay precisely with the exact words? All he had to say was "Would like to, but I didn't realize it was so late. See you later." Why did he have to work so around the conversation?

She gave the next coded reply: "Where will you find me?"

He turned and walked to the door. Outside, a paper boy had been sheltering his newsstand from the rain. He wanted desperately to impress her, make her remember him.

He paused and said, "Oh, I find you–even you go see family ..." He glanced at the newsstand. The headlines of the paper screamed REDS SHELL MUC WA. "... in Muc Wa."

Thi was relieved at last. He had come through with Muc Wa, the countersign.

"Goodbye," she said with a laugh of relief as he continued out of the door. She waited until he was on the street, then picked up the case and ran after him.

"Don't forget your briefcase!" she shouted, but he did not stop. She ran closer to him and thrust it into his big hand. He looked at her blankly.

"You forgot it. Remember?"

"But ..."

She was gone in the crowd before he could answer.

What is this? Crazy girl! I better give it back. Some sort of a mistake. No ... I will bring it back tomorrow. She will be glad to see me. Maybe so glad that she will buy me beer!

Kim crossed the traffic circle at the intersection of Nguyen Hue and Le-Loi, dodging the cyclos, trucks, and taxis. Then, picking his way through the black-market displays on the sidewalk, he entered the North Pole Ice Cream Parlor and went directly to an empty booth. As soon as the waitress had taken his order, he placed the attaché case on the bench between himself and the wall. Carefully he opened the lid and peered inside.

Great Buddha's ghost!

He snapped it shut. Quickly he looked around the room to see if anyone was watching him. The parlor was filled with both Vietnamese and Americans, all eating ice cream and talking. They were oblivious of Kim and his great discovery. Apparently, no one was noticing him. Again he inched open the case.

It is true! My eyes did not deceive me! Stacks upon stacks of 500-piastre notes!

He closed the lid again slowly on his hand. While he looked around the room, his fingers worked some of the bills loose from their neat paper binding. These he pulled out of the case and stuffed into his trouser pocket.

Then he snapped the case closed again. The waitress appeared with his ice cream.

"My check, please."

When she returned, he reached into his pocket and pulled out the wad of newly acquired bills. He peeled off one and threw it on the table. She picked it up and went off to get change. He arranged the other bills into a roll, quickly counting them. They were all 500-piastre notes! Although he was trembling, he tried to eat his ice cream calmly.

What if the case is full of 500-P notes?

His curiosity was almost too much to bear. His crafty peasant mind was working the events over and over.

First, that bar girl did not know what was in the case. Then she wouldn't try so hard that I take it. Second, she must be part of some black market payoff and it will soon be known the payoff was made to me, Kim, not to the right guy!

My life is not worth a grain of rice if they find me with their money. I must keep it hidden! They may follow me, but won't touch me until they know where the cash is. Oh, maybe they will slap me around a bit to make me talk. But only if they get me alone. Now, where to hide this P? It's only maybe twenty minutes since the girl left. So ... no one knows they make mistake. Yet. But soon. Lotsa P here. I wonder how much. Time to move fast. Check this out ...

The waitress returned with his change. Finished with his ice cream, he stuffed the loose money in his pocket and casually left the ice cream parlor.

Slowly, he threaded his way through the black-market American goods displayed on the sidewalk and made his way past the McCarthy BOQ. There, behind the sandbagged guard post was a trash can with a beer carton and some discarded string sticking out of the top. Kim knew immediately what he would do.

"Hey, GI. How about me use box?"

"What? Oh sure, sure. Help yourself."

Kim retrieved the beer carton. The case fit into it exactly. Then, taking some of the string, he tied the carton shut and made a string handle at one end to make it easier to carry.

"Thank you, GI. Now all okay."

"You steal it?"

For a moment, Kim's heart missed a beat.

"Oh no, I buy PX. Now I send my father in Suwon," he laughed as he walked down the street.

Quickly he hailed a cyclo-mi and directed the driver to the East Wind Hotel in Cholon. It was a small, cheap hotel that Kim had stayed in several times when he had a girl and it was after curfew. He walked into the dingy lobby and signed up for a room. The desk clerk knew him and asked, "Where your girl?"

"Too early. Maybe bring in one later," Kim answered with a laugh.

Soon he was in his room and, after carefully locking the door and inspecting the walls for possible peepholes, he sat on the bed, untied the string, and opened the carton. Then he opened the case and emptied the contents upon the bed. Each packet contained one hundred bills, and there were one hundred packets! Kim ruffled the edge of each to expose each bill.

Yes, all 500-P bills! That means ... maybe five million piastres—that's fifty thousand dollars in American green!

In one blind stroke of luck, Kim had become rich. Now his biggest problem would be how to stay rich—and alive. It was dirty money of some sort. Someone would come looking for it. For a moment, he thought of the pretty girl who had given him the briefcase, but he did not think of her for long. Her life did not mean five million piastres to him.

Besides, if she was smart, she could survive the mistake she made. Maybe he would go by and see her in a day or two—after he had hidden the money. If she was cooperative, well, maybe he could make her a deal. After all, he was a man of means now. Giving the money back never crossed his mind. As far as Kim was concerned, the money was part of some black-market deal and it was now his.

His thoughts then turned to the real problem at hand—from his point of view: where to keep the money. It had to be in a safe place, but also a place where he could visit alone without raising suspicion. That was the trouble—he was never alone. In the barracks, there were always many soldiers around. He was alone only in the sedan, when returning from driving Colonel Uhm. However, he didn't always get the same vehicle from the motor pool. Then he remembered Colonel Uhm's room. Often, Kim delivered packages and whiskey there while the colonel was in his office.

One time he had spent over an hour in Uhm's room, looking at the radios, coffee pots, toasters, and irons that the colonel was collecting to take home to Korea. The maid had seen him in the room, but she liked him and didn't tell Uhm. Yes, that was the place. He was in that room at least once a week by himself, and he could always get the key at the desk.

He considered the layout of the room. There were built-in cupboards and shelves, a desk, some rattan chairs, and a couch. Then there was the very large, heavy wardrobe. Once he had to move it for Colonel Uhm. That was it! It had short legs about six inches off the floor, and an ornamental molding that extended between the front legs and along the sides. If he could mount a false bottom under the regular floor of the wardrobe, hidden by the molding ... perfect!

He put the packets of bills in the beer carton and, leaving the briefcase in the room, headed for the Rex Hotel. On the way, he stopped at a small wood furniture factory he had noticed and bought a piece of thin plywood. Then he stopped at the black-market vendor on the sidewalk and bought a screwdriver and wood screws, two small hinges, and two small hooks and eyes.

At the Rex, he picked up the key at the desk and soon was in Colonel Uhm's room. His timing was good. It was early evening and the floor maids were gone. There would be no interruptions. Kim removed all of Uhm's clothes from the wardrobe and then pulled the heavy piece of furniture onto its side.

After brushing away the accumulation of dust and cobwebs, he attached the plywood to the bottom with the hinges along the back and held it in place with the hooks and eyes at the front. He righted the wardrobe and inspected his work. Hidden behind the molding, the plywood was out of sight, even when he lay on the floor. Kim then reached under the molding and disengaged the hooks. The plywood swung on its hinges, down to the floor. He took the money from the beer carton and placed the packets of money on the plywood, keeping back two packets that he placed in his pockets. Then he swung the plywood up against the bottom of the wardrobe and hooked it in place.

Knowing that his money was now secure, Kim felt relief and accomplishment. He regarded the wardrobe from all angles, but could not detect the hiding place. He carefully replaced Colonel Uhm's clothing and strolled out of the room with the empty carton. On the way down the steps, he discreetly dropped it in a wastebasket.

Now I may go where I want in this town. I can go anywhere, eat anything, drink anything, love any girls I want. Tonight … I'm going to the best house, have the best girl, stay all night long!

He turned in the key at the desk and walked out onto the busy street. There were several cabs waiting for customers and Kim selected one. He remembered the name of a certain place American GIs had mentioned.

"Ninety-two Hung Vu'o'ong."

Without a word, the driver guided his little Renault into the incessant stream of traffic.

Ψ Ψ Ψ

Bill Scott stood quietly at the door of the bedroom and listened.

Mark was sleeping soundly. The spectacular two-day drinking bout was over. All that remained was to pick up the pieces and reassemble them once again into the man, Mark Buckley.

Bill gave instructions to the house servants to call him at his office if Mark awakened. All in order, he entered the waiting sedan and proceeded to his office. At noon, he returned to the villa to check on Mark and found him just waking up. After sending one of the servants to fetch the number one masseuse from a massage parlor nearby, he helped Mark into a cold shower.

As Mark dried off, the young woman arrived and was ready to give him a rubdown. She ignored his groans and protestations. She worked on his hung-over body for a full hour before considering her job finished.

Mark sat on the side of the bed. He was gulping down the tall glass of Vietnamese iced coffee, *café da*, that Bill had brought him.

"My God, you could have shown a little kindness by just letting me die."

"That would be too easy on you. I want you to suffer a bit so you'll better appreciate what we've done for you!"

"Thanks."

"No sweat. I've seen worse. What I want to know now is, are you ready to go to work?"

"Let me see if I can walk first."

Mark slowly got up and walked around the room. A throbbing head only made his embarrassment worse.

"That was pretty childish of me. What I mean is that I should've been able to handle this transition without feeling so damned sorry for myself."

"Forget it. It was all contrived."

"What do you mean?"

"Well, I figured that you'd keep resenting the job as long as you were here unless you had a chance to get it out of your system. We didn't want your work hampered by any nasty old bitterness, so I decided to let you get them all off your chest. That's all."

"Fine for my chest, but now how about my head? Wow!"

"You don't have a thing to do for the rest of the day but worry about your head. Tomorrow is your first day of duty. The rest of your stuff arrived from Trong Thoi. It's all pressed and hanging in the closet. Now I've got to get going. Have a meeting with Mr. Han at JUSPAO. See you this evening."

As Bill left the room, Mark sank back on the bed and closed his eyes. He was thankful for Bill's consideration and friendship. Perhaps he could return the favor someday. But now a little more sleep seemed to be in order. It was an easy order to obey.

Ψ   Ψ   Ψ

Bill headed for JUSPAO and wondered if Mark was really over the shock of this change of assignment. He was still thinking about Mark when he arrived and walked into Mr. Han's office. Then all other thoughts vanished as he looked down on a tiny doll of a girl seated very stiffly, almost uncomfortably, at a small typist's desk.

"Major Scott, I am Mai Lei, Mr. Han's interpreter."

"I am very glad to meet you, Cô Lei," he said with a smile. "Is Mr. Han in?"

"We tried to reach you before you left MACV Headquarters. Mr. Han is regretfully delayed for one half hour. It is too bad."

"Not at all, Cô Lei," Bill laughed. "Perhaps we could spend the time having a coke together."

"That would be very pleasant, but I must not leave desk."

"Well, in that case I will get the drinks and bring them here."

"Oh, you Americans. You never take no for an answer."

"I didn't hear you say no."

"Well, it was—how do you say it? —implied, and besides, please make mine orange."

"That's better. I'll be right back."

Mai Lei watched him leave the office. She decided he was very good looking.

Bill returned quickly with the soft drinks. In his absence, she had pulled up an extra chair near her desk.

Mai Lei thanked him for the drink. "We are getting so used to all the cold drinks and refrigeration you Americans have brought. What is to become of us when you leave?"

"Will you be worried more about the lack of refrigeration or the number of Communists?"

Mai Lei laughed, but she also shuddered as a cold chill went up her spine.

"My father says that it would have been better for us if you Americans had not come here."

"Do you believe that?"

"Oh no. By now, we should all be Communists or dead! But you see, my father feels that we must find our own destiny."

"We are trying to help you find it."

"Yes, but, well, I wish someone else would talk to him. I am tired of arguing with him."

"I would like to talk to him. May I call sometime?"

For a moment Mai Lei was silent, as if she was contemplating the question; then she seemed to have made up her mind.

A wide smile covered her face as she looked up at Bill.

"Yes, yes. I think that would be good for him. You must come and talk to him!"

At that moment, Mr. Han entered the office and Mai Lei introduced

Bill. The three of them retired to the inner office and Bill extended Ambassador Osborne's personal invitation to Mr. Han to attend a special reception and supper the following week. It would be at the new US Embassy and would honor the leaders of the Australian Mission.

Mai Lei translated for Mr. Han: "I am sorry, but I must decline the very kind invitation. You see, it is impossible for me to speak English and I would be lost."

"But that is why Ambassador Osborne has sent me here to invite you in person. He is most anxious for you to attend, and thought I could iron out any such difficulties. This will be so easy. Cô Lei could be with you. I will see that an invitation is extended to her immediately."

Mr. Han reluctantly accepted the invitation under those circumstances. He agreed that Major Scott would pick up both of the Vietnamese in an official sedan the night of the function.

His official business concluded, Bill lingered in the outer office with Mai Lei.

"You don't mind if I drop around a little early to talk to your father, do you?" asked Bill.

Mai Lei laughed. "Not at all, but I feel I had better warn you. He is a professor at the Saigon University and very smart!"

Ψ   Ψ   Ψ

Thi heard a key turn in the front door lock.

As she walked across the living room to see who was there, Ahn burst into her flat. Without a word, he struck her hard on the side of the face. She crashed into the coffee table as she hit the floor.

He snarled in Vietnamese: "You stupid little slut! Who did you give it to?"

She looked up at him with frightened eyes, uncomprehending. He kicked her hard in the belly and she rolled on the floor in pain.

"Get up! Ông Duat wants to see you. You will tell him all. I promise you. Move."

Thi, dizzy and nauseous, quickly got to her knees and tried to stop the reeling room.

Give what to? No! Something must have gone wrong with the five million piastres pick-up. But what? God! Did I give it to the wrong person? That's impossible! The big Korean said all the countersigns.

She steadied herself by holding to the back of a chair. Her face stung from the blow and her stomach ached. She wanted to vomit.

"Fix your hair. Get a raincoat. Move!"

Mechanically she did. Moments later, they were in the Mercedes. Tears of anger and chagrin mingled with raindrops on her lovely face. Only the sounds of the street and the loud pounding of the night rain on the roof of the car interrupted her thoughts.

In her mind, she was trying to recreate word for word the conversation with the big Korean. Thi knew that Ông Duat would never forgive her any mistake. She knew enough of his operation by now to know that there was no place for failure in his organization.

Duat survived on perfection. Now her one aim was to stay alive. She knew her only chance was to convince him that she had made no mistake. She would have to prove herself despite the treatment she expected to receive.

The car stopped in front of the Catinat Hotel. They passed through the lobby, crowded with people escaping the rain. She paused at the door of the ladies' room.

Following instructions and for the benefit of the crowd, she spoke brightly.

"Excuse me," she said, looking up into Ahn's face, "I must make a call. See you later."

Ahn was waiting for her when she stepped out of the elevator. She followed him into Duat's living room where their leader was waiting, sitting very straight, his face a mask.

Thi stood before him with head bent and eyes downcast. She knew that the next hour was crucial. Somehow, she must get across in her actions, as well as her reactions, that her actions with regard to the transfer of the five million piastres had been perfect. Plus, she had to show that she was annoyed at being blamed for someone else's blunder.

To accomplish this, she realized, would require the greatest acting performance of her life.

"Five million piastres were mishandled," said Duat in a slow, quiet voice. "It was your responsibility to see that this currency was delivered properly and on time. It is not the loss of the money. Of far more importance is the fact that a mistake was made. I do not allow mistakes. You will now go over your actions at the Queen Bee in minute detail. Begin with your arrival."

Thi raised her head.

Action!

Now, internally, deep in her role, Thi's eyes were blazing with anger, yet her voice was steady, distinct, and very matter-of-fact. She gave an almost perfect account of Kim's arrival and the ensuing conversation. She told of her misgivings when he strayed from the exact wording of the script, but she used examples to illustrate how close he actually was. She stressed the point of his use of the countersign: Muc Wa. She ended her account by stating that Kim had entered the bar at exactly five o'clock and he was the only person to enter the Queen Bee from 4:55 to 5:10. His conversation had identified him as the agent to receive the money.

She then asked, "If this was not the right man, then who has betrayed us and put my whole life in jeopardy? If I am risking my own life, do I not have the right to work with people I can trust?"

Thi's defiant attitude was not a surprise to Duat. He knew her well enough to expect it, and was pleased by her demonstrated ability to throw displeasure elsewhere. Now, this affair had unearthed another problem. Ahn was jealous of the girl. He was trying to convince Duat that her mission with the money had been somewhat less than professional.

As he looked at Thi, behind his cool, expressionless eyes, Duat's mind raced along unexplored possibilities.

Ahn wants her dead. He knows her potential, thinks in time she will be a threat to him. What an interesting entertainment to let them fight it out. Both are bright, yet totally without feeling for others, totally amoral, totally cruel. Yet they are devoted to me. They know it is I who will decide who is to live or to die. They are so attracted to power that they would destroy each other for it; yet they would let my power destroy them without the slightest protest.

He glanced at Ahn. Duat's eyes were that of a stalking snake.

124

Ahn must have some time by himself with her to cement his position in her eyes. A short "interrogation" should be sufficient.

"Ahn, perhaps you should continue the questioning," he said. "Bring her back in half an hour and we will see if there is anything else to cover."

As Duat watched, Ahn led the girl across the terrace.

Ahn knows she must show outward signs of mistreatment when he returns her to me. It will be interesting to see which of our methods he is planning to use.

He looked at the sky. Dark clouds were forming. There would be a storm. He turned and strolled to his quarters and went directly to a small tape recorder that he had placed on the center table by the bowl of white peonies. With a smile, he flicked it on.

"Aren't you a little late?" It was Thi's voice. "Oh, I guess so," said the voice of the stranger, "but maybe my watch stop."

"When did it stop?" Thi asked.

Duat snapped off the machine. "Clever, clever," he sighed. "Cô Thi, you have this little machine to thank for your life."

As Thi walked with Ahn to the office, her thin cloak of bravado was quickly being replaced by one of sickening fear. She looked at the face of Duat's lieutenant and saw anticipated pleasure and excitement in his expression.

She tried to plan, tried to think of some way to escape this madman's wrath. What could she do? To run or to fight would not only write her off as Ahn's enemy, it would also finish her with Duat. She would be better off dead. Try as she might, she could not produce a viable plan. The only thing that seemed to penetrate the cloud of fear was a desire to fight for life and to preserve her esteem in the eyes of her leader.

Ahn knows he can't kill me. No matter what he does to me, I can stand almost anything for thirty minutes.

They reached the meeting room. Ahn slid the blackboard aside and opened a door behind it.

"Come, Cô Thi, follow me."

Thi noticed the thick walls as she entered this hidden area. She was instantly on guard. The room was like a tomb. No sound would escape from here. There were no windows, and only a low wooden stool placed over a small, grilled drain opening in the center of the bare cement floor. Harsh light came from a single bare bulb that hung from the ceiling directly over the stool.

Trying not to be obvious, she looked about for some means of escape. Almost instantly she spotted three large iron rings, equally spaced high up on each of the four walls. The deep, dull thud of the door closing caught her attention. Ahn had left her. She was alone in this room.

Every second that passes is in my favor. The longer he's away from me, the better my chances of surviving the night.

Ahn's voice, loud and harsh, boomed into the room like a clap of thunder.

"Please disrobe completely, Cô Thi."

She looked for the hidden loudspeaker, hoping that the surprise and fear she felt were not evident to anyone who might be watching. Duat had given Ahn the order. She must comply.

Ahn's voice continued: "You are wasting valuable minutes. This is not to be a sexual escapade. Knowing much of your past, I suppose you must be disappointed. Quickly now, remove everything— underclothing, shoes, watch, bracelet. Bring them to the door and exchange them for another garment. You will find our little room becomes very hot for one reason or another. We do not wish to soil the clothing we have provided for you."

Thi's fright left her.

Ha! Liar! Sex! Of course! He's like all men. Says no, means yes. It's my way out! In spite of what he says, I know he's interested in me.

She couldn't suppress a slight smile as she hurried to follow instructions. Completely nude, she gathered her clothes in a neat bundle and stood before the door. It swung open, revealing Ahn dressed in a loose-fitting, sleeveless cotton shirt that hung to his knees. The seriousness of her situation prevented her from noticing the ludicrous picture he made with his bony body in such an outfit.

Without the slightest glance at her, he said only, "Put this on."

Then, taking her clothing, he disappeared through the half-closed

126

door. Thi's head surfaced through the neck of the simple white gown in time to see him return clutching a strange, sticklike device about a meter long. The door closed behind him as he waited for her to adjust her gown.

"Come now, Cô Thi. Our time together is slipping away. Here—sit down on the stool and listen to me carefully."

As she took her seat, Thi tried unobtrusively to pull her garment tightly about her body. Then, crossing her legs, she pulled the hem well above her knee and hoped the pose would attract his attention.

It was wasted effort.

Without even looking her way, Ahn asked the first question: "Who was the person you gave the money to?"

"The man you sent. I don't know," she answered in a low, husky voice.

"That won't do." He brought the baton around and touched the end of it against her thigh.

She gasped with surprise as the pain of an immediate electric shock raced through her body.

"This is your first introduction to the American way of disciplining cattle," remarked Ahn with a satisfied smile.

"A very useful object when modified as we have done here; it makes honest people out of liars of even the worst sort. Notice the small knob on this end. The charge you received was from the weakest setting. Now watch as I turn the knob to the very highest. You can see that we have a great variety of range. Then there is the shape of the instrument—long, round—just the right diameter to fit snugly into the major openings of the human body. Only a physician's examination would reveal the effects of this instrument."

Warming to his subject, the corners of his mouth moistening, Ahn continued.

"I noticed your interest in the iron rings on the walls, Cô Thi. We often use them in conjunction with the prod. Imagine a rope tied to each ankle, then through the rings. A simple hoist which results in our guest spread upside down on the wall, gown tumbled down over the head, and the rest of the body in position and open for the interrogation!"

Ahn's description had the desired effect on Thi. She felt the room becoming unbearably hot. She broke into a sweat. She was so afraid of the prod that she didn't notice that her gown was now drenched.

Good God, I don't want that thing up me; the man is a monster. Doesn't want me to speak the truth. What can I say? What can I do?

"Now again, Cô Thi," Ahn whispered. "Who was the person you gave the money to?"

The girl's frantic mind searched for an answer that would save her from the horrible instrument.

"The man you sent ... he was a ... he was a Korean, a Korean soldier. I don't know his name. I never saw him before," she answered.

Her voice trailed off as fear of the expected punishment overcame her.

"That answer is only half-acceptable," Ahn said coolly. "Therefore, a mid-setting should suffice to obtain a completely suitable answer."

As he turned the control knob, up to half charge, he advanced the prod toward the frightened woman. His eyes roved over the sweat-drenched garment like a bird of prey searching for a target. The prod hovered a few inches from the pronounced curve of her left breast.

"The moist garment will assure an excellent contact."

Thi cringed backward as far away from the torture instrument as possible. His eyes fastened on hers and would not let go. Suddenly a new plan for survival came to her. She acted quickly. As if to defy her adversary, she suddenly moved forward and thrust her breast against the end of the prod. The unexpected power and pain of the electric shock, so much greater than before, rocked her backward.

With a piercing shriek, she rolled her eyes back into her head. Her body stiffened. Her eyes closed. She fell from the stool onto the hard cement floor and did not move.

Ahn at first was pleased with this reaction.

"Get up, you little whore," he sneered. "You'll have to take a lot more punishment than that to survive in this business."

He nudged her with his foot as he looked down upon the wet, helpless figure that had been so beautiful, so defiant. With his foot, he rolled her over on her back.

"I said get up, you slut! Get up and get back on that stool!"

Thi lay limp on the floor, hoping her performance had been successful. Her breast pained her badly, but she dared not move or even twitch. She tried to control her body so that he would hardly notice her breathing.

Ahn kneeled by her and picked up her limp wrist. He glanced at his watch to take her pulse. He realized that only ten minutes remained before he had to return her to Ông Duat. He was in trouble.

While she's in this condition, I can never get her dry, dressed, and in shape to take her back to him. What can I do? I'm sure of one thing. It's better to tell my story, as I want it first, instead of having him come to investigate why I'm late in bringing her back. That's it. The little bitch wasn't even strong enough to take a half charge. She'll never be of any use to us when the situation gets tough. She'll be dead within the hour.

He placed the prod by the door and hurried off to report to Duat.

As Thi heard his footsteps fade away beyond the closed door, she sat up and took the cattle prod. Quickly, she set the knob to the highest reading, and then carefully replaced the prod on the floor so that it was barely within reach of her hand. After making sure she could grasp it with her eyes closed, she resumed her position on the floor and waited, ready to retaliate—to give Ahn the worst the cattle prod had to offer.

When the door opened, however, Thi was surprised to hear Duat's voice.

"Don't touch anything, Ahn. Let me see the situation here."

She felt his soft hand lift her arm gently. He was taking her pulse.

"Seems normal," he said softly.

He dropped her hand. There was silence. She wished she could open any eye, but did not dare to take the chance.

"Ahn, you fool! You stupid, ignorant fool!"

Duat's voice rose higher and stronger as his emotions took over. The shrill uncontrolled screech in Chinese sent shivers down Thi's spine. Evidently, Duat had picked up the cattle prod.

"Come here, you idiot! Does this look like half-charge to you? You've given this girl a full-charge shock! What was your motive? You know you have no authority to do this without my permission."

He continued in a highly agitated voice.

129

"You've never had a full charge, have you? Well, now you are to have one to teach you a lesson. Never let your emotions stand in the way of reason!"

Ahn lamented the loss of face far more than he feared the shock of the prod.

"Ông Duat, I do not ask forgiveness or try to apologize for my thoughtlessness. Please punish me as you believe I deserve to be punished," he said in a voice strained with emotion.

Thi realized that a happy stroke of luck had turned her chancy and imperfect plan into a masterstroke of revenge.

Who would have thought that Duat would return with Ahn; turning the tables on my tormentor in such a positive and effective way! I must see him suffer! I can't let this moment pass.

Without moving, she opened one eye, and then quickly opened the other, so startled was she with the strange sight she saw. The two men had forgotten her on the floor. They were staring at each other, oblivious of Thi and her condition.

Duat was visibly shaking, once again trying to control his anger. Ahn, for once, was bewildered, insecure, trying to comprehend the magnitude of his crime. He was trying to reason why the knob was set to the highest charge, trying to foretell the effect of all this on his future—if, in fact, he had one.

She watched in fascination as Ahn slowly pulled the white, sweat-drenched gown over his head and dropped it to the floor at his feet. He was now naked.

"Oh, noble Ông Duat, I offer my lowly unworthy body to punish as you see fit. I have acted in the lowliest, self-seeking manner, and have made myself unworthy in your eyes."

Duat's reply was a direct and simple one. He silently raised the prod and moved it forward, catching Ahn full in the crotch.

The unfortunate man, although braced for the shock, was still not prepared for the horrible pain, the powerful searing agony that seemed to envelope his testicles. The bone-bruising current burned like a fire throughout his body with the center, white-hot apex of the flame concentrating in his crotch. Ahn felt the room spinning, as his whole body seemed now afire. He screamed, then emitted a low guttural groan as he clutched himself and slowly sank to the floor.

Duat dropped the prod as if it were a filthy thing and gazed at the outstretched body of his lieutenant. Ahn's shaking subsided in diminishing waves. Duat looked down at him with contempt before slowly walking to the door.

Thi remained in position on the floor, afraid to move.

Where will this end? What's to happen to me? To Ahn? My God, he killed him! Run! No. I could never make it. He would kill me then.

The sound of the door brought her back to reality. She felt strong hands shaking her.

"Wake up, Cô Thi. Ông Duat says wake up, get clean, get dressed, go to the apartment, continue your work. Come. Get up. Follow me."

She opened her eyes and confronted two female servants she had never seen before. They helped her to her feet. Her breast stung badly. She couldn't bear to feel even the damp cloth of her garment on the spot where the prod had touched her. As she meekly followed the two women out of the room, she turned to look at Ahn. He was unconscious, splayed on the floor like a dead, plucked chicken. Badly burned, his entire genital area was a deep scarlet color and his testicles hugely swollen. The smell of scorched flesh was overpowering. The enormity of her experience and her own intense pain robbed her of any feeling of satisfaction or revenge.

After she was dressed, she stumbled into the elevator. Outside it was raining hard, but she didn't feel the storm. A cab stopped and she tumbled in. The driver had to tell her when she reached her address. She gave him a large bill, ignored the change, and slowly climbed the stairs up to her apartment. She let herself in and, with trembling fingers, removed her *ao dai*, sat down before the window, and let the breeze cool her body. She tried to fight her reactions, ashamed that she could not keep control of herself. She then decided she would get over it sooner if she gave in and let herself go. The shaking and twitching grew until true convulsions started.

In terror, she tried to regain control of her body, but the seizure had gone too far. Before she blacked out, she remembered falling to the floor. Then no more.

When she awoke hours later, she was calm again. Her skin was damp and cold. Picking herself up from the floor, she stumbled through the dark apartment to the yielding softness of her bed.

Ψ   Ψ   Ψ

Janet Holden looked at the group of earnest young people before her.

They were toiling so hard.

How can people say they are sloppy and lazy?

Janet didn't know that she was a special American as far as the highland people were concerned. She was getting complete and enthusiastic cooperation from them merely by being herself, not trying to impress them in any way. She was a person who respected the ideas of others. It wouldn't occur to Janet to play a false game with these people.

Janet thought their efforts were for their country, for a better life for their own people. She would have been upset to realize that actually they were working, not for those things, but for her personally.

She looked up from the pages of her draft report and scanned the faces of the six young students before her. All were from the Rhade tribe of Montagnards. Right now, this was not so apparent. Gone were the native G-strings and topless sarongs; now replaced, in classic missionary fashion, by white shirts and black trousers for the boys, and white blouses and black satin slacks for the girls.

She loved working with these youngsters on a practical project that might produce immediate dividends. But the day she got the call from Newell Osborne to join up, she was anything but happy. After all, she was having trouble with her own work up in Buon Ho, and talking on that stupid radio didn't make things go well either.

But Newell is a real love and he wouldn't ask me if he wasn't worried and didn't really need me.

So here she was, translating the Bible into the Rhade language. It had been a missionary's project at first and they had been doing well. However, the VC had decided that the Bible was a potential weapon against them and had put terrible pressure on the Rhade not to cooperate. The project requested outside assistance from MACV, was passed on to

CORDS, and that's why Janet was involved. Darlac Province was strategic and a key buffer against the Cambodian border.

So far, she had been down into Ban Me Thuot only once for an initial meeting with Reverend White and his family. She liked them immediately and hoped that Sally White would come up and visit her in Buon Sut Mgra. It was Reverend White's idea to divide the project. The reasoning was good. In the first place, part of Janet's original study was being conducted in Buon Sut Mgra. She could stay in touch with it. In the second place, Janet would have the assistance of the mission-educated Rhade.

As she looked at the industrious youngsters before her, she thanked Reverend White for his decision. It would be hard to leave this wonderful group when the project was over.

Wow. Compared to the hostility of the French Catholic missionaries she had met, who were so sympathetic to the VC, the Whites were great to work with.

She thought of her last two-day trip to Saigon and hoped she wouldn't be called back soon. Newell was very thoughtful about getting her in from the boonies from time to time, but she was entirely content up in the mountains. She occupied her time keeping busy and trying not to think of Ted.

For a moment, in spite of herself, she thought of him. Where was Ted? She couldn't believe him dead. Still, it had been months since even a rumor had come in. She looked at the papers in front of her—*Whither thou goest, I will go.*

Only it didn't go quite like that in Rhade.

Oh, Ted! I really would like to "go whither thou goest"—wherever that is.

"Janet look sad."

Janet was slightly startled. She hoped she didn't show it as she looked up. One of her young helpers stood in front of her desk.

"Must keep my mind on the project, that's all."

"You think of your husband so far way?" the young girl asked shyly.

Janet laughed. "Yes, but I don't think I'm supposed to do that on government time."

"When not government time?"

"That's the problem. Over here, it's twenty-four hours a day."

Ψ   Ψ   Ψ

Poli De Salle had made a bad mistake.

He sat and sulked at his large desk and watched a small lizard move slowly across the wall opposite him.

Yes, the flyswatter was a bad mistake, but how was I supposed to know that these people practically made house pets out of the damned creepy things? They should respect me, but somehow they always seem to be something a little less than respectful. The moment I saw the flyswatter for sale in the P.X, I felt like St. George, and ran back to the office to stalk the dragon with Excalibur. Whatever it was St. George had used to slay the dragons. Some damn snotty, English lit grad student would know and even care.

Disaster. I pictured myself standing in the doorway holding one of the things by the tail, a curious crowd of secretaries, aides, and staff members gathering around to admire me as a man of action. Well, they gathered all right. The commotion I made swatting and chasing the lizard had drawn the crowd. It wasn't until I finally killed it and had almost been sick in my handkerchief that I noticed them. God, their accusing eyes! What's that about? Then someone carried the little twisted body out on my ruler like a dead hero and showed it to everyone in the office! Now they whisper behind my back and stare at me as if I were Jack the Ripper! And they took my ruler!

Now I wonder if this new thing will be out for vengeance. Eat bugs? Really! In an air-conditioned office, there are no bugs, yet that seems to be the official excuse for having the slithery things about.

Ignoring the tiny, live reptile, he jumped into his personal project of the day: how to get an invite to the embassy's reception and dinner for the Australian Mission. The head of the office had received an invitation, but Poli had not. Perhaps it was because he was a consultant and not in the regular chain of command. He hadn't met any of the higher echelon since he had taken this job. He was annoyed that he had not seen Newell Osborne since that luncheon with Janet Holden.

Janet would be invited. Osborne would see to that. Suddenly a plan took shape, and thoughts began forming like swirling snowflakes.

Janet could be the key! I'll write her, saying I would like to talk a little business while she's back in Saigon, and ask if I might escort her to the recep-

tion! She won't know I have no invitation and will be willing to help, as always. Then I'll call Osborne's office—that young army guy, Bill something—and tell him confidentially that Janet has asked me to escort her to the reception and I'm a little embarrassed that I haven't yet received an invitation.

Naturally, I'll say Janet would never ask me to be her escort if she hadn't first checked to see that I was on the guest list. Then that army person Bill whatshisname, being a good friend of Janet's and wanting to help her out, will just go ahead and forward me an invitation.

The plan seemed foolproof. He immediately wrote a note to Janet. When it was finished and ready to go, he rang for someone to come and get it in the mail. The girl who entered the office was new.

"Molly's out for a while. She asked me to cover. I'm Brandy Masters," said the girl with a smile.

She took the letter and left the office before Poli had time to remark what an agreeable surprise Brandy had been. He watched her walk away. The sway of her perfect behind, accentuated by high heels, made the view memorable.

That's one outstandingly built blonde.

He made a mental note to investigate this new addition as soon as possible. In the meantime, the important thing was to get to that reception.

Ψ   Ψ   Ψ

Ahn suddenly appeared without notice at the No. 516 flat several days after his encounter with Thi.

He waited patiently while Thi said goodbye to Sam and the others of the Sixty-Ninth Special Action Group.

"You have been a great help to us, Cô Thi," said Tam, the group's number two, with a smile.

"Yes, your help and advice have been exceptional," added Sam. "We will contact you next week when the items are in place. There are less than six days to go, but our go-ahead must come from our master. We will wait for his word to be delivered through you."

Once more, they all shook hands. Then, in order to keep up the charade, they left the apartment with Thi at the doorway, speaking loudly in English, admonishing them to study their next lesson before next Wednesday.

When the door closed, Ahn looked at Thi for a long moment. She wondered if he felt the pain as much as she still did after all these days and if he felt hatred for her as much as he did before. Outwardly, it looked as if he had decided to let it pass and act as if the session with the prod had never happened.

"Have you ever used one of these?" he asked as he handed her a small .32 caliber break-top revolver.

"No."

"You will tonight."

He looked for a sign of apprehension on her face, but found none.

"Will you teach me how to handle it?" she asked.

"Of course. It will be the technique, not the accuracy that counts. You see, you will be very close."

Ahn looked closely. Still there was no sign of fear, no indication of inability in Thi's face. In spite of himself, her apparent coolness impressed him. He led her to the private room.

In no time, she was expertly handling the gun. It was exciting to her that the first time she fired it, she would be pressing it into the belly of an American soldier.

Ψ Ψ Ψ

Confrontation was its title.

Cy looked at the picture he had just completed. It concerned an incident that had happened yesterday, on his first visit to the Cholon PX. He had a new ration card and ID. The fatigue uniform Hue's friends had "procured" for him was perfectly starched; the staff sergeant's stripes gave him real pleasure; his boots were well shined and he had been given a close haircut by Kam. In short, he was the picture of a perfect NCO.

He made many purchases at the PX and had taken three trips out of the gate to his waiting taxi. Cases of soft drinks and beer and his total ration of cigarettes had almost filled the back seat. Secure in the fact that the cab driver was a special friend of Hue's and would not drive off with his purchases, Cy had ambled back to the commissary to pick up some American food for himself, which he had missed badly during his long confinement.

He was hauling the large bag of groceries out of the compound when he looked ahead and saw Colonel Buckley coming through the gate. Quickly he switched the bag of groceries so that it hid his head from the oncoming officer. Then, pretending it was heavy, Cy grasped it with both hands and walked straight toward the colonel.

"Quite a load you got there, Sergeant. Anything left in the store?" asked Mark as he passed.

"Yes, sir," mumbled Cy who kept moving without pausing.

He continued through the gate, imagining Buckley's eyes following him. Cy felt himself break out in sweat as he reached the taxi, but he had the courage to look back and steal a glance through the wire fence. Colonel Buckley had not stopped! He had not recognized him. With a laugh of relief, he climbed into the taxi and headed for Hue's flat, but all the way there, his thoughts were about what might have been.

Now the painting with its troubled blacks and reds and the yellow-gold sunburst filled his mind. It mirrored his imagination. A true likeness. He put down the brush and crossed over to the bed.

The whole flat was quiet. Hue was out and Kam was downstairs taking her siesta. Keeping busy with his painting and getting ready for the PX trip had made his thoughts of Kam less vivid in the last few days. Nevertheless, she was still in the back of his mind. Now, she emerged in full focus, once the first PX run was complete and his pictures were finished. He thought of her downstairs in her room sleeping peacefully. Cy wondered if he was ever in her thoughts.

Actually, Kam was not asleep. Her room was quite hot and she tossed fitfully on her bed. Her thoughts were almost completely upstairs—with Cy. Over the weeks, her initial fear of the big, black American had turned to a disturbing excitement. Lately, the excitement had changed to a wild fascination, gathering in strength as each day passed.

Often she had thought of starting a sexual liaison with him but she was frightened of what that might do to the relationship between Cy and her brother. Hue was dramatically jealous under even the mildest circumstances. Something like this might drive him to some sort of violence against Cy or herself. She knew Hue was not true to Cy, but Hue expected Cy to be true to him.

To conduct an affair without Hue's knowledge seemed impossible. True, during the day there was plenty of time when she and Cy were alone. But she was afraid that neither she nor Cy could carry it off without making it obvious to Hue. One possibility was that Hue would tire of Cy and replace him with another lover. In such a case, Cy could merely move downstairs at night and work in the studio during the day.

However, Kam realized that Cy was different from any of Hue's previous lovers. First, it seemed to her that Cy was very much a man, and he would not put up with her brother if Hue wasn't a shield against the authorities. Second, Cy was the first American and the first black man Hue had brought home. It was plain that he was still very intrigued. Therefore, the possibility that Hue would soon tire of Cy seemed not realistic.

Still, where was Hue now? Had he found another lover to spend the noon sleep-time with? She thought about that possibility, and the more she thought of it, the more unfair it seemed to her. She heard Cy stirring above her and wondered what he was doing. Suddenly she found herself out of bed and walking silently to the outside stairs.

She was oblivious to the fact that her only garment was a piece of cotton cloth loosely tied about her waist.

Cy had tried to sleep, but found it impossible. In his troubled thrashing, he had removed his terrycloth shorts. Now he lay spread-eagled on the bed, eyes closed, thinking of Kam—imagining her there in his arms.

God, I been patient. I can't wait any longer. I know she wants me. I gave her plenty of time to make her move. Now I just gotta take the chance.

Suddenly he became aware of someone near, someone close to him. For an instant, he thought Hue might have returned, and he experienced a quick, sick feeling. He opened his eyes. He could not believe it! Kam was standing by his bed, head down, eyes averted. She said nothing, but her right hand reached up ever so slowly and loosened the cotton cloth about her waist. It fell to the floor. Slowly, Cy sat up and reached out his arms to her. His hands trembled as he drew her close to him.

"Oh, baby, baby! I knew you'd come, I knew it."

Instantly he sought her mouth with his eager lips, but they lingered there only briefly as he lowered his head and sought her small, firm breasts. His tongue played with her hardening nipples. He felt her arms encircle his big body and her hands caress his moist back. She trembled as he drew her farther onto the bed and laid her down on the damp sheet.

Now his hands were free to explore her complete body, and he thrilled to feel her response to his slow, gentle touch. He heard her start to moan. He was aware of her hands sliding down the sides of his buttocks. Now they were under him—groping, feeling, and then at last grasping his hard, extended member.

"Mau len! Mau len! Mau len!" she whispered.

Cy slid into her. He had forgotten how good a woman was! Kam moved her body with clear experience. This was not new for her and she wanted very much to please him.

She was everything Cy had imagined for all these weeks. He gave himself up to complete pleasure as he drove himself hard into her. He felt her body shudder and twitch as she responded completely to his quickening thrusts. She was loudly moaning now and her breath came in short gasps. Suddenly like a sunburst, his body was consumed in orgasm. He didn't even notice her shrill little cry.

It was some time later when passion had spent itself that they both became aware that, no matter how wonderful their first sex together had been, they were now two very vulnerable sweat-covered bodies clinging together in a hot, rumpled bed. Danger was close.

Big trouble, Xau lam.

"Oh Cy, Cy. We no tell Hue. He get very mad. He maybe kick you out."

"You are so right, honey. You are so right. Mums it's gotta be. Just you and me, Kam baby."

They quickly became aware that to stay together this way any long-er was senseless because Hue might walk in at any moment. Kam got up and retied the cloth about her waist. With a last smile for Cy, she ran downstairs to her room to prepare to return to the kiosk.

Cy straightened up the bed before he started preparing a new canvas. He laughed as he worked.

"Well, you sure fixed up your sex life, Cy baby," he muttered to himself. "Now you got a day and a night schedule. Guess you're going to be the *numbah one* GI lover in this old town."

He looked intently at the blank canvas. He knew this next picture was going to be a happy one.

Ψ Ψ Ψ

Ahn drove the Honda motorbike with Thi riding side-saddle on the rear seat.

He wore a wig and she was dressed in the traditional French-style garb of the Vietnamese schoolgirl: white blouse and dark blue pleated skirt. Thi had braided her hair in one long plait down and in front of her left shoulder to hide the scar on her cheek. She wore bobby socks and white sports sneakers.

In her lap were five schoolbooks strapped together the way schoolchildren do it, the world over.

She was eager to kill Americans. She was more eager to prove to Duat that she was capable of doing this job—or any other job—without question, without hesitation, without remorse. She pushed her finger beyond the false back of the middle book and felt the cold metal of the pistol. It gave her a feeling of power and strength.

They swung out into Ham Nghi. The street was filling with people homeward bound from their offices and places of business. In the tangle of motor vehicles, exhaust smoke hung like thick fog in the air. Crowds of people were an asset to their operation because they were counting on them to cover their getaway. Ahead, Thi could see the old embassy building. They were approaching the target. Ahn pulled over to the curb and waited. Apparently, they were a little early.

Ahn looked over his shoulder. How different she seemed with the long hair of a student.

"Ready?"

"Yes."

"Now remember. Wait for the loud backfire explosion at the eastern end of the building. It will take attention away from us."

"There he is," she hissed in Ahn's ear.

He nodded, and urged the Honda forward again, staying close to the sidewalk. Their timing was very nearly perfect. They could see the soldier approaching them through the traffic.

Where's the backfire?

She reached in, slipped out the pistol, and held it under the books. The sergeant was almost upon them now. He was big and black. She recognized his face from the pictures Ahn had showed her.

Bang! The loud sound of the backfire frightened her for a split second, but it had been effective. Even her target turned to see the cause of the noise. She reached out and as she pushed the muzzle of the weapon into the sergeant's soft belly, she pulled the trigger.

Pop! The small gun bucked in her hand.

Then she plunged the pistol back into the book. They were past him now, but from the corner of her eye, she saw the big sergeant hesitate, take one pace forward, and sink to his knees. He lay on the pavement. Blood spread across the front of his uniform shirt.

The rush of traffic had carried them on to an alley. They turned into it and drove directly into the third doorway. It was dark. The sound of the Honda echoed off the narrow walls. Ahn ripped off his wig and his outer shirt. He dropped them in the cardboard box lying in the corner as Thi hopped off the motorbike and then dropped her books in the same box. Ahn drove the Honda alone out from the doorway and back up Han Nghi Street.

Through the exhaust haze, he could see a crowd of people and automobiles forming on the other side of the street. Thi had done her job well. As he drove on, he heard the siren of an ambulance approaching.

Thi left the building, walked the length of the alley, turned the other direction, and finally emerged on Chuong Cuong Quay. She hailed a cyclo and headed back toward her flat.

As she was being pedaled back down the alley, she saw a ragpicker emerge from the same doorway, carrying the box on his *don gan*, the shoulder pole with the balanced loads on each end. She heard another ambulance siren off in the distance as she arrived in front of her flat. She paid the cyclo driver and went upstairs. It wasn't until she opened her door, that the whole reality of her act hit her.

Her heart pumped adrenaline through her system at a triple rate. Her breath came in hard, quick gasps. She slammed the door behind her and locked it. Thi entered the secret room and removed the student uniform and the simple, children's underclothing. Naked, she sat before the makeup mirror and shook her hair out of the loose braid. Then, with trembling fingers, she exposed the moon-shaped scar. She smiled back into the mirror, a smile of complete satisfaction. At last, finally, she was getting revenge.

Only the beginning.

Ψ   Ψ   Ψ

Sam and his men entered Thi's apartment at the appointed time for their "English lesson."

They quietly took seats in the living room and waited. Thi had important details to pass on.

"The day is to be Saturday. The time is to be 12:21."

"I will be on the roof opposite the park. I will be the timekeeper and will raise my hand to my eyes, as if to shield them from the sun. Then I will lower my hand and leave the roof. You should watch me from your observation points. When my hand lowers, count forty-five seconds. This will give me time to reach my apartment.

"After the first bomb goes off, I shall reappear on the roof as part of the curious crowd. I will be able to determine when the most rescuers are in place and will determine when it is best to give the second signal. I will be holding a peasant's straw sun hat. When the time comes, I will drop it over the side of the roof. Then fire the second group of claymores."

"That should work well," commented Sam.

Thi continued, "The master feels that, if for any reason it is necessary to postpone the attack, he will do so by reaching me any moment up to thirty seconds before zero time. So pay close attention to my signal."

"What should we do in case there is no signal? Where shall we reach you? Surely we should not return to your flat."

Thi smiled. "No. Return to your lodgings. We will contact you."

She was pleased with this plan. It was well conceived and, best of all, she was a star in it.

Ψ   Ψ   Ψ

The next meeting between Thi and Duat was very different from their last encounter.

Duat quizzed Thi at length about the killing of the soldier. He wanted to examine her inner reactions. Did she feel revulsion? Did she have guilt feelings? How did she feel about future operations?

Thi was extremely cool and direct in her answers. She was honest about the reaction alone at the No. 516 flat after the encounter with Ahn, but quickly added that she did not expect a similar weakness in subsequent operations if she had the honor to be chosen again.

Duat allowed a slight smile to cross his face. He was pleased with Thi and was strongly considering her for many far more dangerous missions in the near future.

Never once was the affair of the lost money brought up. Thi did not expect an apology, but she thought that some acknowledgment of her proven loyalty should be in order. There was one thing certain–she would never bring up the subject. Now she knew that she was fully trusted and her abilities appreciated. Consequently, she had the feeling that she had an advantage. She had caught them in a mistake; they had not caught her in one.

Thi wondered if Ahn's sadistic action with the cattle prod on that evening of the money transfer had been with Duat's consent or if it had been his own idea. Whatever the case, she had not forgotten it, nor did she intend to. Although she had managed to even the score with Ahn, she wondered if Duat would take Ahn's side the next time.

Duat quickly brought her thoughts back into focus when he said,

"But we have a new assignment for you. Go now and see Ông Ahn."

Thi bowed her goodbye to Duat and crossed the garden to the offices. Ahn was seated at a worktable. Without a word, he motioned her into a chair opposite him. She murmured a greeting as she sat down, but she did not smile. It was all business with Ahn.

"Your English is presentable," he commented without looking up from the papers in front of him. "Presentable enough for you to be an interpreter for the US Information Service. You will act as one at an American reception next Friday night. Here is your invitation, your USIS identification card, and your official English-Vietnamese dictionary. Please note these two pictures. This is Ambassador Osborne. He is slated for, ah, extinction in the not too distant future. Here is Major Scott, of Ambassador Osborne's office. The major is young. Our records show that he does not have a girl and he lives in a villa in the city. We think he is vulnerable. You will attend the reception and dinner, posing as an interpreter, but actually, we want you to get to know Major Scott—very well. We want certain information from him which we will describe in detail after you have, ah, shall we say ..."

"Compromised him?"

"Ah, yes. That's a nice way to put it."

"How about Osborne? Shall I, ah, work on him too?"

"No, not now. We just want you to know who he is and report on any word you hear about him. However, do not actively pursue this man. Is that clear?"

"Yes, Ông Ahn."

"Remember, you are a guest, but you are also on hire. You are on duty. If you are offered a drink, take a Coca- Cola, and do not become the center of attention. Be attractive, but studious. Perhaps a pair of glasses and an *ao dai* of not too brilliant color ... introduce yourself as Cô Dao Thi, interpreter. You are the passé film actress once called Solange working for the Americans—doing her part to win this war."

"Yes, Ông Ahn."

"One more thing: when you entertain Major Scott, do not use No. 516, use your own flat. Although this is part of your official duty, consider it private from the start. Your private affairs, as you know, must happen in your own place. Later we may change this after the compromise."

Thi was furious at this condescending attitude of Ahn's, but she would not give him the satisfaction of knowing it.

"Yes, Ông Ahn," she said softly.

Ψ   Ψ   Ψ

Bill Scott opened the gate to a small courtyard and walked to the modest house. Before he could ring the bell, a small boy opened the door and gazed up at him with wide eyes.

"Hi. Is Cô Lei at home?" Bill asked.

The small boy disappeared behind the open door. Bill could hear a long string of excited Vietnamese chatter trail off, through the house. Evidently the boy, like a Vietnamese Paul Revere, was dashing about warning everyone that the Americans were coming.

After a few moments, Mai Lei appeared at the door.

"Please come in, Major Scott. I see you did arrive early. That is very nice. My father is anxious to meet you. He has many questions to ask you."

Bill was struck with Mai Lei's beauty. During his short visit to her office, he had become very much aware of her good looks, but now he saw again that she possessed the classic willowy figure of a young Vietnamese woman: a slim, graceful flower-stem beauty displayed so well by the yellow *ao dai* she was wearing. Her wide-set eyes were reflecting the merriment of her smile as she spoke. Obviously, she was anticipating the encounter between the two men with some enjoyment.

Bill followed her into a small living room. It was completely functional, with simple furniture and a rush rug. High on one of the walls hung a picture of the Buddha sitting under a tree, looking down upon the room with benevolent calm. The couch was a common iron frame covered with woven plastic. One large, Western-style easy chair occupied the corner of the room. On either side of it were two low tables, piled with newspapers and books in comfortable disarray. Almost lost in the corner of the chair was a very small man in a Western suit, nearly hidden behind a large book.

Mai Lei approached him, and she spoke softly in Vietnamese.

The little man slowly lowered his book into his lap. For a moment, he observed Bill over the top of his glasses. Then, without rising, he offered his hand.

"I am glad to meet you, Ông Bu," said Bill.

The old man replied in English, haltingly and with a French accent. "Draw up the small chair, young man. You are the first American with whom I have had the pleasure of making—what you say—small talk?"

"This is my first opportunity to speak with a Vietnamese gentleman on a subject other than my business."

"And what is your business? I hope it is not bombing villages."

"No, sir. I work at CORDS."

"Oh, yes. Civil Operations Revolutionary Development. I know about that project. Very noble, but I am afraid too noble for *we poor Vietnamese*. You Americans will soon find that only those on top will benefit. The poor workers and farmers, seeing only the rich ones become wealthier, will lose faith and fall back, and that will be the end. You see, you have at last recognized that this is a people's war and you want to get our people involved. But they are too smart. If the benefits were for them, they would rally. But already they have seen the same old corruption develop and the same people come out on top, therefore they will not follow."

Bill replied, "We are trying our best to keep this program a meaningful one, totally without corruption, but with something of this magnitude, we cannot really know all those with whom we work. We cannot, in most cases, discover the dishonest ones right away."

"That is the Americans' problem—too much money to give. No way to know who to give it to…" the old man replied.

"Now wait a minute, Ông Bu. Our program is based upon full Vietnamese participation. Vietnamese instructors teach Vietnamese teams. The teams go to the farmers. They go to the villages. They try to get the people involved, to teach patriotism …"

"As I say, Major Bill. Your program is quite a noble one," Bu broke

146

in, "but not a practical one. Consider your own country. A little village in East Dakota. Suddenly twenty young people, all fat with good food, all from New York, come and tell the people of the village how to be good farmers, how to resist bandits, how to be patriotic."

Bill smiled over "East Dakota," but Bu's point was well taken.

"We know we have made mistakes," he answered. "And we hope in time to discover and eliminate them. We hope that you and your people will help us in this."

"Our enemy," said Bu, "has the great advantage of the people's support. We do not. Victory can only be achieved with the people's support. That applies to either side."

"Sounds like Mao Tse-Tung."

"Yes, Mao and George Washington and Francis Marion, and Castro and Stalin, and everyone who truly grasps the concept of a people's war. You see, in a people's war the people are the decisive factor. Your approach will never win a people's war. Too much heavy weaponry. Artillery. Tanks. So much. They should be reserved for wars between nations."

"We fight in the only way we know how. Firepower, mobility, surprise ..."

"You have forgotten the way you once fought at Lexington, at Trenton, at the Cowpens. Even more recently, in the Philippine hills against the Japanese occupiers. You have now concluded that all wars are the same and should be fought the same. You have forgotten ..."

Mai Lei came into the room. She was carrying a small black purse. There was the faintest tint of lipstick on her lips.

As a courtesy to Bill, she spoke in English: "Father, I must remind you that it is past the hour and time for us to go. We must not keep Mr. Han waiting."

"Gosh. That's true. I didn't realize it was so late," added Bill, checking his watch.

Bu smiled. "Your friend is most interesting, Mai Lei. Please bring him back soon."

Then turning to Bill, he said, "Please come back. I am very interested in you Americans. The next time I shall let you express yourself more, and perhaps I shall get around to my questions."

"I enjoyed it, sir."

As he left the room, he looked back. Bu had already lifted the large volume from his lap. His focus had returned to his book. Bill and Mai Lei were already far from his thoughts.

Ψ   Ψ   Ψ

Mark Buckley made one last check in the men's room mirror at the United States Embassy: hair brushed, nails clean, new suit properly pressed, dress shoes shined. He was ready.

"New embassy, new suit, new job," he said to himself, almost out loud. Then he added, "But the same old Buckley!"

He walked out and headed to the reception room for one last check on the refreshments and the serving staff. There was still a quarter of an hour before the guests would be arriving, but Mark was new at this business and wanted to make sure everything was in shape before the reception began.

"Hello, I am Cô Thi. I was asked to arrive a little early."

Mark turned around and saw a young girl smiling behind heavy-rimmed glasses. She was holding a small purse under a tiny, well-used dictionary. Her royal blue *ao dai* was perfectly plain, except for a spray of small golden flowers embroidered across the front. At first glance, she looked to Mark like a somewhat intense, very earnest intellectual, but a fast appraisal of her lovely figure made him change his mind.

Thi started fumbling in her purse. "I am from the US Information Service. I am an interpreter. Here is my identification. Are you … ah … Major Scott?"

Mark grinned, broadly. "No, but I know him well. He and I are housemates. I'm Colonel Mark Buckley."

She held out her hand and Mark took the pass, but did not glance at it. Instead, he looked directly into her eyes.

"Here. Put it away. That thing could be a forgery for all I know about it, but I certainly like the Information Service's choice of interpreters."

"Well, I'm new. This is my first job."

148

"Mine, too," broke in Mark. "Say, this could be fun, pushing cookies for the first time with a beautiful girl."

"Push–what?"

"You know. That's American slang. We call helping out at these things 'pushing cookies.' That makes me a cookie pusher."

Thi laughed with Mark over the poor joke. She thought him most attractive for an American, and wondered if Duat might allow her to make her acquaintance with him instead of Major Scott.

"Are you Major Scott's boss?"

"Oh no. We work together–on the same level, as we say. But he knows all about the work and I am a greenhorn in this side of the business."

Thi started thumbing through her dictionary.

"Greenhorn, greenhorn …"

Mark laughed again. "You won't find it in there; it's more slang. Means new on the job."

"Greenhorn. Cookie pusher. I must remember them!"

They both laughed.

"Well, you're a greenhorn, too, if this is your first job. Just stick with me and we'll both be thrown out together."

Chatting, they walked over to a large table laden with hors d'oeuvres.

How easy this is going to be. By the time the guests arrive, I will be a regular fixture.

Mark and Thi tried several of the snacks.

I wish he wasn't so pleasant. I wish to hate him so much.

A few people arrived and clustered by the entrance.

"There is Ambassador Osborne. Come on over and I will introduce you," Mark said, as he gently guided her to the doorway.

"Please, Colonel Buckley. Remember, I am not a guest, I am a worker here!"

"Hell, Cô Thi, we are all workers here. Come on."

Newell Osborne saw Mark approaching and smiled, "See, Mark. I told you this job was going to have its compensations. Already you have a beautiful girl on your arm."

149

"Sir, may I present Cô Thi? She is an interpreter from the US Information Service."

"Very happy to meet you, Cô Thi. It is a pleasure to have you with us today. I believe there will be many opportunities for you to assist in our attack upon the language barrier."

Newell laughed lightly at his own joke, then turned and said, "Well, the show is about to get on the road. I see the protocol people looking at me anxiously. Goodbye, for now. I hope Mark doesn't keep you working too hard."

As Newell left to form the receiving line, Thi followed him with mild eyes that belied her real feelings.

They are so pleasant, so nice to me. I wonder what they would do if suddenly they came to know that I shot one of their sergeants last week!

A faint trace of a smile appeared on her face and quickly faded.

The room was gradually filling with people. Newell had the chief of the Australian Mission with him at the door, as well as two Vietnamese government officials. Mark saw Bill Scott bring in Mr. Han and Mai Lei. As they met the guests of honor, Newell asked Mr. Han to join the line, thus leaving Bill and Mai Lei free. After promising to stay close at hand, they walked over to Mark and Thi.

"Now I understand why you deserted and made me set up this whole thing by myself," said Mark to Bill as he met Mai Lei. "I don't blame you."

Mai Lei looked at Thi carefully.

How do I know her … Ah, yes. She's that would-be film actress who used the French name and didn't quite make it. Her personal reputation wasn't the best. I wonder how she got this job.

"Are you still in films, Cô Thi?" she asked quietly.

Thi was waiting for this question. "Oh, no," she replied with a laugh. "I'm afraid I wasn't blessed with the talent for films. But I'm happy to have had the opportunity to try."

"Gee, a film star!" Mark said with humor. "I've never met one before. Would it be okay if I asked for an autograph?"

His smile puzzled Thi. Was he serious or was this an American joke? Then there was the possibility that she was now a suspect. She decided to dodge the question.

"Oh, that was so long ago, and I was so poor in my films. Your request embarrasses me."

"Now see what you've done, you bully," Bill broke in. "You've embarrassed this pretty girl, you clod!"

Both Americans laughed and Mark apologized to Thi, thus making both Vietnamese women laugh, although they didn't quite understand the meaning of the conversation.

The two Americans intrigued Thi. She would have a lot to tell Ahn about this party. Mark–older, more mature, bigger physically, and good looking in a rough sort of way. Bill: very smart, more cultured, handsome, but younger and somewhat inexperienced. They both should be exciting subjects on which to work.

Mark, turning to look at the arriving guests, caught sight of a mass of red curls.

"Say, who's that girl going through the receiving line?" he said, not attempting to conceal a certain level of interest.

Bill followed Mark's glance and spotted Janet Holden smiling up at Newell Osborne. The ambassador leaned over and kissed her and, after a few words to the very thin man with her, placed her in the line with him. Bill's gaze lingered on Janet Holden just for a moment.

Maybe just a tiny bit less than beautiful but many, many times pretty. But that amazing red hair and her inspired curiosity reflected in those green eyes make her absolutely ...

"That's Janet Holden. She has a social science program she's doing for USAID. I see the Ambassador has taken her over," said Bill.

"That must be the guy we got the invitation for. A Dr. De Paul?"

"No, Dr. Poli De Salle."

"Oh right. He looks a little put out over the loss of the lady."

"Wouldn't you be?"

"I would be if I didn't know the lady's occupation. You know how I feel about all these social science people over here."

"Oh, come off it, Mark. You don't know anything about her or her work."

Mark realized that he was off base and smiled. He put his hand lightly on Bill's shoulder.

He grinned. "Sorry, old man. I'll watch my manners."

Thi, who had felt a little jealous over Mark's original interest in Janet, was secretly happy that Mark found fault with the American woman. She covered a brief smile with a bland, less telling expression. The four young people separated and went about their duties. Many guests were paying their respects to Mr. Han, and both Mai Lei and Thi were busy interpreting for the numerous Americans and Australians who required their assistance.

Mark and Bill circulated, making introductions and getting drinks, but they found themselves returning to the two girls, to bring another soda or just to talk. At one point Newell Osborne called for Thi to assist in a conversation with the Vietnamese minister of health. She was thrilled with this opportunity and knew that Ahn would be impressed.

Mark checked at his watch. In ten minutes, the curtains at the end of the room would part, and the guests would move into the dining area. He hoped everyone had taken note of the table seating diagrams placed about the room.

"Maybe we'd better pass the word about the seating arrangements," he suggested to Bill as they met briefly in the crowd.

Thi had seen the diagrams and said that she would leave the party when the guests started in to dinner.

"Don't be silly," said Mark. "See those two tables in the corner with no names on them? Well, they're for the hired help. You stick with me and you'll eat. Besides, 't ain't a fit night out for man nor beast."

Mark was referring to the heavy downpour that had just started and was audible throughout the room.

He escorted Thi to the porch and for a moment, they stood behind the cement security screen and watched the rain. The wind whipped the panels of Thi's *ao dai*, revealing her slim waist and shapely hips in the tight satin trousers. Mark couldn't help but notice her provocative figure. He had also noticed a rather knowing expression about Thi when she was looking at other men. There was a lot about her that attracted him, but it wasn't all nice.

The ex-actress seems to have been around a bit. Wonder what's going on in that little mind of hers.

He made a mental note to complete this investigation at a more opportune time. As the couple came in from the porch, they met Newell Osborne and Janet Holden speaking to some of the Australian officers. Newell stopped to introduce Mark and Thi, and as the group chatted about the rain, Mark took the opportunity to observe Janet. His first impression had been correct. She was a truly beautiful woman.

Janet, on the other hand, was slightly confused. This Cô Thi looked familiar to her. She felt she had met this Vietnamese woman before, but could not remember the occasion. She wanted to think about it, but the presence of Mark Buckley, whom she found most interesting, dissolved thoughts of anyone else.

Thi was looking at Janet very critically. She noticed the pale green satin Chinese sheath dress with a modest split at the sides. The light red hair was in small natural curls, like a young boy's haircut. The gold jewelry was small and very plain, but Thi decided Janet Holden really didn't need the help of jewelry. Her own fresh looks were more than adequate.

Yes, this girl is very attractive to the American, and that is not good for me.

Mark was intrigued with Janet. She was a small woman, an attractive woman. Her personality seemed perfect to him and her fine sense of humor quickly became evident as she enjoyed a small joke one of the Australians told.

Why in hell would she come all the way over here to catch a husband?

Mark then noticed the gold ring on her left hand and assumed that she had a husband somewhere in the States.

Probably was too smart to come over here. But he let her come alone. Why?

At this moment, the curtains parted and Newell and Janet led the guests of honor into the dining area. After Mark got Mr. Han and Mai Lei seated properly, he joined Bill and Thi at one of the far tables. From this vantage point, they watched the other guests find their seats.

The room settled down to murmurs of conversation as the guests enjoyed the first course. Janet looked across the room from the head table, hoping to catch a glimpse of the Vietnamese girl to see if she could remember where she had met her. She found the table, but her eyes strayed from Thi to Mark Buckley. She could see him in animated conversation with the others at the table.

"Why is it always more fun to sit below the salt at these parties?"

Janet glanced at Newell; she only half heard his musing question.

"My, you're far away. Your thoughts still in the highlands? Remember, you're supposed to win their hearts and minds. They aren't supposed to win yours!"

Janet laughed, "You are the only one who could ever win both my heart and mind, but you're married, you rogue. I was just thinking about that girl over there with Colonel Buckley. I think I've seen her somewhere before."

"I doubt it," said Newell. "She's brand new from the Information Service."

"Well, tell me about Mark Buckley then. I think he's most interesting."

Newell gave Janet an abbreviated version of Mark's career, including a redacted version of the trouble at Trong Thoi and his subsequent assignment to Newell's office.

"Do you think it was unjust to relieve him of command?"

"I don't know, but it certainly was expedient. You can't fool around with a US senator like Joe Masters. Besides, I think Mark is great in my office. He's a combat guy. It gives us the balance we need."

At the far end of the room, Thi sipped her glass of red wine. It was delicious. She hadn't enjoyed wine so much since Paris, when she was the actress, Solange.

How I'd really take the time to enjoy this wine the way the French do. These Americans, they drink it as if it were their vile Coca-Cola.

She looked around the room.

These damned glasses make everything a bit blurry, but I can't take them off.

She scanned the room again.

Tomorrow some of these people will be victims of the Rex Hotel bloodbath. Wonder which ones will die? What a wonderful game! If I can only get a guest list and mark my guesses, then compare them with the actual casualty list!

She looked about, her eyes jumping from table to table, missing no one. They settled on Janet, who was smiling at her. Thi smiled back.

Smile, you American bitch. You must be one of the victims. You must be!

She glanced at Mark.

Thi smiled up into Mark's face. "Colonel Buckley, do you think it would be improper if I should ask for one copy of the seating diagram to take as souvenir of my first job? I would like it so much."

"Of course it would be okay. Please take this one. I have no use for it now."

Thi thanked him and put the piece of paper in her purse, but not before she had carefully written in the names of everyone seated at the two tables that did not have place cards. This task required the assistance of Mark and Bill and lasted almost to the end of the meal.

Those at the head table rose and left the dining room, followed by the other laughing, chatting guests. The evening was over. Following the guests of honor, the others quickly departed. Janet and Poli were all that remained. The plan was that Newell, Mark, Janet, and Poli would stop by the Hangout before curfew for a drink and a critique of the evening. Bill was to join them after he had dropped Mr. Han and Mai Lei off at their homes.

Mark had asked Thi to come along also, but she made her excuses and left the party shortly after the guests of honor departed. Desiring to see her again, Mark obtained her address and he gave her his phone number. She promised to call in a few days.

As the group was preparing to leave, Newell was called away to take a phone call. Slightly annoyed, he returned to the group.

"I have to stop by Westy's for a while. Mark, you take Janet and Dr. De Salle over to the Hangout and I'll join you there."

"Don't stay too long, Newell. Remember, you can't win the war in one night," Janet said as he departed.

Driving to the Hangout in the Ford sedan should have been very pleasant for Janet and the two men since the streets, still wet with the recent rain, gave a cool freshness to the city. The many lights of Saigon sparkled in a million ways as the car slowly made its way through the crowded streets. But Mark, not having had the opportunity to talk with Dr. Poli De Salle during the evening, was suffering his first exposure. It was not pleasant.

"I find these people completely unfit for the democratic process,"

155

declared Poli to no one in particular. "Most of them actually are illiterate subhumans–puppets to be manipulated by a few prurient individuals who are smart enough to gain from this mess a lucrative living. The fact is that the words 'freedom,' 'democracy,' and 'vote' mean nothing to them."

"How long have you been in country, Dr. De Salle?" There was an edge to Mark's voice.

"Long enough to know that this is a hopeless case. These people don't deserve any assistance from us. They abuse our aid. They don't understand our ways."

"That's right, they don't understand our ways. But do we understand their ways? And more to the point, do we try to understand them?"

"Look, Captain Markey, or whatever your name is, we are spending a lot of money and lives on these people. I don't think we should do this to foster practices which we as a nation do not endorse."

"That's Buckley, Lieutenant Colonel Mark Buckley. What practices? What things are they doing that you find so repulsive?"

"Oh, come on, Colonel, you certainly are aware of the corruption of all these officials, the money stolen, the Swiss bank accounts ... this is a corrupt nation. We should pull out all of our support."

"On that basis, our own government does not deserve our support. You seem to forget the Billy Sols, the Senator Dodds, the Bobby Bakers ..."

"Gentlemen, gentlemen," said Janet as she grabbed their arms. "It's lucky I am sitting between you or you would be trading punches! Let's think of more pleasant things."

It was clear to her that she still didn't know why Poli was in Vietnam.

How many Americans over here agree with Poli?

She was glad to see that when they arrived at the Hangout, Bill Scott was there to give them a smiling welcome. She glanced at Mark. There were dark clouds of anger crossing his face. She smiled at him, hoping he would return her smile, but his thoughts seemed miles away. He looked at her, but did not seem to see her.

After they were all seated in the Hangout's living room, Poli again dominated the conversation in spite of Bill's lighthearted attempt to keep things bright and pleasant. In a distant room, a phone rang, and Bill left to take the call. Shortly he was back, announcing that Newell Osborne would not be able to join them. Everyone was disappointed. Poli especially was upset, and bore down on his favorite theme again with vigor.

Janet noticed Mark's discomfort. Sometimes he looked as if he was about to speak, perhaps to register a denial or protest, but he seemed to check himself before the sound reached his lips. Bill made several protests, but Poli ignored him and continued his long lecture.

Finally, Mark rose from his chair and said, "Excuse me please, ladies and gentlemen, but I am afraid I must leave this charming company. I have a long day tomorrow and must turn in."

Janet was sorry to see him go and wanted to salvage the evening, if possible. She made a vow to put a stop to Poli's diatribe because she knew it to be the only way she could induce Mark to stay. She took his arm in her own and guided him away from Poli.

"Oh, Mark, please ... we must go along soon. Please try to help me get Poli out of this rut."

"I would like to, Mrs. Holden, but ... well ... I'm afraid that ..."

"Afraid to hear the truth?" sneered Poli, who overheard Mark's protest.

Now it was way beyond the tipping point for Mark and his eyes blazed.

"That's the trouble with the whole goddamned system over here. They let half-baked, little maggots come over to 'study the people' as if they were so many ants between two pieces of glass. Then after the first week—when they have successfully managed to make a trip to the PX all by themselves, with only the help of a native driver and a US Embassy sedan—they become experts.

"What in God's name are you doing here? Talk about stealing US money; you commit larceny every time you cash your check. This is a war. Do you understand that? People die. You are mad because they don't understand what democracy means. Stop staring down that long nose of yours and try to tell them ... try to help them."

"Oh please, Mark," said Janet, "We are trying to help them. We have to identify the differences in order to make the learning process easier for them so we can teach them. That's what we are here for."

"That's what you are here for? Lady, that's a laugh. That's as funny as the phony professor here, passing himself off as an expert on Vietnam. I'll tell you why you are here. You're over here because in this small, American community you can get noticed. The competition isn't much here and you can get special treatment; it's always the way in a society of men. There's a certain type of woman who manages to wander in and take over the dominant role. Well, lady, that's okay by me if you'll face up to the truth and admit it, but Jesus, don't hide behind a phony social study and pass yourself off as Madam Smartass."

"Colonel, I suggest we change subjects." Bill was on his feet and he crossed the room until he stood very close to Mark.

"No," said Janet coolly. "It's not enough. It's too much; please explain to Newell why we couldn't stay."

She went to the door.

"I think you have a car out here we can use, don't you?"

Poli, ashen-faced, went quickly to Janet's side.

"This is not good," hissed Bill as he left Mark and went to see Janet and Poli off.

Mark heard Bill, using great skill, try to apologize for him. Their voices sounded very far away, as he stood alone in the room. Angry. But in his own mind, clear.

Ψ Ψ Ψ

It was a beautiful, bright, wonderful morning.

Half-awake, and comfortable in her bed, Thi slowly realized that this was finally the day of the largest terrorist bombing of the war. She stretched out and felt deep pleasure. A slight breeze moved the curtains of the bedroom window, causing the sunlight to fall in diffused, dappled patterns on the floor. The breeze also brought the street sounds into the room to remind her that she must be ready for her part in the explosion.

Most on such a day would have slept little or fitfully, their thoughts constantly going over and over all the details. Thi was not like them.

No time to lose.

She washed and dressed quickly and put on the clothes of a Saigon housewife: short white blouse and black satin trousers. She planned to carry a broom and leave her feet bare.

The kitchen was cheery and fresh in the morning light. As she prepared her simple breakfast, she began thinking of the multiple explosions. There would be many innocent Vietnamese victims and that was too bad, but there would be many Americans, and Vietnamese working for the Americans, hurt and killed. This was the real payoff. When blood filled the circle and ran down Ngyen Hue, the reality was that the blood of the enemy would mix with the blood of the innocent.

That's the way that it had to be.

Her thoughts wandered to Mark Buckley and Bill Scott and suddenly she felt a twinge of conscience, but automatically her hand touched her scar and the weakness disappeared.

NO! They were Americans and they must die. If not by the claymores, then in some other manner.

A strong vision of Janet Holden flashed before her eyes. For a moment, Janet was smiling, then suddenly there was a loud explosion and Janet's face disappeared behind a curtain of blood.

"That's what she deserves," she sneered out loud.

Thi looked at her watch. There was more than an hour to wait. She decided to busy herself with the partially made dress on the form. Soon she was engrossed in her work, almost forgetting that she was to be the key figure in a most horrible bloodbath.

There was a knock on the door. Thi glanced at the time. It was 11:50. She hoped it would not be a message from Ông Duat, calling it off. Scissors in hand, she went to the door.

It was Ahn. Behind him, there were other people in the hall. Some were on their way to other apartments, and some were going downstairs.

"Good morning, Cô Thi," said Ahn politely. "Am I early for my English lesson?"

"No, sir, you are right on time. I hope you studied."

Once the door was shut, Ahn assumed his usual, businesslike attitude.

"Ông Duat has requested I make one final check. All seems to be in order, and we are still on schedule. You should be almost ready to go to the roof. Where is your hat?"

"The hat is not used for the first operation," replied Thi, coolly.

She obviously relished letting him know that she was the better prepared.

"Of course. When you go back. Well, I must be gone. Ông Duat wishes me at Xa Bui when the event occurs. Good day, Cô Thi."

Thi opened the door for him. "Good day, sir."

Ahn hurried down the corridor and out into the bright street.

It was 12:05 when Thi reached the roof. It was hot and clear. She looked south down Nguyen Hue toward the river. Large white clouds were forming and they looked like mounds of cotton against the blue sky. A small storm was on the way.

There will be rain to wash the streets clean.

Thi looked over the roofs of the buildings and then made her way across the tops of the buildings to the end of the block.

There were several other Vietnamese women on the roof, putting clothes out to dry on makeshift lines or gathering in dry clothing. Several children were playing among the skylights, gables, and water tanks that comprised the landscape on the tops of the buildings. Soon Thi reached the east end of the structure.

She was alone. Directly in front of her across the narrow park was the Rex Hotel and Cinema Building. Many sedans were pulling up to the end of the park. It was lunchtime and the place was teeming with American, Australian, and Korean officers. Next to the Rex Hotel, hundreds of people were coming out of JUSPAO. Thi checked her watch.

12:16

Plenty of time for Sam, Tam, Wok, and the others to see her. The breeze blew her hair away from her face and exposed her scar to the hot sun. She was happy about it. She hoped that every American down there would look up, see the ugly blemish, and shudder in horror. It would be the last thing they would do in their lives.

12:19

The mid-day crowds were at their peak. The traffic jam around the circle broke up a bit and trucks started to move again. She wondered where the team members were located. Up high, she supposed, to escape the shrapnel.

She trembled as she glanced at her watch. Slowly she raised her hand as if to shield her eyes from the sun.

Her signal.

She dropped her hand and suddenly turned to start her retreat to the other end of the complex of roofs and her stairwell.

As she walked briskly, she counted "Thirty-one, thirty-two, thirty-three, thirty-four ..."

She opened the trapdoor to the stairs. "Forty-three, forty-four, forty-five!"

She held her breath for the loud explosion.

Nothing!

She listened carefully. Faintly she could hear the usual outdoor sounds. She dashed up the stairs, automatically grabbing the straw hat that was ready for signaling the second blast. It was unbelievable! The various women were still on the roof, the children playing. She carefully crossed over to her position facing the Rex Hotel, affecting a casual demeanor.

There were police and bomb disposal vehicles by the North Pole Ice Cream Parlor and by the Air Vietnam office.

She did not wait to look for more evidence. A shiver went through her in spite of the heat on the roof. She made her way down to her flat and threw herself in a chair.

Quickly she reviewed her general instructions: if things did not go as planned, or it seemed that any part of an operation had been compromised, she was to remove any personal items from the No. 516 flat. Then, take her name off the front door, dress as a woman street laborer, and wait by the statue of the Madonna in front of the cathedral on Tu Do Street. Someone would contact her there. The current week's countersign would identify any agent personally unknown to her.

Following her instructions to the letter, she changed clothing and placed her few personal things in a small rag-wrapped bundle. Thi walked to the rendezvous and began listlessly sweeping the sidewalk in front of the large Madonna. Occasionally she would stop and look at the crowds of people making their way home to lunch and the afternoon siesta. After about one hour, she noticed a man approaching the statue. He was dressed in a white linen suit and carried two cameras.

It was Ahn.

"Excuse me, woman. Will you take my picture for me, please?"

"Ah, sir, I do not know how to use the camera."

"It is easy. Here. I will set it and all you have to do is push the button."

They were very close now looking at the camera.

Ahn spoke quietly, "Xa Bui is safe. Go there as soon as I leave."

He posed in front of the Madonna and Thi took his picture. With a brief bow, Ahn retrieved his camera and went on his way. Thi returned to sweeping the sidewalk. Slowly she drifted away from the statue, and soon was walking toward the Catinat Hotel and the welcome safety of Xa Bui.

Ψ   Ψ   Ψ

Newell Osborne wished, just this once, that he were an army officer.

He looked across his desk at Lieutenant Colonel Mark Buckley. If so, he could merely correct Mark and dismiss him.

Dr. De Salle had called him. It was an unbelievable story that he finally worked out of Bill Scott. Then, of course, there was the rest of the story. Mark had not been told the "Holden saga." If he had known it, he probably would not have said the things he did.

Newell had come to like Mark. He considered him a typical American military sort, a type whom two years ago he had looked upon with either scorn or amused disdain, depending on the circumstances surrounding the encounter. The longer he worked with these men, the more he had gradually come to realize that they were usually straightforward and methodical in their thinking, dedicated to their work, and completely self-sacrificing in their application to the mammoth tasks they were assigned.

Often blunt, sometimes profane, they were also intelligent and well prepared for the positions they held. He badly needed Mark on his team.

Mark was standing at rigid attention before Newell's desk. His jaw was grimly set. He had just formally requested relief from his assignment on grounds that he was incapable of handling the job, and the longer he stayed the more likely would be the chance of further embarrassment to the Nation, the Army, and to Ambassador Newell Osborne.

"Goddammit, Mark, this is not a military office and I'm damned if I'm going to say 'at ease.' You have no reason to extend me military courtesies and, what's more, I won't take them from you."

He rose from his desk, walked over to the divan behind Mark, and sat down.

"Come over here and sit down in this chair and—have a cup of coffee, and that's an order!" he added with a grin.

Mark turned around and took a seat at the coffee table. Taking a cup, he poured himself coffee from the pot in front of him.

"Now lean back and relax. I have a long story to tell you, and I want you to listen and put away the ramrod in your back."

Mark listened while Newell told how Janet and Ted Holden had worked for one full year on the original Montagnard study that had become the American and Vietnamese textbook in their relations with the hill tribes. The recommendations in the study had been followed to the letter, and by these actions, the Montagnards had been turned away from Communism and become indirect allies to the South Vietnamese government. They were now fast friends of the American Special Forces so at least they were fighting the same enemies as the Saigon government, if not exactly for the same cause. Saigon was far away. The VC were right there.

"It was Ted and Janet who kept the Montagnards from revolting. Through them, we were able to keep them unified against the Viet Cong—instead of against us.

"Both anthropologists, Janet and Ted worked as a team. Ted was a dreamer, the visionary, if you will. His ideas were always original, but somewhat impractical. Janet, on the other hand, always has her feet on the ground. As a team, they were superb; Janet could control Ted and guide him.

"About six months ago, Ted went out alone. He had taken pre-med training as an undergraduate years before and medicine was always dear to his heart. Here in Vietnam he often acted as an aid man in the remote villages. Some of the natives had requested that he visit a small mountain hamlet to the west, near the Cambodian border, to help some sick people. He never returned. He was either killed or kidnapped. We don't know which. Whatever the case, there's been no trace.

"Poor Janet was beside herself for a long while. Her love for Ted is very deep and real. Finally, she decided that she would continue their study on her own. She chose to do this because if she didn't have an official reason for being in Vietnam, she would be sent home. She had to be near—just in case. In addition, she felt that the government had contracted for an additional study, and she wasn't about to let the government down.

"I know how you feel about all of the social science work being done over here, but this time, Mark—believe me—you're very wrong."

There was a brief silence before Mark finally spoke, "What can I do?" he asked quietly.

"Well, in the first place, I want you to apologize to Janet Holden. She's a person who will accept a sincere apology with good grace. In the second place, I want you to stay out of De Salle's way. In spite of his academic reputation, I don't think he's being very effective here. In the third place, I want you to go back and start doing your job."

"But Mrs. Holden—Janet—I must talk to her but I understand she left for the highlands this morning."

"That's right. Schedule yourself on the courier flight tomorrow. We'll expect you back sometime Monday or Tuesday—and Mark, keep that Irish temper of yours in check, will you? Remember it's the VC we're fighting—the *VC!*"

"I'll try my best, sir, and thanks."

Suddenly Mark felt better. The feeling that he had been a first-class slob was still with him, but now there was a way to make amends.

Ψ   Ψ   Ψ

Thi stepped out of the hidden elevator and went immediately to the office.

Ahn met her, handed her a simple, black *ao dai*, and led her to a small dressing room where she washed away the makeup and changed. When she stepped back into the office, Duat and Ahn confronted her. They were both grave.

After Thi described the sequence of events by the Rex Hotel, both men remained silent for some time.

Finally, Duat spoke. "Sometime during the past two days, the team was compromised. The city police knew where the location for each charge would be and traced the wires. This morning, when our men brought in the claymores, hidden in boxes and baskets, the police allowed them to make the connections and to proceed almost up until the last moment. Then they took them."

"I wonder if they will talk," said Ahn.

"Of course they will, but they will use the cover story. It's more sensible than the truth."

"But if they defect?"

Thi broke in, "Then are we all in danger? This place, all our contacts, everything?"

"No. They did not know this part of Saigon at all, and they couldn't have associated Xa Bui with any specific location. The one time they came up here, they came up by the long tunnel. It's doubtful if they even looked for landmarks with which to get their bearings while they were in the garden.

"The only place that could really be compromised is your No. 516. We will put a watch on it for several weeks before we risk moving you back. You will use your own place until we reopen the flat or abandon it for someplace else. Be sure to tell your old neighbors that you have returned from Hue and you have decided to start teaching English and French. That will explain your visitors.

"The important thing is to get closer to the Americans. Begin with Major Scott. Later we may switch you to this new officer, Colonel Buckley, when we find out more about him."

Thanks to Duat, Thi now had quite a stack of money to make her flat more presentable and to buy new clothes. In a taxi on her way home, she allowed herself a thought of Sam and his team. She had liked them. They were so brave. But, a feeling of defeat slowly surrounded her like a black cloud. She could not shake it. She decided that when the evening coolness came, she would go to the Cercle Hippique to exercise her horse. Somehow working with Prince always cleared her mind. How the horse felt about it did not cross her mind.

Ψ Ψ Ψ

Corporal Kim was making himself at home at "The 92," which was his name for 92 Hung Vuong Street, the best whorehouse in Saigon.

He was finishing a game of pool at the oversized table that dominated the north side of the large courtyard. Kim had gotten off early to run Colonel Uhm's errand, which was to get him a girl for the evening. Now he was waiting for the crowd to arrive and the action to start. He sank the last ball, then carefully hung up his cue and walked over to a small table and sat down. Instantly, a young, attractive girl came up for his order. He brushed her away with a smile.

How he loved this place. The large mimosa tree in the center of the courtyard shaded everything nicely, and the three stories of rooms with balconies that made up the west side of the courtyard gave the place a lot of privacy. He glanced shyly at the girls seated on benches on the south side of the yard.

All the girls are number one!

He was careful not to smile at any one of them, because he knew that, with even so little an encouragement, one of the lovely young women would come to his table. He didn't want to get involved just yet.

He was waiting for his new American friends, Red and Dave, to see what their plans were for the evening. He remembered standing outside of "The 92" on that first day, his pockets stuffed with piastres, working up enough courage to enter. Then Dave and Red had come up. They didn't even know him, but each grabbed one of his arms and propelled him through the gate, past the main house, and into the courtyard.

Red was big and strong, maybe three inches taller than Kim. He was an army sergeant, first class, with a red crew cut, gigantic red mustache, and many freckles on his face. Dave, on the other hand, was small and dark. He was a sailor and wore his white cap over his left eye.

That first day, they had brought Kim in as their guest.

They said, "The drinks, the chow, and the first piece of ass are on us. After that, you gotta pay your own way."

They had all laughed very hard as they passed the pool players and sat down at a round table. The first beer appeared without their ordering, and more kept coming. Kim couldn't believe his luck. His new friends were like American GIs he had known in Korea when he was a boy. They made him one of them. He glanced at the girls. One look and he knew his troubles with Colonel Uhm were over!

Then Ba Thoa had come to the table. She ran the place. Dave called her Madam, but Red called her Ba Thoa and slapped her on her bottom. She was sitting on Red's lap when she met Kim for the first time, but she didn't pay much attention to him then because Red was running his mustache across the low-cut front of her dress and tickling her breasts. She was laughing and pretending to be mad.

It had been a great night. The greatest night in Kim's life. After that, the three had become close friends and they met at "The 92" every night they were off duty.

"Where your friends, good lookin'?"

Kim looked up and saw Ba Thoa standing very close to him.

"Hiya, beautiful," he said in his close imitation of Dave.

"Where your buddies?" she asked again.

"Oh, they come along soon."

"Say, look, no more beauty contests. Make the girls jealous. Understand? You tell Red?"

"No, you tell Red. This your place."

They both laughed, but suddenly Ba Thoa became serious.

"Okay I sit down?"

"No, please. Come sit."

Kim had wanted to ask her as Red did, but he was too shy.

"Look, handsome, I see you here every day. You spend beaucoup P. Where you get all that P?"

"I told you. My rich old aunt die."

It was an expression Dave had told him to use, and he used it all the time.

"What girl you send over to your boss tonight?"

Kim scanned the girls quickly. "Maybe tonight I send two."

"What you wanna do, kill him?"

They both laughed and Kim said, "You know, I tell him I make good friends with Madam. I tell him I make Madam give boss number one girl. Boss no have to pay."

"Why you no let boss pay? Why you pay all time, make him think no one pay?"

"This way him no ask questions and leave Kim alone. Boss like, I like, Ba Thoa like. All okay!"

"I think you crazy, but you very nice."

Ba Thoa looked over the crowd of girls again. With a small movement of her finger, she summoned a short, rather well filled out Chinese girl with short hair and merry, laughing eyes.

"This Miss Win. How about her for colonel boss tonight?"

Kim looked her over carefully, and then patted her breasts to see if they were false.

Nope. All number one.

"Looks like a winner," he said in imitation of his American friends. "Send her the regular time. He will be standing by the MP blockhouse."

"No worry. All be taken care of."

She accepted the money from Kim and sent the girl back to the bench. Thoa liked the personal service jobs, especially when they paid so well.

The afternoon was waning and an evening coolness was in the air. The courtyard was starting to fill with customers. Thoa, contrary to her usual custom, remained seated. She seemed to have something on her mind. Unobserved, she ordered a beer for Kim. He was surprised when it arrived.

"On house," said Thoa proudly.

After Kim had tasted the beer, Thoa reached across the table and patted his hand. He instinctively withdrew it. Then, with a smile, he returned it to touch hers.

"My girls say you number one lover."

Kim laughed and looked at the table.

"Why you not stay here with me all night? You try me. We like each other, we make good deal. Okay?"

Kim looked at the attractive, round face. Thoa was older than the house girls. Maybe thirty-five, but she looked very good in her Western clothes, and he had often wondered if she was still available.

She has a number one ass. All of her is number one, I bet.

"What kind of deal?"

"Well you know. You make this your night home. You sleep with me. All free all time. Food free, laundry free, best fatigue starch job every day, boots shined–all free!"

Kim looked carefully into Thoa's eyes.

"What if I want other girl? You get mad!"

"Oh, you want other girl, you pay. Me no get mad if you pay."

"Sounds okay, but my boss not let me. He say I stay barracks."

"We'll fix him. You say no more girls free if no let you stay!"

"Maybe work. I see."

Thoa looked toward the entrance.

"Ah! Here your friends."

She left to greet Red and Dave. Although Red tried to be playful, Thoa cut him short and made a big play for Dave. Delighted with this unusual turn of events, Dave acted the great lover and sat her on his lap at the table. There, amid many tickles, slaps, pinches, squeals, and laughter, Thoa entertained the three men and several others at adjacent tables.

Ba Thoa knew her business, however, and did not linger very long at their table. She was soon on her way, supervising all things of her establishment. After she had left and the first *Ba Mui Ba* beer arrived,

Red said that tonight they were all going to the Plaza, his billet, because there were steaks for dinner and a good "round-eye" floor show.

"Just to show you how on-the-ball I am, I even got the colonel's jeep for the evening!"

"How in hell did you get that?" asked Dave.

"It wasn't easy," answered Red.

"You tell colonel you have high-ranking Korean—to drive around!" added Kim.

They all laughed as they left the table and threaded their way through the crowd.

"We'll be back by ten," said Red, as they filed past Ba Thoa.

As he passed her, Kim reached out and patted her on the bottom. This was his first physical imitation of Red and Dave and he was anxious. He caught Ba Thoa's eye. She smiled and he smiled back.

Okay! I'm number one, too!

Yes, it was a wonderful war. He was a very lucky corporal. As the American GIs said, he had the world by the ass and he wasn't about to let go.

Ψ   Ψ   Ψ

The next morning Kim had never seen Colonel Uhm in such a good humor.

He was driving his boss around Saigon. Things had started to go well right after Kim's three-day pass. Ever since then, Uhm had been satisfied with the girls and, best of all, this ended the frantic after-curfew dashes about town. Kim's evenings were now his own.

Uhm leaned over the front seat and spoke to Kim familiarly.

"That Chinese girl last night. What a lovely creature! I asked her to return tonight. I am the envy of the whole billet! They wonder how I do it. Of course, I am not telling."

"Ah, Colonel, sir! I hope it can continue."

Kim hadn't intended to bring up the subject at all, but to his surprise, he had blurted it out.

"Why? What do you mean? What's the trouble?"

"Well, sir, the madam, the one I was telling you about. The one that well … loves me. She has become more demanding of my time. She wants me to spend nights with her when I'm not on duty."

"That's impossible. It takes special permission to stay out of barracks overnight."

"That's what I told her, sir, but she says colonels can do anything and that if you wanted to continue with the situation with the girls, you could get me a special pass."

"Preposterous! What situation?"

"You know, sir … the girls … for free."

For a long time they drove in silence. Finally, they arrived at ROK Headquarters. The colonel said no more, but he left the sedan, his face an angry thundercloud. Kim was very worried.

"I think I blew it," he sighed aloud.

He wondered if he would ever see "The 92" again.

It was almost an hour before Colonel Uhm reappeared. Kim threw him a smart salute as he held the car door.

"To the Rex," ordered Colonel Uhm as he settled back into the seat.

When they drew up to the first stoplight, Colonel Uhm tossed something over onto the front seat. It was a coveted Blue Pass!

"If you are ever caught out after curfew, if you are picked up drunk, if that place is raided some night and you are caught, if you step out of line one little bit, it's a court martial for you, understand?"

"Oh yes, sir, clearly understand. But not to worry, I will get in no trouble. The 92 will not be raided. One of its owners is the Secretary of Interior Affairs."

It was the next day that Kim found the piece of paper lying on the front passenger seat of the sedan. The message was in English.

Why did you lie to me?

You agreed to meet me in Muc Wa.

Please meet me in the May Moon restaurant at Le-Loi and Pasteur at nine o'clock tomorrow evening.

We have much to talk about.

(Signed) The Girl without briefcase

So she had found him.

Kim had known that this day would come, sometime. But, he was not disturbed. He had planned to play this one out to the end. He knew one thing for certain: he would not be poor, ever again.

He would die before he gave up that money. He did not care who the money belonged to. After all, it was crooked. Kim knew he was safe as long as the location of the money was secret. He could see no harm in going to the restaurant and talking to the pretty girl. A very pretty girl.

Chapter IV

AUGUST

B randy Masters gave her living room the once-over.

They designed these USAID billets to look like stateside living. Somehow, the whole rig gave her a guilty feeling. Perhaps it was because she had known the other side of Vietnam: the stinking, humid dressing rooms, the dusty roads of the Delta, the crummy hotels, the makeshift stages with the bugs trying to get the lights and the bats trying to get the bugs. But most of all, the sweaty, grimy men in stained fatigues, all looking at her, all wanting her, each one a potential lover. Yes, she missed it all very much. That was a life that was real. That had guts. This new life was sterile and not interesting.

She had spent a lot of time on her apartment. The drapes, the rug, the new furniture—all were very modern, very colorful. The local art fit in well. She shied away from the usual sidewalk stuff of sailboats and rice fields, but bought extensively the Vietnamese impressionists. Some, she thought, were fair, even good. Her eyes turned again to the large, rather wild and colorful painting with the red Ψ mark in the lower corner. She liked it, but sometimes wondered what the kooky artist could have been thinking.

She had avoided knowing her neighbors, because she wanted to be free to entertain whomever she wanted, when she wanted, without answering questions.

Most of the people on this floor are married, and wives are always a pain in the ass, the way they guard their husbands. Now, the two bachelors who share the apartment at the end of the hall ... that's a different story altogether. I'd love a three-way with those guys. There's plenty of time to work it out before they head back to the States.

Right now, however, she was concentrating on her flat because she wanted everything perfect for her little party.

It's all a show so I can get to know that new guy, Dr. Poli De Salle. He's interesting. He's sort of like Peter Charles, only with a background and education.

There's something about his personality that interests me. He's not evil ... that's too strong a word for such a weak man. Perhaps immoral, even dissolute, certainly dishonest. The way he talks, you might think he slept with Ky, Westy, and Bunker every night! God, how insufferable he was after that reception for the Aussies. He talked about it for days! Well, tonight I'll give him something to think about, even if he doesn't talk much about it. I'm going to wear his nasty little butt out. That's what.

Unconsciously, she slowly rubbed her palms on her blouse, over her breasts, feeling the friction on her nipples, which quickly became large and hard. This added to her dreamy excitement.

Only six people. That's all the air conditioning can really handle for a long period. Besides, I want the others to clear out by curfew. Lots of martinis, followed by a buffet ...

She left the living room to bring in the ice. For a moment, she watched Ooogg, her Vietnamese cook, making the shrimp curry.

"Ooogg," of course, was not her real name, but it was as close as Brandy could come to it. Ooogg's husband was also there helping for the party.

Every time I see him, I think of that night in Trong Thoi. He looks like one of the soldiers. Maybe a cousin? They all look alike, especially in the dark.

Quickly she picked up the ice and, after telling Ooogg that everything was *number one chop-chop*, returned to the living room and prepared the bar.

She had just put on a stack of records by her favorite French vocalist when Jim and Bette arrived. They were a young couple, each with jobs with Agriculture. Bette had a degree in botany, but she was actually doing clerical work. Jim was "on the staff." Posted to Saigon only a couple of months ago, they were still experiencing culture shock.

Gerald and Toni appeared before Brandy had mixed the first round of martinis, so she added two more glasses.

Gerald, according to Gerald, was an old Southeast Asian hand. He was well into his second year in Vietnam, and often talked about how it was back in the early days when he was in Da Nang. Sent there during his third week in country for a short stay as an advisor to some USAID people up there, he still had not recovered from the shock. Gerald was in Political Development and Brandy thought he should get along well with Poli.

Gerald had met Toni after his first year. She was a librarian, and was on an interesting project of starting up public libraries in Vietnam. They had been thinking about marriage, but both doubted if they really would.

Secretly the girls were wondering who Brandy's date would be, because there had been some vague gossip about her when she first came to USAID and, although no one could pin down the real story, she was rumored to be a rather wild person. Her long blond hair and curves certainly caused much comment and interest.

They soon found seats and the drinks were passed. Although everyone in the room was acquainted, there was a moment of awkward silence.

"Well, here's to air conditioning, that great American contribution to Vietnamese culture," said Toni, raising her glass in an effort to start the conversation.

They all followed suit and murmured, "Hear, hear."

Gerald got up from the couch and walked to the window, "Do you ever use your balcony, Brandy?" he asked without turning around.

She gave the sort of answer that she knew they would like to hear.

"Not if I can help it!"

"Ours is impossible," interjected Bette. "The odors from that native settlement. Once the air conditioning went out and we had to open the windows. Believe me, my dear, we almost went mad. Finally, I told Jim to close the windows. I would rather die of the heat than be gassed by the smells of this town!"

"There's a whale of a storm coming up," declared Gerald, still at the window.

"Good! Maybe it will wash some of the filth from the streets."

The rain arrived in sheets of water that periodically lashed the concrete building. Brandy was worried about Poli. Unless he had managed to get into the building before the rain, he would be a mess. That would ruin his mood.

"This it, Brandy?" asked Toni.

"Just one more to even things up."

"Oh, good! Six is the right number for air conditioning. Any more and it gets awfully sticky."

"It's lovely here now ..."

There was a knock at the door and Brandy quickly opened it. Poli was standing in the doorway, wet but not drenched. He had almost beaten the rain.

"Oh, you poor man," Brandy cried as she led him into the room. "But before I introduce you, I'm going to let you visit the powder room to repair yourself. Here, follow me. I'll bring him back in a minute, girls."

Grateful for this chance to dry off, Poli arranged his clothes and combed his hair. He looked around at the plumbing with real envy.

How lucky these people were in the USAID billets—first class—everything like the good old USA.

When Poli reappeared, Brandy made the introductions. He immediately tried to take over the conversation. However, not knowing the time-honored ritual of USAID parties, he made an unwise choice of subject. The result: the others, who were following the regular format, ignored him.

First, at USAID parties, one always spoke of the inconveniences encountered in Vietnam. Each had a new story concerning the difficulties of everyday life. The commissary had been out of a certain cleaning powder for weeks; the street in front of someone's billet wasn't paved, and you could lose your car in one of the potholes; the water was out again in another part of town.

When each guest had been given a chance to recite the latest indignity he, or she, had endured, it was on to the next phase.

Part Two: Everyone's Vietnam story. It usually concerned his sole encounter with a native in the last forty-eight hours and the story could be hilarious, tragic, disgusting, or sad. Hilarious stories were preferred.

Part Three: The subject of the war was brought up, and usually each person had a rumor to distort a little before it passed on to eager ears. They hashed out and rehashed any local terrorist incidents in the last day or two.

Part Four, the closing act: Arguing the future of Vietnam, with each person acting as a soothsayer. These prognostications generally mixed in everyone's opinion of the Vietnamese people, their government, their economy, and their weaknesses. Result: a happy future for South Vietnam was rarely forecast, by anyone.

Only in this fourth phase of the party was Poli able to hold forth with conviction. As supper was finally served, all of the guests were spellbound with his scathing accounts of a people he seldom spoke to or cared to try to understand.

Brandy, who knew Vietnam and the Vietnamese people better than anyone in the room did, kept quiet. She did not agree with anything her guests had said, but from her low position in USAID, she could not speak with authority. Anyway, she did not intend to differ with Poli this evening. She had other plans for him.

During supper, the subject of conversation was Jim's coming trip to the Delta. He was going to Can Tho to see a demonstration at the agricultural school there. He was very nervous about his trip because there was talk of a side visit to some of the *agrivilles* near the Cambodian border. These were small towns built and populated with refugees. Started up to support the agriculture projects started during the Diem regime, most of the little hamlets had done well and they were a subject of interest. Could it be that Diem, now marked a crook and thief, had actually done something right?

"Don't go, Jim. Just refuse to go," suggested Bette as she sipped her wine. "After all, there's fighting there. You aren't a soldier."

"They say that if the chopper flies over five thousand feet, it's safe from small-arms fire."

Toni shuddered. "Well, you have to get up to five thousand feet— and you have to come down. What's to protect you then?"

"Will you be going anywhere near Trong Thoi?" asked Brandy.

"Where is it? Never heard of it," replied Gerald. "Can't be much there or I would know about it," he quickly added.

"Oh, I don't think it's very big. I have a friend stationed there. Thought you might say hello."

Suddenly the electric power went off and the room was plunged into complete darkness. After the usual, "Oh God, not again!" and "Dammit to hell!" Ooogg brought in two candles and an uneasy conversation started about how long this would last. It was Poli, however, who went to the window and saw that it wasn't just a section of town, but all of Saigon was in darkness.

"Well, our car lights will work won't they?" asked Bette.

"Of course they will. I wonder if we shouldn't go home," Jim added uneasily.

"It may be the VC," offered Gerald. "You know, when I was in Da Nang they tried ..."

The room without the air conditioner began getting very muggy, and soon the guests were remarking on the discomfort. Perhaps they should be going home.

"Please everybody," exclaimed Brandy, "You must stay at least long enough to try Ooogg's dessert. It's absolutely superb. Gentlemen, take your coats and ties off, and I will open the windows."

Immediately after the guests gulped down the dessert, Bette and Jim made an abrupt departure. Brandy gave them a candle to light their way out to their car. Gerald and Toni soon followed, with the old Southeast Asia hand sporting a pencil flashlight for emergencies such as this.

Poli, however, agreed to stay awhile after Brandy professed fright and "didn't like the look of things."

There was a small wind stirring, which did not relieve the uncomfortable situation for those used to air conditioning but, to take advantage of it, Brandy led Poli out onto the balcony to escape the closeness of the room.

Poli remarked on the blackout and wondered aloud if there was any danger. Suddenly Brandy realized that Poli was afraid to leave the apartment.

Well that works. Here we go.

"Poli, I'm very frightened tonight. I've never seen the city quite like this. I wonder could you, would you mind staying here tonight?"

"Why, Brandy, under the circumstances I think it would be perfectly proper for me to stay. After all, this is war, you know." He was greatly relieved.

Brandy smiled in the dark as she moved nearer to him. These inconveniences certainly made it convenient for her. -

Ψ   Ψ   Ψ

Kim walked into the restaurant at exactly nine o'clock. Thi had already arrived.

She was surprised to see him wearing a light blue sport shirt and gray slacks. She had only seen him in his fatigue uniform and she was pleased with his good looks.

He walked over to her corner table and, without any greeting, sat down.

"Nice of you to come. I hoped that you would find my note."

"Glad to see you again," said Kim.

Since they had to talk in English, he decided to emulate Red and Dave as much as possible.

"You some chick! You English very good. You turn me on something big."

"Let's get down to business," said Thi with a smile.

In spite of herself, she could not help feeling very warm toward him.

"What did you do with that briefcase you took?"

"Wait a cotton-pickin' min, baby. You gave it to me. I tried not to take, but you put into my hand."

"Well, what did you do with it? You see, there was a mistake—it was supposed to go to—someone else."

"Well, I said 'Kim, that chick has blown her mind. She gave me this case and it not mine,' so I took to the police."

"Police?" she had not thought of that possibility. "Didn't you open it? Didn't you look to see what was in it?"

"I thought maybe you bad girl, make bomb, blow up poor Korean boy."

Thi was incredulous. Could he really be so naive?

"How's about egg roll and a *Ba Mui Ba?*"

"What?"

"You know, chow. Want to eat?"

"You mean food?"

"Yeah. Come on, let's have a beer."

Before she knew it, Thi was enjoying the food, and especially enjoying Kim's company. The more she came to know him, the more she was sure that he could not give away the briefcase without opening it. Moreover, if he had looked in it, he would not have given away the money. He was smart. It might take some time to get into his confidence. It might take time and a lot of female persuasion. As she looked at him across the little table, she decided that at least that part might be enjoyable.

Kim, on the other hand, was finding out quite a lot about Thi. He soon discovered she wasn't a typical bar girl. She was beautiful, but she was also very smart. He'd better watch his step. What a conquest she would be. What a gem to show off to Dave and Red.

Nevertheless, his crafty peasant mind was flashing danger signals and he was inwardly heeding every one of them. He wondered whom she worked for and what her real game was. No matter; he hoped he could convince her that he was only a stupid Korean GI, who might give a briefcase to the police, as he had said.

"Come on. You like to cop outta here?"

"Do you mean leave? Where will we go?"

For a moment, she thought of him at the Cercle Sportif or the Cercle Hippique and she almost laughed aloud. However, she looked at his handsome, trusting face and the crinkles around his eyes when he smiled, and she could only smile herself as she awaited his answer.

"Well, how about high-class dancing place? You like Blue Moon or Paradise?"

Thi had never heard of those places, but she assumed they must be typical soldiers' hangouts and wanted none of them.

"I think I better go home. It's getting late. Why don't you come with me?"

Kim was again on his guard, but he could not let this opportunity go by. It was obvious she did not believe the police story. Therefore, she was still after the money. How would she try to get it? His guess was there were two games: have the location of the money beaten out of him or seduction.

He had learned long ago not to travel unarmed. When in uniform, he kept the US Army MK-2 combat knife he'd picked up at the PX in his boot. In his civilian clothes, he carried a switchblade. He patted the knife in his right pocket. He wasn't too worried about a fight, and as for the other option, well, he was ready for that, too.

Kim laid some piastres on the table and got up, "Let's take off, hon, and check out you pad."

By the time the taxi that Kim had hailed had driven to Thi's flat in Cholon, it was after ten o'clock. Kim was glad of this. If he didn't like the looks of the situation, he could always make a hasty retreat, begging curfew. If he did like the looks of things, he could stall and insist on staying because of the curfew. Either way it worked.

They walked up the stairs and were soon in Thi's living room. He agreed to try brandy and soda with ice because she had no beer, and because she was going to have one. He followed her into the kitchen. He wanted to make sure that the drinks were both made the same.

No funny business.

He noticed her small refrigerator, like the ones for sale in the PX.

"You have American GI boy friend?"

"No, I got it on the black market."

"Very expensive on black market. Maybe you get tips in Queen Bee."

Thi thought a lie was better than the truth in this case. She laughed and said, "Well last year, I had an American boyfriend, but he went back to the United States."

Drinks in hand, they returned to the living room and sat on the couch. Suddenly the room was in blackness.

Kim was instantly on the alert; with his right hand, he pulled the knife from his pocket and made it ready. With his other hand, he snatched a couch pillow to use as a shield.

"Oh! Another blackout," moaned Thi. "I hope this one won't last long. It's always this part of the city. Here, I have some candles handy."

Thi rose and slowly moved to the sideboard where she opened a drawer and struck a match.

Kim put the pillow down and hid the knife under his leg. Thi, engrossed in lighting the candles, didn't notice. She left one on the sideboard and placed the other on the coffee table in front of the low couch.

"Look," she said, "the whole city seems to be out."

The glow from the anti-infiltration flares was adding a little light to that part of the city, but their effective illumination area was south and east of Cholon.

"You know, with this blackout, it won't be wise for you to travel about tonight."

"Yes, it be very bad. I never find cyclo or taxi, and cannot go quarters by curfew."

Both of them were serious as they considered Kim's dilemma. Thi was looking directly into Kim's eyes. They were sitting quite close to one another. The candlelight cast their silhouettes, large, on the wall.

"Do you have room for me?"

"Why, of course. Come see." She got up and carried her drink in one hand and the candle in the other. Kim followed, carrying his drink in one hand and his knife in the other.

Thi put the candle down on the dresser and started to undress. Kim sat on the edge of the double bed and watched her carefully. She hung her *ao dai* over a chair and removed her black brassiere. Her full breasts were perfect in the warmth of the candlelight.

Number one! She's got some Western blood in her from someplace.

So, it was to be the second choice after all. Kim slowly lowered the knife to the floor beside the bed.

Then, after a long pull on his drink, he got up and removed his sport shirt, shoes and socks. As he took off his trousers, he noticed the light in the room change. He turned to see Thi near the bed, nude except her sheer white low-cut panties. She was without doubt the most beautiful woman he had ever seen. Thi placed the candle on a small bedside table and arranged herself with great deliberation on her back on the bed.

He fumbled with his trousers very briefly and then approached the bed wearing only his shorts. He noticed a smile on Thi's lips as she looked at him. Then she turned and blew out the candle. He reached for her in the darkness.

She was waiting.

Ψ   Ψ   Ψ

Ambassador Newell Osborne had been working his people around the clock.

The presidential elections were less than a month away and he was trying to ensure that in all the provinces in South Vietnam, the elections would be free, honest and, as far as possible, safe from the VC. Rumor had it that the VC were rigging the election for Tran Van Huong, a popular candidate who was very outspoken against Generals Thieu and Ky.

Osborne sent out detailed instructions to all province advisors on how to counter these rumors. Mark Buckley made a tour of the "problem provinces" to monitor the counter-rumor operation. Heading south by chopper from Kon Tum, Mark was looking forward to stopping in Ban Me Thuot, and hoped he would be able to get up to Buon Sut Mgra to see Janet Holden again.

He remembered too well their first meeting, and the fool he had made of himself later that evening at the Hangout. She was a wonderful person to forgive him with such kindness and understanding when he had flown up later from Saigon, on Newell Osborne's suggestion, to apologize.

On that visit, the two had time for some good conversation, and Mark quickly saw that Janet was a person who worked well with the Vietnamese. She and Mark both felt that the Vietnamese people were worth helping in any way possible. They both deplored the heavy-handed "do it my way" approach that the official American effort had lately advocated. Both wanted more Vietnamese ideas tried, with American assistance and encouragement to Vietnamese workers.

"I realize that this is a state of emergency and we don't have time for a lot of teaching in many cases, but let's start a foundation of instruction where we can teach—not only the American way, but ways familiar to the Vietnamese, modified to be compatible with American tools, equipment, and supplies."

"I know what you mean, Janet," agreed Mark. "We should go back to equipment we used in our country around the turn of the century and introduce that first. For instance, it's too big a step to have them jump right into our sophisticated farm machinery. There has to be a step in between. These people have native mechanical intelligence. Give most of them a simple gasoline motor, and they can manage a complete overhaul with no trouble at all. With the proper training and equipment, they quickly could go right up the scale to the most complicated stuff."

Mark had spent the day with Janet and her staff of locals on that trip. He found that he enjoyed himself more than he had in years. When he returned to Saigon, a lively correspondence had developed between them and, as a result, he had made plans to stop over on this trip.

After the chopper dropped him off, he found a Tri-Lambretta heading for Buon Sut Mgra. It was an arduous trip of many stops and changes of passengers, the five-mile journey lasting well over two hours.

"Without my bag, I could have walked it and made better time," muttered Mark to himself as he left the Tri-Lambretta.

It was afternoon when Janet looked out of the window of the little chapel schoolroom and saw Mark walking up the dusty road. Her little cry of delight aroused some of her helpers from their midday rest; they got quietly up from their straw mats and watched her run down the steps to meet him.

Janet threw her arms about Mark and kissed him. "Oh, I guess I shouldn't have done that," she said, somewhat embarrassed, "What will the students think?"

"Well, as long as we are giving them a show, we might as well do it right."

He dropped his bag, swept her into his arms and kissed her soundly.

They heard the giggles of the students and Mark gallantly raised his fatigue cap in salute.

"Oh, Mark, you perfect fool," laughed Janet. "But you know we shouldn't have done that. It's just that I was so surprised and happy to see you."

"Well, no harm done. In fact, I think it was good for us."

He had brought along gumdrops for the student helpers. This gift disrupted their rest hour and the work schedule for the rest of the day.

"Look what you've done, Mark Buckley. This whole place is a complete shambles. The only thing I can do is declare a holiday."

Janet resumed her teacher persona. "That's all for the day. Tomorrow we will start promptly at eight o'clock. Be sure to close the shutters and lock the door."

With polite murmurs of happiness, the workers put their papers and books away, and all trooped down to the town with Janet and Mark.

"Howard Shultz, the district advisor, promised me transportation to Ban Me Thuot whenever I wanted it," said Janet when Mark explained that his chopper would be leaving at four-thirty. "In that way, you can stay longer. We will stop by his office first, then you can take me to our restaurant and buy me a cool drink."

Soon, they sat at a small, wobbly table under a mimosa tree in the restaurant's courtyard.

Over their not-so-cold beer, they continued their conversation of the previous trip, but try as they might to control it, the subject always became personal, more intimate. An eavesdropper would have thought they were lovers.

The truth came to Janet: it would be wrong to continue in this manner. Rather than deceive Mark, she wove Ted into the conversation. Mark slowly realized that Janet had seen the path their relationship was taking and had deliberately brought up Ted in order to put all the cards on the table.

"He must be a wonderful person," commented Mark, sadly.

"Thanks for putting that in the present tense. Sometimes it's hard to keep thinking that he's still alive. Yet in my heart, I know he is."

"You're quite a girl to hold on this long ..."

"It's not a question of holding on. The love is still there. I have no choice."

Mark added nothing, but patted her hand. They turned to safer subjects until the jeep arrived.

When they said goodbye, Janet reached up and brushed Mark's cheek with her lips. She stood in the dusty road and watched until the jeep disappeared around the bend.

Ψ   Ψ   Ψ

Hue scratched his head and scowled.

He was looking at Cy's latest work.

"This very good picture, Cy. Hue no understand why your pictures no sell very much."

Cy stood with his arm on Hue's shoulder. He knew why only two pictures had sold.

"Look here. It's easy, see. You know who buys pictures? GI soldiers, that's who. What do they want? Souvenirs of Vietnam. They see junks, palm trees, rice fields, water buffalo, pretty Vietnamese girls. That's what they want. Maybe I will change–start doing your stuff, too."

"No. Never happen, Cy. You making good money on black market with PX stuff. You bring cigarettes, whiskey, wine. I make money on pictures. You keep paint like now. Someday we get professor at academy. Put on one-man show at Alliance Française. No sidewalk stuff like I do now. You wait. You see."

Cy was discouraged, but as long as Hue was happy, he wasn't about to change. He was doing what he liked, he was living high, and he had a sex life that would be the envy of every dogface in Vietnam. This was a good life. He liked it this way.

Hue showed Cy the new art supplies he had bought, then went over to work on his own canvas.

Cy lay down on the bench and picked up the Saigon Daily News, one of the few English-language papers printed in Vietnam. Kam picked up a new copy for him, daily. He liked to follow the progress of the war, as well as news of the various candidates in the national election. The News also covered items from America.

Cy eagerly followed the social unrest in his country and the surge of black power seeking recognition and equality. His hatred for the honkies back home grew daily. He believed that many black Americans were dying in Vietnam for the economic advancement of American business. White businesses.

The Vietnamese national elections first caught Cy's attention when he read a funny column on two candidates who were using the water buffalo as their party symbol. The only difference was that the horns of one animal turned up, while those of the other turned down. Soon he was aware of the many different political parties. He found it interesting to relate them to the Vietnamese people and their first real chance to select their own government. He would often tell Hue and Kam that this was their opportunity to vote out the present government.

They could replace them with others who would end the war and give the poor people a break. If their country started out right, they could work it so everyone really was equal and had an equal chance.

Hue and Kam, however, knew their people far better than Cy and, although they smiled and agreed with him, they realized that for the present, the Americans would be the deciding factor in their government, no matter the election outcome. Without them, the country would be Communist. For them and many others, a red take-over would be far worse than the present state of affairs.

The bell rang. Cy and Hue knew that Kam would be coming up. In a moment, she entered the studio apartment with Qui, a slight young man whose eyes were always in motion, missing nothing, seeing everything, who was now their black-market contact.

For Qui, information was not only power, as it is in all places high, low, east, or west, but also, sometimes, a matter of life and death. In his eyes, Cy was not only a black-market business resource but also a possible source of some bit of information that, added to others he vacuumed up, could be useful. Useful to Qui.

Cy, Hue, and Qui sat around the table discussing what Cy should pick up during his next visit to the PX. He was working three false ID cards now, and three corresponding false ration cards. Cy was a sailor at the Cholon PX, an airman at the Brink PX, and a soldier at the Tan Son Nhut PX.

Qui brought the military payment certificates for purchase of the items. He also gave Cy a list stating the type and amount of each item required.

Cy never knew who supplied the MPCs or who determined what items to buy. He really didn't care. All he knew was that he was making a pile of dough with this operation.

Cy always went to the PXs in civilian clothing now. He had several different combinations that lessened the chance of anyone recognizing him. He knew, for instance, that his picture, along with all other deserters, was at every MP station and major security point. Consequently, his false ID cards showed him in heavy glasses, and he wore them on these trips.

For Cy, Qui was interesting to have around because he always had a lot of intelligence on what was or was not going to happen in Saigon. This information, for the most part, came from his many black-market contacts. But at some point, the black market and the VC blurred lines, providing whispers and gossip from that world as well. Some bits proved to be correct, while others were not. However, Cy thought Qui's credibility score was high, and so he took great stock in his information.

Qui was also a bit of a showoff. And what he had to brag about was insider knowledge. Or at least what he thought sounded like it. In capitals the world over, little cogs in big machines chatted up this sort of material to impress others, to seduce women, or to obtain riches. For Qui it was about respect. As a mere, if effective, conduit for American PX goods, he had only a little. He wanted more.

Today Qui talked mostly of the election and terrorist activities that had been going on in order to keep people from voting.

"The number one terrorist is a girl."

"Girl?"

"Yes. She number one! Already she kill American sergeant in daylight time, she throw grenade into police station, she help blow up theatre, she shot American guard by Ambassador Hotel, she ..."

"Wait a minute, I read all about those, but they were by different people: a young girl, a schoolboy, an old woman ..."

Qui laughed, "You not so smart GI. You like police. Think all different. I say all same-same!"

"You got to be kiddin'!"

"No. Kid you not. She fool everyone. She number one!"

"You are damned right she is, if what you say is true," Cy replied.

"You wait, GI. She really make bang-bang over this town before election. Make people scare of vote!"

Qui left the list of items to buy and departed. He felt a delicious but small taste of power that came from showing off his knowledge of the VC's secret world.

Just a hint of course.

Cy knew it was time for him to risk his neck again. He and Hue made arrangements for the special taxi to pick him up in the morning.

Ψ Ψ Ψ

Mark Buckley and Bill Scott were sharing a table with two sergeants at the small cafeteria in the headquarters.

The room was packed with officers and soldiers who had been on duty all night or had arrived for duty without breakfast.

"As long as Janet's husband has a chance of being alive, she won't consider getting serious about me," said Mark, as he stared into his coffee cup.

"Well, how about Cô Thi? Doesn't she keep your mind away from Janet? Hell, I thought you'd moved into her place a couple of nights last week."

Mark gave a bitter laugh. "How wrong you are. Hey, I thought you were chasing her."

"Me? Hell, after one week she dropped me like a hot rock and jumped right at you."

"Well, I'm glad she dropped you–if she did–because you should be paying more attention to Cô Lei. She's really a fine girl. If I were you, I'd be getting serious after all this time."

189

"All joking aside, Mark," Bill replied, "what would you think … I mean, how do you feel about … well, mixed marriages?"

Very seriously, Mark said, "I think that mixed marriages have a better chance for success if one member is male and the other is female."

The two sergeants looked at each other with wonder. Then Mark and Bill laughed.

"Stop it, you imbecile, I'm serious. How do you think the Army would take it?"

Mark was sober now. He looked directly at Bill.

"If you two really love each other, you won't care what the god-damn Army thinks." Then, with a smile, he got up and said, "Come on. We can continue this conversation over a couple of martinis tonight."

As the two officers left the table, the two sergeants looked at each other.

Finally the younger one said, "See, Sergeant, it's like I told you. These officers ain't with it. They got one round-eye and two slant-eyes between 'em and they think they gotta get married!"

"Yeah. Makes you sad, doesn't it? Them missusin' all that valuable property!"

Ψ Ψ Ψ

Thi looked at herself closely in the mirror.

She was almost ready. The American-style silk dress had worked out well after all. She turned and looked at the fit across her backside, and was satisfied that it was not too tight. During the several times she had been out with the American officers, she had noticed that American women's dresses were cut a little fuller over the backside so that they did not cut in below the derriere as the Vietnamese imitations did.

She did not dream that the American women were envious of the slim hips and small bottoms of the Vietnamese women, or that their main objection to the tight dresses was that they could not wear them without looking like a football player in ballet tights.

She thought of Kim and hoped he would come by that night. She was very much in love with him and wondered if Ông Duat's people

190

had reported her affair yet. Since there hadn't been any restrictions placed on her private life, she intended to continue until told differently.

One thing worried her greatly, however, and that was the money. Kim had never mentioned it to her, and she had been unable to bring herself to pursue the subject. She reflected on her initial plan. Originally, she had designed the affair to get the money back from him.

Yet after that first night, in the darkness of her flat with only an occasional infiltration flare to paint the room with crazy, swinging yellow light, she somehow didn't really care what he did with the money, so long as he continued his visits whenever he could. Kim took her right to bed every time. She quickly suppressed that thought as a familiar pleasant itch started beneath the silk dress.

She had thought at first of telling Duat that she had located the man she had given the money to, but later realized that Kim would meet with some very rough treatment from Duat's people if she identified him.

Lately, she had been having daydreams that she and Kim might somehow use the money to purchase Air France tickets to Paris. She envisioned the two of them living in a swank apartment off the *Place de l'Etoile*, but she knew she was playing with fire. Duat's men were everywhere. If he ever found out that Kim had the money and she was living with him, Duat would never believe that it hadn't been a conspiracy from the start.

Her thoughts returned to Kim. Not a demanding or jealous lover, he seemed content to share her with others without being too inquisitive as to who they were. "Two American colonels" was enough of an explanation. In fact, he seemed honored and almost happy to be on par with such high-ranking people. Perhaps he bragged about it to his friends in the barracks—she did not know. Whatever the case, she was happy that he had other places to go and people to see when she was with the Americans.

Those two Americans! How easy it would have been not to hate them. When she first met them, she was surprised. They were polite, considerate, friendly, and generous.

191

Then, of course, she realized that these were the very reasons that they should be despised. She would often think of the horrors they and their comrades had wrought upon her country, her people, and upon her. The great contrast of their actions to the false face of their personalities was enough to make her loathe them. Her scar was symbolic of the atrocities her country had sustained at the hands of the US soldiers and airmen. It was her constant reminder of their wanton conduct.

As she regarded her reflection in the mirror, she lifted her carefully combed hair and again exposed the scar.

"What do you think about this, Colonel Buckley?" she said out loud, as she gazed at the angry red groove.

It gave Thi great inner pleasure to be able to profess interest, admiration, and even attraction, when her feelings were of repugnance and a desire for revenge. She considered her association with both Mark Buckley and Bill Scott nothing but an assignment that she must complete before she would be given duties more to her liking.

She knew sex was part of this assignment but, so far, she had not let her relationship with either man reach that point. Tonight, she planned to consummate her relationship with Buckley at her apartment. It was time for this. He was showing too much interest in Janet Holden. She knew that if she did not sleep with him now, she might never have the chance and would have to report to Duat that she had failed. Duat did not tolerate failure.

Ψ   Ψ   Ψ

Across town, Mai Lei was also preparing for the evening.

Bill Scott was to take her to supper at a Vietnamese restaurant. Mai Lei planned to surprise Bill by wearing a new American-style dress. It was a simple, white sleeveless sheath, with an oval neckline and a broad, wine-colored silk scarf tied as a belt. Her new slippers matched the scarf.

She regarded herself in the small mirror of her room and wondered if Bill would approve. Probably, he would politely say she was stunning, but she could tell by his eyes if he really meant it. She smiled to herself in the mirror.

Downstairs her father was also eagerly awaiting Bill. He had come to enjoy his conversations with the young officer and insisted upon a fifteen-minute talk each time Bill called. Bu had started serving Bill expensive rice wine liquor which came from Red China. Bill knew he was being highly honored when Bu served this rare cordial, and always made flattering remarks about the drink, even though he found it repulsive.

Bu was sitting very straight in his chair; the usual clutter of papers and magazines on the little table was gone, replaced by the bottle of liquor and small cups. Mai Lei ushered Bill into the room. Bu glowered at his daughter to let her know that he had reserved this time for himself. She was not to intrude.

Mai Lei smiled at her father's attitude and seated herself quietly. She knew that Bill enjoyed these conversations as much as her father did.

Bill took his usual seat across from the old man. After the brief greetings were over, he said, "The national elections are almost upon us, sir. I trust you are ready to cast your first ballot for freedom and democracy."

Bu smiled. "If the VC will let me, I shall certainly vote."

"Ah, we expect some trouble in the country, but I think you will be perfectly safe here in Saigon."

"Young man, do you really think that you Americans control this city that well? The papers are full of terrorist activities uncovered by the police. Think of the ones that are not uncovered!"

He picked up a Vietnamese paper and lightly tapped the page. "Look, twenty-three terrorists arrested for death plots."

He pointed to the paper again. "Here. Here Dragon Lady now carries rifle."

"Yes," replied Bill with a smile, "but she didn't hit anyone with the rifle. Things are getting better!"

"Perhaps she is only practicing now. She will improve by Election Day. I wonder why you Americans call her Dragon Lady. Dragon is a symbol of good luck to the Vietnamese."

"It comes from an old American World War II comic strip, *Terry and the Pirates,* I think."

"Ah, yes. I forget your rather strange sense of humor."

"Well, whatever terrorist activities happen on three September, I feel that they won't be able to stop the people from getting to the polls."

"Why do you think such thoughts, Major? Look at it from—what do you Americans call him? The little street walker?"

Bill laughed. "I think you mean the man in the street."

"Yes, the man in the street. What has he to gain from voting? Nothing, except perhaps a piece of shrapnel, a lost leg, or perhaps death. What has he to lose by not voting? Nothing! All Vietnamese think that the Thieu-Ky ticket is the one that the Americans will support. They will vote for that ticket because of the necessity for survival. Most Vietnamese hate the Thieu-Ky ticket. They see no democracy, no freedom there."

"Well, why don't they really organize to vote them out?"

"Major Bill, don't be naive. Anyone who would strongly organize against them would be branded as against the government and be shot—or at least jailed. The strongest opponent to Thieu-Ky is Truong Dinh Dzu. He had better be careful or he will be in custody soon. He is very outspoken."

"Tell me, Ông Bu, if they had their free choice, who would the people of South Vietnam vote for in this election?"

"Ho Chi Minh."

"You must be joking," said Bill with a shock of disbelief.

"Why not? He is the father of the Vietnamese people, north and south. He is loved, honored, revered. With a man like that leading us, you could observe the patriotic fervor you say we lack. Remember, he was our leader before the Americans came over here, and if you Americans had not assisted the French at that time, he probably would have been fighting beside you now. He is our George Washington.

"It is most unfortunate that his country was divided in the middle. What would your Washington have done if, after Lexington, the British had divided the colonies in the middle and prevailed upon the northern half to fight the southern half?"

Bill laughed. "He would have gone to the southern half. He was from Virginia."

The complexity of the argument was too much for Bill to tackle. He decided to ignore the new direction this discussion was taking.

"Let's forget Washington for the present and confine our talk to this election—what it means to South Vietnam. Let's consider this election as the first step in obtaining a workable democracy. Let's assume that, very soon after the winning party gets into power, it starts introducing policies that the majority of the people do not like. What would happen then?"

"Well, in your country," replied Bu, "the people would wait four years and elect someone else. In my country, it isn't the concern of the majority. In my country, if a few strong generals want a change—poof—a coup!"

"But that ends your democracy."

"Yes, the baby may die before it learns to walk."

Bill stood up. It was getting late and he was feeling the strong, if nasty tasting, rice wine liquor.

"Well, let's hope we bring forth a strong, healthy baby that has a chance to grow up. I'm afraid, sir, that Cô Lei and I must be going. Perhaps we can continue our discussion very soon."

"Ah yes. I have kept you too long. But before you go, one more point. Remember this: the baby that has the best chance of survival is not a baby at all. It's the monster that is presently in power. Even so, such a rebirth may be for the best, as long as the American nurse remains to suckle the brat!"

Ψ   Ψ   Ψ

Thi hoped that the anger that seethed inside her was not visible to Mark Buckley.

They had gone to the International House for supper and it had been a pleasant enough evening until Mark had gotten on two subjects—Janet Holden, and the battle raging south of the DMZ. Most of the conversation concerning Janet Holden was one-sided, for Thi merely smiled while Mark extolled her many virtues. He seemed unaware of the extent that he was discussing her or her project. Inwardly,

195

raging purple jealousy had taken over Thi, but outwardly, she was calm, serene, and smiling.

The development of the battle up north was another matter. Mark longed to be there. He felt that all the young, able-bodied men he saw around Saigon should also be there, or should at least be bearing arms for their country. He had rambled at length about the VC, citing case after case of their atrocities, their despicable treatment of whole villages.

At first, Thi had mildly agreed but then, as her anger rose, she brought into the discussion several cases where ARVN or American troops had caused death and destruction to friendly areas.

Mark agreed with her, though he argued that these cases were accidental, whereas there was proof that the VC's were intentional.

Several friends joined them at their table during dinner, bringing a respite from Mark's bitter denunciation. In spite of her boiling hatred, Thi was determined to carry out her plan. Years ago, she found that men could be controlled in a manner very similar to the way she controlled her horse, Prince. In both cases, the secret was in the proper use of her body. It always amused her to recall that the shifting of her hips, the pressure of her thighs, the use of her legs and arms was so effective in both cases. She felt a sense of superiority when transforming a strident, domineering male into a docile, soft nonentity.

Mark had been watching Thi closely throughout the evening. He found it difficult to keep his eyes off the beautiful Eurasian. She certainly was desirable. For the moment, he could forget his frustrations with Janet when he looked at Thi's lovely body. Yes, it was about time to bed her down for the night. If she had the same idea, he had better get off the subject of the war and get on the subject of love.

The music started again, a slow number. He reached across the table and patted her hand. "How about a dance?"

"I thought you would never ask," she replied with a smile.

Close to each other on the dance floor, Mark felt her soft belly and thighs against his legs. He suddenly realized how short she was. The floor was crowded to the point where dancing was impossible, but no one seemed to mind. Even when the music stopped and couples were leaving the floor, some remained and continued their body movements. As they walked back to their table, Mark whispered, "Let's finish our drinks. It's getting close to curfew."

They drove in his jeep to Thi's apartment in Cholon. Mark had finally dropped the subject of Janet Holden and the fight in "I" Corps, but Thi could not rid herself of the hate she had for this American. She watched his face as he drove the jeep and thought of what a pleasure it would be to kill him. If she ever had that honor, she hoped that she would be able to look into his eyes to see that expression of incredulous disbelief in the split second when he realized that he was dying by her hand.

Her little flat was very uncomfortable compared to the coolness of the air-conditioned club, but they didn't mind. They made drinks. Mark made a rather clumsy pass, and Thi accepted it. They kissed for a long time in the close, sticky night air.

The thought came back to her that she probably could get away with killing him. She remembered Ahn's instructions of months ago: "If, for any reason, it becomes necessary for the good of the cause to liquidate someone not scheduled for termination, contact me as soon after the act as possible. The organization has means of disposing of bodies."

She could make up a good reason. She could discover that Buckley had inside information on the "Dragon Lady" and was questioning her closely. Any number of reasons. She also felt that she could withstand scrutiny by the police or an American investigating team, if it came to that, claiming that they had said good night and he had driven off. The police couldn't prove otherwise.

At present, her hatred was strong enough to allow her, if given the chance, to perform the act without a qualm. This was not wild, emotional hatred that produced irrational action. No, it was deep-seated loathing that motivated a contrived act of revenge.

She finished her drink and granted Mark's request to remove his coat. When he had laid it across the chair she came to him, removed his tie, and unbuttoned his shirt. He had perspired through it.

"My, you are wet. Here, remove it and I will give you a towel."

She unbuttoned the cuffs and pulled the shirt from his trousers. Carefully she hung it over a wooden chair to dry and went to the bathroom for a towel. He followed her as far as the bedroom, and then waited there for her return. It became obvious to Mark that Thi had the same idea that he did when she returned with the towel and began wiping off his chest, back, and arms.

"It's getting late, Cô Thi. I think I should plan on staying here–that is, if it's okay with you."

"But of course it's okay," she laughed as she dropped the towel and allowed him to hold her close.

Do I want this of him? I find him despicable, yet I'm very much attracted to him. When I walked through the bedroom, I decided to kill him. I even saw myself in the act, using my very sharp steel letter opener with the ornate jade handle, on the dresser. I planned to insert the blade just below the center of the breastbone and thrust up into the heart, as Ahn explained to me once during training. Now, in his arms with my head on his chest, I can hear his heart pounding!

With his arms about her, Mark's hands were slowly undoing the hooks and zipper on the back of her dress. She allowed him to remove the dress from her shoulders and pull it down over her black nylon pants. Her full breasts strained behind the tight brassiere. He reached to remove it and then, naked to the waist, she stood close to him. She gave a little shudder when Mark pulled her soft body against his. It would be difficult to carry out her plan after this.

Suddenly she knew what she would do. She would let him decide his own fate! Slowly she worked his body until she was leaning against the dresser. The scar would determine if he lived or died. With her right hand, she felt for the letter opener. With her left, she deliberately lifted her hair, exposing her cheek and the red jagged crescent. Her eyes watched his expression intently, ready to detect the slightest flicker of rejection. For an anxious moment, she waited.

Mark was not concerned with the small, tiny disfiguration that the girl, for some reason, felt she must show him. He leaned down and kissed the scar. Thi was at once thrilled and disappointed. Her hand shook as she carefully returned the weapon to the dresser. He picked her up and crossed the room to the bed.

Later, for the first of several times that night, she realized she was not sorry at all for her choice.

Chapter V

SEPTEMBER

E lection Day in Saigon broke clear and hot.

The sky was a dark robin's egg blue, and a brisk breeze ruffled and pulled at the panels of the women's *ao dai*s as they walked through the city to the voting polls. In the background, over the usual rumble of the traffic, truck-borne loudspeakers exhorted the people to get out and vote for one of the hundreds of candidates for the senate and their choice of the several presidential tickets.

From the beginning of that day, it was obvious that the people were going to speak and speak strongly.

History would judge whether they had spoken correctly. In spite of the terror campaign conducted by the VC and the NLF, the people were not intimidated. The bombings, shootings, kidnappings, and un- provoked terror of the last four months had intensified to an unbelievable crescendo during the last week in August. The VC plan for Election Day was a bombardment of the city with 57 mm recoilless rifle fire. However, a miscalculation in plans spared the city this finale of terror. Untrained VC allies had brought up the wrong caliber of ammunition. Consequently, the city had to contend only with the reg- ularly scheduled bombings of polling booths, random shooting into crowds, and hidden grenades aboard buses and taxis.

The election was the prime subject of discussion that morning in the art studio, as Hue and Cy were finishing breakfast. They were sitting side

199

by side on the bench at the table. Cy was reading the paper Kam had bought up with the food and Hue was trying to associate the printed English with what Cy was reading aloud. He could follow the headlines, which had only necessary words. The tight paragraphs with complete English sentences lost Hue.

"Large Turnout Hoped For in Election Today," read Cy as Hue traced each word of the headline with his finger.

Cy paused to bite into a peeled mango, and then proceeded to read aloud the whole article. Hue lost interest in the words that followed and turned to the food before him.

"Remember, today is your day to tell those mothers off. If everybody vote, everybody be equal–got it?"

He turned again to the article, but even quotations from Ambassador Newell Osborne lost Cy's interest.

Kam sat in the open window and watched the two men. Her thoughts were far from the election. She wondered if her brother, so small, so seemingly insignificant beside the big black man, knew about the affair she was having with Cy. She had worried about it for some time now. At first, she did not feel that Cy would be a good enough actor to carry off the deception. Was he able to continue his activities at night with Hue after he had been with her at the noon rest time, or earlier in the evening when Hue was away? This was something she could never bring herself to talk to Cy about, and he never discussed his and Hue's relationship with her.

Cy finished his mango and licked his fingers, then ran his tongue around his lips. The fruit had been very ripe and some of the juice had dribbled down his chin to his chest.

"Cy wants more mango," said Hue to his sister in Vietnamese. The girl smiled and went down to the kitchen for more fruit. When she had left the studio, Hue leaned toward Cy and kissed away the river of juice, starting with Cy's chest and working up to his lips. Startled at this unexpected expression of desire, Cy could not move for a moment.

"No. Not now, man," he managed to say as Hue finished and resumed his seat. "Why you go and do a thing like that?"

Hue looked directly into Cy's eyes. His small fingers grasped the huge black hand of the American.

"Maybe last chance Hue have to do. Cy, you still love Hue?"

"Why, sure. You know I do. Didn't I prove it last night?"

He returned Hue's gaze and saw tears in his eyes. A warning flashed in Cy's mind. He had to be careful now, very careful. He put his big arm about the little body and gently pulled Hue toward him.

"What's got into you, man? What you tryin' to tell me?"

"Hue not tell yet. Maybe tomorrow. Maybe next day, Hue tell."

"Well, how about Hue? You still love Cy?"

Hue smiled up at Cy. His tears had made his eyes red. "Oh, yes. Hue always love Cy."

Cy sensed an uncertainty and decided to press his advantage. "You not cheatin' on ole Cy, are ya?"

Hue looked troubled. He did not speak. Again, Cy changed his mind. Evidently, the subject was too painful for Hue to discuss further.

"Cy always love Hue. Hue teach Cy all 'bout painting, 'bout mixing paint, 'bout colors. Hue number one artist!"

Cy got up from the table and crossed to his latest picture. He looked at the work critically. It was better—more professional. He was saying what he wanted to say more subtly, but still with power and a quieter depth of meaning.

Hue joined him, smiling as he looked at the picture.

"Cy very grateful of Hue. Cy thank him for his help. Cy want stay here very much, work, learn more from Hue."

"Okay, okay! Cy stay. All time stay, okay."

Kam, who had quietly returned with the mango, paused at the door of the studio so as not to intrude upon what she knew to be a very personal encounter between the two men. However, as with most oriental women, it was her nature to eavesdrop, and she had heard most of the conversation. Now she felt it was proper to make her presence known.

"More fruit?" she asked, as if ignorant of the words between the two. She smiled, but in her heart, Hue's words troubled her. She feared that there would soon be bad times for them all.

Ψ   Ψ   Ψ

When Bu and Mai Lei returned from the polls, Bu turned on the radio to hear the commentary.

He was still full of exhilaration, excitement, and surprise from the crowds around the polls. It seemed like a very large turnout, in spite of the VC's terror.

While he had lingered, waiting for Mai Lei to vote, he had talked to many people. Somehow, everyone was friendly, interested enough in this election to converse easily and honestly with others. He listened to a young man's transistor radio—government warnings to vote promptly, and not to linger about the polling places, as there had already been widespread bombings at several voting places throughout the city. Nevertheless, for some reason, as if drawn by a mutual camaraderie, the people felt it was more important to show their determination to vote than to show fear of enemy retribution.

Now, as Bu sat in his chair at home and listened to the early returns, he admitted how wrong had been his judgment of his countrymen. He felt a wave of shame for the cynical opinion he had expressed to Major Bill Scott about the Vietnamese people. The unwelcome truth came to him: he did not know his countrymen at all, but he had been closer to them there at the polling booth than in years. He tried to analyze his feelings out there at the polls—a feeling of oneness, of togetherness, of defying, accomplishing something good.

It seemed almost like ... like ... patriotism?

Mai Lei came into the room and sat quietly, listening to the radio with her father. For a long time both of them were quiet. In the distance, they heard a dull explosion, followed by the whine of the ambulance sirens. Finally, the young girl turned to him.

"Father, what is it I feel? I feel ... almost like I am watching a birth."

"Perhaps we are, daughter, and perhaps not. But whatever happens now, at least we can say that for one short, bright moment in our long history, our people have caught a glimpse of liberty."

For a time he was silent. A great realization came to him. "The people," he said aloud. "The people! They are the real heroes of this election. Tell that to your Major Bill Scott!"

Ψ   Ψ   Ψ

Poli De Salle unfolded the rumpled letter for what he thought must be
the thousandth time. He smoothed out the pages before him and cursed as he read:

Sir:

Your article in *National Affairs* of May 1966 was plagiarized from
the letters of a deceased soldier, Pvt. Gene Winters, who wrote
them from Plei Ku in the winter of 1965. Although Private
Winters had written the letters to you, and in this sole sense,
they were your property, you had neither the grace nor the integrity to acknowledge their source.

Other than an introductory paragraph and several transitional
passages, the contents of your article are in the exact form and
content of Private Winters' letters. As a professional educator, I
consider your actions to be inexcusable and far beyond the
realm of good ethics. I fully intend to prosecute unless you can,
by adequate defense of your actions, convince me to do otherwise. Contact me at your earliest convenience.

Sincerely,
Stephen K. Bromfield
President
Kingstown University

Poli shuddered as he remembered the first time he had read this
letter back in the States. He had actually blacked out at his desk. He
had no idea how many minutes he had remained unconscious, but he
remembered the sunlight reflecting on the desk set and hurting his
eyes. Then slowly the sounds of the students walking outside the academic building on that bright spring day came through to him, and he
was there at his desk with the letter before him.

He could not remember Gene Winters as a student.

The man had not made any impression at all upon the professor. However, as is often the case, the professor had impressed the student. The following year Winters wrote Poli from Vietnam. The first letter had been an introductory one, which stated that Winters had been a student of his, had not agreed with the professor's thesis that democracy was an impractical form of government among emerging nations, and was going to send De Salle writings from time to time, arguing the De Salle thesis. Poli had forgotten that the letter also mentioned that Winters was going to send copies of the writings to Stephen Bromfield. Poli had tossed the letter away without even answering it. To him, it had been merely an ex-student's silly idea that would never happen in the face of a bitter war.

How surprised he had been when the next letter appeared. It had been a well-written, interesting paper. Poli had written to Winters, countering some of the points he had made, but the next paper had addressed itself to those points and, by using examples, had refuted the arguments.

In the end, there were four letters. They were outstanding work. Poli saved them because he recognized their value, but not for an instant did he agree with their content.

By chance, he learned that Gene Winters had been killed in action. Then, Poli considered using the information as his own. It made no difference to him that his own beliefs were opposite to those of Gene Winters. In early 1966, it was fashionable in government and academic circles to be optimistic about the possibility of making South Vietnam a democracy. Poli's interest was an appointment to one of the various social science advisory committees in Washington. He needed recognition. Perhaps an article, which reflected the proper attitude, would do it. He remembered the Winters letters and, with minor editing, submitted the article as his own.

After receiving that letter from Bromfield, Poli moved to see him as soon as possible. The first meeting with Bromfield had been almost too much for Poli. His attempted defense of his actions crumbled when he learned that Gene Winters was, in fact, Bromfield's nephew, and Bromfield was preparing the articles for publication under Winters' name when Poli's article appeared. Bromfield showed De Salle the letter he had been writing Winters, asking permission to use the papers, when he had heard of the young soldier's death.

Stephen Bromfield loved his nephew very much, and was brutal in his treatment of De Salle. He felt that De Salle owed it to Gene Winters to become directly involved in the Vietnam War. By being directly involved, he meant that De Salle should take at least a year's sabbatical from his post as senior professor of political science and give a year of his time in Vietnam, aiding the US and South Vietnam cause. Upon his return, De Salle was to write an article expressing his true feelings, based upon his own experiences, and to dedicate the article to Gene Winters. If De Salle agreed to these terms, the plagiarism would be buried. If De Salle did not agree or if, in fact, his performance in Vietnam came up short, Stephen Bromfield would assure the professional demise of Dr. Poli De Salle.

Although this had happened over a year ago, Poli remembered the meetings with Bromfield as though they were yesterday.

Poli's thoughts returned to the present.

God, I'm starting the fourth month of my Vietnam "sentence" and it already seems like ten years. I'm only a third of the way through. That position as member of the Advisory Committee surely wasn't worth all this. Now here it is Election Day, and these miserable slant-eyes are going out and making a mockery of the whole democratic process. How incredibly stupid the US has been to get involved over here in the first place!

Poli went to the window of his office and looked out into the crowds of people below him.

This mass is supposed to vote intelligently. And if this isn't bad enough, what will go on in the villages? The ignorant people there don't even know what democracy means. Of course, I haven't been to any villages yet. In fact, I haven't been out of Saigon yet. I know that I'll have to make a trip or two eventually in order to write some sort of authoritative article, but I don't relish the idea. Perhaps if I could travel along with the military at the same time that Mark Buckley seems always to be going up to see Janet ...

The loud thud of an explosion drew his attention to the far end of the street. He could see the police running and the crowd spreading out in all directions. In the cleared space, he spotted two people lying on the ground. They were very still; there was blood. He left the window feeling ill and returned to his desk.

"Oh God, oh God! Is this the way these people are going to express their will?"

Ψ   Ψ   Ψ

Thi awoke at nine o'clock on election morning.

This time, alone. She had been awake when Kim left her at six, but she hadn't let him know it. She loved to look at the tall Korean when he was unaware of her watching. She loved following every step of his dressing routine, because she thought him so handsome. However, if he spotted her watching he became shy, and his actions lost their natural grace which so excited her.

After Kim left her flat, she had slipped back into sleep. But now, finally awake for the rest of the day, she went over her schedule. It would be quite busy, as she had two special jobs to do before evening. Then, she had to vote. Duat insisted that all his people register and vote as good citizens. It was part of the cover.

The first job was the hardest. Dressed as a student, she and two others were to take over the microphone at a student rally at Saigon University.

She was to wave the Viet Cong flag while the men gave pro-VC speeches. Then, amid the confusion of the crowd, they were to escape through an unlocked side door, secretly opened for them. Timing and a quick change of clothing would be difficult, but they had worked out the plan well and gone over the actual ground several times.

The second job was a simple grenade drop in front of a polling booth in Cholon. The grenade was in a common clay Nuoc Man pot. It was to "fall off" the Honda as she passed by. She judged this operation to be routine. Her only concern would be the police. There was to be a diversion at the corner to draw everyone's attention ... timing again ... so important.

Thi dressed quickly. She first put on a short, American-style dress. Over this, she wore the traditional student's pleated black skirt and white blouse. She combed her hair, thinking about her date with Mark that night. Supper at the Cercle Sportif, and later, most likely, the night in her apartment. As she cleaned up her flat, she checked the scotch and the brandy.

She was looking forward to moving her operation with Mark to the No. 516 flat. Duat had told her it would be all right after the election. She wondered about Duat's remark and the possibility that he might have some plans that could prove unpleasant for Mark and for her. She had not been able to obtain information from Mark, as Duat wanted. It was because Mark did not fear discovery of their affair. Most unattached Americans were in similar situations. It was common knowledge to their associates.

Duat was not pleased with her lack of progress, but he had not expressed impatience with her. She was always careful to offer Mark as much time with her as he wished, in spite of the fact that she would rather spend her nights with Kim. Mark was quite a dynamic lover, but every time she looked at Kim, well, he was just so beautiful.

Thi went to her balcony and looked down at the crowded street below. If all of these people voted, the polls would be full in spite of their terror program. It was a shame the artillery wouldn't be available.

The wrong ammunition!

The poor fool who made that blunder must be either in agony or already dead.

Her thoughts returned to the people.

How many will vote? How many will brave the threats, and the bombings? The whole thing is stupid! It is an exercise in futility. No matter who gets the most votes, the Americans will see to it that the winners would be Thieu and Ky!

Time to go. She picked up the folded parasol that, inside, had a cleverly concealed, large Viet Cong flag. In a few minutes, she was in a cyclo, heading for Saigon University.

Cy and Kam were standing on the terrace of the studio. They stood close, each with an arm about the other. Up here, darkness meant safety and protection.

Down below on the streets there were lights and laughter, and the incessant high-pitched bark of gasoline engines. People were celebrating election night.

Cy and Kam had been to bed and had made love. Afterward they bathed each other in cool water. Now dressed, Cy was calmly smoking while Kam led him about the terrace. Occasionally she looked down at the street.

"Where Hue? He now *beaucoup* late very much."

"Yeah. It's almost curfew."

"Maybe he stay all night."

"Wish we could count on that." He squeezed her about the waist.

They had returned to the studio when they heard the distant sound of a police siren. It was a familiar sound on the Saigon streets and neither paid attention to it until it was clear that the vehicle was coming down their street. They heard it stop at the entrance to their building. Kam felt her heart miss a beat as she left Cy and hurried to the edge of the terrace to peer over the side. Two policemen got out of the jeep and hesitated just long enough to look up before they entered the building.

Kam ran to Cy. There was terror in her face as she looked up at the big black man. Cy knew exactly what he must do. Quickly, he gathered his American clothes and other belongings and put them in a cardboard beer carton. Then, with the box, he stepped onto the terrace. He reached up and slid the box onto the flat roof. Finally, he swung himself up into the darkness.

The police had come to the door and were talking to Kam, but Cy was now so far away from the living room he could not hear very much of the conversation. He could only guess what was happening below. The tone of their voices sometimes gave him an idea of what the Vietnamese were talking about in everyday conversation. He listened carefully, but he was too far away even for that. He thought of the police dragging Kam off to jail for questioning, and tried to visualize how he could protect her from any harm they might do her. Then again, it might be a black-market raid. If so, no sweat. Qui had picked up all the articles of his last haul and the place was clean. The boxes of unopened cans of beer, and the food and soft drinks that were for their own use would not cause any trouble. It was not unusual for any Vietnamese family to have a small number of illegal products in their home.

He listened intently for some sign of action or noise downstairs, but could hear nothing. A feeling of complete frustration and uselessness came over him. How inadequate he was in this position.

Finally, he knew that he had to look. Not knowing was too much for him to endure. Silently he swung down from the roof and, keeping to the shadows, descended the stairs to the main floor of the flat. There in the darkness of the lower terrace he could see the two policemen and Kam sitting about the table in the living room. There were papers spread before them and some other articles. Cy was too far away to determine what they were about, but not too far away to see tears in Kam's eyes.

Suddenly the men got up, and with a final word, they left the apartment. Kam slowly rose and made her way to the terrace. She seemed to expect Cy's presence when he stepped out of the shadows and took her in his arms.

She buried her wet face in his chest. "Hue ... Hue die."

Quietly Cy picked her up and carried her to the studio, where he laid her on the bed. As he tried to comfort her, thoughts of the consequences of Hue's death raced through his mind. He wondered if Kam could keep the apartment. He tried to remember if Hue had said it belonged to him or to both of them.

He wondered if there were other relatives who would lay claim to it. He sat upon the edge of the bed stroking her back, trying to tell her that everything would work out, but he did not sound very convincing. In a few minutes, Kam got up and dried her eyes. She seemed to pull down a blank mask and her sorrow disappeared within her.

Cy never saw her cry again.

"Kam go now get people, get men for put in ground."

Cy realized that evidently Kam had to identify the body and arrange the funeral. He wondered if she could make it back before curfew.

"Kam go now. Come back soon. Cy stay. All okay. Cy no worry. Kam back one hour. Police give paper—Kam no curfew."

209

Kam did return in an hour. Cy was waiting for her.

That night they were together in Kam's bed, both silent, both wondering what would become of them.

It was several days before Cy got the whole story of Hue's death. Qui told him that, officially, Hue was one of the victims of a terrorist bomb that exploded as he passed a polling place. Someone said that a girl had dropped the bomb off a motor scooter, but no one was sure. Several people were killed, more were injured.

Then, making sure that Kam was downstairs beyond earshot, Qui came close to Cy and whispered additional information. Hue, escaping from the wrath of a jealous lover, died by the bomb.

Qui was eager to tell the story. This man, Lan, was angry that Hue had left him for a young university student. Hue was in a bar with the student lover when Lan came in and started an argument and pulled a knife. Hue fled into the safety of the street, only to be killed by the bomb.

Qui sighed. "If Hue not caught with new and old lover at same-same time, he be okay now."

"Yeah, but what would've that jealous mother done to me? Probably called the MPs," said Cy with a shudder.

"Oh, he no know 'bout you. He think Hue all time with student."

Later that night, in the darkness of the bedroom, Cy held Kam in his arms and in quiet tones told her Qui's story.

"Poor Hue. He 'fraid long time of kill by Lan. But he escape Lan and get it by vote bomb—and he never even vote."

"You know this guy?"

"Oh yes. He sometime live here with Hue before you come."

Cy kissed Kam tenderly. In the darkness, he couldn't see the tears in her eyes.

Ψ   Ψ   Ψ

The message was urgent.

This time there was no mistaking the undertone of distrust that ran through the text. Duat read it several times. He did not like this arrogant

210

command: "You will do away with Mr. Newell Osborne before the last day of October ..."

Always before, individual assassinations had been left to Duat's discretion, in order for him to pick the time and place best suited for the safety of his people. Now the leaders of the VC were adamant. Osborne must be out of their way, and by the first day of November.

Was he really that strong a force in the Pacification Program? That important?

Duat reviewed his own knowledge of VC-projected activities from the present up to the time of Tet, the Lunar New Year celebration. He knew there was talk of a big, nationwide VC offensive during Tet, but he was skeptical.

Many times before, the North passed the word about grand offensives, but they never seemed to materialize. Somehow, the VC could never get enough weapons and people in the strategic places at the proper time. Duat was tired of always doing his part, only to wait in vain for the big attack.

Whatever the case might be, the VC now considered Newell Osborne's Hamlet Evaluation System and his Revolutionary Development Program two strong reasons for peasant loyalty. Osborne's death would do two things: first, it would be an indication to the farmers of the strength of the VC, and second, it would be a great assist in discrediting the Revolutionary Development Program. Without strong leadership, it would be impossible to keep the program going against the doubts already prevalent among other Americans, who did not understand and therefore did not value the program. The VC had no such misunderstanding about it.

Duat knew all of Newell Osborne's major movements very well. He had kept Osborne under surveillance for many months now, and Duat took pleasure in observing Osborne's promptness. He was so unlike most of the Americans in his punctuality. For official meetings, he arrived at exactly the right time. At social functions, he arrived exactly five minutes past the invited time. It seemed to be a fetish, thought Duat—and one so convenient for Duat's purposes.

If he was typical of the other USAID, diplomats, or other civilian contractors ... well ...

After checking his acquired copy of Osborne's appointment calendar, Duat decided on the reception at the Embassy of the Republic of China on September 19th as the best time and place to eliminate Newell Osborne. An opportunity to embarrass the Taiwan Government would please Hanoi's friends as well.

The planning started immediately. Duat summoned Thi. She would be perfect to do this one with her coolness and great dedication.

So, the Americans call her Dragon Lady. From their graphic comic works for children, I understand.

They do not suspect I even exist. If they did, perhaps they would call me L'Ombre Jaune, the Yellow Shadow ...

Duat's eyes lost focus as his mind turned to a long-buried memory from his youth: French pulp fiction stories of a Chinese mastermind. The Yellow Shadow had perfect control of both mind and body. Seeking world domination, he commanded super-science that bordered on black magic, including a way to cheat death. His dogged opponents, the British, never succeeded in destroying him. Duat had eagerly learned French so that he would be able to enjoy the stories.

Duat smiled. He turned and looked into a wall mirror. Yes, there was the Shadow's rounded bald head and also there were dark piercing eyes that his minions avoided.

The Yellow Shadow?

Yes? Perhaps if I could make my eyes seem a bit more hypnotic ...

No, enough of this nonsense. Let the Americans chase their Dragon Lady. This Yellow Shadow will remain unnamed.

Ψ   Ψ   Ψ

Settlement of the legal matters around Hue's death was surprisingly easy.

Hue's father, aware of his son's unstable nature, had willed the apartment to both his children as co-owners. Kam was now the sole owner.

The lack of more of Hue's paintings for sale in the kiosk was a problem now for Cy and Kam. Most sold in the second week after his death. Soon, the few remaining ones would be gone.

At first Cy tried to imitate Hue's style, but this work was mediocre at best. Cy would never be successful doing pictures that way. Consequently, he resorted more often to the black market to bring in money.

Kam thought through this situation as she sat in the kiosk with the paintings. She didn't like it. Any man working six different ID cards would be caught in a matter of time. She would rather have Cy safe in the studio, painting his impressionistic canvases, than going to the PXs to make money.

It was a quiet morning on the street. The rain had scattered most of the Americans, and they had not returned, although the sun had broken through and the street glistened with bright, steamy puddles. Despite the heat, Kam brought out the pictures from the kiosk and set up her displays again.

"Hello, good lookin', 'member me?"

"Hello, number one Korean GI. I no see you for long time."

"I busy winning war. Say, what happened your pictures? Your brother quit, go to war?"

"No. Brother killed by VC. Now no have pictures."

"Oh, too bad! Strictly for birds. I sorry."

"Come on. You buy picture. You buy this one."

"What is it?"

"What you want think it is."

"It's my stomach after beaucoup brandy!"

They both laughed. Suddenly Kim thought he would like to buy a picture. He could put it in Thi's place. He had time to run over there and put it in her apartment before he was to pick up Colonel Uhm. They bargained over the price of several paintings. After careful scrutiny of the many choices of Cy's work, he picked one called "Blues." They finally agreed upon 1500 piastres, which Kim grudgingly paid.

As Kam was wrapping the picture in cheap brown paper, Kim noticed how happy she had become.

"Who paint this picture? Who this?" He pointed to Cy's Greek trident symbol in the corner.

"My ... my ..."

"Boyfriend?"

"My uncle," stammered Kam, as she handed him the wrapped painting.

"Say, where you live now? Still up there?"

"Yes, with uncle ..."

"I come see your uncle. I say I want marry with this girl. Here, I pay 100 P for this girl!"

"That too much! Me number ten!"

"Say, how about you have supper with me some time?"

"Never happen. I busy all time."

"Too bad, baby. I know best places." He looked at his watch. "Say, I gotta go. Stay loose."

Kam watched him disappear among the now fast-filling streets. She realized that she liked him very much, and hoped he would stop by again.

Ψ Ψ Ψ

Mai Lei and Bill Scott often met at midday in a small city park a few blocks from her office to share a quick lunch.

Bill always arrived first, bringing sandwiches and soft drinks, while Mai Lei, who had less freedom at her office, came as near to twelve o'clock as she could. If there was time she stopped at a street vendor and bought some fresh fruit for their meal, but most often, she had no time to make a purchase.

On this day as she hurried across the grass toward their bench, she could see Bill waiting for her. He waved as he rose to welcome her.

"I was hoping you would call 'bout lunch today," she said with a smile as she approached.

He took her by the hand and guided her to the bench.

"I brought your favorite," he said as he took his place, separated from her by the modest lunch he had brought.

"Peanut butter with grape jelly! Thank you, Bill."

He unwrapped a sandwich and handed it and a cold orange drink to her. Conversation lagged as they concentrated on the food.

Bill obviously had something on his mind because he ate with a detached, mechanical effort, apparently ignoring the pretty girl by his side.

"What's the matter, Bill?" Mai Lei, noticing his preoccupation, had a note of worry in her voice.

Bill turned and looked directly at her, searching her face for a long moment.

"Darling, it's about us. We have got to face the future."

"Oh don't, Bill," she interrupted. "Don't start that again. You know it's impossible. My father would never allow us to think of marriage."

"That's just it, Mai Lei. I don't know it's impossible because I haven't asked your father. You won't let me talk to him."

Her voice was barely audible above the sounds of the city. "Bill, Bill, you know it's just because I love you so."

"But, darling, what makes you think he will forbid us to see each other if he should find out that we are thinking about marriage?"

"I know my father, Bill. I know how he thinks about things. He likes you as an American and as a friend. He doesn't see you as his daughter's husband. That would be too much for him to understand–too strange for his ways. It would be a problem. One that he must be rid of. To do that, he would tell me not to see you ever again."

Tears came to her eyes and she turned away so that he could not see her dry her eyes.

"I don't believe your father is that much of an old-school conformist. I know him pretty well, too. I'm willing to take a chance. How about it? Don't you think I'm worth a gamble?"

"Oh, Bill, don't joke about it. Let me think. Let me prepare him just a little then we shall see!"

It was time to leave. They silently gathered the remains of their lunch.

Mai Lei had lost her appetite. She wrapped her uneaten sandwich separately and put it in her handbag.

He pressed her arm tenderly. "Okay, darling, but don't make me wait too long. I love you so much."

She looked up into his face and gave him a faint smile.

"Try not to."

She turned away and started back to work.

He stood and watched her cross the lawn and disappear into the crowds on the sidewalk.

Ψ   Ψ   Ψ

Thi understood why it was necessary to use Chinese accomplices for the Osborne operation.

It gave a plausible reason for her and two others to be at the embassy. They were to appear as Chinese nationalists in the process of obtaining exit visas to Taiwan. The visa office was next to the stairs that led to another office area above. They had practiced for several days in an abandoned house with a floor plan somewhat similar to the Chinese Embassy. Huong would do all the talking. Dien was to stay outside and provide exit cover, as well as give the signal.

They might be capable men but, as far as Thi could see, they were not pros in this business. They were nervous, and she didn't trust them. Ahn explained that they were expendable, and then Thi understood.

They hadn't been in Xa Bui, and Thi was always dressed as Chuan when they were about. It would be up to her to see that the satchel bombs were in place and the timers set properly. Only she knew that Ahn would be on the Honda around the corner waiting for her—while Huong and Dien remained to fight off anyone who tried to interfere with their getaway.

The time envelope was eight minutes for Newell Osborne. That is, he was vulnerable for the first eight minutes after he arrived at the embassy. During that window, he would leave his car, enter the building, be met by embassy staff, and finally walk up the stairs. The bomb was lethal enough to kill anyone on the outside stairs, in the foyer, or the inside stairs. It was set to explode six minutes after the timers were set—enough time for Thi and the two Chinese to escape.

That is, if all went well.

Ψ   Ψ   Ψ

Newell Osborne left the council meeting at the US Embassy at precisely 4:15.

He found his car and Vietnamese driver waiting.

216

Next appointment at five. Damn! Too little time to go to the office and too early for that reception. I have a good mind to miss the damned thing and go back to the office.

The driver was slowly proceeding down Thong-Nhut toward the palace, awaiting instructions.

"Here. Turn down Tu Do."

Newell had decided to go to the reception, because he felt it was an important one. He would see some of the city during his forty-five-minute wait.

As the vehicle approached the park at the river end of the street, the traffic slowed to a halt. A stalled truck was ahead.

It might be a long wait.

For some time Newell stayed in the car going over work papers he had with him. The heat, however, made it difficult for him to concentrate, and he put the papers away. Then, looking out the side window, he noticed an art display a short distance up a side street. Some of the pictures looked interesting.

"Look, driver. I get out, go there." He pointed to the kiosk. "You cut around block, pick me up. Okay?"

In a second, he was out of the car and walking toward the paintings. He noticed a few of the typical "boats and paddies" pictures, but the others, the rather good impressionistic paintings, were what caught his eye.

"You like picture? That number one."

"It's very nice. *Confrontation.* American paint this?"

Kam suddenly became frightened. For a moment she could not speak.

"Who is artist? Who paint? You know?" Newell pantomimed an artist with brush in hand.

"I no know who paint," said Kam, smiling. "I no know."

"All right," replied Newell with a laugh. "How much you want for this?"

"Four thousand P."

"Four thousand P? You little robber. I should have you arrested. I will give you two thousand, and that's too much."

"Three thousand with frame."

"Two thousand and you can keep the frame." He started to walk off.

"Okay, okay," said Kam quickly. She knew she had gotten the best of the deal.

As Kam removed the cheap frame, Newell looked around. His car was waiting. He looked at his watch.

"My God, I'm going to be late. No, don't wrap it. Here's your money. I'll take the picture as it is."

He ran for the corner and placed the picture by him on the seat.

While Newell was purchasing the painting, the two Chinese men carrying school bags, and Thi, dressed as a Chinese school girl, entered the embassy. The weight of the bags suggested that they held only school books.

Although Newell Osborne had met her at the reception for the Australians several months ago, Thi was confident that her disguise and the different surroundings would minimize any chance of recognition.

The trio entered the building and at first glanced about as if uncertain of their destination. Finally, the men placed their satchels in the corner at the foot of the stairs and told Thi to wait there with them.

The two then went to the office to inquire about the visas. They took forms to fill out, and it was at this time that Dien said he was going outside to check on their motor scooters.

Thi looked at her watch. It was exactly five minutes past the hour. Dien's whistle announcing Osborne's arrival should sound now. She listened intently. She glanced at the satchels. The two strings that controlled the timers were visible. A minute and thirty seconds had passed.

Osborne was late! Suddenly she heard the shrill signal—or did she? She looked up and saw Chuong leave the little office. She pulled the strings that armed the device and followed him out of the door. As she did so, she brushed past an American speaking to a staff member at the foot of the stairs. Was it Osborne? She did not dare to look, but continued out of the building. Chuong and Dien were waiting for her, and they started to walk briskly down the street.

"Stop them!" cried someone from the embassy.

218

Thi glanced back and saw the embassy staff member racing toward them. She broke into a run and did not stop, although her two companions drew pistols and turned and fired. She heard the shots as she turned the corner. Suddenly there was a terrific explosion. She saw Ahn ahead of her with the Honda's engine running. People were coming toward her now, dashing to the scene of the explosion. She jumped on the back of the Honda and held tightly to Ahn. They were away.

The explosion met Newell Osborne as his car turned onto Nguyen Hue. The shockwaves shook the car. Ahead he could see debris flying out of the black smoke, which poured from the Chinese Embassy. The driver stopped, and for a moment, Newell waited to see if he could be of any assistance, but the police arrived almost immediately and put a cordon around the building, so there was nothing for him to do but return to his office.

As the car made its way through the traffic, Newell looked down at the picture.

"I'm not sure you're art," he said aloud, "but you were a real life saver for me."

Chapter VI

OCTOBER

E veryone wanted to see the painting that saved Newell Osborne's
life.

His story about the art with the intriguing Ψ signature quickly made
the rounds of the American community. Most of the people in MACV
Headquarters made some pretext for dropping by Newell's office to see it.

Newell had placed the picture above the couch in his office, and often during the day he found himself studying it, fascinated by the use
of color and the rather unconventional composition.

Finally, the number of visitors became so distracting that Newell
had the picture hung in the outer office. Mark Buckley made a sign
under it reading, "This is it! Admire it and get back to work!"

Several people with interests deeper than those who had merely
heard Newell's story evaluated the picture as an artistic effort. Most of
them gave the painting high marks, and thought they would like to
purchase one by the same artist.

Remembering the pretty girl who had sold him the picture, Newell
felt he would like to help her. He made a note to revisit the little kiosk
and tell her to raise her prices on the pictures painted by Ψ, whoever
he was. He thought of this again, when Mark brought in some papers
ready for signature.

"I wish we could charge admission to see your painting. I think we
could all retire on the profits."

"You know, Mark, I was just thinking about that little girl who sold it to me. I think she unknowingly is about to have a run on those paintings. Don't you think we should tell her to get ready for a wave of brisk business, or at least to raise her prices?"

"Well, sir, wouldn't the eggheads down the hall call that 'fostering inflation'? You know Premier Ky won't have that!"

They both laughed, but Osborne became thoughtful again.

"I really ought to go by there and at least thank her."

"Say, I'm heading for JUSPAO, this afternoon. Why don't I give her your message—after I buy a 'Psi' for myself, of course!"

"What a thief you turned out to be!" said Newell, laughing.

"No, I won't buy one. I'm no art fancier, but I will pass on a message for you."

"Here. I will write one. I have a strong hunch that the artist is American or English or someone with an American or English education."

He took a piece of official paper and wrote:

Dear Miss:

Thank you for saving my life the other day. Because I stopped to buy *Confrontation* from you, I was late for an appointment at the Chinese Embassy, and missed an explosion.

Many people have admired my painting and have asked where they may purchase one like it. Therefore, you should have many customers soon. I hope you have lots of business!

Sincerely, Newell Osborne
Dep. Ambassador for CORDS

He placed the letter in an envelope and handed it to Mark.

Ψ   Ψ   Ψ

It was a typical American cocktail party given by Americans for Americans.

This one was to celebrate the successful installation of the computer at MACV Headquarters. Most of the IBM people were there, and a good turnout from the US Embassy, JUSPAO, and USAID balanced the large military contingent.

The plants and trees in the central courtyard of the Continental Hotel sported several additional strings of colored lights for this party. The hotel had added three large serving bars.

Newell Osborne was not present, but his story about buying the picture and escaping the explosion was retold, repeatedly. Most of the guests had seen the painting, and several had tried to buy one by "Psi," as the symbol was now commonly called.

"Don't waste your time going to the kiosk looking for a Psi," one of the American women said to a group of officers. "It's been closed every afternoon for the last week. The people in the shop next to it always say the girl will be back tomorrow, but she hasn't been."

"She's probably Psi, and is busy at home producing more masterpieces to sell to gullible Americans!"

"I wonder who Psi really is!"

"The whole city is wondering. Did you read that article in the News today? There are several theories. One is that Psi is a high-ranking member of the embassy who's sneaking off to Vung Tau to RDV with a beautiful Cô, and painting between wild love orgies."

"Painting or panting?"

"Sounds like fun. Let's all become artists."

"I like the theory that Psi is that American nurse who went AWOL and is living with a Vietnamese colonel in a love-nest studio behind the Buddhist temple on Le-Loi."

"Well, I think you real art buffs ought to be able to figure out from the paintings an awful lot about Psi. You know, the influence on the work by what schools of painting, the power of the brush strokes, the ..."

"Just what is an art buff?"

"You know, silly; someone who has posed for a picture in the buff!"

"Well, that lets me out. I wanted to, but no one would paint me."

"You didn't pay them enough!"

Brandy Masters listened to this conversation in bemused silence.

I wonder if anyone here has ever been to Vũng Tàu—or even out of Saigon, for that matter. Most of the USAID parties are so dull I can't stand them. I wish Poli hadn't insisted on bringing me to this mess. He promised that it wasn't strictly USAID but it's just as bad. Where the hell is Poli now? Probably at the bar. He never seems very far away from one now, ever since the election. When he drinks too much, he's so useless in bed.

What would these people do if they knew I had a Psi! And what's more, if they knew I bought it several months ago, before the Osborne incident. Well, it might liven things up.

"Of course, I haven't seen Ambassador Osborne's Psi, but I like the one I bought several months ago. It's a ..."

"You mean you actually own one?"

All conversation stopped in the ring of men and women. Several of the men laughed. The women, already envious of Brandy's stunning figure and long blond hair, quietly wondered how she could have had enough sense to buy such a picture.

Brandy waited to observe the reaction, and then replied, "Of course, I don't know if I have it hung upside down or not, but it looks good."

Everyone laughed, but the young man on her right said, "Well, I'm pretty good at distinguishing tops from bottoms. Why don't we go and see your picture? I may be of some help. And by the way, I'm Bill Scott."

"How do you do, Bill? I am Brandy. Brandy Masters."

For a fleeting moment, there was a stunned look in Bill's eye. Brandy caught it.

Here's someone whose memory extends beyond last May.

Forcing a smile, she looked directly at him. "When will you be over, Bill?"

"Well, perhaps after the party we could see it. How about it, Cô Lei, would you like to see her picture?"

The young Vietnamese girl smiled and said it would probably be too late, but perhaps they could arrange it some other evening.

A few moments later, Bill excused himself from the group, and he and Mai Lei crossed the courtyard to another, smaller gathering. Brandy followed them with her eyes.

This guy Scott is going to tell somebody that Brandy Masters is alive and well and living in Saigon, attending this very cocktail party. I wonder ...

It was fairly dark in the corner where Bill Scott was heading, and Brandy had difficulty in distinguishing the various people. She followed Bill a little way for a better look at the faces.

My God. It's Mark—Mark Buckley.

Instantly she turned and joined another group of guests.

Mark took Bill's whispered message coolly. His eyes searched the courtyard.

He turned to Janet Holden and said, "Had enough of this? How about going to the Mayfair for a bowl of French onion soup? It's the best in Saigon."

Janet looked up at Mark. She couldn't help the warmth she felt when she looked at him.

I wonder if I have a right to have such a warm feeling toward this guy whenever I look at him. Newell insisted on this three-day trip to Saigon. I put it off as long as possible because I can't trust myself with Mark. My plans to leave the highlands while Mark was on a trip to the Delta sure didn't work out. How would I know his trip was cancelled?

"I'd love some soup ... how about Bill and Mai Lei joining us?"

Mark looked at Bill. "How about it?"

Bill was hesitant, but Mai Lei seemed anxious to leave the party. "It would be very nice," she said, smiling.

After thanking their hosts, the four friends walked to the end of the courtyard. Mark felt eyes upon him. When he reached the open lobby, he turned and looked back at the crowd. He couldn't miss her. Instantly their gazes met. Brandy, now caught, stared wide-eyed at Mark before she glanced away.

The Mayfair restaurant, a short walk from the Continental, seated fifty people at the most. A few framed French prints on the wall gave the place some vague resemblance of a fading Gallic past. It boasted one long, narrow aisle, tables for four on one side, and tables for two on the other. A very small bar occupied the left rear of the room.

Mimi sat on one of the three bar stools, overseeing the clientele.

Half-French, half-Vietnamese, and attractively plump, Mimi had been raised by the French owners of the Mayfair. Now she was one of the Vietnamese staff that had taken over when the owners returned to their homeland. The original chef had taught his Vietnamese apprentices well, but over the years, a slight oriental flavor had crept into the once-pure Gallic cuisine. Most Americans found this a delightful variation, and Mayfair was one of the most popular bistros in Saigon.

Mark led his group into the small room, met by friendly Mimi, who had left her bar stool to welcome the newcomers. There was a table available and they took it.

Across the narrow room, Kim watched Mark at the table. Something about the big American reminded him of a GI he had known many years ago as a young boy, during the Korean War. The longer he watched Mark, the more he felt that he must be the same man.

"What are you looking at?" Thi, facing Kim, could not see what interested him so much.

"American man came in with three people. Think I know him *boo koo* years ago in my country. If he's the same, he's some pretty great guy. I was little boy. It was very cold. He put me in his jeep with many blankets, gave me food. I stay with his outfit over two years. Then pow! He get it and go to hospital.

"What's his name? Buck ... Buckley!"

"Buckley?" Thi couldn't help saying it. She looked around to see Mark staring at her.

Kim jumped to his feet and walked over to Mark's table.

"Captain Buckley, sir. You remember me, Kim, your houseboy?"

For a moment, Mark, very surprised to see Thi, could not concentrate on the big Korean, but finally he dragged his mind back to Inchon in 1951, and the little boy he had picked up cold and hungry.

"You can't be little Kim!"

"Yes, yes sir. It is I, little Kim." He held his large hand down low to show his height so many years ago.

"Kim, Kim! My God! I've wondered for years what happened to you. Now look at you!"

226

He left his chair and stood next to the Korean.

"Why, look how tall you are now!"

He embraced the big Korean, and then stood off to look into his face.

"Must have been C-rations you feed me. Right, Captain? You still captain?"

"No, I finally made lieutenant colonel."

"Oh, you have battalion now?"

"No. Wish I did. I'm out at MACV. On the staff."

"I'm corporal. I drive Colonel Uhm."

"Good for you, Kim. That's great. Look, I want you to meet my friends. This is Kim, my houseboy, when he was young. This is Janet Holden, Mai Lei, and Major Bill Scott."

Kim shook hands vigorously with all of the people at the table, then said, "I want you meet my girl friend. I get her."

He went to bring back Thi.

Thi had caught a glimpse of Janet Holden, and purple, hot jealousy was consuming her. By the time Kim returned to the table, she was fighting a monumental rage that threatened to engulf her, in spite of her efforts to cover her feelings.

Kim, overjoyed to find the man who had been both father and mother to him so many years ago, was oblivious to Thi's feelings.

"Come, Thi. He's same man. Come meet him and his friends. He's number one. Great, I tell you."

Thi turned on Kim with eyes blazing.

"Let me alone, you fool. I'm not going over there. I'm leaving here. Now!"

Kim, being a true Korean male, was not going to allow any woman of his to talk to him that way, no matter what her nationality. His happy, carefree manner immediately turned to anger; he grabbed Thi's arm in a hold that made her wince. He did not release the pressure.

Thi thought that her arm would break. The pain—the searing pain—became her paramount feeling, pushing the jealousy and hatred back into her subconscious. Tears came to her eyes. She rose to her feet.

"Yes. Yes, Kim. I will come," she gasped.

Kim released her arm and gave her a moment to compose herself. Now, all smiles, he returned to Mark's table, Thi following, her eyes downcast.

She heard Kim say, "I want you to meet my girl friend, Cô Thi."

Ready for them now, she raised her head with a broad smile. "It's nice to see you again, Madame Holden, Cô Lei, Colonel Buckley, Major Scott."

She turned to Kim. "I have had the pleasure of meeting your friends before."

Her eyes turned to Janet. "Colonel Buckley has told me about your wonderful project in Buon Ho. He speaks of you often. Now, if you will excuse me, I must leave. I have a terrible headache. Kim, please stay. I know you have much to talk about with your old friend."

She gave them each another friendly glance before she left the table and hurried out into the street.

Kim made no effort to stop Thi or to escort her out. As if not hearing the protests of the Americans he merely smiled and looked raptly at Mark. For the moment, Thi did not exist.

"How about joining us? Here, pull up a chair," said Mark, taking a chair from a vacant table and putting it next to him.

"Shouldn't you go with Cô Thi?" asked Janet. She felt somehow that Kim's love life might be in trouble if he did not.

"She go home. I go there later. By morning she be okay."

Mark and Bill looked at each other, and neither could help smiling. It became obvious to Mark that he was not Thi's only lover. He was amused that his rival was this boy whom, he remembered fondly, he had taught how to brush his teeth and bathe in the field, sometimes under fire.

While Mark's party finished their soup, he and Kim revived memories. Finally, Kim said good night, but not before he and Mark had agreed to meet at the Victory restaurant for supper the following night.

As they watched Kim leave the restaurant, Janet said, "You must have been a good papa, Mark. He is a fine young man."

Ψ   Ψ   Ψ

Kam was mystified and more than a little frightened.

Mark Buckley explained Newell Osborne's note as best he could, and added that Mr. Osborne said, "Thank you."

Kam still was worried. Consequently, after Mark left the kiosk, she closed it for the day and went home to have Cy read the note.

Cy was at first surprised and puzzled.

I know all about Osborne. There's not a day when he's not in the News or the Saigon Post, one or the other. How the hell am I supposed to feel good about this big guy in the crackers' camp when they's such sons a bitches? Why would a guy this high up do somethin' nice to a little Cô off the street? Wonder if it's got strings attached.

But Cy knew that if Kam was to be calmed down, he had to convince her that Osborne was a good man and the letter would mean no harm to them.

"Mr. Osborne good man?" she asked Cy for the thousandth time. Her eyes were wide with uneasy fear.

Cy paused. This time he had to answer. He didn't want to give an unqualified yes or no, but he realized that any other answer would continue her fears.

Finally, reluctantly, he admitted that Mr. Osborne must be a good man, because his programs all seemed designed to help the Vietnamese people to live better.

It was Kam who brought to Cy's attention the fact that Mr. Osborne was trying to help them by indicating they should raise the prices on the paintings. In reading the note, Cy had not been as much impressed about the money as he was about the possibility of becoming successful as a painter. He wondered if Newell Osborne's prediction would come true. Whatever the case, it sure wouldn't hurt to be ready. As soon as he could, he prepared four canvases for painting, all set up at different locations in the studio.

It was the next morning that Cy read the first article about himself in the paper. A bold headline asked, "Who is Psi?"

The story recounted Ambassador Osborne's purchase of the picture, the subsequent bombing of the Nationalist Chinese Embassy, and the resulting popularity of the picture among the foreign community.

It mentioned that the picture vendor did not seem to know the identity of the artist, and ended with a plea to the artist to make himself known so that he could receive some justly deserved praise.

There was also an article on the same page about Newell Osborne visiting the Revolutionary Development school at Vung Tau. The item explained in detail the life of the students, their dedication to the school, and the work of the subsequent teams formed by the students for duty in the provinces of South Vietnam.

Cy's new interest in Osborne resulted in his reading every word. Although he did not like the ambassador for what he was, he began to respect him for what he was doing and, from that day, Newell Osborne became Cy's new interest. He saved every newspaper article that mentioned the ambassador, and every picture of him that appeared in the papers.

One Sunday the news did a feature on Osborne that outlined his private life and covered his career in the US Foreign Service. Cy read the account several times, learning that Osborne was a Harvard graduate, married, and the father of three boys in school back in the States.

He noted with approval that Ambassador Osborne chose not to have his wife join him in Vietnam because the US military were not allowed to have their wives in country.

On the same day that Kam received the note from Osborne, she and Cy had a long talk about what she should tell people when they asked who painted the pictures.

After discussing several alternatives, Cy said, "Since your brother got me started painting again, let's give him credit by saying 'from Hue.' People will think you mean the city, but we know you mean your brother."

Kam was delighted with this idea. She practiced several times saying, "I don't know. Pictures come from Hue. Take very long time for pictures to get here."

This statement also gave them a good reason for the lack of paintings if ever the demand exceeded the supply.

As the days passed, the little kiosk began doing brisk business with Cy's pictures. The two had taken Osborne's advice and raised the prices to five or six thousand piastres. This depended upon the size of the work or, sometimes, upon artistic quality. The curious came only to look, but there was a good chance that the twenty-five pictures ready for sale would be gone in a week or two, if business continued so well.

More articles appeared, speculating on the identity of "Psi." These were rumors resulting chiefly from cocktail party conversation. Each article, of course, brought more customers and Kam finally had to announce that no more pictures had come from Hue, but maybe next week there would be more.

Cy was ecstatic, living an ideal life, perfect in every way. He spent his days painting the impressions gleaned from his artist's vivid imagination. He knew that his work was good; it had made him famous. At first, it was frustrating for him not to be able to receive acclaim, but later talking to Qui he discovered he had achieved a certain special fame as a figure known all over Saigon—yet still unknown.

Qui normally would have shared this in many low places, but had kept his silence about Cy to the others in his circle only because of the potential for an American MP investigation if Cy was taken. The distance between Cy and Qui was too short for even the GIs to miss, in what would surely be a high-profile affair.

Soon cheap imitations of Psi originals began appearing at other art displays. Most of these were quickly spotted as frauds. The result was more publicity for the original Psi paintings.

One day a distinguished elderly Vietnamese approached Kam during a quiet moment at the kiosk. After identifying himself as Professor Loy of the *École des Arts Appliqués de Gia Đinh*, he proposed to give "Psi" a one-man show. It would be on behalf of Orphans' Relief and presented under the sponsorship of Madame Ky. Sale prices for pictures would be doubled, and Orphans' Relief would receive fifty percent of the take. Professor Loy expressed the hope that Kam would think seriously about this proposition, as he considered the work by "Psi" the most promising in Vietnam.

Finally, the old man smiled and said, "You know, Cô Kam, years ago I taught your brother. This 'Psi' is the most promising artist since Hue's early work."

Kam was exhilarated with this great chance for Cy, but she remembered how Hue had worked to be ready for his show; Cy would have to have more than twenty pictures finished before such an exhibition.

"Ông Loy, as you know these pictures are sent from Hue. As you see, there are only two left here. My other pictures are by different artist who pay me a commission. I must keep the next two or three shipments off sale until I get enough for such an exhibition as you describe. Please give me time to think. I must contact my … ah … business associate in Hue."

"Of course, Cô Kam. Please take as much time as necessary to consider this proposition. And I hope you have good luck in contacting your friends in Hue."

Professor Loy smiled and handed her his card. Then, after a slight bow, he was lost in the crowd.

Ψ   Ψ   Ψ

Bill Scott had promised Bu and Mai Lei that he would cook a real American barbecue grill dinner.

He was to bring wine, French bread, margarine, and steaks. Bu was not truly interested in an American dinner, which he had heard to be heavy and lacking in flavor. However, he was most interested in spending a whole evening with Major Scott. It was always pleasant to have Bill around to exchange ideas and to hear about the war from an American's point of view.

But today Bu had heard some disquieting news. His longstanding idol, André Maurois, was dead.

Ah, such a sadness, this fine man—gone. He is the one who let me see the Western way. How they do things. If it weren't for Maurois, I would have a bad, French-style idea of the Yankees. I wouldn't have let Mai Lei work for the Americans. Even if we were poor as street sparrows, I wouldn't have let her work there. Now Maurois is dead. What did he once write? Oh yes: "In literature as in love, we are astonished at what is chosen by others."

Bu went to his bookshelf and picked up *The Silence of Colonel Bramble*. His soft dry hands leafed through the well-worn pages.

How I enjoyed this book! How amused I was! Colonel Bramble was the first Englishman I had known. He prepared me for some delightful acquaintances with real Englishmen when I was at the Sorbonne.

"Father, would you like me to fix you some early supper so that you won't be hungry in case you do not like the American food?"

"No, daughter, that would not be fair to our friend the chef. But perhaps you should have something ready that might be prepared quickly after he leaves."

Mai Lei smiled. She had often been Bill's guest at American messes, and was familiar with American food. For this reason, she assumed her father might find it unpalatable.

The radio was loudly proclaiming the virtues of a candidate for office when Bill arrived. The national and senate elections had been a great success. There had been a large turnout of voters despite the VC's best efforts. Now, fifty days later, the lower house elections were to take place. Since such a great effort had gone into the September 3rd election, it was becoming very difficult for the government to stir up the same enthusiasm for this election, which most Vietnamese considered less important. There were so many running for the seats that some candidates appeared on radio or television almost continuously.

Bu turned off the radio as Mai Lei ushered Bill in, carrying two large paper bags.

After the bustle of bringing in the food and preparing the portable charcoal grill that Bill had brought, the three sat in the living room sipping a cool white wine.

"Oh, quite delicious. Not since France have I had wine like this," said Bu.

"I'm afraid, sir, this is American. From Northern California. A little area called the Valley of the Moon."

Bu looked surprised; quickly, Mai Lei said, "I like it very much," and smiled at Bill.

"Valley of the Moon, something to do with your Jack London as I recall," mused Bu.

Outside a sound truck barked its message, and Bill turned searchingly to Mai Lei for a translation.

"It's another one of the candidates. I will be glad when it's all over."

Bu was not following the conversation.

Suddenly he said, "Major Bill, did you know that a great man of France died today? Did you know that Andre Maurois died?"

"Why, yes. As a matter of fact, I read it in this morning's paper."

"Were you familiar with his work?" asked Bu.

"I read—let's see—*Prophets and Poets* and *Olympic*, but that's all. He is not as popular in America as he is in France, I suppose."

"It is men like Maurois who could solve the differences of thought between people in our world and his kind, more than the politicians or the soldiers. By reading Maurois, the French understand the British and the Americans the British and the Americans understand the French ..."

"Oh, but who will make the Americans understand the British?" asked Bill.

Bu laughed at Bill's joke and added, "Who will make the South Vietnamese and the NLF understand each other?"

More noise came from outside. It was another loudspeaker truck passing the house and proceeding slowly down the street.

"Oh, this election—less than two weeks away. I wish it were over, then our government would be formed and they could stop all of this shouting and get down to business," said Mai Lei with a sigh.

"That's when the shouting will really start," said Bill.

"Yes, but it will be confined to the one building which we can all avoid," added Mai Lei.

"I wonder if there will be a Dzu in the lower house elections," mused Bu, as he looked at his wine. "Remember what I told you during the national election? If anyone who was against the Thieu-Ky ticket showed real power, he would suffer. Well, look at Dzu ..."

"I read he was released from jail last week."

"Yes, but to house arrest. He is a very sick man."

"Do you think that he was guilty of illegal money transactions?"

"We are all guilty of illegal money transactions. Every time you buy a Vietnamese paper with your military payment certificates instead of piastres, you are guilty. Our president-elect should not invent 'evil reports,' but instead look for the good sides of fellow beings!"

234

"Maurois?"

"No, Buddha."

Bill smiled and picked up his glass. "Now it is time for us to go to the garden while I cook the steak."

"Is this the American way?"

"Oh yes, we all sit there and talk while I burn up the dinner. That's the way we do it at home."

Bill checked the charcoal fire. The coals were glowing red in the fading twilight. He placed the three small T-bones on the grill.

"How do you like your beef, Ông Bu?"

"I do not know. I never have had it in big chunks."

"I think you should cook Father's the way I have mine," said Mai Lei.

Bu was dumbfounded.

"All this food, all this food. There is enough meat there to feed a Vietnamese family of six for over a week."

After cooking the steaks, Bill realized that he had forgotten knives and forks. Mai Lei produced three kitchen knives, and they used chopsticks. Then they ate sitting around a low stone table in the garden by the light of a single candle.

At supper, the subject of conversation was the coming election.

"There are *beaucoup* parties," complained Mai Lei. "I cannot keep them all straight."

"There are only over a hundred candidates," joked Bill. "I don't know why you should have any trouble."

Bu laughed. "We are very new at your game of politics. It seems that almost every candidate has his own party. There are oh, so many. Perhaps when the inauguration is over and the members of both houses are in their seats, some of the smaller political units will form into larger parties."

"When will they settle on a date for the inauguration?"

Bu replied, "It was first decided that it would be November 1st, but that is the last day of the lunar month, which is not considered a very auspicious day. Premier Ky says that General Nhuyen Bao Tri has been instructed to consult the top astrologer for a better date."

"He must be fooling."

"Not completely. It is part of our culture to do things according to the phases of the moon. It results in a more tranquil life."

"Speaking of a more tranquil life, I hope you have noticed how few instances of terror have been conducted by the VC."

"Perhaps Hoang Diep—your Dragon Lady—was liquidated by one of her own bombs."

"I doubt it," declared Bill. "I think the VC came to realize after the presidential election that their activities only galvanized the people to greater solidarity and determination."

"Maybe a couple of well-placed bombs are what we need to get more interest in this election!"

In the distance, the distinctive wail of a siren hovered over the sounds of the city.

"Sounds like the demolition squad," said Bill.

The three listened again, and there was silence around the table. Bill sat watching Bu struggle to eat more of the steak.

Then he said quietly, "Ông Bu, I think now is the time for me to bring up a question which I do not think will be a surprise to you. It is the matter of my great regard for your daughter, Mai Lei. I greatly desire to make her my wife, and so … well, I am asking you now for her hand in marriage."

Mai Lei was completely surprised. Bill had not told her he had chosen this evening to talk to her father about their future. A small gasp escaped her lips as she excused herself from the table. She was rising to leave when Bill reached over and put a restraining hand on her arm.

"No, Mai Lei. We have talked it over many times. You know all my thoughts in the matter. Please stay, unless, of course, your father desires to talk with me alone."

Bu was silent for a long time.

Then he looked at his daughter and said, "Mai Lei is my only child. She has been carefully brought up in the Vietnamese way, and is not fully aware of the American way of life. I always planned that she would marry a physician or a professor and somehow we would all live happily here with her children. That is what an old man wants—to end his days quietly with his grandchildren about him. But these are unsettled times. Our countries are locked together as partners. Perhaps for many years to come. It is only natural for some young people from each country to unite. But for my family I do not know. I admire and like you very much, Major Bill Scott, but I must think. Please go now and do not return to see my daughter until I call for you by message through Mai Lei. I hope you have considered Mai Lei's future and her best interests."

Bill rose from his seat. "I promise you, sir, she will have the best of care and the most protected life that I can provide."

He looked at Mai Lei. She remained seated, tears in her eyes. Bu was very grave. He rose and offered a badly shaking hand to Bill.

Bill walked through the house and let himself out the front courtyard gate. He turned to see Mai Lei running through the house. When she reached the front door, she stopped and waved. There were still tears in her eyes, but he could see that she was smiling.

Ψ   Ψ   Ψ

Duat and Ahn studied the streets carefully.

The map covered only the area of downtown Saigon within a mile of the palace, but the scale was of such size that individual buildings were readily recognizable. It also covered a portion of the Saigon River and the canals that bordered the southern part of the city.

Duat made a simple compass of a black crayon and a piece of string and drew a circle with a half-mile radius, using the palace as center.

"That close?"

"Yes, Ahn, that close. This man is a real artist with the mortar. He has requested as short a range as possible. Then, his accuracy will be far better, as there will be less chance of winds to affect the rounds. Now, what buildings do we have within this circle?"

"How about our tailor shop on Hong-Thap-Tu?"

"Perhaps. But remember, we need a secluded place where rounds can leave the tube with little chance of being heard and have a clear path to the target. I feel that if we find the proper location, our gunner will be able to get in ten rounds of corrected fire before the police close in. We will have observers on high buildings to phone in the shots, over or short, right or left."

"That four-story house on Ton That Dam would be perfect. The mortar could be located off the third floor on the upstairs sundeck. One would have to be on the fourth floor to observe what was going on, and we would clear that."

"Yes, that has possibilities. When the young gunner arrives tomorrow, show him that house first. The other places we select should not be mentioned unless he turns this one down. If the first round falls while the car is drawing up to the building, we have a good possibility of getting our old friend Osborne and Vice President Humphrey by the third shot."

Duat circled the tiny square that symbolized the four-story house.

"If our friends like the location, move them right in the house. The present tenants must not know. Tell them the house is unsafe, and they must move out for ten days while repairs are made."

Ψ Ψ Ψ

The lower house elections on October 22nd were held without major incident.

It was so quiet election day that everyone wondered about the Viet Cong. What were they up to? The truth was that the VC had decided not to waste terror tactics on this event. Word had come from Hanoi to save harassment for some later occasion.

Bu returned from the polls in deep thought.

Every day I weigh the big question of Mai Lei's marriage to the American from both sides. Mai Lei says they wish I would go to America with them, if I let her marry. But how could I leave my country! I could not leave. Perhaps when the war is over and all is well, I could make a short visit, but not to stay.

If Major Bill and Mai Lei were to marry and go to America, I would stay in Vietnam, perhaps live with my old friend in Nha Trang. There I would teach English, French, and maybe Vietnamese to the Americans. I am too old to continue at the University anyway.

238

My daughter has been a joy to me. She has filled the void as best she could when my wife died. Now I want her to find happiness, but that is the real question. Would she find happiness in a foreign land, a foreign culture? It is not a matter to be taken lightly.

Ψ   Ψ   Ψ

Cy looked at the painting on the easel and smiled.

Then, he turned to look at a group of others and flipped through them like the pages of a large book. Since they were his best efforts, he was saving them for the show.

He turned again to the easel.

Perhaps this one wasn't quite good enough to join the paintings for his show, but it would get a fine price at the kiosk. He paused again to reconsider, carried the painting over to the waning daylight, and then placed it in half shadow. He would wait for Kam's decision. She seemed to have Hue's appreciation of what was good and not so good. He checked his watch. She should be coming in soon to start supper. He was hungry after working through lunch and the afternoon rest time.

Cy heard voices on the stairs. Kam was with someone—clearly, someone he knew because they were coming right up to the studio.

Qui. Right.

Of course. He had forgotten about the black-market run he was to make to the exchanges.

The two hurried into the studio. Kam was full of happiness, effervescent with a special joy that was contagious enough to bring smiles and laughter to the always-dead-serious Qui.

"Oh, Cy! Good news! *Beaucoup* good, good news!"

She ran to him, the bright green panels of her *ao dai* flying behind her.

Cy caught and hugged her, the sweat of his body making dark wet areas on her clothing. The big man picked her up, off the floor.

He put her down and sat down himself on the wooden bench.

"What happen, Kam? What happen to make you so happy?"

"Today I close kiosk *ti-ti*, early, go Ông Hao. He number one ...
how you say in distance see?"

"What? What you talkin 'bout?"

Qui, as excited as Kam, came over from the doorway. "Americans
call Ông Hoa 'Toothsayer.'"

"Toothsayer?"

"He look in distant time."

"Ah, soothsayer. Ông Hoa is a soothsayer!"

Kam could not contain herself. "Yes, yes. Ông Hoa number one!
He give me good news. I ask him my boy friend will be *beaucoup* great?
I no tell him boy friend paint. He say boy fren paint pictures. Paint
good pictures. Very best Saigon have show. Everyone come. All people
Saigon come. New president come with wife. High American come,
even Westy! Even your fren, Osborne!"

"He's not my friend. He don't know who I am."

But Cy was pleased, and a big smile wandered across his face.

"Hong Hoc say everyone Saigon know you and have picture of
you!"

"They may know me as Cy, but not as Ned Green—and I hope they
do have one of my pictures, but not one of me."

But Qui was musing over Kam's remarks. "Maybe Ông Hoa wrong."

"What you mean, Qui?"

"Well, your show come after 31 October, okay?"

"Yeah, it not until 15 November."

"Well, Hoa say Ambassador Osborne go show. He not go show. He
be dead."

"What you mean dead?" Cy almost shouted the words.

Both Kam and Qui, startled at Cy's reaction, stared at the black
man openmouthed, while Cy, realizing that he had frightened Qui into
denying the truth, finally brought his emotions under control before
he spoke again.

"Tell me what you know," he said quietly.

Qui had no strong reason not to tell Cy, as he knew the AWOL soldier was not in a position to take counter-action, and if he did, Qui
couldn't care less if Newell Osborne lived or died. Qui's first interest

was always his own safety, especially if it ever got back to the VC that the plot failed because he had passed on the information.

At least a bit of the story.

"I jes want to know what's goin' on, man," said Cy with a smile. "Give me all the scoop."

Qui slowly started a story constructed of what he had heard from several sources and places, but it wasn't long before Cy realized that he was holding back.

"Look, Qui, you 'n me been friends long time, see. You always tell Cy *beaucoup*. Now you not tell all you know. Cy no like that. Maybe not go PX for you no more."

Qui never looked too closely at what must be the highest level connection between his world and the Viet Cong, but always assumed there was money being made off the VC to handle certain tasks within Saigon. He could care less which side did or did not succeed. As long as he made money it was all the same to him. His point of view was shared up and down the black-market chain. But sounding as if you were in the know was a common source of pride and some things leaked within the black-market brotherhood.

Qui took delight in piecing together many threads to make a story he could tell well.

But Qui got Cy's point. Here was a direct source of his income at risk. So he blurted out more of what he had heard from his black-market associates who, in some fashion or another, knew others who worked on behalf of the VC.

The attack was to be on Independence Palace during the reception on October 31st, the evening of Inauguration Day, the day before the National Day ceremonies. All gossip agreed on that. The story was that the VC would bring their top mortar gunner into the city. They would use a picked location nearby. Observers would radio correcting information in azimuth and elevation, so that by the time he fired the third round, his mortar would be zeroed in on the palace entrance. He would fire the first round after a signal that the sedan carrying the American Vice President Hubert Humphrey, along with Ambassadors Bunker and Osborne, approached the entrance. Since the gunner would know the exact distance from the mortar location to the palace, there was a good chance that the first round would hit the car. If it did not, the corrected range would certainly bring the fire on target before the VIPs could take effective cover.

The VC had chosen a 60 mm mortar because of its accuracy and, most importantly, because ammunition was readily stolen or bought for them by their black-market connection from the ARVN. Orders had been placed. Payoffs made. Shells had been secretly stored. Word got around.

The real gem was the probable mortar location: the third-floor terrace of a house at 143 Ton That Dam Street near the old US Embassy. The terrace was out of the way of police patrols, hidden from the street. Apparently, a delivery of some sort had been made there by one of Qui's associates and that likely location had now become part of his story.

The VC needed these black-market operators inside Saigon and this weakness, again, created a small window into their operation. Fear of both the VC and of the hidden power of the organization was supposed to keep the silence. It had not, at least with Qui who had relished putting all of these scraps together in his tale to make him appear to be "in the know."

Cy listened carefully to all of this as he left the bench and crossed to his easel, picked up his palette and brush, and started to paint—an effort he hoped would cover the intensity of his feelings.

When Qui had finished, Cy casually discussed the real value of his paintings to bury the importance of the coming assassination attempts among the trivia of gossip. Qui finally turned to the subject of tomorrow's PX purchases and, after leaving the military currency and shopping list, he left.

Kam, knowing Cy, was apprehensive and conflicted about the fate of Newell Osborne. To allay her fears, Cy joked about the "stupid plot" and told her it was a poor way to try killing anyone.

Slowly, Kam forgot about the VC plan, but had she looked closely at the picture Cy was working on while talking with Qui, she would have discovered the words "143 Ton That Dam" were painted in tiny letters on the canvas.

Ψ   Ψ   Ψ

October 31st was nearing before Cy decided what he would do.

If I do anything, I must do it alone ... One thing is certain: I don't give a shit about Humphrey or Bunker. But Osborne is something else.

Cy's decision on whether or not to take action was partly based on Osborne's comments about his art and on the help he had given to Kam. The primary motivation came from Cy's gradual realization that Osborne's Refugee and Revolutionary Development programs were as important to a positive future of Vietnam as was the outcome of the actual war. For these reasons, he also felt Osborne must not die.

Cy did not know much about his own nation's history. But, he had somehow made the comparison of the South Vietnamese peasants to his own people during the American Civil War, but he had reversed the geographic positions of the two opposing forces. Thus, a victory for North Vietnam would be like a victory for the South, extending the slavery of his people—people he had come to know like Hue, Qui, and Kam. This he saw with great clarity. His vivid imagination spun a complete full-color story of future events blended with his own version of America's past.

Newell Osborne was a sort of Abraham Lincoln to Cy—almost a modern Lincoln with a reconstruction program capable of bringing real freedom and equality to all the people in the South, not just to the privileged classes.

There. It's necessary for old Cy to do something to save Newell Osborne. An whatever plan I decide to follow gotta be kept completely secret—even from Kam. I know she would protect me, but if I fuck this 'n up she ain't gonna suffer for it—only me.

He racked his brain for some possible line of action. He ruled out anonymous letters to the local police. He had read that they received thousands of such letters a day. Since most of them proved to be false, many being planted by the Viet Cong, the policy had been not to follow up on any of them, even ones written in English.

Next, he considered contacting Newell Osborne directly, but Cy knew that after the Chinese Embassy bombing, Osborne would be well protected. He would only be wagering his own freedom against long odds that he would ever get to Osborne anyway. A bad bet.

His final thought was to turn himself in to the military police and tell his story. But would he reach anyone high enough to listen to him? Who would lend credence to some crazy story told by a black deserter?

For two days, he struggled alone with his problem. Then one morning he picked up the Saigon News and an article caught his eye—716th MPs Guard vs. Terrorism.

He read about the battalion whose beat was Saigon. There were several paragraphs about their duties and past operations. In addition, there was a description of the battalion commander, Lieutenant Colonel Morgan D. Row.

That was it! Why not come into headquarters, not as a deserter, but as the best-turned-out MP sergeant in Saigon, up from Can Tho with a special message for LTC Row. Once he got in to see him, he could convince him that the mortar attack on the palace was real, and that at least it would be imperative to keep the house at 143 Ton That Dam under surveillance. He might even be able—in the confusion of headquarters activities—to walk out and disappear again.

Have to play that part by ear.

Whatever the outcome, he was prepared to give himself up and establish his true identity, if it came down to that, to convince the colonel that he was telling the truth.

That afternoon he asked Qui to come up with a complete MP sergeant's kit and a corresponding ID card. Cy created a story for Qui that he had almost been recognized during his last PX trip, and thought the PX guards would less closely check him if he appeared for a while as an MP.

Qui bought the idea without a question. Cy hoped Qui's always unnamed black-market bosses would do the same.

In a few days, Qui started delivering portions of the uniform. Cy worked hard on the brass and leather, while Kam washed and pressed the trousers and shirt.

When Qui dropped off the white helmet, Cy tried on the whole uniform. He looked at his reflection in the studio mirror and, after a careful inspection, he decided he was well satisfied with the result.

"You pretty sharp GI," said Qui, watching. "Everything fit number one!"

"This is a pretty good .45 you get. This any problem?" asked Cy.

"No. No problem. Can get any American stuff you want."

Suddenly Cy had an idea. "How 'bout ammo?"

"No sweat, GI. You see, I bring you two clips .45 auto."

"No, I mean like grenades—maybe other stuff."

Cy moved over to the studio door to see if Kam was about.

No.

Returning, he spoke to Qui, very quietly. "You see, I can make number one lamp as surprise for Kam out of mortar shell. I number one mortar man. I take live mortar shell, remove all explosive, get wire, light bulb, make very pretty."

"That number ten. Go bang. No more Cy, no more Kam, no more black market!"

"No sweat, Qui. I expert on shells. I study long time in army. Special Forces. No go bang. How about you get me one but you make secret, okay? Besides, if you bring two, have extra one if I make mistake!"

Both men laughed and Qui promised to bring him a mortar round in a day or two. Now he had a story for his pals about a crazy American who made lamps from explosives.

Cy, now on a new course of action, felt he had a greater chance of success. Even better, this did not require him to give up his freedom.

In the following mornings, while Kam was working at the kiosk, and he was supposedly painting, Cy would don civilian clothing and walk about Saigon to reconnoiter the area near the old US Embassy. He especially checked the vicinity of 143 Ton That Dam.

Ψ   Ψ   Ψ

Janet Holden lay in her bed, alone, sleepless, staring into the darkness.

Why did I accept Mark's invitation to come to Saigon for the Inauguration and the National Day ceremonies? Perhaps it was because I've known for a long time that I must solve the problem of Ted, Mark, and me before I saw Mark again. But I know I could never bring myself to the point of facing this problem. This date in Saigon tomorrow is a definite deadline and there is no way to turn away from it. I must choose.

She finally resolved to have it out with herself as she was preparing for bed that evening. Then, she admitted to herself that she had fallen in love with Mark Buckley.

Hours later, one more time, she restlessly turned to the wall as she again reviewed the situation. Her thoughts centered on Ted and the wonderful life they had together.

What a perfect team we were! He needed my stability. My meat and potatoes, every day, solid strength that complemented so perfectly his mercurial, brilliant, but not always practical mind. I knew I was important to him. I developed his fuzzy ideas into workable theories, and I loved the fact that he knew and acknowledged this strength. We were ... yes, we! We were a perfect team— mutually supporting and mutually dependent. This team must continue to function—it's our very life.

Mark, on the other hand, is from a different world. There could be no mutually supporting team with his strength—he and he alone runs the show. No wife of Mark's could ever achieve equal status with him on a professional level. The military is, of course, not open to such an arrangement and in the second place, Mark's personality would never allow it. To be Mark's wife would mean being totally subservient to him. I wonder if I could ever exist in such an environment.

Yet Ted might be dead and our perfect team, gone. This is the hard point of fact that, in the past, I've never been able to face. It would mean making one of two hard choices: to carry on as a second-rate anthropologist without Ted, always lacking the originality he supplied—or to become Mark's wife and possible mother of his children.

Neither of these prospects offers a completely satisfying existence. My future happiness depends wholly on Ted. He must be alive. He must return.

She stared into the darkness, thinking about her situation, balancing Mark's great personal magnetism against a vision of day-by-day life with him as a soldier's wife. Her mind wandered to some of the other wives of soldiers she knew. They seemed happy enough when they were with their men. But what about the others? Those whose lot was similar to hers—the wives whose husbands were prisoners of war or missing in action.

What do they do when they finally face the stark, grim fact that their men are in the limbo of the un-dead, yet un-alive? Do they stand fast, never giving up hope and never yielding to temptation, or do they allow themselves an occasional romantic interlude to help ease the loneliness? Most of these women have children to bring up—children who need a father. Perhaps it would be better for them to write off the father as soon as possible and find a new one while it was still possible to attract a man.

God, what a thought! What a horrible position to be in. It makes my problem seem tiny in comparison. I'm at least close to where Ted vanished. I'm working in the environment of the war, while the other women are ten thousand miles away, living in an apathetic, alien society, just waiting, each day listening to the news media tell them that their men were stupid and immoral to fight and perhaps die in this wasteful war.

She dismissed these thoughts and then turned her mind to Mark.

If only he had proven to be a mean or undesirable person! If only he had not been so sweet and so interesting. If only he had not proved to be so—well, so damned sexy.

A smile came to her lips. She closed her eyes and ran her hands down the front of her thighs. Languidly, she stretched and rolled over on her side.

Steady, Janet. That's not like you; you with your PhD, fantasizing all over the place!

She dozed, and in a half-sleep envisioned herself in a long-established, happy relationship with Mark. They are together in bed, awaking on a bright, sunny morning.

Suddenly Ted appears at the bedroom door.

He stumbles into the room, dirty, thin, sick, and looks at her with hollow, accusing eyes, then turns and leaves. She turns to Mark, who looks at her with the same hollow, accusing eyes and follows Ted out of the room.

With a little cry Janet opened her eyes and, wide awake, came to the realization that there could never be any sort of temporary arrangement with Mark. It was up to her to see that none ever developed. She would have to make Mark understand. She would wait with the others. She would wait for Ted.

Sleep finally came to her—but she knew that she had solved every-thing, yet she had solved nothing.

Morning came. As she prepared for the trip to Saigon, Janet re-viewed her final resolve of last evening. She was now determined to face up to the situation with Mark. He must promise not to see her for a while. They both must agree that their relationship would not move forward until Ted was proved to be … yes, until Ted was proved to be dead. She reminded herself of this that afternoon as the helicopter brought her toward Saigon.

Mark, ignorant of Janet's decision, was overjoyed with her visit. He was at the landing pad waiting for her. As soon as the Huey touched down he rushed, under the whirling blades, to gather her into his arms, and kissed her passionately.

Then, he swung her through two complete turns before her protes-tations managed to get through to him. Reluctantly, he put her down.

"Mark, you fool! These people will think we are married or some-thing!"

"Well, if you won't agree to marriage, I'll settle for the something!"

"You are horrible, simply horrible! You are right now so horrible I want you to kiss me again."

Still feeling the second kiss, Mark ducked back to the chopper and picked up her bag. As they walked to the jeep, Janet was trying to calm down to prepare him for a serious conversation. During the drive to Saigon, Janet considered that this ride might be her last chance to talk to Mark alone for a while. Although the noise of the city wasn't helpful to quiet conversation, she thought it better to start now before the holiday got too far along. Or he kissed her again.

"Mark, I've enjoyed your friendship so much that I hesitate to jeop-ardize it with what I have to say."

He glanced at Janet and noticed that her words were coming out very hard.

"Honey, if it's that serious, this is no place for talk. We have a little time now. I know a bar that should be quiet at this hour. It's on the way to the Hangout. Why don't we talk there?"

He pulled off Cong Ly and parked in front of a small hotel with a sign that blared: "Great Girls, Drinks, Food" in that order. Mark escorted her through the air-conditioned bar to a tiny walled garden. Several small, empty tables were in a group, under a large mimosa tree.

The sun was low in the sky and, although there was still too much light to produce the desired effect, the proprietor switched on a string of colored lights for his first two customers of the evening.

Mark ignored the tree and chose a table in a corner by the wall. He ordered two beers. He followed closely Janet's quiet admission of her growing love for him, her love for Ted, and her faith that Ted must still be alive. He held her hand while she explained that it was not fair to any of the three to continue this relationship, and then demanded that Mark hold off on any further meetings for now. They must wait until Ted's fate was clear.

"But Janet, that might not be for years."

"I know, Mark, but what else is there for me to do? Ted was in good health when last seen. There is no reason to believe that the Viet Cong would wantonly kill a civilian like him."

"I hate to say this, Janet, but he may have been shot while trying to escape."

"I've thought of that. Many other things as well. He could have died of some illness, blood poisoning–there are so many, many possibilities, but one fact remains. When last seen, he was healthy. In my thoughts that's how he will be until I see him again."

"I understand you've used official channels and the Red Cross."

"Oh, yes. All of the many international organizations and several so-called underground groups as well, but the answer is always the same: no knowledge."

Mark mulled over their discussion for a long time. It was only because of his love for Janet and his desire to protect her feelings that he agreed not to see her after she returned to the central highlands.

But Mark Buckley was not a man to give up easily. In his mind was the outline of a plan which, if he could bring it off, might break this logjam in their personal future.

Ψ   Ψ   Ψ

Inauguration Day was a quiet celebration throughout Vietnam for those not directly involved in fighting the war.

In Saigon, there was a happy spirit of "a change for the better" among the people. Most well-read Vietnamese realized that there probably would not be any real change in the nature of the government at first. They were hoping that, in time, the National Assembly's upper and lower houses would grow in power. Finally, the will of the people would be felt.

The only large dissident group in the city was the militant Buddhist faction, who had quietly demonstrated in front of Independence Palace all week. Their leader, Thich Tri Quang, accused the government of shirking its responsibility in the matter of the new Buddhist charter, but most Saigonese were willing to overlook the Buddhists' protests in favor of the activities of the new government.

Twenty-two countries had sent representatives to attend the inauguration ceremonies. Vice President Hubert Humphrey of the United States, Premier Chung Kun of Korea, and Foreign Minister Paul Hasluck of Australia were, of course, the three most important. Their countries were the three greatest allies to South Vietnam.

The new government chose this moment to announce two programs, which drew mixed reactions from the people. The first was a new draft law lowering the age from twenty to eighteen years, and making veterans of less than thirty-three years of age eligible for recall. The idea was to increase the South Vietnamese armed forces to 700,000 men. The second program was more popular: amnesty for over 500 criminal prisoners, 5,000 political prisoners, and 250 prisoners of military courts.

Many VC suspects were among those released, causing many Americans to believe this act extremely ill advised.

In Lam Son Plaza, long red and yellow cloth streamers dropped vertically from the high portcullis of the government assembly house and formed a striking backdrop to the speaker's stand. Staffed South Vietnamese flags of red and yellow decorated the edges of the plaza. Flags also flew from the Continental and Caravelle Hotels, which fronted the north and south sides.

Several thousand people started forming early in the morning to watch the spectacle. Security police were everywhere. All knew that the inauguration ceremony would be a prime target for the VC.

Thi looked down on this scene from the living room window of her No. 516 flat. It certainly was an impressive sight with all the banners and decorations. She coolly noted that from her window, with an automatic weapon, one could have liquidated most of the new government in forty-five seconds. Duat had warned her not to try anything on her own, no matter how tempting the targets looked. When he explained that hidden security guards were watching each window facing the square, instructed to shoot at the slightest suspicion, she understood his warning.

The police had visited her that day. The orders were clear: no one would be allowed to enter her building before the ceremonies were over, and that, if she left, she could not return until the end.

All the dignitaries were in the stands now. She could see Vice President Humphrey, Ambassador Bunker, General Westmoreland, and Ambassador Osborne. Would Humphrey and Osborne be alive at this time tomorrow?

Then she saw Generals Thieu and Ky arrive. Thieu stepped quickly to the speaker's stand. He raised his right hand and took the presidential oath.

There was a roar of cannon fire as the twenty-one gun salute began. Then, just as suddenly, there was silence and President Thieu began his short address.

The amplified words echoed off the buildings. Thi listened with complete disdain.

A pledge to end corruption! Well, that's about as original as advocating motherhood for women.

Next, the president followed with his outline of social reforms, economic austerity, and administrative reorganization.

She was bored long before President Thieu got around to his peace proposal. Then the band played the national anthem. When it was over, the mass of people began leaving the plaza, and the troops marched off. Thi glanced over at the grandstands again. She could see Mr.

Humphrey with a small group of Americans slowly moving toward their government sedans.

Wasn't that Mark Buckley? Why, yes it was and ... it's that little red-headed bitch with him!

Thi felt the old jealousy boil up within her. She lit a cigarette with trembling hands. Then, while she blew out a long stream of smoke, her free hand unconsciously reached for the scar on her cheek and she ran her fingers the length of it.

Ψ   Ψ   Ψ

Cy was ready long before dark.

That afternoon, while he was alone, he had carefully removed the safety spring on the fuse of the 60 mm mortar round. This had automatically lined up the powder train and made the round "unsafe": capable of exploding on impact. He then wrapped the projectile in a roll of newspaper. He was careful to recess the nose at least two inches in the paper. Finally, he hid it in a paper bag, along with a small pocket flashlight and his combat knife in a leather sheath.

At supper, he casually told Kam that he would be out for an hour, but back before 8:30.

Outwardly, Kam had listened quite calmly. Inwardly, she had much on her mind. Up to now, Cy, knowing that every time he left the studio he jeopardized his safety, had seldom gone anywhere other than on PX runs. The few times he had gone out at night, Kam had been with him.

Still, she made no protest and asked no questions. She was not aware of the mortar round. If she had been, she could not have been so calm.

At exactly 6:45 he put on a pair of black slacks and a dark blue shirt, then picked up the bag and left.

Kam missed nothing.

What is in the bag?

Filled with apprehension and dismay, she rushed to the terrace to watch him as he went down the street. Cy hailed a taxi and headed for the corner of Tuc-Khang and Ton That Dam Streets. Soon he was entering the open shell of a building under construction.

He now had to avoid being spotted by a watchman. There had to be one in the structure. Inside, it was much darker. He tried to distinguish the street sounds from all inside but couldn't do it. Quietly and very cautiously, he proceeded up several flights of concrete stairs until he reached the top floor. For a moment, he paused in the darkest corner and again he listened. All seemed quiet. He went to the edge and looked over to the next building. As he had expected, it was about four feet down and only two feet away.

He spent some time searching the roof to try to spot any sign of a lookout or guard. There was no one in sight. Cy opened the bag and slipped the knife and flashlight into his pocket. Then he stepped over and down to the next roof; he was on his way.

Ψ Ψ Ψ

They gave Janet Holden the best room in the Hangout and, being the only woman, she always had access to the bathroom first.

Those were the rules. She had left Bill and Mark downstairs with their drinks while she went upstairs to get ready for the reception and ball at Independence Palace.

Mark told Bill about Janet's request and his determination to honor it.

"Knowing you, I'm sure that this isn't the end of the road as far as you're concerned," said Bill.

"You're certainly right. If I sit idly by, it would mean losing the most wonderful girl in the world. I figure that if Ted won't come to us, maybe it's time we went to Ted."

"What do you mean? What are you going to do?"

"Now, don't get excited. I'm merely going to do some sleuthing via the intelligence boys. Nothing out of line."

"Of course."

"Of course."

"Bathroom clear!" Janet called from the head of the stairs.

"You take it, Bill. Now that we've split into two cars, you'll have to leave here first."

"That's right. Remember 1930 hours at the gate. That will put us both at the palace at 1935. You know how punctual the boss is about these things."

"Yeah, it's liable to be the death of us, one of these days," Mark muttered to himself.

Ψ   Ψ   Ψ

Cy was hiding behind a large water tank.

Most houses had one on their roof for auxiliary water supply. He checked his watch: 7:15. He had made good time until, two houses from his goal, he suddenly came across what had to be the VC lookout.

As luck would have it, the guard was with a young girl who had the guard's attention, completely.

If it hadn't been for that young Cô, I'd have run right into him and be one dead guy right now.

His hand trembled slightly as he checked his watch. It was nearly 7:20. He couldn't wait much longer.

Cy reviewed his plan. In thirteen minutes, he had to dispose of the guard and probably the girl, crawl over two roofs and kill the mortar crew. Right then it seemed an impossible task.

The tone of the conversation of the two Vietnamese seemed to be changing. God, how he hoped that girl would leave! He didn't think he could kill her; yet he knew she must not be around to see him and raise the alarm.

Suddenly there was a third voice—an older woman calling. The girl answered. The woman threatened. There were muffled goodbyes, after which the girl ran to the edge of the roof, waved, and disappeared over the side.

Thank you momma!

Cy edged around the large water tank. The Vietnamese was still looking toward the ladder as Cy approached him from behind. The VC seemed not to have a firearm of any kind.

Now the big black man appeared out of the darkness and towered over the little Vietnamese, the unsheathed long combat knife in his right hand. In one movement, he coiled his huge arm about the guard's neck and tightened it. He lifted the man from the roof.

There was no sound as the man struggled to get loose, his legs flailing in the air.

Cy saw the guard's right hand move up as if to strike. He had managed to pull a knife from his belt. Cy warded off the blow, then plunged his own knife into the guard. The struggles ceased. He lowered the dead man to the roof and looked around, shaking, covered with blood and sweat.

He glanced at his watch. The time was 7:30.

Late, man.

Cy picked up the paper bag in one hand and the VC in the other and started across the last two roofs. The dead body appeared almost weightless in the big man's grasp. There was a crash of thunder and a flash of lightning. Large raindrops started to fall. A few feet from the edge of the roof, Cy laid the corpse down and crawled to the edge with the paper bag.

The unmistakable pop of a mortar told Cy the first round had been fired.

"Sweet Jesus, I'm late," he muttered aloud as he ripped open the bag and slipped out the modified mortar round.

Two more rounds went off. It was pouring rain now as Cy, standing on the edge of the roof, poised his mortar round for a perfect drop. Below, he could see the mortar crew hesitate as they waited for fire correction.

Their small radio crackled with the lightning of the storm.

One of the crew looked up and spotted Cy, who appeared as a gigantic black god, silhouetted against the lightning and the storm clouds.

"Look!" he cried in Vietnamese as he pointed.

The others got a glimpse of their killer as Cy carefully dropped the mortar round and dove down, prone on the roof.

Instantly, there was a flash and explosion. Cy heard shrapnel whistle by. Then he was up again. He grabbed the dead guard, threw the body down onto the terrace, and turned and ran, keeping low along the roof.

He heard excited Vietnamese voices coming from inside the building as he jumped back into the welcome, deep blackness of the half-completed structure. Rain was coming down in torrents after he returned to the sidewalk to walk through darkness to the studio. It wasn't eight o'clock yet. He wondered if the three rounds had been effective.

Had he acted in time? The walk back was good for him.

It's too early for the MPs to be looking for AWOLs and anyway, in this rain they'll be hiding out in some bar. Real brave of them. The rain might wash some of the blood off my shirt and trousers.

That reminded him of the knife blade. He pulled it from his pocket and held it in the rain while he ran his fingers down the flat of the blade. Then he returned it to its scabbard and to his pocket. He bounded up the stairs to Kam's flat, but did not have to knock on the door. She opened it as he approached. She must have been watching from the terrace, because she was as wet as he was.

"Oh, Cy," she cried as she threw herself into his arms.

He laughed as he kicked the door closed behind him and held her close, their bodies leaving a puddle of rain water on the floor.

Kam, her emotions a mixture of joy and apprehension, murmured a long string of Vietnamese at him, but he kept holding her, caressing her, and telling her everything was all right.

When she had quieted down, they went up to the studio and removed their wet clothing. Kam got dry towels. Soon they were in Hue's bed, warm and dry and holding each other, while the rain beat down upon the roof above them. The thunder crashed about them, and the lightning sent stabs of brilliant light across the heavens.

Ψ   Ψ   Ψ

National Day, November 1st, dawned clear and cool.

The bright sun and a pleasant breeze soon dried the streets, wet from the storm of the night before.

Cy asked Kam to go out early for a morning paper. When she brought it back, he scanned the front page, which was almost completely devoted to the elaborate National Day celebration activities.

"Ah, your shirt number ten. Me throw away!"

Cy looked up from the paper and watched Kam rip up the shirt. It was her way of destroying the evidence.

He glanced back at the paper. The article he was searching for was on the bottom of the front page. The headline read:

COMMUNISTS MORTAR INDEPENDENCE PALACE

He heaved a big sigh of relief. There were no casualties at the palace. The crew aim had been poor and they did not have time to make corrections. It was the last paragraph that interested Cy:

Police quickly found the mortar site at 143 Ton That Dam Street. The three-man mortar crew was dead beside the mortar tube. According to reports, they must have had trouble with the projectiles and it appears one exploded prematurely, killing the crew. Near the bodies were twenty additional live rounds ready for firing. Many casualties would have been suffered at the reception if providence had not given them one faulty round.

"With gunners like that, I sure didn't have to risk my ass," muttered Cy to himself as he put the paper down.

There was a knock on the door below. Soon Kam appeared with Qui, who was trying to act casual, but clearly had a lot on his mind. He rattled Vietnamese to Kam, who disappeared downstairs.

Then he turned to Cy. "Where lamp you make for Kam? It all finish?"

"No, Qui, I had to get rid of it."

"She no like?"

"No. One day I work on it. I carefully start taking it apart, suddenly it go, 'tick, tick, tick'! I hurry up to put it under water and it stop. I take it out of the water and it go 'tick, tick' again. I put it back in bucket filled with water and carried it out to storm sewer."

Cy escorted Qui over to the terrace and pointed to the hole in the gutter that drained into the underground sewer.

"Then I poured bucket down the hole. Down goes the mortar. No go bang!"

Qui looked at Cy quizzically; he could not believe the story but wasn't quite sure that he had understood Cy.

Cy turned serious. "I kid you not." He hoped that Qui had so little knowledge of ordnance that he would accept this absurd explanation.

"Hey, look," replied Qui, in an effort to get to the rest of the story—and the real reason for his visit.

"Hey, look yourself. I'm not making any PX runs this month. Almost got caught last time."

"No PX. You know, I tell you about mortar of Vice President long time ago?"

"Yeah, I remember, but VC have number ten gunner."

"How you know?"

"I read it in the paper. Look. See."

He held up the paper and pointed to the article.

"VC have lousy gunner."

"Yes. Number ten."

"Number ten thousand, you mean! You tell me best VC gunner coming to do the job. If that the best they can do, they have lost the war!"

"Oh, they can do better, but not so much mortar." Qui brightened up in telling one of his stories. "You see, they good shot rifle."

"Yeah, I doubt it."

"You see today. They no do job last night, but they do today. Best shot do it."

Cy felt a cold chill, but he showed no outward sign that this new information had affected him.

He tried to control his voice. "Who they try to get today?" emphasizing the "try."

"Oh, they have orders get American Osborne or else."

"Yeah? That crummy gunner gettin' another chance?"

"No. No gunner. Rifle today. Much better. Best shot do today. No mortar."

"They can't get a rifle on Osborne, man. This is shit. He's covered by guards all 'round."

"You forget, GI. Today big National Day parade. Osborne stand up with new president and vice president—be easy target from roof of Shell building."

"Ha. Look, if they have the chance to kill those guys, they'd go after Thieu or Ky, not an American."

Cy knew he had to play to Qui's ego to get the whole setup without scaring him off.

"You don't get it, Cy. Thieu and Ky made *beaucoup* mistake. They not make South Vietnam strong. They die—US put other like them in place. But Osborne, he make South Vietnamese people strong. Make stand up, fight. That bad for VC. They say he gotta go."

"There's no way they can get a guy past the guards and put him on the roof of the Shell building. The whole route's been inspected and scrubbed down for weeks. You know it. No rifle. No shot."

Qui's ego and enthusiastic desire to be seen as "knowing all," now completely blinded him to the risk of any later question about his poking his nose in affairs that were not his concern.

"Easy for VC. Cleaning man in Shell building have pass, everything. He no cleaning man, he VC. He good shot. Bang bang, that do it!"

"Maybe, but how they get rifle in?"

The eager Qui continued, "No sweat, GI. Rifle been in *beaucoup* months. Every building in Saigon have some hidden."

Cy now realized that what Qui was saying was true. He wondered briefly how he got his information, but did not dare to ask. After a few more challenging questions, he was able to find out that the plan was a simple one. The shooter had to keep hidden until the time to fire because lookouts and guards on other buildings would spot him and fire on sight. He was to remain out of sight until he heard the Revolutionary Development Cadre band strike up their official march just before they passed the reviewing stand. Osborne's interest in his cadre would bring him forward on the reviewing stand. The assassin's cue was the music. Halfway through the first chorus, he was to pop up and fire two quick rounds.

"How he know the music?" asked Cy.

"Oh, everyone know the RD Cadre march."

Qui started to hum and Cy recognized a tune he had heard many times on the radio.

To cover his anxiety and assure Qui that he was not personally concerned, Cy jumped up and said, "Tell you what I'll do, Qui. I bet you even odds they don't get Osborne at the parade."

"What you mean?"

Cy went over to a cupboard and drew out a 500-piastre note. "Here. I bet you. If Osborne shot, I give you. If Osborne not shot, you give me."

Qui's eyes lit up. "Oh, bet. I see. I make you bet. Okay, okay."

Cy knew that Qui, like many Vietnamese men, loved to wager on almost anything. This would go a long way to explaining Cy's curiosity.

"Right, Qui, see you later. Going to rest now."

Cy went over to the bed and lay down. He put the morning paper over his head to shield the light.

As soon as Qui left, Cy was instantly alert, trying to think what he should do. This one was clearly for the MPs, but there was no time.

Then he lay back on the bed.

Wait a minute, man. They're goin' ta be after this guy Osborne from now on. What you goin' ta do, show up like the Lone Ranger every time you hear about it and save his white ass? It was luck last night. Your luck can't last.

What you do this time is impress on the MPs that this guy Osborne is a prime target from now on out, and they gotta get with the program.

In the distance, he could hear military band music. Maybe it was too late anyway. He glanced at his watch: 0900 hours. Cy picked up the paper and found the schedule for the parade. He learned that Thieu and Ky were due to arrive at 0900. After short speeches, they would pass down the parade route. Then they were to return to the reviewing stand for the parade. He looked at the list of units marching, scanning the list quickly, and came to the Revolutionary Development Cadre. The band was also mentioned.

This was it. Damn.

The parade was to last one hour according to the paper. Quickly he counted the marching units and found RD cadre just after the middle. They should be in front of the stand about thirty minutes after the start.

Cy figured he had about thirty minutes to save Newell Osborne. Should he try it? He thought of last night and the risk he had taken and decided that it was worth one more chance—but right after this one he had to think seriously of getting word to Osborne that he was a marked man—if he didn't get it already.

He went to the closet and pulled out the MP uniform and pistol belt, dressing as fast as he could.

Kam entered the room from below with wet laundry to hang out on the upper terrace. Surprised to see Cy in the uniform, she put down the laundry.

"You go PX today?"

"Yeah, yeah, honey I go PX."

"You have list! Where list? I no see list."

"Already in my pocket. I gotta go."

"PX closed today."

"No, only the Brink PX. Tan Son Nhut is open for people flying home."

Cy paused at the steps and looked back at Kam. There were tears in her eyes, but otherwise she was hiding her emotions with that placid mask which oriental women use to deceive their men in times of stress. He returned, picked her up and kissed her very tenderly, then ran quickly down the steps.

Kam rushed to the terrace and watched Cy disappear in the crowds of people heading for the parade. She heard the band again—playing the Vietnamese National Anthem. Tears were running down her cheeks as she stood quietly, straining to see Cy once more. Somehow, she feared this might be for the last time.

Cy knew that if he rushed through the crowd in his MP uniform, it would cause too much attention, but every second counted. Therefore, he walked as fast as possible, dodging food vendors, balloon sellers, and school children. Finally, he found that he could make better time walking in the street.

"Hop on, Sergeant."

Cy looked around. A weapons carrier of MPs had pulled up by him. *Great!*

This would give him several minutes extra to get to the Shell building. Automatically he jumped on the running board and the vehicle took off. Using a siren and the horn, the driver made good time through the crowd until they reached Thong Nhut, the parade route.

Although Cy's plan did not include a confrontation with Colonel Row, he asked, "Where's the boss's position for this shindig?"

"You know he's got a roving command post. I don't know where he is now," said the very young-looking lieutenant sitting by the driver.

Cy looked at his watch.

"That's right. It's later than I thought. That's my position—over there, by the Shell building. Thanks for the lift, buddy."

He jumped off the vehicle and vanished in the crowd.

The huge size of the parade became suddenly apparent to him. He passed between the grandstands of people and took a position on the edge of the street. There were Vietnamese MPs there, keeping the people on the sidewalks from getting into the cleared street. Cy stepped onto the pavement and helped a small Vietnamese soldier motion people to move on. From this position Cy could see the reviewing stand and, across the street, the Shell building. He noticed several small utility structures on top of the building and decided that the rifleman was hiding in one of them.

He thought over his next move. Trying to find Colonel Row, the commander of the US security battalion, was out of the question. He glanced up at the Shell building. There was still time to get that guy—if he could get up there. He looked up the street to see a small convoy of vehicles with motorcycle outriders approaching. Each vehicle had a yellow-and-red-striped South Vietnamese flag flying. It was Thieu and Ky. They had driven down the line of spectators and were now returning to the reviewing stand.

The Vietnamese MP near him faced the street and came to attention. Cy followed his example. As the motorcade approached, the people in the stands rose and started cheering. The military personnel saluted.

Cy saluted with the small soldier on his left. After the motorcade passed, the street was again empty. Cy checked his watch: 0925. In about ten minutes the RD Cadre band would be passing the reviewing stand.

He took a deep breath. Then, as if on duty, he walked directly across the street. He had never seen so many people in one place in all his life. The stands were full. Flags of all the allied nations were on stands along both sides of the street. Long streamers of the Vietnamese colors draped the buildings, and two large balloons tethered to the reviewing stand suspended long, light blue cloth banners marked in black with traditional Chinese good luck symbols. Large clusters of different-colored balloons were also tethered about the stands. These would be released on cue. There was an air of gaiety and happiness that was quite contagious, and Cy felt it also.

Cy managed to get through the crowd and passed behind the grandstands. He turned left and headed for the Shell building. He went to the front door and found it locked from the outside with a bar and chain. There was an official police notice in Vietnamese and English. The building was closed and locked down for the parade. He hurried around the side of the building. There was a service door—also locked.

He tried the door. It was steel and did not budge. Quickly Cy circled the whole building, looking for any opening. All windows on the ground floor had iron bars, all doors were of steel.

The Shell Company had done a good job of defending from outside attack. In desperation, Cy stopped in the shade to think what he should do.

Shoot the lock with my .45? No, looks like that wouldn't work …

There was music coming from the street now. The first of many bands had already marched by and several units had followed, marching past the reviewing stand. He glanced at his watch: 0942.

"Oh shit," cursed Cy out loud.

I wasted too much time. There's only one thing left to do, and that's to get to Osborne and warn him!

Osborne was on the other side of the street and Cy knew it would be difficult for him to re-cross, now that troops were marching by.

If I'm going to do anything, I better move right now.

He plunged back into the crowd packed between the bleachers.

Soon he was by himself between the edge of the crowd and a large marching group of VC defectors, dressed in brown pajama uniforms and straw conical hats. To his right he could see a group of news cameramen, who had been inching farther and farther out into the street to get better angles for their photography. He walked down to them and held up his arms.

"Back, fellas, get back to your spots. Boss says you're getting too far out."

Grumbling, the cameramen moved back. Cy stayed on the edge of the group and waited for his chance. His watch read 0946. He looked down the parade route.

The RD Cadre couldn't be too far away. He had to get across that street. He waited for what seemed a long time before there was a break in the parade.

One marching unit must have been late, because there was quite a gap between marching troops. This was the time. He walked directly across the street into the crowd on the other side.

Right then he heard a band and realized that the RD Cadre had been the late unit. They had just started their own theme music. There was only one thing Cy could do now. Keeping on the edge of the crowd, he outdistanced the band as he ran to the reviewing stand.

Seated on the right side of the stand were many high-ranking Vietnamese officers. In the center: the Vietnamese President Thieu, Vice President Ky, and their cabinet. Finally, on the far end were high-ranking American officers and civilians.

Newell Osborne was in the front row on the far end.

"Hey, they're playing my song! Here come the best troops in the parade," Newell announced and leaned forward.

Cy ran below the stand until he was directly in front of Osborne. He looked up. The stand was four feet above the street.

He called, "Mr. Osborne! Mr. Ambassador!", but with the confusion and noise of the band, Newell did not hear his cries.

In one motion Cy jumped up, caught the railing, and swung himself up beside the Ambassador. In the excitement of seeing the passing units, no one paid attention to the MP sergeant.

"Mr. Osborne, get down! They're going to shoot you!"

Newell looked at Cy as if he must be out of his mind. "What are you doing here, Sergeant?"

There was no time for talk. Cy stepped in front of Osborne, then turned and pointed to the top of the Shell building. The noise of the band muffled the two shots, but their effect was all too apparent. Cy, who took them both in the chest, crumpled and fell over the railing into the street below.

The young men and women of the RD Cadre marched smartly past the stand, hardly noticing the commotion among the high-ranking spectators. But the lookout guards located across from the Shell building noticed the two shots. Quick counter fire killed the would-be assassin of Newell Osborne as the local military police carried Cy behind the stand.

Mark Buckley, at the rear of the crowded stand, had watched the MP sergeant jump up beside Newell Osborne. Instantly sensing danger, he moved, reaching Osborne's side in time to see the sergeant step in front of Newell and to hear his warning. When he saw the bullets hit, Mark hustled the Ambassador off the stand, then returned immediately to the wounded sergeant.

"My God, it's Ned! Ned Green! What in the hell are you doing here?"

Cy looked up at Mark Buckley and smiled briefly.

The pain was extreme when they moved him around to the back of the stand. Newell Osborne appeared and knelt down by the side of the stricken man.

"Mark, do you know this man?"

"Yes, sir. He is Ned Green. He was one of my best corporals down at Trong Thoi."

"Did you see what he did for me? Did you see him? This man saved my life. He didn't know me. Why would he take two slugs that were meant for me?"

"I don't know, sir. Ned, can you talk?"

Cy tried to talk, but words would not come out. He wanted to talk. He had much to say. But his mouth moved and nothing came out. Someone lifted his head to give him some water. He choked it down.

Then he saw the red on his chest. Slowly he somehow raised his right hand until the fingers were in the blood. Then with great effort, he traced the symbol Ψ on the smooth sidewalk by his side. He smiled as he watched the look of recognition come to Osborne's face.

Then he closed his eyes and died lying on the streets of Saigon.

Ψ   Ψ   Ψ

Bu sat in his easy chair and listened to the sounds of distant, happy people outside.

This National Day was the fourth anniversary of the overthrow of the Diem regime and considered, therefore, as the fourth anniversary of Vietnamese independence. He had mused most of the day upon his country's future. His conclusion: there wasn't much he could do about it personally. He wished there was something he could do to help his people build solidarity and honesty and patriotism.

Bu picked up a copy of the English-language Saigon News that Mai Lei was always bringing home, and turned to Cong Trinh's column, which he often found amusing. Today Trinh was asking a question: "Which way is it to be?"

The article read:

Two ways now stretch ahead. One is the easy, effortless way in which failure to take responsibilities, disregard for the interests of the majority of the people, preference of flowery words and empty promises to action and results, sloth and personal safety and interest are forever put first, in which declining standards of life and morals are taken for granted, and no effort made to overcome them. The other route, far tougher, is for patriots and democrats.

It is for men who do not accept arbitrary acts and arrests, social injustice and inequality, poverty and misery and hardships as a permanent way of life.

It is for men who have pride and faith in this Vietnamese land, not for men who, while speaking of patriotism and lofty ideals, keep their minds and eyes turned outward when they will flee when the going is tough.

It is for men who see its vast, untapped potentialities, and the heroism of its people to weather the storm blown up by the Communists, and who are determined by personal effort in and out of the government to build a sovereign, free, democratic, and prosperous country, in which our children will nevermore know want and fear.

Which way is it to be with the formation of the new government? How we choose may determine whether Vietnam lives or dies.

Bu put down the paper and stared for a moment into the lengthening shadows of late afternoon. The house was silent, but in the distance, the muffled sounds of bands and cheering people made a muted backdrop for his words. Aloud, but quietly, Bu spoke to only himself.

"Oh, Vietnam, Vietnam, why do you still sit and weep? Your children have been weeping for over twenty years. Now we must stop our weeping. Now, now, before it is too late, we must dry our eyes and stand up and fight!"

Chapter VII

NOVEMBER

I t all changed in one night.

Ned Green's decisive actions and his death went unnoticed by most of the spectators at the National Day parade. Then, the press went to work and by morning, the story was on all the newsstands. By the end of the day, a hunted deserter in life became a hero idolized in death.

Kam suffered terribly over Ned's death. It had been her dream that, once the war was over and the Americans were gone, she and Cy would be married and live happily in Saigon. Or maybe Paris. Now her dream was shattered and she was alone. There was no one to comfort or advise her.

But there were people interested in Kam because of her relationship with Ned. They were not interested in her feelings.

These were the Saigon police and the American Military Police. Following up on the contents of Ned's pockets, they arrived at her flat within hours. Because she and Cy were not married, they did not consider her worthy of pity, respect, or much of anything else. In fact, they saw her as a prostitute living off an American.

They gave no thought to her personal feelings. They searched the flat roughly, thoroughly, and maliciously. They interrogated her concerning one Corporal Ned Green, US Army, a person she did not know. All she could give them was meager information about an artist named Cy.

This dodge of Kam's (as the police saw it), only increased the heavy handedness of both police forces. They became more brutal with her and her personal belongings. It was during their "inspection" that the charcoal sketches of Cy were found and were to be impounded as "evidence."

Rescue, in the form of Ambassador Newell Osborne, stepped in.

The impact of seeing Ned's symbol drawn in his own blood had a deep and lasting effect on Newell. The young black soldier had given his life to save him. He wanted to do something to repay this debt. He remembered the young girl with the kiosk where he had purchased the Ψ painting, and he surmised that she must be Ned's lover.

He imagined what hell the authorities must have been giving her, so he sent Major Bill Scott to act as protector until the police could be called off. Newell demanded the address from Colonel Ross, got it in moments, and sent Bill Scott on his way.

Bill, looking for any excuse to see Mai Lei, called her, explained that this was an official duty, and asked if she would act as interpreter for a few hours. Mai Lei, happy to see Bill for any reason, rushed to Kam's flat.

Bill's orders were to comfort the girl and perform a holding action with the police until Newell could persuade the Vietnamese and American security forces to back off and leave the girl alone.

What good was she to them now that the man was dead?

Both Bill and Mai Lei marveled at the number of Ψ paintings in the studio that Ned had completed for his show. Another surprise was Hue's fine work. The two carefully put all of the paintings and sketches away after persuading the police to vacate the premises and to leave Kam's possessions and the artwork alone.

Mai Lei took an immediate liking to Kam, and stayed with her that first night. After that, Kam carried her sorrow stoically and bravely, as became a Vietnamese, and outwardly regained control and composure. She realized that her life had to go on, and it would be best for her to keep busy at her work and try to forget Cy as soon as she could.

The people of Saigon had other ideas.

The mysterious painter Ψ had captured their imagination. Then, finding that he was an American deserter who had loved one of their people, who had died heroically to save the life of one of the few Americans they thought sincere in trying to help them, was too much for even normally stoic, or even cynical, Asian minds to ignore.

Their emotions boiled over with admiration and uninhibited hero worship. Copies of Cy's pictures appeared everywhere. On sale on every corner were poor, hastily done paintings of black men, supposedly of Cy.

Professor Loy from the College of Fine Arts appeared again at Kam's apartment, and reminded her of the show. He was delighted to find all of Cy's pictures stacked there and, by careful persuasion, was able to convince Kam that this show would be a great tribute to the artist and should go on as planned.

"Both Madame Thieu and Madame Ky have requested to co-sponsor the show and, considering the story, believe it would be only proper to raise the prices of the paintings quite a bit higher."

"Sir, if you please, I wish to let you handle such things. I feel inadequate and incapable of handling any of the affairs of the show."

"To be sure, Madame, I certainly understand, and will be happy to take over settling all matters of the exhibition for you."

"Sir, I have another subject which I would like to discuss, if you please. You were once a good friend of my brother's and spoke kindly of his early work. Please look at these and tell me how I should dispose of them."

Kam brought out several of the sketches, and unrolled them on the floor. For a moment, Professor Loy did not speak. He gazed at the pictures. Encouraged, Kam produced the whole set and placed them side by side with the others. Finally, Professor Loy broke his silence.

"At last, at long last, your brother was able to realize the promise he showed so long ago. His true ability finally came to harvest. There is no finer work of this kind being done in Vietnam today."

Kam smiled for the first time since Ned's death.

Professor Loy proposed a combined show, with the work of both men, each complementing the other. The mere fact that the sketches were of Cy would be a lure. The people of Saigon were bound to flock to the show to see, at last, what their new hero actually looked like.

Kam, who was not ready emotionally to comprehend the magnitude or even the real purpose of the show, again thanked Professor Loy for assuming the responsibility of the undertaking.

The next day Loy brought a photographer to the flat. He took photos of the sketches and two of Cy's paintings. The photo story soon appeared in every paper in Saigon, and most of those in the provinces. Even more interest and excitement resulted. Madame Thieu suggested that the show open as soon as possible, in order to take advantage of the publicity.

Kam was a source of curiosity herself. After all, she was the lover of this new hero. She ignored the curious who came to ask questions or just to stare at her. One result: when she returned to the kiosk, many artists requested that she handle their pictures.

Being a sharp businesswoman, she demanded and she got fifty percent of the sale price on each picture.

Newell Osborne knew of the coming art show. He suggested that those who owned original Cys loan their paintings to the exhibit, thereby allowing many Americans to participate in this Vietnamese charity. The next day an appeal appeared in the newspapers requesting the loan of any Ψ paintings.

The response was immediate and strong. Now, the larger number of pictures required more space. The Central Information Office on Tu Do Street became the show site. The exhibit was set to open the first week in December.

Ψ   Ψ   Ψ

Brandy Masters sat alone in her apartment with a drink.

While she waited to leave for her class in spoken Vietnamese, she thought of her "new life," as she called it. This reminded her of the reformed prostitutes she used to read about in lurid paperback novels.

Certainly, by this time I've proved to Uncle Sam that I am truly a good person, capable of doing meaningful and worthwhile work in the cause of Vietnamese freedom. Ha! I've not been able to convince myself.

What I've proved is that I've been able to hold down a job in what I thought to be a strong and necessary part of US policy in Vietnam. Now I see that the whole organization is extremely ineffective and amazingly wasteful.

Many of the Americans in Saigon who came here to run USAID's programs are basically "takers," as opposed to "givers." This is the real, underlying problem. These types give nothing of themselves. No overtime, no personal feelings, no real contributions of time, effort, even compassion. They just take the money.

All right, girl, just where do you fit in? Aren't you one of them also? What have you contributed? Isn't this really why you came over here in the first place—to help? Then, for God's sake, find some job, some real job, where you can give something of yourself.

Brandy thought of her qualifications and a rueful smile crossed her face.

"My best qualification," she said aloud with a laugh, "is one they won't let me use, even though for a while it certainly helped a lot of soldiers."

She thought of Trong Thoi and Mark. Briefly, she recalled that night in the village so long ago.

It's funny how things seem to encircle me, even engulf me, then pass by, leaving me untouched, but leaving others badly hurt, sometimes for life, here, now, and in Paris years ago.

She looked up at her painting and thought of the artist, Ned Green.

The newspaper stories have made it plain that this GI had already left Trong Thoi before my visit. If I had gone there in May, would Ned have been one of my men that night? I bet I would have inspired at least one of his paintings.

She smiled and crossed the room, picked up the newspaper, and re-read the article about the exhibition.

I'll certainly lend my painting. Wish I had known him. Wish that he had been among the men that night. He seems to have been a real man. I would have liked to have worn out that strong black ass.

No. Stop that. The man's a real hero and he seems to have given so much of himself to this effort over here. Newell Osborne owes his life to this guy. The orphans will get a lot of money from his pictures. The people certainly are getting a real shot in the arm out of the whole affair. All of these things are coming about because a black corporal went AWOL and shacked up with a young Vietnamese and his sister. But, most importantly, he gave what he had, what he knew, whether he was aware of it or not, he hit upon the right combination to be a real help in this war.

Her thoughts returned to herself.

Isn't that what I was trying to do with the singing act? Or was it just an easy way to meet GIs and get laid? Even so, isn't that what I was really trying to do that night in the village? But then, is that all I have to offer? There are certainly a lot better secretaries around! What have I really wanted to do—ever?

She thought of her girlhood and her early resolve to be a veterinarian. She had always loved animals and wanted to help them. Later, she had gone into nursing.

I probably would have graduated and been a good nurse if I had really needed to make a living. But the best part became taking the interns into storage rooms and partying away. They really got turned on by the student white uniform and the black French underwear. They had never seen anything like it. Or like me.

But after I had run through most of the staff and some of the patients it just got boring there. Time to leave. Then it was more fun working in Uncle Joe's campaign headquarters. But later he sent me to Paris to get me away from ... what was his name? I remember his face. Anyway. Paris. Uncle Joe had to help out with that too. Maybe then, I should have gone back to school and finished. God, it seems foolish from this point in time. Don't know if I even remember the rudiments of my nursing courses. I sure studied! I was always near the top in my class—and I gave it up because Uncle Joe wanted me to work for him that fall. At least that was the reason I gave at the time. But now I know there was that other reason.

She looked at her watch—almost time for her class.

She finished her drink and called *Toi di nura* to her servants as she picked up her books.

Soon she was outside among the crowds in the street, walking too fast in the humid weather.

It's funny that I get so wrapped up in these language lessons. But really ... originally, they were only a means to get rid of Poli De Salle. What a bore he became. The sex wasn't even marginal. I had to work so hard to keep him focused. He was always afraid that he would be attacked while we were at it. Every creak of the bed convinced him that the VC were creeping up on him and he would stop right there and lose it. Who needs that? I wasn't giving him the best piece of blond American ass in Saigon for his political commentary.

His dark obsession about these people gave me the idea—to see less of him, I saw more of them. But that was the big surprise. I really enjoy meeting the Vietnamese—meeting them on their own terms, in their own homes, and the more acquaintances I've made among them, the fewer Americans I see in my time off.

Gradually her social life had changed, and she was enjoying the friendships she was making, even though her mastery of the tonal qualities of the language still was a challenge.

Her thoughts turned to her lesson as she approached her teacher's home. Rapidly, she reviewed all the sentences of her homework assignment while she threaded her way through the crowd.

Ψ   Ψ   Ψ

There were other parties in Saigon interested in the art show, and for narrow reasons.

Duat's plan to assassinate Newell Osborne had failed and now Duat had lost much face. Outwardly, he showed no sign of this terrible, unaccountable defeat, but inside all was turmoil.

Then word came from the NLF that Osborne was now one of the three best-protected Americans in South Vietnam, and would be almost impossible to kill. Duat was further informed that all attempts on Osborne's life would cease immediately because of the danger of exposing Duat's organization through capture. This welcome news restored some of the lost face, and Duat regained his confidence and his disdain.

I will make one more attempt on Osborne. But the North will only know if it succeeds. If not? Well, it was someone else. But no one must know, for now. Ahn ...

On command, Ahn brought out the Saigon street map once again. Duat studied it for a moment and then pointed to the Tu Do Street location thoughtfully listed in the newspaper articles.

"Ahn?"

"Yes, Ông Duat?"

"I need you to do many things quickly. There is time. But not too much."

"Yes, my Master."

"Ahn, no one in the North need know of any of this."

"Master?"

"No one."

Duat sat down in his favorite chair. He leaned back, closed his eyes, and started to dictate to Ahn.

"First we will need the right sort of person. Not very bright, of course, but enough to drive a vehicle."

Duat allowed himself a small smile.

Helpful that so many of them will be in one specific place at one precise time. So very helpful …

Ψ   Ψ   Ψ

Kim had worked an outstanding deal, one rarely, if ever, equaled in daring and cunning in the history of the whole ROK Army.

He was very proud of himself. Kim had managed to maneuver his boss right into the arms of Ba Thoa, the operator of the house at 92 Bung Vu'o'ong. This had not been easy to accomplish. In fact, it had required the help of Red and Dave, and probably would never have come off without them. His American friends had given him confidence. They made it sound so easy. But, best of all, they had talked Thoa into letting Uhm use the private entrance to her room on his first visits. Then it was Dave's idea that Thoa should pretend she was being seduced. That's what made it permanent, as far as Colonel Uhm was concerned. The surprise came later! Whoever would have thought that Thoa would be happy with Uhm as a lover on a more or less permanent basis?

Of course, the best part of it was that Colonel Uhm no longer expected Kim to supply girls. Now, Thoa wouldn't always be asking Kim to move in with her. He thought of the several times he had stayed with Thoa, dressed in the black silk robe that she had always had him wear as they sat at the table drinking beer and looking out at the activity in the courtyard. He smiled as he visualized Colonel Uhm in that robe.

He must look lost in it! But Thoa is a practical woman. She no doubt had several sizes of robes to accommodate her various lovers.

Now, as he turned off Tu Do Street, he could see the familiar kiosk, its green roof well above the crowd. He wondered if the girl was there, or if she had vanished after the death of the black American. As he got closer, he could see the paintings on display and a rather large crowd about the kiosk. Soon he was near enough to see her very beautiful face, which somehow he had never been able to forget, even when he was with Thi or Ba Thoa or other girls.

Kim pushed his way to the front of the group.

"Good afternoon, number six and one half!"

She turned from her prospective customer, caught his eye, and smiled. "Ah, Corporal Kim. I am so glad you have returned."

She was truly happy to see him again and almost forgot the customer in her excitement.

"Please, in a minute. I would like to talk to you," she said.

Then she returned to the American sailor, who now moved on from his original choice of pictures and began looking at another.

"This by that Green guy? Ned Green?" The sailor's smile had a knowing air.

"No, sir." Her face went blank. "By fine young Vietnamese artist. Cy pictures–Ned Green pictures–all gone now. You look some more. I be over here." She returned to Kim.

"I think maybe you number five now. No more six and one half," Kim said.

She laughed so quietly he could not hear her above the noise of the street.

"Oh, I like that, I like number five!"

"You do? That's pretty bad."

"Better than six and one half."

Both laughed shyly. The sailor came up carrying a painting and quickly peeled off 6,000 piastres.

"Here you go, honey. I think this's one hell of a picture."

Kam took the money, amazed that he did not bargain with her.

Americans.

"How about have dinner with me tonight?" asked Kam, happy the sailor had gone.

She thought about the last time this Korean soldier had asked her out, and though she had not wanted to go, she had worried about his coming to the studio and running into Cy.

Now there was nothing at the studio except loneliness. It would be nice. She felt his hand rest tenderly on her arm.

"Look, Cô Kam, I know all about sad time you have, so I say maybe nice outside dinner good deal for Kam. Make her happy again. Look, we go first-class joint, I betcha."

He had a big grin on his face, his eyes almost completely shut with pleasure. He looked up to her flat and pointed.

"See, I remember. I come up get you seven-thirty." He didn't wait for her acceptance, but walked off through the crowd.

"Baby, if he don't show, how about me?" a big soldier asked with a laugh.

Kam was very happy. The smile she gave the soldier was radiant.

"I no worry, GI. He come okay."

Ψ Ψ Ψ

Poli De Salle had never in his life loved anyone or anything more than his new lacquer coffee table.

His hands caressed the cool, smooth surface as he gazed into the underwater scene of red-gold carp swimming among waving water plants. Somehow, the sun seemed to have found this dark pool, and a few filtered rays highlighted the fish and some of the long leaves of the vegetation. He enjoyed looking into the scene and almost felt as if he were swimming down there amid that serenity, away from the problems that seemed to plague him in the real world. The table had cost a fortune in piastres, but to him it was worth every one.

Considering the fact that piastres are coming to me so easy these days, the actual cost doesn't seem like very much. You have to be realistic and see things for their real value over here.

If anyone had ever accused Poli of participating in the black market, he would have denied it with every ounce of fervor he could summon. He merely had a convenient arrangement with Soo, his servant, who traded US dollars for piastres at an extremely high rate.

It was unlawful to have US currency in South Vietnam. Poli knew this very well, but he considered the military payment certificates that everyone had to use as just an instrument of the Army to keep soldiers from throwing dollars around on payday, and to keep natives from robbing them when they were drunk.

Most of the people in USAID have dollars because they're in and out of the country all the time ... Besides, I'm not in the Army and don't feel obliged to use MPCs except in the PX and those boring army messes. Ugh.

He took a drink from his tall glass and carefully replaced it on a coaster on the corner of the new table. He had to be very careful until the plate-glass sheet he had ordered was finally delivered and in place. Nothing must mar the quiet serenity of his private, underwater lacquer world.

Briefly, he thought of Brandy, and wondered if she was still trying to learn this overly complicated language. He missed her, in a way. He considered her still sort of a friend, but she was certainly no longer a lover.

The affair lasted longer than it would have if she hadn't worked in the office with me. She sure was careful in the way we broke it off, almost as if she had been the one who had called it quits. But what a woman! Certainly not on my intellectual level, quite obviously, but extremely accomplished in the bedroom.

My God, the noises she made and the words she used in bed. And she expected me to keep up with her demands. My God! All night sometimes. She did things I never heard of before and certainly none of my graduate students ever offered to do for a better grade. That was probably the key: she always wanted control. Well, no little bitch controls Dr. Poli De Salle. Not even a wild blonde like that with those amazing breasts, those huge nipples and well, that incredible ass. The way she moved when she climaxed and ...

"Soo!" Poli loved to spit out the word with all the contempt he could muster. He liked Soo because he was servile, respectful, and never laughed at him. The old Vietnamese appeared quietly in the doorway and awaited instructions.

"Another drink before I start work."

Now this was being in control. And I like it. Too bad I can't take him home with me. Hurry up, little yellow man! I am waiting.

He rose, went to the window, and looked out upon the crowd of people hurrying through the noonday heat to their homes for the rest period.

"That's it, you little bastards! Run home and make *beaucoup* so we will have to ship more food here and have even more mouths to feed," he said aloud.

He intercepted the drink from Soo's tray and again turned to view the crowd below.

Animals—they are animals—and we are over here killing our own men to save them. We should easily be able to control them—make them produce more, fight harder, be more loyal to our cause. In short, the Americans, of superior intellect, should be able to use them more efficiently. They should not be using us.

He thought of an academic study of an anthill that he had read years before. In each case, when danger threatened, they had mobilized within themselves to combat the threat. A curious expression appeared on his face.

He went quickly to the smaller bedroom in the apartment, which he called his study. He forgot his drink. Poli found two articles on the political situation in South Vietnam and a book on the government of the provinces and districts of the country. There was also an excellent series of provincial maps and a short book on administration of the districts and municipalities of South Vietnam.

Poli, underneath all a born scholar, had finally worked out a way to solve his difficulties, a way to square himself with Stephen Bromfield, to enhance his position in the social science community, and possibly to depart from Vietnam a hero.

He smiled as he drew forth a pencil and a large yellow tablet. For the first time since he arrived in Vietnam, Poli De Salle felt good.

Ψ   Ψ   Ψ

Kam was dressed in her best wine-colored silk *ao dai*.

She had brushed her long black hair back from her face and held it in place by a tortoiseshell band. Her high-heeled slippers matched her black silk trousers. She was elated with the idea of going out with the big Korean soldier. It had been a long time since a man had asked her out, and she was aglow with happiness.

Her wooden slippers made a light clack-clack as she walked the tile of the studio terrace, and from time to time, she glanced over the side of the building to see if Corporal Kim was arriving.

Again, she looked at the tiny gold Seiko PX watch Cy had given her. The corporal was fifteen minutes late. Suddenly an American jeep careened around the corner and came to an abrupt stop in front of her building. She saw Kim jump out and wave the jeep away.

"Don't take wooden Indians!" he yelled as the jeep drove off.

Then he knocked at her door. Kam clip-clopped across the living room to let him in.

"You very pretty. Wow! You number one!" Kim gave a low whistle.

"You say today I number five."

"Now you sumpin' else again. You really number one bit of fluff. Zowie!"

When he finally managed to take his eyes off her, he wandered about, looking at the few furnishings, and every now and then glanced out the window.

"This studio?"

"No. You want to see studio?"

"Is okay?"

"Is okay. This my house all alone now."

Kim caught the note of sorrow in her voice. She led the way through the living room, across the lower terrace, to the outside stairs. They proceeded to the studio, where the paintings caught Kim's interest.

"You like Coca-Cola?" she asked.

"I like very much."

Kam left him in the studio and returned shortly with two cokes, served in glasses with ice cubes.

"Say, this number one place."

They strolled out onto the studio terrace and then leaned over to watch the people in the street below. It was getting dark. A street vendor with single-stringed musical instruments was scraping out "Yankee

Doodle" on one of them. Somehow, the sound managed to escape extinction by the other noises of the street and drifted up to the terrace.

They sipped their cokes. Kim felt very much at ease here in the studio. There was a feeling of remote, quiet security about the place that was new to him. He was reluctant to leave.

Kam was fighting a shyness that she always experienced when alone with someone new to her. She was quiet for a long time.

Finally, she managed to look at her watch. "It very late, maybe we go?"

He looked at her and smiled. "I like you place. I hate leave. But we gotta get goin'. I take you to meet my buddies."

The restaurant was Chinese, atop a five-story building that had an ancient elevator right out of an old Marx Brothers film.

"Dave, my buddy, say you get fly-boy pay for ride in this."

Kam said nothing. She was terrified by the swaying, jolting, open cage. As they ascended she could hear a loud band playing American songs, and she was afraid Kim would expect her to dance.

"You like dance?"

"I no dance American," she answered.

"I no dance. I watch. Come on, elevator no go all way. Now we walk."

They climbed a flight of stairs to the restaurant. A confusion of light and sound greeted them and assaulted their senses.

"Welcome to Bong Lai Restaurant," she heard someone say in English.

Instinctively she clutched Kim's arm. He was pleased. She did not see him look down at her and smile.

The waiters seemed to know Kim, and guided them to a table in the corner of the roof. In the semi-darkness Kam could make out two Americans and two Vietnamese girls seated there. The two Americans jumped up and Kim introduced Kam to Red and Dave.

Kam then turned to the girls and the Americans clumsily introduced their dates. After she was seated, Kam had a moment to look at the roof garden. It was a large L-shaped place with many potted palms and bougainvillea vines along the railings. At the far end of the "L," on a raised bandstand, a very loud and brassy orchestra was playing. Some couples were dancing in the cleared area immediately in front of the band. Tables of all sizes, each covered with a white tablecloth, filled the rest of the room. There were strings of multi-colored lights everywhere.

Having only been in quiet little restaurants before this, Kam was impressed, somewhat overwhelmed, even a bit frightened of this garish, noisy place. She moved closer to Kim. He put his arm around her waist and pulled her to his side. She found this reassuring and managed a smile, first at Kim, and then at the other two men.

"So this is the little gal who lived with Ned, Cy, what's his name."

Kim felt Kam stiffen and grab his arm.

He understood perfectly, answering, "That all over, GI. No good talk. Make sad."

Red was sorry that he had brought up the subject. He reached over the table and patted Kam's hand.

"Sorry, baby. I didn't mean to cause you any hurt."

"Dumb ass," said Dave. He reached across and shot Red's shoulder a hard clout.

The two Vietnamese girls, however, picked up the remarks and were most impressed. They started jabbering at Kam who immediately withdrew into the "know nothing, express nothing" fortress of her being which she had used at the kiosk when people asked her questions about Cy.

Kim realized what had happened and he said in a loud, stern voice, "First one who talk about this, I cut out his tooth!"

"You mean tongue?"

"Yes. I forget. Tongue. Tongue, tongue, tongue."

"What is this, this tongue?" asked one girl.

Soon they all had their tongues sticking out and were laughing. Kam began to laugh also.

Suddenly she liked Kim very much, and she liked his friends. She was awfully glad she had come tonight. Something told her that the future was going to be very happy for her.

Ψ   Ψ   Ψ

Mai Lei was playing a waiting game with Bu.

She had told him that she was meeting Bill Scott in an official capacity in conjunction with her job. However, she carefully complied with her father's wishes and did not see Bill at all during off-duty hours. In this manner, she had cleverly handled her father's decree that they should not see one another until he had made up his mind about their future.

This was vexing to Bu, as now he didn't see Bill at all. He missed their discussions.

"Did you see Major Bill at work today?"

"No, Father."

"Why did you not?"

"Our office had no work with his office today."

"When you work with his office, do you speak only of the business to be done?"

"Yes, of course, except when ..."

"When what?"

"Well, when all of us go to lunch, the Americans always talk of other things, and they expect us to express ourselves also."

"Perhaps the next time you work there, you could ask Major Bill his impression of the new cabinet—and the new prime minister."

"Perhaps I could ask him to stop by here to see you when he is out in this vicinity and not too busy."

"That would be most forward, Mai Lei. Do not do such a thing."

"He asks about your health, Father, whenever he sees me."

"He is most thoughtful."

"Father, I think it would be proper for Major Scott to visit us here at home. After all, he is a guest in our country. It is only right that we be hospitable."

Bu knew that he was the real loser in his own edict, but it was foremost that he save face. His daughter was giving him a way to do so. He accepted her suggestions calmly and without hesitation.

"I will write him a note. Please help me with the English. I think I will invite him to supper next Wednesday."

Mai Lei, afraid to reveal her happiness, measured her steps as she went to the cupboard to get writing paper.

Ψ   Ψ   Ψ

Mark Buckley had wangled a trip to Pleiku Province, and then added on six days' leave.

He spent most of his time at a Special Forces camp off Highway 19, about fifteen kilometers from the Cambodian border. For several days, he talked to the locals about the situation in Cambodia and the different tribes that drifted back and forth across this abstract political boundary.

Finally, members of one tribe, whose village was in Cambodia, came to the camp for medical attention. Mark, having assured himself of their loyalty, arranged to visit their village.

He traveled with the group of natives and worked hard during the trip to get to know the people and gain their confidence to the extent that they would talk freely with him. When this moment finally came, he had his interpreter ask the question that he had been waiting to ask since his arrival in the province.

"Do you know of an American man living across the border?"

The tribesmen looked puzzled and did not answer.

Again, the interpreter tried. "It is said that an American man lives across the border with Vietnamese. Do you know of such a man?"

At last, one of the men replied, "There is such a man—a white man like this American, but he is of the nation of the old conquerors."

"The French? Does he mean the French?" asked Mark.

"Yes, Ông Buckley, it is a Frenchman."

Mark was both relieved and disappointed. However, he had to make sure that this Frenchman was not Ted Holden. He learned that the man was in the village of Phum Lun. This place was within a few days' journey on foot from his new friends' village. It seemed a small enough risk to take in order to establish the man's identity.

At sunup, with some villagers whom he trusted, Mark left for Phum Lun. He was back at the Special Forces camp two days later minus two cartons of cigarettes, four cakes of soap, and a box of tropical chocolate bars, all of which he had given to his native friends and to one half-mad, but very grateful, Frenchman.

Now Mark, returning by chopper to Saigon, tired and dirty, wondered if the Special Forces camp commander would report to higher headquarters Mark's visit, his mysterious disappearance from camp, and subsequent return.

Bill, the only person who knew Mark's real mission, met him at the heliport, anxious to know the outcome. As they drove through the darkening, crowded streets toward the Hangout, Mark filled Bill in with the details of his trip. A large black thunderhead loomed above the city and a strong wind suddenly whipped through the streets, hurrying people to places of refuge.

"I'll bet that Frenchman was surprised to see you."

"Surprised and scared to death. I think he felt that some of the natives might report my visit to the VC."

"But he took all the goodies you brought."

"Hell, yes! Not at all up to his standards, as he made sure that he told me, but grabbed everything. You know the French."

The storm broke over Saigon with a vengeance as Bill pulled into the driveway of the Hangout. Both men made a dash for the wide porch the moment the jeep was parked, but they were still wet to the skin before they reached the house.

When they had changed out of their wet clothing and Mark was thinking of a hot bath, Bill came to the door of his room and handed him a tall gin and tonic.

"I'm sorry things didn't work out, Mark, but I hope you won't take any more risks like that."

"Now wait a minute. Things didn't work out badly. What if that guy had been Holden–alive? That would have been the end of everything for me."

"I realize things could have been worse, but I know you want to end this uncertainty, this waiting. Say, why don't you join me in a visit to Mai Lei's tonight? Get your mind off your problem."

"Not on your life. That gal of yours wants to see me about as much as she wants to see the VC. Besides, this rain isn't going to let up for another three hours and all of Cholon will be washed away again, including Ông Bu's place! Now, get on your way, oh Lochinvar. All I want is a hot bath, another drink, and about eighteen hours of sleep."

Ψ　Ψ　Ψ

It was all because of Kim.

That's why Janet had accepted Mark's invitation to come down to Saigon for the last weekend in November. She liked the big Korean whom Mark had helped as a small boy, and she felt that, because of Mark, Kim had become a very fine man, loyal to his own country and friendly to hers.

She had elected, however, to stay at the Embassy Hotel instead of the Hangout because she was determined to keep her interest in Mark from getting out of hand. It was just too tempting.

Kim had sent an invitation to Mark to a party "to meet his new bride," and asked in the note that he "bring his number one girl."

Mark picked up Janet and shortly they were climbing the stairs to the studio. As soon as Mark saw Kam, he remembered her as the young girl involved with Ned Green, but he did not mention their previous encounters. It was Kam, later in a moment of quiet, who recalled to him the note he had delivered from Newell Osborne.

The upstairs studio was decorated with many colored lights and hanging lanterns. Kam had made several large flower arrangements. All evidence of an artist's studio and Hue's large bed had been removed. Now there were several tables and chairs. Janet was interested in the diverse group of guests who milled around the large room, occasionally sampling the wide variety of Vietnamese, Chinese, Korean, and American foods arranged on a long table in front of the windows. On the terrace, a bar offered a staggering variety of drinks.

She was the only American woman; the rest were Vietnamese. There were American, Korean, and Vietnamese men. Since they all wore sport shirts and slacks, she had no idea what ranks they held or what service each represented. She didn't care.

A big redheaded American came up with a very small, very lovely Vietnamese girl. He introduced himself as Red and said he was one of Kim's best friends. Later a smaller dark-haired American, with an equally attractive Vietnamese girl, introduced himself as Dave, and suggested that she not believe anything Red had told her. Both of these men seemed to know Mark and spoke to him with deference, never failing to add a "sir" when it was proper to use one. Obviously, Kim had told them about Mark.

Kim told Mark of his marriage to Kam. It had been a simple ceremony, performed by a Buddhist priest, and kept very quiet because Kim had not been able to get permission from the Korean authorities in time to make the date.

"My colonel, Colonel Uhm, he make okay for me."

At that moment a rather short, attractively round Vietnamese woman in a tight, American-style silk dress, joined them.

She was with a chubby Korean, introduced as Colonel Uhm, Kim's boss. The Vietnamese woman, Ba Thoa, did most of the talking for Colonel Uhm because his English was poor. The fact that the two seemed to communicate when one could speak only Korean and the other knew no Korean was one of the lingering mysteries of the evening.

Later Janet found herself on the terrace in spirited and warm conversation with Ba Thoa.

"What you do in Vietnam, Madame Holden?"

"I am an anthropologist. I study your people and try to help them."

"That very nice."

"It's very hard work sometimes. Now I am in Buon Sut Mgra, where I work on a book for the Montagnards."

"That very nice."

"Thank you. And what do you do, Ba Thoa?"

"I run number one whorehouse."

"That's very nice," said Janet, not losing her poise.

"You bet, baby. You come visit. I show you around," said Ba Thoa proudly.

Later there was dancing and some singing. All the guests were enjoying themselves because they were happy for Kim and his bride. Just before curfew broke up the evening, Kim drew Mark aside and talked to him earnestly.

"I like you number one girl. You like her too?"

"Yes, Kim. She is a wonderful person. I want very much to marry her."

"Then you go, marry her. She sumpin pretty good."

"Yes, I know, but there are—well, some complications. You know?"

"Oh, that too bad. She best one for you."

$$\Psi \quad \Psi \quad \Psi$$

The next day as they were driving out to the heliport, Janet finally allowed herself to be alone with Mark.

She saw this as a necessary break in her vow because of some disquieting news she had received from Newell Osborne.

"Mark, I have been talking to Newell and, well, he says he thinks you are taking undue risks because of me."

Mark looked at her sharply.

"Not for you. For us, darling. But how did he know?"

"He just put a lot of things together and came up with the answer. Please, Mark, please promise me you will stop this. I don't want anything to happen to you or Ted. I'm afraid that if you get things stirred up, Ted or you might end up suffering for it. I don't want that, Mark. Let things work out naturally. Otherwise you may do much more harm than good."

"Janet, if there is information available concerning Ted that I did not try to uncover, I would never forgive myself. Remember this: your happiness is my greatest desire. I only hope that someday I will be able to play an important part in that happiness," he replied.

Janet was quiet for a moment. She was choosing her words with care.

"I must warn you again, Mark. My happiness is concerned first with Ted. It will always be that way as long as there ... as there is Ted."

Mark, realizing how hard it was for her to speak of the possibility of Ted being dead, thought it best not to press her further. He reached over and patted her hand.

Chapter VIII

DECEMBER

The opening of the Ned Green art show was the biggest event in Saigon that December.

There had been an unofficial preview one day earlier for all those who had personally assisted in organizing the exhibition. Kam attended this function.

She wanted to be there to see Ned and Hue honored because she knew this would be her final farewell to them. She also wanted Kim to attend with her, because he was so much a part of her present happiness.

As they entered the exhibition hall, Kam was startled to see the large portrait of Cy smiling down at her. The committee had chosen this drawing of Hue's to be the central theme of the show.

It was a good choice because it was a happy picture and gave a lift to the visitors. Over the drawing, a small sign read "Honoring Theodore Cyrus Green, who gave his life that another might live."

On each side of the picture were crossed United States and Vietnamese flags. Below it was a large painted red Ψ in the style of Cy's distinctive signature.

Passing to the right of the picture, Kam and Kim entered a large L-shaped room which displayed all the pictures Ned Green had created for his exhibition. Kam noticed that on the right-hand corner of each picture was a small card reading, "Starting at 20,000 piastres" or

"Starting at 50,000 piastres," prices the committee had suggested. Below each was a small box.

"What these for?" asked Kim.

Kam was bewildered. "I not know."

Kim turned and spoke in English to a lovely Vietnamese woman standing close by.

"Excuse, Madame. You know what for this?"

Kam looked over at the woman and instantly grabbed Kim's arm. "No, no, Kim, it is …!"

However, the woman smiled and held out her small hand. She spoke in Vietnamese.

"I am Madame Ky. You must be Cô Kam who owns these paintings and, of course, knew the artist, the American Ned Green."

"Yes, Madame Ky, that is correct," stammered Kam.

Then Kam motioned to Kim and said, "This is my husband, Corporal Kim. We are just married."

Madame Ky turned to Kim and said in English, "Congratulations to you both. I hope you will be very happy."

Sensing that both Kam and Kim were ill at ease, Madame Ky laughed and continued speaking in English.

"You asked about the signs and the boxes. Well, you see, we decided that the paintings and sketches should go to the ones who would pay the most for them. Each person who has an interest fills out these little cards. Then on the day before the exhibition ends, we place the highest bid received on each picture. After that, everyone who wishes can bid again, and the highest bidder gets the picture."

Kim was astounded.

What a way to make money!

An idea started to materialize. After taking a pen from his pocket, he picked up one of the cards and began to copy down the minimum price of each picture. Even after the charity cut, he realized Kam was going to become a rich woman. His focus on the show vanished. His mind was busily planning for the future. He barely acknowledged Madame Ky's farewell.

Kam liked the exhibit. Pictures were grouped mostly by color.

With each group was one or two of Hue's sketches that was chosen to match or at least complement the mood of the oils. Thus the brighter paintings were hung with the more active or happy sketches, while the more somber groupings were placed with the more pensive ones.

Off the main gallery was a smaller room. Here hung over twenty Ψ paintings, loaned for the exhibit by their owners. As Kam saw them, she tried to remember the person to whom she had sold each one. Then she spotted Newell Osborne's name next to one and her mind returned for a moment to that day when he had visited the kiosk. It had been the start of Cy's success.

"Do you remember that day?"

Kam turned and saw Newell now standing beside her. He smiled and held out his hand. As she took it, she returned his smile and called for Kim, who had lagged several pictures behind.

"This Mr. Osborne. He Colonel Buckley's boss."

"That's right, Mark works for me."

"This is husband."

"Oh yes, Mark told me about you. So this is Corporal Kim."

"Yes, I Kim. Colonel Buckley my good friend. He number one man. I know since little boy in Korea. Why you no make he chicken colonel?"

Newell laughed and said that he hoped that would happen some day soon.

"You will come to the big opening tomorrow night?"

Kam shyly shook her head and looked at the floor.

In a low voice she said, "Many people come. They see me. Think I still sad for Cy. They no know I marry number one Korean corporal. They no understand."

"Of course. I certainly understand, and I know others will also as soon they are aware of the circumstances. By the way, do you know that the Army has granted a full pardon for Ned, er, ah, Cy? That means he is no longer a deserter."

Kam smiled. "That mean he now good man?"

"Yes, Kam. He's now a good man."

"Then what you think, Mr. Osborne? Look."

She led Newell back to the other room and stood before a large, rather somber painting. Newell noticed that Cy had named it "Homesick."

"How about if you send this picture to Cy Mom and Papa? Could do?"

Newell realized that Kam was making a very generous and considerate gesture, and for a moment, he could not speak.

Finally, he said, "I think you're doing a very thoughtful and kind thing; I'll see that the picture is taken down and placed in the other room, marked as your property. I'll tell the committee of your change in plans."

"Tell them I give them all money on number one high price picture in all of show, so orphans do okay."

After talking to Professor Loy and several other guests, Kim and Kam left and headed back to the studio.

Kim was deep in thought as they walked through the crowded streets. Suddenly he grabbed Kam's arm to stop her.

"Look, Kam, you go back to flat. I leave you now; see you there in sec."

"You go work now?"

"No I be there pretty quick-like."

Kim tore off through the crowds.

Kam had finished a Coca-Cola, removed her green *ao dai*, and was lying on the bed when she heard the front door open and slam closed. There were hurried footsteps on the stairs before Kim burst into the room, carrying a brown paper grocery bag.

He dumped the contents of the bag on her. She was buried in 500-piastre notes.

"Here, Kam, here all my money. We gonna do okay. I got plans, baby, I got plans!"

Ψ   Ψ   Ψ

Brandy Masters was delighted when the Doms accepted her invitation to join her at Cy's exhibit.

It gave her a chance to return the many kindnesses of Madame Dom, her language teacher. Her visits to the Doms' two-room flat were like walking into another world. As her Vietnamese improved, she began to enjoy their company and become an active participant in their social life. Mr. Dom was an ex-soldier who, because of his invalid status and good war record, had a modest government position. The Doms were members of the young middle class that was emerging in Saigon. This was a class with a modern outlook, serious about politics, and sincerely trying to make a better world for themselves. If not necessarily pro-American, they realized that the presence of Americans in Vietnam allowed them to live as they wished.

The art exhibit had been enjoyable and exciting, and the three friends were talking about it as they left for dinner. Brandy had chosen the Golden Lotus because it was located just across the plaza. The food was good and it never seemed to be too crowded. As they dodged the cars, the Doms began to chatter excitedly about the many well-known Vietnamese and Americans who had attended the function, but Brandy was not even trying to follow the conversation. She was deep in thoughts of her own.

A hard rain had fallen while they had been inside, but now it had slackened to a fine mist that turned to gold in the automobile headlights. Ahead of them was the open veranda of the Continental Hotel. The little orange lights on the tables looked inviting to the three as they walked by. Brandy almost suggested they stop by for a drink, but the Golden Lotus was very close and it was getting late.

The air-conditioned restaurant provided welcome relief from the humid plaza. Shortly the three were enjoying a French-Vietnamese supper. The art exhibit dominated the conversation, but Ba Dom could see that Brandy did not understand too much of it. The thin, elegant woman switched to English.

"Cô Brandy, what seems to be the matter? I think maybe your mind not with us, although you are here."

Brandy smiled. "Ah, Ba Dom, you can tell. Yes, I have something on my mind. Something important that I forgot. Don't worry; there will be time for me to get it done after we finish here."

The Vietnamese couple smiled at Brandy. Her gaiety returned; she concentrated on her guests.

Ψ   Ψ   Ψ

Despite the rain, Hieu peddled his cyclo as if a demon straight from hell was in pursuit.

The bulging cords in his strong, wiry arms showed the force he was exerting, holding on to the grips of the handlebar as he steered the careening pedicab through the crowded streets of Saigon. His eyes were cold and focused only on the road ahead. Between his clenched teeth was an unlit, and now soggy, Salem cigarette. His traditional peasant hat barely hung on behind him on his shoulders, held by an old, knotted bit of string around his neck.

The street was nearly empty due to the downpour, but if any of those forced to leap out of the way of the racing cyclo had taken the time to look, they would have wondered what the hurry was, for there was no one holding on in terror to the seats.

It was empty.

Hieu was not risking his life and his cyclo for a passenger's P. It was a wager.

Moments before, several cyclos were waiting at the curb and, despite the rain, competing for fares on Tu Do Street near the Caravelle Hotel.

"Hey, don't go him. He too old and slow," Nguyen said to two American GIs hurrying by on the sidewalk.

He turned to Hieu and in Vietnamese said, "Old man, why don't you take that ugly cyclo and get off the streets?"

"Hey, I'm still faster than you," Hieu yelled back.

The two Americans, amused, stopped and watched the action.

Chien chimed in, "He's right. You're a disgrace. Time for you to junk that wreck and stay away."

"Hey, I'm faster than either of you."

"Not so."

"Yes, I am"

"I bet you are not."

"Bet?"

There was a long pause as Chien considered the matter. A wager was a very serious business, after all.

Finally, he narrowed his eyes and replied, "Five P says you can't go down Tu Do to the river, back up Pasteur to Le-Loi, and back here faster than Nguyen."

"Twenty-five P!"

"Ten P!"

"Twenty P!"

"Twelve P!"

"Done!"

The Americans had been joined by a small group of Vietnamese who were now making side bets and arguing over the odds. Some rule clarifications were required and the route and terms were set.

Moments later, the two were off, peddling in a frenzy south on Tu Do, weaving around Tri-Lambrettas, larger vehicles, bicycles, and pedestrians. Hieu, with many more years of experience on these streets, had an edge anticipating the parts of the mosaic of traffic he could intimidate and those he could not. As a result, by the time he reached the right turn onto the riverside road, he was twenty feet ahead.

Hieu was long gone around the corner when Nguyen's drive chain jumped off the well-worn gearing and his cyclo swerved to a stop, nearly running down an elderly Vietnamese woman who then stood in the rain and took several minutes to berate him and his ancestors, in colorful detail.

Of all this, Hieu knew nothing. All he knew was that he was in the lead. A few moments later, he skidded around the corner at Le-Loi. He ignored the policeman's whistle and the bleat of the horn of the Tri-Lambretta he had cut off.

The strong rain had changed to a thick mist.

Blinking water from his eyes, he could see the Caravelle two streets away. Hieu found something more within his old, stringy body and pressed on.

Ψ   Ψ   Ψ

When they left the restaurant, Brandy accompanied the Doms to their parked Honda. She declined a lift, made excuses, and said good night.

Then she returned to the art exhibit.

The show hall was now jammed with both Vietnamese and foreigners, but Brandy had to find Professor Loy.

Finally, she bumped into him and he did not resist her invitation to join her in a quiet corner of the room.

"Professor Loy, I have been thinking about my painting."

The professor had spent many long hours listening to aggrieved painting owners' complaints.

"You do not like its location?" he said with as much politeness as he could muster.

"Oh, that's not it at all. The displays are wonderful. You see, what I would like to do is to, well, donate my painting to the Orphans' Relief. You could sell it also."

Loy brightened up, "Ah, Cô Masters, that is very generous. Are you sure you wish to do this?"

"Yes, Professor Loy. I've made up my mind."

He smiled and held out his hand.

"These kids need it more than I do. Would you take care of the arrangements for me?"

"Of course, Cô Masters. I will take care of it right away and thank you for your kindness."

Professor Loy smiled broadly, musing about an old Vietnamese fable about the one good chicken in the flock.

Brandy worked her way through the crowd to take one last look at her picture. She was going to miss it. She had grown fond of the painting, her symbol of one good thing that had been done in Vietnam—a man who once had been against this war to the point of desertion had suddenly turned and become completely committed.

As she approached the painting, she thought she recognized one of the Americans in the crowd looking at the paintings. Was it Mark Buckley? It was. Impulse drove her to leave but, for some reason, she found herself coming closer to him.

"Hello, Mark."

She couldn't believe her own voice.

He turned and smiled down at her.

"Hello, Brandy. That's a nice thing you did–lending your painting to the show."

He's so composed. As if Trong Thoi had never taken place.

"Well, I got to thinking about how little I was really giving of myself to this war, and it seemed a way to do something, however small."

"Every little bit helps."

Brandy detected a bit of sarcasm in his voice. She wondered if he was remembering picking her up off that table in the bar and then carrying her naked body through the town at Trong Thoi. Or was it after the whole affair, when she had tried to damage him.

Either one would probably do it. Damn.

Suddenly Professor Loy broke through the crowd. He was carrying a small sign and a box which he taped to the wall below the picture.

This painting has been donated to the Orphans' Relief through the generosity of its owner, Miss Brandy Masters. Those wishing to acquire it, please place your bids here. Starting at 60,000 P.

Mark read the sign. Touched by Brandy's sincerity and generosity and ashamed of his remark, he turned, but Brandy was gone. He glanced over the heads of the people in the crowded room and saw her heading for the exit.

"Brandy, wait, wait a minute," he called.

By the time he got to the exit and looked out in both directions along the wet, crowded street, Brandy Masters was gone.

"Dammit," he muttered, "I've got to let her know that I approve of at least one thing she's done over here."

Ψ   Ψ   Ψ

Phuc stopped himself from pushing the green button on the dashboard, for the thirteenth time.

He struggled to remember why he had to wait.

I want it now. But I must wait. Why? Oh, he will hurt me again if I do not wait.

299

So instead, he pushed down on the small accelerator pedal of the small, old French Citroen H delivery van. The hard rain had stopped, becoming a fine mist. He could now see better out the nearly vertical windshield. The one working wiper rattled across the glass, digging deeper into it, the few remaining bits of rubber on it almost worthless.

Phuc did not notice the rattle made by the rusted-out vehicle with corrugated metal sides. These had been freshly painted with signs that said, "Saigon Flowers – Delivery Today."

No, that was not quite correct. The right corrugated panel side of the van had been cut away. A canvas piece painted to look like the original metal and with the advertisement, had been mounted by Ahn and the men tasked by Duat for this project.

Concealed within was a large, thick metal plate, braced by welded bars twelve inches from the false, fabric wall. The face of the plate featured eight nearly flat, rectangular US Army claymore mines, easily obtained by Duat's organization from a supply depot outside of Saigon.

"Our drug trade is most helpful at such times," Duat had commented to Ahn.

When triggered, the mines would send shrapnel in a forward direction for quite a distance. Far enough to enter the exhibition hall lobby and tear into all standing there, attending the Ned Green art show.

With luck, this would include Newell Osborne and many of the top officials of both the US Embassy, MACV, and the Saigon government.

Wires led from the claymores to a small battery and then under the front seat, ending at the green button.

All Phuc knew, or could sometimes remember, was that he had to wait to press the green button and then he would get more of his favorite treat, a crispy, baked banana cake, Bánh chuối nướng.

Why must I wait? Oh, yes. He will beat me ...

Ahn had found the perfect tool, and his master, Duat, had complimented him for an inspired choice. Phuc was a young man who had the misfortune of being too close to a bar bombing in Saigon some months ago. Concussion. Confusion, fogginess, headaches, vacant stares, and sometimes slurred speech had resulted.

But he could still drive a motor vehicle.

"Well enough and long enough, anyway," Ahn had told his master.

After Duat's organization had stolen an old, tired delivery van and started turning it into a weapon, Ahn and his men had searched for a driver. They found Phuc. Penniless and living on the streets, they trained him with reward and brutal punishment. Banana cake and beatings. Finally, after several trial runs, they had their man.

The day of the Ned Green show, Phuc was to drive from Cholon to the exhibition hall on Le-Loi Street at a specific time. Once there he would pull up in front of the entrance at the curb. Several of Saigon's "white mice" had been bribed to look the other way when the "florist delivery" arrived.

After stopping the van, Phuc would press the green button to receive his reward. He remembered, dimly, that if he did not do exactly as he had been told and trained to do, more beatings and no cake would be the result.

And he loved the freshly baked, crispy cakes that Ahn had provided, between the beatings.

Left out of Phuc's training was the detail that under the Citroen's small front bench seat was another claymore, facing up, and also wired to the green button.

"No loose ends," Duat had told Ahn.

The crew that had modified the van and recruited Phuc had already been eliminated.

Ahn suspected that this whole operation, one more attempt on Newell Osborne's life, had not been authorized by the North. If Hanoi found out Duat was behind another failure, and acting alone, Ahn was sure they would eliminate him, Saigon drug organization or not.

Ahn savored this. He felt a tingle of real power.

I must save this for the proper time. If it fails then, after a word in the right ear, that Chinese dog will be at my feet. Then we will see how much pain he likes before he dies. I will like living above Saigon and having all men fear me. Especially that Thi. What I will do to her! Perhaps keep her naked and chained, waiting for my next amusement.

Phuc dimly remembered driving down Le-Loi before. Actually, he had taken this route over twenty times with Ahn riding next to him.

He glanced down at the green button again.

Must be soon. Ah, yes, that large sign over there ... not far to go.

Ahn had made up a story for each block along the way, incorporating commercial signs and other markers to keep his driver on the right path. They had only risked it once before with Phuc alone. Now, so far, it was working.

The small van came up behind a cyclo. Phuc could see the driver peddling in a frenzy. For a long moment, he stared and wondered about it. Then, the fog lifted again, and he remembered.

Let no one stop you from your task. Stay to the right. Do not slow down. Do not stop. If you fail ...

Phuc hit the horn button, and a tiny sound of Paris streets bleated out in Saigon.

Hieu heard the noise behind him. Only a street to go before he would win. He ignored it.

Go to the devil!

He pressed on. The Salem was still in his mouth, limp and soggy, the tobacco half fallen out. The filter tip had now become almost flat between his clenched yellow-stained teeth.

Phuc stared at the back of the madly pumping cyclo driver just a foot in front of the short hood of his van.

I must not be late. No cake. Hurt. Let no one stop me.

With a left jerk of the steering wheel, Phuc swerved into the lane on his left. The van skidded on the wet street, rocked, and tilted. He spun the wheel back to the right and the Citroen, off balance due to the modifications, tilted over on its side and slid to a halt.

Hieu peddled on. In the van, Phuc was dazed and scratched but unhurt.

Stopped. The cake. Now.

Bleeding and lying against the shattered right window, Phuc reached over for the green button.

He could already taste the warm, crispy Bánh chuối nướng.

Ψ Ψ Ψ

For some time, the NLF had concentrated all efforts on a gigantic attack on key points in the country.

Bit by bit, they slowly shared more information. Duat then concluded that this latest plan, which included an attack on Saigon, was for once, more than an idle wish on the part of the NLF. This time they claimed to have the equipment, manpower, and real desire to mount a concerted attack that could result in the fall of the city.

Still, after so many attempts, Duat was not going to risk himself without a firsthand assessment of the plan by one of his trusted people. He selected Thi for this job. Duat had many reasons, not the least of which was the fact that she was becoming too close to a Korean corporal. That the corporal's interest in her was solely physical made the situation worse from Duat's point of view.

He knew that sooner or later the Korean would leave her, causing Thi's unstable emotions to erupt so violently that she could not be relied on to behave rationally. There was no room for such a person in his organization. Normally Duat did not care to "save" people if they became too widely known or developed problems that might jeopardize his organization. They were simply killed, or sacrificed.

Thi is different, unique. A replacement as fearless, clever, and capable would be hard to find.

Her personal acquaintance with many high-ranking Americans makes her invaluable. I made a great exception in her case, against my better judgment. Yes, Thi will live and work for me, for the moment, at least until after this new attack on Saigon. Then ...

Duat moved quickly. Thi was summoned. He told her that Corporal Kim was a member of a Korean espionage unit and had been assigned to report on her activities to the allies. A fabrication, but an effective one.

"I do not have to tell you what this means—once you are a police or intelligence suspect."

Thi froze. Her breath stopped for a few seconds. She shivered slightly, then quickly got control of herself and regained her composure. She heard Duat continue:

"But you have proved yourself to be extremely valuable to me and, for that reason, I am suspending my usual rule. You will continue to be of use to us. However, it will be necessary for you to leave Saigon for a period of time. When you return you will meet the young Korean once again. You will accuse him of being unfaithful to you in your absence, and you will quarrel. At this time you will break off the liaison once and for all."

Duat watched Thi closely for her reaction to his instructions. He noticed the pupils of her eyes dilating for the instant before she cast them down. It was her only outward sign of emotion. Inwardly, Thi was angry beyond measure. Many thoughts raced through her head, all concerned with the perfidy of the big Korean.

I will kill him on that last night. I will kill him slowly and painfully. I will . . .

Then she heard Duat's voice again.

"You will leave the city tomorrow morning with the sunrise. See Ahn for the details of your duties."

That day, at dawn, Thi left the city dressed as a farm girl and easily made contact with the VC north of Gia Dinh. She entered their underground training camp and took the sappers course, Duat's idea, and a masterstroke.

Although the VC knew she was one of Duat's group, they thought she was a recent recruit, and thus still apart from Duat's independent ways. Quickly, she became trusted by the NLF. When school was over and she started her trip, she was marked loyal to the cause. The resulting ease of access spelled unqualified success for her throughout her reconnaissance for Duat.

Ψ   Ψ   Ψ

The day of the Ned Green art show, Thi was again in Saigon, with anger welling up in her like a gnawing, rapidly festering wound.

Before reporting to Xa Bui, she had been merely tired, sore, and dirty. Now she was all of that, as well as humiliated. The four weeks in the field, first going to school and then traveling about to contact the VC unit commanders had been a rough, filthy business. She felt entitled to more respect than the cold brush-off received from Ahn.

"You are filthy. Ông Duat never receives anyone in your condition.

Go home and wash. Rest. Return here at eleven tomorrow evening and I may have further instructions for you."

She was still enraged as she got into a cab and headed for her flat.

"I didn't expect a bouquet, but a pleasant word wouldn't have been too much. I've heard him give that to a dog."

"What's that, woman?"

The cab driver wasn't civil either. He had taken her for a beggar, demanding to see the fare before taking her to her address.

"Nothing that concerns you, pig. Just drive me to the address I gave you."

He grumbled and proceeded through the darkness. A heavy rain began to fall, striking the little Renault like a thousand tiny hammers. Infiltration flares illuminated the southern end of the city. There was sporadic small-arms fire in the distance across the river. Nothing had changed in Saigon in her absence.

"That might be part of Won's probe to test the southern defenses," she mused as she leaned back in the seat and momentarily closed her eyes.

Then the driver pulled up in front of her building and stopped. Thi paid him and ran through the rain to the doorway. She burst into the living room of the No. 516 flat. She peeled off her black pajama trousers, dirty white blouse, and well-worn underwear. Finally, she removed the bandana around her hair and let it fall about her naked body. She stood among the filthy wet clothes, head down and shoulders slumped forward.

She dragged herself to the windows and threw them open wide, hoping that the storm might create a breeze. Then she headed for the bathroom and climbed into the empty tub. The cool porcelain soothed her aching body. She lay there with no desire to move. Finally, she reached up with her foot and started warm water, waiting for the heat to flow over her.

It was an hour before she emerged from the bathroom. She wrapped a towel about her waist while she brushed and combed her freshly washed hair.

Then there was the sound of an explosion.

That's not far. Wonder which team it is. Target?

Sirens and noises from across the plaza attracted her attention and she moved to the open window to hunt the source of the commotion. By leaning far out she could see a large crowd in front of the exhibition hall. The nearby sound of the explosion and the hard rain that had turned to a fine mist did not seem to dim the enthusiasm of the people.

What can that be all about? Some sort of event. Ah, that dead black American artist.

Seeking a sign of the explosion, she leaned out. Off to her right, a block down the street, she saw smoke and a tangle of traffic, and the remains of some sort of small vehicle on its side. This made no sense to her.

She felt the dampness on her naked torso, breasts, and shoulders. Disappointed, she retraced her steps to the bedroom.

Not here. Damn. A great target missed. Hopefully many dead Americans there.

She dropped her towel, sank down on the bed, and fell into exhausted sleep, lying naked on the bed. She did not notice the brightness of the lights she had left burning.

Ψ   Ψ   Ψ

With a good night's sleep behind her, she was ready to face Ahn. She would see Duat later, in the evening, when he started his day. Ahn met her in the office section of Duat's penthouse and started the interrogation. This reminded her of the cattle prod affair. At least this time there would be no torture. Thi was still annoyed that not one word of welcome was spoken—not one word of concern for her well-being, not one word of praise.

Within, Ahn was ecstatic that the bombing of the art show had failed. Of course, no outward sign must be allowed. That would be fatal. Duat had forbidden any mention of it.

As he put Thi through her paces, Ahn's narrow, cold eyes masked a hidden warm and luxurious feeling of personal power that washed over him. In her pique, Thi did not notice the barest trace of a smile as Ahn savored the future betrayal of their master.

306

Not this day, but when the moment is perfect ...

All day, Thi kept tracing her route of travel on a large map and indicating units, names of commanders, and locations of weapons and food caches. At noon, they took a break for a simple lunch. Only then did the subject change.

"Ông Duat tells me that you have made a poor choice of lovers."

Thi did not answer.

"There was some consideration of eliminating him."

"I also have been considering it," she admitted.

Ahn smiled. It was not the answer he expected. He had forgotten that Thi was not like the others. Her sense of revenge, already highly developed against the Americans, was easily switched to the Koreans. He knew that it could just as easily be switched toward himself—or even Ông Duat. He still felt the results of the cattle prod and could not help thinking Ông Duat had made a serious error by not eliminating her.

Thi took advantage of the pause in conversation to change the subject.

"I have never spent time as a peasant before."

Ahn merely grunted; otherwise, he ignored her observation. The quiet period gave Thi a chance to think about her visit to the country. The few hours back in Saigon had already started to bring the trip into a false perspective. The worst aspects of her travel in the heat and rain had already begun to fade in her mind, while the more pleasant memories of the nights with new comrades in secret camps, and the endless discussion of the New Vietnam to come, were still bright and shiny.

Above all in her memories was Trun Du, one of the Viet Cong leaders. It had been near the little village of Bao Tre that a young boy, her guide from the last VC unit, had left her.

"You walk that road," he had said, then turned and disappeared into the jungle.

Down the road, a peasant woman stepped out of the brush and escorted her into a small village. For a long time she waited. Finally, a man on a Honda stopped and told her to hop on. It began to rain. In short order, she was drenched. A large convoy of American trucks crowded them off the narrow, muddy road, and they cursed the Americans. After the trucks had passed, they rode on for almost ten kilometers before her driver stopped and told her to get off.

She stood in the rain and watched him disappear down the muddy road. She was cold, muddy, hungry, and very low in spirit. The only shelter was a small lean-to along the bank of a stream. Thi headed for it.

"We've been waiting for you."

The voice came from an old farmer sitting far back in the shadows of the shelter. The lean-to was the entrance to a large cave complex. Thi was ushered into the underground world of the VC, where after she cleaned up, was given dry clothing.

The cave complex was the headquarters for a VC regiment. Its myriad rooms and chambers included the facilities for a complete community.

That evening Thi met Trun Du. He was lately down from the north. In appearance, he was a tall man and powerfully built. Sitting at his desk when Thi first entered his office, he reminded her of a kindly teacher she had known in elementary school. After the two days of her visit, Thi found him to be shrewd, domineering, and sometimes brutally harsh.

She was instantly attracted to him. She considered herself very lucky to share so much of his time. Often her thoughts wandered to fantasies of this powerful man taking her. Possessing her. Dominating her. Allowing her to be completely and wantonly a woman under his strong hands. Beneath his hard body.

And then his . . .

"Back to the map, Cô Thi."

Ahn's voice broke through her reverie and brought her back to the present. They worked through the afternoon, with him asking the questions, making her remember, relentlessly drawing out of her information she had already forgotten.

At six o'clock, Thi, exhausted from the ordeal of Ahn's interrogation, was taken into Duat's presence. With the map she and Ahn had drawn and the voluminous notes he had taken, she repeated the story of her trip. This time the words came easier, they seemed to flow out of her. She realized that resulted from her work with Ahn and despite her hatred for him, she silently thanked him. When she came to that point in her narrative concerning the tunnel complex at Bao Tre, she seemed to forget her fatigue. Duat noticed her eyes light up with unusual interest the moment she mentioned Trun Du.

Duat stopped her and asked for a detailed description of the man— even to details such as how he held a cigarette.

When she had finished, there was a long silence.

"So he has really come this time. At last General Du has come south."

"General Du?"

"Yes, Cô Thi, General Trun Du has come south to lead the Viet Cong in an assault on Saigon."

Ψ   Ψ   Ψ

Kim pulled his army sedan up in front of the Rex Hotel.

He seldom came here anymore because Colonel Uhm spent his time either at the office or at "The 92." He hoped that the colonel wouldn't be too long, as he wanted to get back to the flat, to Kam. He got out, stood on the sidewalk and joked with two American drivers.

"You get around this town a lot. I seen ya on Tu Do with a real hot babe."

"What day you see me?" Kim asked.

"Think it was Wednesday."

"Ah, Wednesday. That was number one girl."

"What you mean? Thursday you have different one?" The stocky American driver was getting into the pidgin English.

"You get picture, GI. Every day I get different girl. That much better."

"You know it, lover boy, but how you support them all?"

"I no support girl friends. Girl friends support me. They give me money. Say 'Please, Kim, let me be next.'"

"Goddamn liar!"

Kim looked beyond the soldiers and saw Thi standing there, watching them. She was very beautiful in an *ao dai* of lime silk with white trousers. Her long hair hung straight down her back, secured with a matching lime ribbon.

Without a word, Kim left the soldiers and went to the girl. The soldiers were astounded by Thi.

"Well I'll be a ..."

"That son of a bitch was telling the truth."

Thi was angry with Kim, but relieved that she had been able to attract his attention.

"Where have you been? I have been expecting you for five days."

"Where you been? You are one who took off."

"I had to visit my aunt in Hue. Listen, I have to see you. When can you come by?"

"Well, this ... I have great news. I am very happy. You see ..."

Thi interrupted, "Look, I haven't time to talk. Will you be by tonight?"

"No, I try to tell you, I ..."

"Don't tell me now. I have got to see you today. Will you be getting off at noon? I must see you."

Thi had been frantically trying to find Kim ever since her return to Saigon. Every day Ahn asked her if she had ended her affair with that "big Korean." She had to take his scathing rebuke as she admitted that she hadn't been able to find him. She was relieved that the search was over, but Duat's report that Kim was an intelligence agent who paid attention to her only to report on her activities still rankled. She vowed that she would kill him as soon as she had a chance.

"I get off at noon. I have an hour and a half, but your flat too far. I cannot get there and back."

Thi did not intend to lose Kim now. Taking a tablet and pencil from her purse, she quickly wrote down instructions.

"I want you to go to this address; it is my aunt's place, very close to here. Fifth floor. No. 516. Go in and wait for me. She said I could use it when she was away. Be there, darling, please."

She wrapped something in the paper and thrust it into Kim's hand, then hurried away.

Kim opened the paper and inside found a door key. He pocketed the paper and key and rejoined the soldiers.

"Wow, lover boy. How in hell you do it?"

"Jeeze, if you got any left over I'd like that one; try and remember your old buddy."

"Well, she great but I got to tell her I don't play house with her any more, cause I married," Kim said.

"Married?"

"Yes."

"You married? To who?"

"Girl you see me with on Tu Do Wednesday."

"My God. You got all this and screwed it up by getting married?"

Kim noticed Colonel Uhm approaching.

"So long, fellas. Here comes boss."

Kim dropped Colonel Uhm at "The 92." Then he stopped at a small sidewalk shop and had a duplicate made of the key that Thi had passed to him.

It just might come in handy some day.

Ψ　Ψ　Ψ

Thi had found Kim.

She did not consider it too much of a risk to give him the key to No. 516. She had carefully kept knowledge of the new flat from him because she considered him her personal property. Since Kim was not a target, Duat and his men had seen no reason to interfere.

But now, as an accused spy, he became very much part of her secret life. To follow her orders to terminate her relationship with him, she had to resort to using No. 516. The more she considered the whole matter, the more it seemed a masterstroke. She would kill him this noon, soon after she left her meeting with Ahn.

Yes, she would kill him and drag his body into the secret room. To-night Ahn could dispose of him through the roof access. If not tonight, then tomorrow night. The small risk of discovery was acceptable.

She grew excited as she thought of the jade-handled letter opener on the dresser in her old flat. It was so sharp, so thin, so delicate, yet so deadly. She had to stop by and pick it up. He must die with it. No spy, no man was stronger and more intelligent than she. No man would make a fool of her or betray her.

She smiled. She would use him once more. Men are the most vulnerable when they are making love.

The fools. All of them are so simply led. And killed. One lesson I learned in Paris.

Kim parked the sedan in front of the Rex and walked down to Tu Do. In no time, he had found the flat. He tried his new key copy and it worked perfectly. He slipped it in his shirt pocket and walked into the living room.

Kim gave a whistle. "Her aunt must be rich. I think maybe aunt not aunt. Is uncle–but not uncle," he laughed.

He explored the kitchen, the bath, and the bedroom. He found the bar and mixed himself his favorite drink, a brandy and orange soda. The flat was warm. Kim shrugged off his fatigue jacket, hung it over a chair, and sat down to leaf through a magazine. Soon he was up again to use the bathroom. This was the nicest, most modern one that he had ever seen.

Kim wandered into the bedroom and entertained himself in front of the large mirror. He tried the bed. It was cool and soft. Slowly he removed his boots and fatigue trousers. He carefully folded the trousers over the back of the chair and placed his boots side by side, near the bed. Then, remembering his jacket, he fetched it from the living room and hung it with his trousers. Kim felt wonderful and cool without his clothes. He stretched out on the bed and soon dropped off to sleep.

The opening of the unlocked door awakened Kim.

Thi ...

He decided to let her think he was asleep. He heard her close the door and throw the bolt. He arranged himself sprawling on the bed, with his arm over his eyes in such a way that he could watch her unobserved. Thi called softly and then came quietly into the bedroom.

Again she called his name but, noticing that he did not move, she stood at the side of the bed and looked at his sleeping figure. Her thoughts turned dark.

I should go ahead now and kill this Korean bastard while he sleeps. It would be so easy.

She planned to use a technique well known in the Far East: a blade inserted in the soft area directly behind the ear and into the brain.

But for Thi, he was too beautiful not to use one more time. She removed the letter opener from her purse and placed it under the other pillow, next to Kim.

Kim had watched this unfold through nearly closed eyes.

One bad-looking knife. One very bad girl.

Thi turned and undressed. Completely. Now nude, she slipped into bed and nestled beside him. She allowed her erect nipples to brush his chest. Then she moved closer.

Kim pretended to stir and slowly moved his body to cover her, nearly. His arm crossed over her and reached for the blade under the pillow while the other arm slowly caressed her body. As his hand found cold steel, he opened his eyes.

"Thi, I thought you never come."

Whispering to her and caressing her to divert her attention, he pushed the knife down between the sheets so that it would be impossible for her to retrieve it. He was over her now. His hands grabbed her hands and placed them on his lower back. Each time her hand left his body and reached for the pillow, he used some ruse to distract her. Once he rolled over completely on her arm and pulled the girl on top of him.

Thi's struggles to get the knife became less determined as Kim brought her to a high threshold of desire. She knew she was losing control of the moment, but now, she did not care. She was annoyed with herself, but for a reason she could not focus on. All that was in her mind was to be fully taken by this man: to lose herself wildly in his arms.

Kim looked down on Thi. She was trembling, starting to twitch. Fascinated, he watched her breasts quivering. He moved his hand to her wetness and heard her gasp and moan. Then he leaned down and kissed her breasts. With his tongue, he teased her rock-hard nipples. Her moaning started to become pleading. She had started to work herself against his leg, up and down. His body responded.

He buried his head between her breasts and felt her arms leave his buttocks and move toward his neck. She grasped his hair, raised his head, and kissed him. Kim felt her sucking in his tongue. Suddenly she disengaged her lips.

"Now, now," she called out hoarsely. It was a command.

Kim watched her head fall back to the bed and writhe in a torment of desire.

"Now, I said now," she said, louder.

Kim did not take her. Her hands were on her inner thighs, spreading them wider for him. His fingers penetrated farther this time. He found her spot, just inside. It was small, hard, and round. His fingers caressed it as his thumb found her clitoris outside and above. His fingers moved slowly in both areas. Softer, harder, slower, faster. He watched fascinated as her body responded to his every move. More inside, less outside, then the other, then both.

He owned her. She was at his command. Kim smiled and laughed.

He watched Thi's face, twisted with the pain of her pleasure. Her hips began to buck and her body closed around his two fingers inside her. From deep down in her throat, a guttural growl came. Her lips opened and her breathing came in quick short bursts. Suddenly she raised her head and took the left side of his chest in her teeth. She bit down hard on his small brown nipple. He felt the sharp pain and saw the blood ooze from between her teeth. She smiled a cruel smile.

He slapped her, and as her head fell back, he took her nipple between his teeth and bit her sharply. Her cry was uncontrolled and piercing. Her breath came in gasps of terror, pain, and desire. Her eyes were wide. The pupils were black pinpoints. Kim, aware of the madness of her desire, knew this was the right moment. He guided her hand to his swollen stiffness. She grasped it and thrust it into herself. No longer a rational person, she was completely an animal. Her only thought was sexual gratification and the quickest way for her to get it.

He rolled over on his side, then onto his back, pulling the girl along and finally up on top of him. Now straddling him, she took the initiative. He looked up at her. Her long hair was hanging down, lashing him as she leaned over him and swayed from side to side. Her body was covered with sweat and rivulets ran down her hanging, swaying breasts. He noticed her head swaying, keeping the rhythm of her undulating hips. Some blood from the bite he had given her joined the sweat and dripped from her nipple onto his chest. It mixed with his own blood. Now her hips moved forward and back in a rolling, rocking motion, stroking him deep inside her.

Thi now began emitting sharp little cries as she increased the tempo. Kim raised his hips into her, supporting himself with his legs. He started pushing upward in quick strong thrusts, the angle allowing him to find her spot, and he hit it again and again.

She screamed in a mix of French and Vietnamese he did not understand. Her body convulsed. He could feel a sudden rush of wetness from deep inside her.

He reached orgasm in an explosion just as Thi suddenly froze on him, then ground herself against him for a long moment, gasping more French. Then, with a small cry, she fell forward, spent, limp, exhausted on top of him. For a long time Kim let her lie there as he absently caressed her round, firm behind, enjoying the muffled small whimpers Thi made into his chest. He lay there enjoying the continuing sensual echo of his experience. Enjoying the momentary power he held over this beautiful, arrogant woman.

A strong knock on the door brought both of them back to the real world. They heard men's voices speaking in Vietnamese.

"Who they? What they saying?" Kim demanded.

"They are the police. Quick, take your clothing."

Thi left the bed and pulled back the silk tapestry that revealed the door to the hidden room.

"In here!" she hissed to Kim as she helped the naked Korean gather his clothes and hide.

Then she called out in a loud, sleepy voice, "In a minute, in a minute."

She grabbed a dressing gown and headed for the front door.

"Please stop pounding. This is rest time."

She opened the door in complete apprehension, but tried to give the impression of annoyance for this invasion of privacy. Standing in the hall were three young Vietnamese soldiers, obviously drunk.

315

"Ah, Cô Thi," slurred the leader. "We wish ... we wish an English lesson."

It was a moment before the surprised Thi realized the situation. Drunken minions of Ông Duat. Looking for a woman. Later they would pay dearly.

"You are not police," she said with chagrin. "Why, you impostors, leave my door this instant before I call the police. Go! Now!"

She slammed the door.

While Thi confronted the soldiers, Kim was feeling the walls of the dark room for the light switch. When he finally found it, he put on the lights and dressed. He glanced about the room as he put on his boots.

What a strange place—the mirrors, the makeup area, and the wigs. She must be some kind of actress.

Kim heard the door slam. Quickly he turned off all the lights as he adjusted his trousers and stood in the darkness. The door opened and Thi, in a high state of agitation, pulled him out of the secret room by the arm.

"It's dark in there. I couldn't see to lace my boots."

Panic seized Thi. Had the room been compromised?

"That's my aunt's secret closet. She thinks she should hide canned goods in there to prepare for a famine. Couldn't you find the light switch?"

"No, couldn't find, who at door?"

She was relieved that Kim hadn't seen the room.

"Some damned drunken soldiers. They said they were the police. God, I could cheerfully kill them!"

Kim wondered if she would do it with that sharp, jade-handled letter opener. He said nothing until he had completed dressing, and then turned to her with a smile.

"I must go but, say, I no get chance to tell you. I maybe never see you again. I married now. That's some sorta great!"

This news exploded in Thi's already confused mind like a grenade.

After this last time with him ... I didn't think I could ever kill him—or even part from him. I've been ordered to accuse him of unfaithfulness and to get rid of him. Now he's telling me that he's married! I'm mad enough to kill him.

316

Now, since I know he's an intelligence agent, assigned to spy upon me, he should be killed before he can file a report. I don't know what to do ...

The tough, vindictive Thi dissolved in a flood of tears. She was facing a situation that she could not cope with. She reached a chair in the living room and sobbed into her hands.

"But why you cry? I not your only boyfriend. You have others. I not number one in your book!"

"Oh, Kim, Kim. Don't you understand? I love you. You are the only man I have ever really loved."

Kim ignored her statement and continued his own farewell: "Well, I married now, baby. You great kid. Wow! You some wild crazy piece of ass!"

He rubbed his wounded nipple.

"Hope I don't get scar," he grinned. "Be seein' ya round! Oh, here's your key."

He dropped the original key she had given him in an ashtray and walked out the door. He could still hear her sobbing behind the closed door as he left.

Later she would tell Ahn that she had gotten rid of "that big Korean," but she did not tell him that Kim had been in the secret room.

Ψ Ψ Ψ

Many threads wove together in Saigon as the Western calendar year of 1967 neared its end.

Bu decided to host a special dinner party to celebrate the Christian Christmas season. He chose Tan Loc, a popular Chinese and Vietnamese restaurant, to provide the meal. The staff promised to serve only food that was popular with the Americans.

Bu chose this restaurant for another reason. The owner was a distant cousin of his wife's father's brother's wife, and it was always good to keep things in the family.

Mai Lei hoped that her father had created this occasion to announce good news regarding Bill's marriage proposal. This possibility also visited Bu's mind. Ever the careful, methodical scholar, he felt he had not completely pondered all aspects of Bill's request. Therefore, he was not ready to give his answer. He knew her hopes, however, and spoke to her before the party in order to save her disappointment.

"One must not consider this problem lightly, daughter. You must remember that you are my only direct descendant, and only through you will our bloodlines continue."

Mai Lei murmured her agreement and looked down at her folded hands. She knew the pride her father had in their family, and the veneration he had for his ancestors. This would be a big factor in his final decision—perhaps the greatest factor—even greater than his regard for her happiness or his great loss in the event she married Bill and left for America.

Janet was coming to Saigon for Christmas, but would not stay through the New Year. Mark was so happy to have her near him for even a few days that he was determined not to nag her into changing her plans. The dates of Janet's visit in the end determined Christmas Eve as the date for Bu's party. Mai Lei had mentioned Janet Holden to her father, and he was eager to speak with a well-educated, attractive Western woman. This was a pleasure denied him since his student days in Paris.

Kim and Kam would join the party as well. The original guest list had included only Bill, Mark, and Janet, but Bu remembered the story of Kam and the help Mai Lei had given her after the shooting of the artist, Cy. Therefore, he told Mai Lei to include her in the party. Misgivings arose when he heard that an invitation to Kam must include her Korean husband.

Bu, like many Vietnamese, was afraid of Koreans and avoided them whenever he chanced upon them in his travels about the city. Slowly, however, his natural inquisitiveness overshadowed this fear and he began to look forward to meeting this Corporal Kim.

Kim had plans of his own and had been unhappy about going to Bu's house for the party until he heard that Mark Buckley would be there. Recently, the two had had a few brief encounters in front of the Rex Hotel. The tall Korean soldier had proudly displayed his new, customized US Army combat knife. Kim felt proud when Mark complimented him on his choice.

He also had a party planned for that night. He had invited Red and Dave to the flat where he expected to surprise them with a real Christmas tree, gifts, food, and drink. Kim's memories of American Christmas parties in Korea were among the happiest moments of his childhood. He longed to duplicate those wartime Christmas festivities as best he could, even to the music which he remembered the American soldiers singing. For weeks, he played the record of Christmas carols that he had purchased at the PX over and over on his stereo. As he listened, he noticed that the songs were the same as those in his memory, but they sounded better on the record and some of the words seemed to have changed.

In particular, he could remember singing, "Go rest your hairy gentle lamb, let nothing Buddha say," but the record seemed to say, "God rest you, merry gentlemen ..."

Since Bu's dinner party was for the early evening, Kim decided to go ahead with his plans. He would start his party later and have his American friends stay the night because of the curfew. Generous to a fault, Kim, at the last minute, hired the two most popular girls at "The 92" as all-night partners for his two friends. It was going to be the best Christmas ever—for all of them.

Ψ   Ψ   Ψ

Duat's own Christmas cadre all began arriving at Xa Bui, unobserved and quietly, precisely on schedule.

Thi, as Chuan, was dressed as a poor woman. She took her place in the large room and watched as the room slowly began to fill.

For Thi, it was a long hour before everyone assembled and Ahn stood before the group. In a quiet voice, he made two obscure announcements, which Thi did not understand. She then realized that they were code, directed to unidentified individuals in the room whose work did not involve her in any way.

Suddenly Duat appeared before them. His very presence electrified the group. Thi could feel the change in the room as the people came to realize that this was a moment of great importance to them all.

Duat signaled to Ahn, who drew open a curtain to reveal a large colored map of South Vietnam. Across the top in red letters, it said: The Winter Offensive.

Without emotion, Duat addressed the crowd: "In the very near future, our allies from the North will mount the first real full-scale offensive against the cities and provinces of South Vietnam.

"This offensive will cause the collapse of the present government, and gain support of the people in such numbers as to assure the takeover of all authority by Viet Cong and North Vietnamese units.

"We have been promised similar offensives before, and each time we have been disappointed. However, this time I have assurance that things will be different. This offensive will go! We will capture the seats of government. All of Vietnam will be ours!"

Ahn pulled another curtain to reveal a large map of Saigon and surrounding areas. With a start, Thi recognized the map as the one she had worked on with Ahn after her visit to the VC and NVA units.

"One of our group has completely circumnavigated Saigon and visited the various units located outside the city. The mission of these units is to take over Saigon as the major thrust of the coming offensive."

He pointed to the various symbols drawn on the map. "These units are real. They exist. Our brothers are there awaiting the signal to attack. And when they attack from without, we shall attack from within. Be ready. Our cause depends on each of you."

Without another word, Duat left the room. Ahn waited silently, out of respect for their leader, as well as to let Duat's dramatic words take effect. Then he described the various units, using the information Thi had furnished. Her face flushed with pride as she heard a particular phrase or opinion of hers spoken.

When Ahn spoke of Bao Tre, Thi's thoughts returned to the cave complex and the wonderful hours she had spent there with General Trun Du.

Her visit there was far too short, but the recollection of her departure would always be in detail, bright and clear.

Du had walked with her to the exit, stood, and talked with her under the lean-to shelter. He wore the field dress of the North

Vietnamese Army, but no insignia. As always, he was immaculate, with boots shined and uniform freshly washed and pressed. That morning she had recognized something in his manner—perhaps an air of easy assurance—that so closely resembled Mark Buckley's ineffable magic. This was a quality belonging only to the professional soldier. Men like that are never owned by any woman. It was this quality that separated them forever from ordinary men.

That morning, General Du looked deep into her eyes when he said goodbye.

"Do not worry, little Chuan. We will rescue your city. We will deliver it to you all wrapped up as a New Year's present."

She did not trust herself to answer, but turned and started down the road. After a long moment, she found the courage to look back. He was still standing there, watching her. Although she knew she was being forward, she raised her right hand slightly in a final farewell. Tears came to her eyes and her heart skipped a beat as she saw him raise his hand in a salute, then turn and re-enter the cave.

Ahn's words brought her back to the real world of Xa Bui ...

"... during the next two or three weeks. You will receive these instructions in the usual way. Those with special tasks will return here for a final meeting. Whatever the case, do not leave Saigon without our permission. Remember, our great chance has come at last. There will be no failures."

Ψ   Ψ   Ψ

When motivated, Poli De Salle could be a very fine scholar.

Then his work was well conceived and meticulously executed. But, like most scholars, De Salle required a mentor or professor to guide his work properly if he was to keep within the bounds of practicality. Right now Poli was highly motivated. Unfortunately, there was no one to channel his efforts.

This was to prove disastrous.

For days, he had spent every working hour on his project. At last, it was taking shape. Immersed in the details of his plan, he lost all concept of time, all desire for food. The work was to him purely an academic exercise, divorced from the reality of the Vietnamese people. He congratulated himself for being so cleanly "objective" in his outlook.

Many days passed before he sent a note to his office, stating that he was working on a special project and would be away for some time. His associates at USAID worried about his absence when the days became weeks and Poli was still missing. Finally, they sent someone to his billet to inquire about his health.

They sent Brandy. She volunteered because she too was worried. From experience, she knew Poli to be extremely erratic in his living habits. Her first knock on his door went without answer. As she was about to knock again, the door opened a small crack and she saw the startled eyes of Soo staring out at her.

Brandy spoke in Vietnamese, "Open the door, Soo, and speak to me! I am worried about your master. Is he here?"

Soo smiled and opened the door. He had always liked Brandy.

"Ah, Cô Brandy speaks good Vietnamese now."

The grin that spread across his thin face revealed several missing teeth.

"Not very well yet, Soo, but every day I am improving. Your master, Ông De Salle, is he here?"

"Yes, Cô Brandy, he is here, but very busy. He works every day all the time on his most difficult creation."

"Do you think I could see him ... that is, would it be all right?"

"Oh yes, think so. Please step inside and I shall announce you."

It was some time later that Poli came out of his study to greet Brandy. She was shocked at his appearance: two weeks' growth of beard and dark rings under his eyes deeply accented his gaunt face. He had thrown on a thin silk dressing gown over his T-shirt and boxer shorts.

"Poli, my God! What has happened to you?"

He seemed not to hear her question as he took her outstretched hand in both of his and kissed her cheek. His beard scratched her and his smell, a combination of stale cigarettes and body odor, repulsed her. She was alarmed as she pushed him away.

"Poli, whatever are you doing? I'll bet you haven't had a real meal in days. And, well, you need to clean up."

"Brandy, at last I have a plan to really change the whole face of this war. Not militarily, but politically. Here, please sit down and I will describe it for a moment, then I must get back to work. I want to present it to Newell Osborne just as soon as it is finished, but there is much to do."

Her blue eyes blazed.

"Look, Poli, you stink. Literally, stink. Go and take a bath and shave. Then have some lunch with me while you tell me about it. I mean this! Go in there and clean up or I'll walk out."

She turned for the door. Poli was so eager to tell someone about his plan that he quickly agreed and dashed off to the bathroom.

Brandy headed for the kitchen to instruct Soo, but found him in the dining room, eavesdropping. Then, as he heated up a can of soup, he explained to Brandy that every day he had made full meals for his master, but Poli hardly touched his food.

By the time the meal was ready and places set, Poli returned, washed and shaved, dressed in slacks and a shirt. Brandy noticed that he had lost considerable weight.

"Now before you start talking, start on that soup. The bread and butter won't hurt you either."

Poli quickly attacked his soup. God, he hadn't known how hungry he was. Halfway through a second bowl, he got up and went to his study. In a moment, he was back with two large maps that he spread out on the empty part of the dining room table.

There was a great gleam in his eyes. A strange gleam. It worried Brandy.

"What I have done here is to devise a completely new system for measuring pacification progress. It is a new way of dividing each district politically into spheres of GVN influence.

"See, here is the regular pacification map for Binh Long Province. You will note all the symbols indicating areas that are pacified, or questionable, or under VC influence. Now, note this other map I have drawn. Look here at An Loc District. The town of An Loc is considered completely pacified. These areas to the west are questionable on the

323

pacification map. But on my map, I have extended the administration area of the town to include these questionable areas. In this manner, the town's influence will extend to these areas and the whole, new town will be pacified."

"But, Poli, what makes you think that just because you have extended the town's influence on a piece of paper, the VC will also honor the new boundary and give up and go elsewhere?"

"It's not just the map. It's the actual administration of the completely new area. The people there will fall under the influence of the town. It's a matter of psychology—you are part of the town. The town is loyal to the GVN. Therefore, you are also loyal—or get out. Over a period of time this will happen because people want to be with the majority group."

"Won't this take a lot of extra troops to enforce the system?"

"No, that's the beauty of the plan. It's just a gradual assumption that becomes a reality. First, it comes out on all the maps, then, the administrative directives and laws of the town take over. The people, like so many ants, merely start complying.

"Oh, I realize that this won't be a universal take-over by the GVN. Some areas will be easy. Some will be more difficult. But the administrative pressure will be on them all ..."

"Poli, I realize that this is not my bag. I'm just a poor secretary trying to improve my typing so I won't get fired, and I don't really understand your scheme, but I think you've overlooked the VC."

His tone became condescending.

"Look, I have only outlined the basic premise for you. I haven't gone into the political and psychological aspects of the total plan. The example of just one village is not really valid. Just imagine a whole map of South Vietnam comparing the pacified areas according to the old plan with the pacified areas according to the new plan. The effect will be very dramatic: the map alone will sell this to MACV."

"Well, Poli, I hope your plan is successful. God knows, we need something to get this war off dead center."

Brandy rose from the table.

"Go to bed and get some rest before you go back to your maps. I'll tell the office that you're okay. When will you be back on the job?"

"Tell them that I need a couple of weeks to finish, and that I hope to have it in shape to brief Osborne by mid-January."

Suddenly Poli was tired. The conversation with Brandy had unwound him. He felt ready for rest. When she left, he headed for the bedroom and in moments, he was in a deep sleep.

Ψ   Ψ   Ψ

Saigon had been preparing for Christmas for almost a month.

At first, there had been only a few ornaments for sale in the sidewalk stores on Le-Loi and Nye Hue. However, as the weeks went by, a few old French ornaments appeared, with faded cardboard likenesses of Father Christmas and a plaintive NOEL in dim letters below the once jolly face.

In mid-December, new shipments arrived from Hong Kong and Red China. The merchants who owned the sidewalk stores transformed their drab, portable, old-army-poncho-covered stalls in one afternoon into gaudy, multi-colored arbors of ersatz Christmas cheer.

About a week before Christmas, real pine trees arrived from Delta, to be stacked in the old flower stalls in the park that ran down the center of Hyena Hue. Once called the Street of Flowers because of the blossoms sold in the central park, the influx of American soldiers, who had little use for flowers, caused a change of merchandise to cameras, phonograph records, small radios, and souvenirs of Vietnam.

The pine trees were a gamble on the extent of American homesickness; but with a temperature of ninety-five degrees and a clear, blue tropic sky, most Americans found a pine tree as incongruous as a snowman. By Christmas Eve, unsold and unwanted, the trees were on the street in unsightly brown piles.

Red and Dave walked through the crowd that jammed the sidewalk stalls on Le-Loi. Above their heads was a web of light rope and twine on which were suspended a hodge-podge of ponchos that shaded the sidewalk. From the ropes, the merchants hung long garlands and festoons of bright gold, silver, and green tinsel. Everywhere were displayed small sets of electric lights, glass and plastic ornaments, wreaths, and trees. In one booth, a whole tray of small mechanical Santa Clauses popped in and out of plastic chimneys, their oriental faces half-hidden by cotton beards. A little boy in shorts was in charge of this display. He kept very busy winding up the toys.

As the two Americans made their way slowly down the street, Red, a tall man, had to duck frequently due to the maze of ropes above the sidewalk. They stopped in front of the display of mechanical Santas.

"Boy, I got to send one of these to my niece."

"How old is she?"

"Too old for you, scabby—she's six."

"Smart ass!"

"Hey, GI, you want buy?"

"How much?"

"Two hundred P."

"Two hundred? You little robber! I call MP, lock you up!"

"Not too much. Come all way Canton—no, Hong Kong."

Dave ignored the banter and tried to move Red along.

"We aren't going to find anything here for Kim and his wife. Why didn't you get that electric frying pan at the PX, like I told you?"

"I didn't have the MPC then."

"Well, how 'bout we get 'em one of these Santy Clauses?" asked Dave sarcastically.

"Don't get smart, swabby, or I'll tell the Navy where you've been hiding out, and they'll finally send you back to sea."

"Look, Red, we're supposed to be at Kim's place tonight. It's Christmas Eve. Let's grab a cyclo and get out to the Cholon PX and get a real US-type present."

Red put the toy down on the tray and winked at the small boy. "You're right, Dave. Let's go. The roof in this place is too low for me anyway."

He stuck his head through a plastic wreath that was hanging from the ropes.

"How's this for two hundred P?" He grinned widely.

"You like?" An old woman who was selling the wreaths pushed toward them.

"What he really needs, Mama-San, is a horse collar. You have?"

"What you want?"

"Oh, nuthin'. *Cam o'n ba. Chao.*"

They pushed their way to the street and crowded into the seat of a cyclo. Soon the driver behind them was peddling the ancient vehicle on to Cholon with all possible speed.

Ψ Ψ Ψ

All was in order for Christmas Eve at the house of Ông Bu.

Mark, Janet, and Bill arrived at exactly 5:30. Mark was able to park the jeep in front of the house only because Bu had blocked off a small portion of the street with cardboard boxes and string. There was a sign in Vietnamese reading "Reserved space for honored American guests of high rank and importance."

Mai Lei, on the lookout for Mark's jeep, rushed out and removed the barrier as Mark drove up.

Mark was full of cheer: "Merry Christmas, Mai Lei! We brought Mrs. Santa Claus two helpers."

Janet climbed out of the jeep, kissed Mai Lei, and handed her the presents they had brought. Everyone was laughing as each entered the house. Kam and Kim arrived by taxi moments later.

With everyone assembled, Bu led the way to the garden where a dwarf pine had been decorated. Under the tree was a present for each guest. The gifts that the guests had brought for Bu and Mai Lei had also been placed under the tree. After a waiter from the catering service brought a tray of cold rice wine, the group drank toasts to Christmas, to the United States, to Korea, to Vietnam, and to victory.

Bu was fascinated by the Korean. He had been surprised that Kim spoke like an American until he heard about Kim's boyhood and Mark's help during the war. He had not considered the American influence on young Koreans before. How much permanent influence would the Americans have on small boys in Vietnam? His mind skipped forward twenty years and he saw the Americans fighting Communism in another country with Vietnamese units assisting them ...

"Father, do you not think we should eat now?"

Mai Lei's question brought Bu back to the present.

"Oh yes, my dear. It is time."

He led the group into the small dining room.

Bu sat at one end of the table, Mark at the other, with Janet on Bu's right and Kam on his left. Mai Lei sat on Mark's right and Kim on his left, while Bill was between Kam and Mai Lei.

During the soup course, Janet and Bu spoke of Paris. She had spent a year studying there. By the time the roast duck appeared, they were talking like old friends. Later, during the crispy Chả giò, Janet described her project with Reverend White at Buon Sut Mgra. Bu was intrigued with the work, the more so when Janet promised him a signed copy as soon as the Rhade Bible was published.

Many times during the meal, Janet engaged Kim in conversation. She found him shy, but anxious to talk with her, seeming to want to know her better. Kim felt grateful for her attention and was careful to use his best, most refined English.

After the duck, rice, and vegetables, a lavishly decorated rum cake appeared, all ablaze. Bu beamed with delight at the astonished murmurs of approval.

Kim, dazzled by the party, thought of his great luck.

This is best party of my life! Never before have I been to a party with officers and their ladies, or a college professor like Ông Bu. Janet Holden is a lovely lady. Just right for a wife for Colonel Mark! Maybe her husband will turn up dead soon— or if he turns up alive, well, he can be made dead! That's easy in Saigon! I can tell by way Janet and Colonel Mark look at each other that they are in love like Americans and have a mutual attraction like Koreans. My friend Colonel Mark must have this lovely lady. It is pre-ordained. I will make a special prayer to Buddha.

Now Bu was rising. At his request, the guests followed him back to the garden. The last patches of light were just visible in the sky. Candles were burning in the flowerbed and tiny lights covered the little Christmas tree. In the humid darkness, it glistened like magic. For a moment, they all gazed upon it in silent wonder.

"Perhaps tree makes one think of more pleasant Christmas at home," said Bu quietly.

"My dear friend," said Janet, "To be sure, we are thinking of other Christmases, but–thanks to you–there could be no more pleasant moment than you have given us here."

"Thank you, Ba Holden. It has been a great pleasure for me to arrange this party," said Bu.

Then he announced that it was time to open the gifts.

Mai Lei passed them out. She and her father were slightly embarrassed by the number of presents their guests had brought them, but they managed to open them all and to show delight over them. Bu was especially pleased with a book of Shakespeare's plays that Bill had given him.

"I noticed, sir," said Bill, "that in your library, you have a volume of Shakespeare in French. I think of all authors, Shakespeare should be read in his native tongue."

Bu agreed, but privately wondered if his English was good enough.

Mai Lei excused herself for a moment and returned with an American-made guitar. Quietly she strummed, singing the traditional old French *Carol of the Birds* in a soft clear voice.

> Angels and shepherds, birds of the sky,
> Come where the Son of God doth lie;
> Christ on earth with man doth dwell,
> Join in the shout, Noel, Noel!

When the song was over, she said, "That was for my father, who always requests it each Christmas. Please tell me your favorites and I will try to play them for you."

Soon the Americans were singing the familiar carols. Kim proudly offered his versions remembered from his boyhood.

The singing ended. Kim explained that he and Kam had to go back to receive friends. Mark and Janet also made their farewells. Since Bill had decided to stay awhile, Mark offered Kim and Kam a ride in his jeep. They drove off laughing and waving to the people clustered about the door of Bu's house.

As they traveled toward the center of Saigon, they noticed that people had a festive air about them, and many more were on the streets than usual.

Mark spotted the large increase in Hondas and Suzukis. These were all driven by young people and going around and around the main thoroughfares of the city. The noise was a steady roar that was impossible to ignore.

Near the city center, the sidewalks were jammed with people. Pedestrians spilled into the streets as well as cyclos, automobiles, and jeeps. Everyone was in a happy mood. There was singing and much laughter and joking. Finally, as in a gigantic puzzle, the key car stopped and the traffic came to a standstill. The press of people and vehicles caught Mark's jeep and stopped it cold.

Thi was returning from a special meeting with Duat. She abandoned her taxicab to return to her flat on foot. There was much to do when she got home, and she was furious with the crowds wandering about the city. The surge brought her up against Mark's jeep. Before she realized it, she found herself face to face with Janet, who recognized her at once.

"Merry Christmas, Cô Thi. Here, get in before you are crushed."

Janet moved toward Mark in order to share her seat with the girl. Thi's frown changed to a facsimile of a smile. Quickly she glanced at the other occupants of the vehicle. Everyone began to talk at once. Thi found it a strain to be lighthearted and friendly to these people whom she loathed completely and wished dead.

"Cô Thi, you meet with my wife, Kam."

Kam nodded and smiled. Kim turned to his bride.

"This pretty girl I tell you about."

Good God, his damn wife! This is the final stupid indignity.

Thi had not seen Kim since that last day in the new flat, the day of her discovery that she could never be able to kill him. Now, she was not so sure. She looked over at Kam and thought that she would rather have Kim dead than with this new wife.

Unconsciously she pressed her fingers against the envelope inside her blouse. It contained her special instructions for the offensive, received just a half hour earlier and not yet read. But whatever else she was to do, she hoped that she would still find a way—and the courage—to end Kim's life.

"Come on, get in! The traffic's started moving again."

Cô Thi shook her head.

"No thanks. I have only a little way to go. Merry Christmas to you all! It has been a pleasure to meet you, Ba Kim, and to see you again, Ba Holden."

In a moment, she was lost in the crowd. Once she looked back at the jeep, caught a glimpse of Janet's curls, and became almost nauseous with hatred.

She touched the scar on her face. Then she vowed that somehow, by heaven or hell, she would get to them—all of them—and they would pay and pay and pay.

Chapter IX

JANUARY 1968

M ai Lei knew that she must do everything to perfection or their kitchen god would not be pleased.

It was the twenty-eighth day of the last month of the lunar year and she was being especially careful in her preparations. She placed the three crude terra cotta lumps that represented the kitchen god on the hearth and put the dish of nuoc mom before them. The crude lumps of clay had represented her family's kitchen god further back than anyone could remember. The ritual that Mai Lei carried out extended back even further, through the dim mist of time to the earliest traces of Vietnamese culture.

Next, she transferred a large red carp to the family's nicest platter and set it by the nuoc mom. It was the largest and best carp that she could find in the fish market. She hoped that the kitchen god would be pleased with her choice. Mai Lei could picture him now, his belly full of the wonderful food she had left him, mounting the back of the carp and urging it out of their house and upward through the still night air, far beyond the moon-tinted clouds into the misty realm of heaven and the palace of the Jade Emperor.

Mai Lei hoped that the kitchen god's disposition would be happy as he gave the exalted one his yearly report on Bu and herself, the members of the little family of which he was in charge.

Knowing that the Jade Emperor would use this report as a basis for administering the next year's fortune to the mortals of his charge, Mai

Lei wanted to be sure that everything at the ceremony would be done without error. There was so much at stake this year. The Jade Emperor could bring her happiness by influencing her father's decision regarding Bill.

She remembered the remaining little dishes of food and hastened to place them around the big platter. Crab, rice, corn, spiced chicken, Chả giò, minced beef, and several kinds of fruit. It was a beautiful display designed to satisfy and please the kitchen god, yet not so auspicious as to hint at bribery.

When all was finished, she looked at the result of her efforts and spoke quietly, "Have a safe journey, and hurry back to our hearth."

Satisfied with her preparations for the commencement of Tet, Mai Lei joined her father in the living room.

"Have you finished the offering, Mai Lei?"

"Yes, Father, and I think our kitchen god will be most pleased."

"Does Major Bill understand our celebration of the Lunar New Year?"

"Yes, Father. I believe so. Last week while we were working together, the subject of Tet came up and I explained that it was the most important holiday of the year for all Vietnamese and Chinese people."

Bill was actually somewhat perplexed by Mai Lei's description of the holiday and took time to investigate on his own.

He found that Tet was best described as a combination of birthday, Thanksgiving, and Christmas. Families make every possible attempt to gather in order to honor their ancestors. The dead commune with those yet to be born through veneration offered by the living. It is the time of year to settle all material, financial, and spiritual accounts.

In peacetime, the celebration period lasts from the twenty-third day of the last month until the last day of the first month of the new lunar year. During wartime, the period of celebration was reduced to three days, starting on the last day of the lunar year. Although the celebration was curtailed in the war year of 1967, most of the Vietnamese in Saigon had started planning for Tet early in the month. Decisions had to be made as to the places where families would gather. Letters were written to relatives in far-off places, begging them to return home for the holidays. Certain foods were required for the very special meals. Family budgets were bent and stretched to accommodate the purchase of new clothing.

Ψ   Ψ   Ψ

Duat was working on his own special Tet preparations. These differed dramatically from those of Bu, Mai Lei, and most Vietnamese families.

Duat was in charge of receiving weapons and food supplies coming from the North and caching them in selected locations about the city. He was responsible for seeing that the invading army would be well fed and armed, once they smashed their way into Saigon. Duat conceived the plan of using false funeral ceremonies as a means to transport the weapons and ammunition—the graveyards being a convenient place to store them.

The supply plan was simple. Sampans with cargoes of rice approached the capital from the northwest using the Saigon River. Concealed in the cargo were thousands of weapons and tons of ammunition of all sorts, which had been brought down the Ho Chi Minh Trail to the loading point in Cambodia.

At a place north of Gia Din, the munitions were first unloaded and hidden in caves and tunnels. Later, hundreds of large trucks carrying plants and potted flowers into the city for sale for the Tet celebration also carried the weapons, hidden under false truck beds. When the plants were unloaded, the "empty" trucks went on to Duat's warehouses, where weapons were packed into coffins. This resource was one of the major reasons Hanoi had taken a risk and allied with Duat's organization in Saigon.

Fake funerals were held all over the city, and the "bodies" were buried with appropriate ceremonies, including priests, mourners, and bereaved families of the deceased. Locations of the cemetery plots were sent through the underground to Trun Du's staff. The attacking NVA army knew exactly where their weapon caches were located.

The normal activities of Tet were perfect cover for the VC. People carrying large bundles were traveling in all directions at this time of

335

year. No one thought for a moment that the VC and the NLF would violate the national customs of well-being and non-violence at Tet. For, even though the North and South Vietnamese were political enemies, they would always be spiritual brothers.

Always ...

Ψ   Ψ   Ψ

Mark Buckley stood on the helicopter landing float below the high mud walls of Trong Thoi.

His thoughts went back to that gray day nine months before, when he had stood on this same spot and returned the farewell salute of the Vietnamese and American soldiers. He glanced up at the empty parapets high above.

Major Ho, standing beside him, seemed to sense his thoughts.

"Today happier day than last time. Colonel Mark smiling."

Mark had reason to smile. He had been in good spirits ever since he had received the message from Major Ho a few days before, and had hopped the first chopper he could commandeer to get to Trong Thoi.

An hour's visit had convinced him that Ho had a real lead on Ted Holden. In another hour, they made preliminary plans for two days hence. Now Mark was on his way back to Saigon.

The chopper was waiting. He shook hands warmly with Ho.

"Yes, I am happy. You have given me hope."

"But I still not understand. You bring husband back, then you can no marry lady."

"Well, at least I'll get our future off dead center. I'll make that bastard come back and be a husband or divorce Janet—one or the other. At least I'll have a fifty percent chance for happiness. As it is now, I have none."

"Americans very strange. Why you no let me make arrangements finish off this man? Would not be hard. Would cost very little."

"Now don't start that again. I know you're trying to be helpful, but I can't go that route. It has to be this way."

"Okay, Colonel Mark. You are boss."

Mark boarded the Huey and Ho scurried back up the wall as the chopper revved up. In one moment, Ho was a waving speck on the wall. In the next, Ho and the fort were part of the muddy scar on the green bank of the Mekong.

Back in Saigon, Mark put in papers for ten days' leave at Vung Tau. He had no intention of going there. Instead, after his leave was approved, he headed for the delta town of Chow Doc, close to the Cambodian border.

The USAID chopper dropped him on the dirt strip several miles out of the town. It was a gray, overcast day and, after the chopper disappeared in the distance, Mark felt completely alone. The strip, made of mud dredged from the swampy backwaters of the Bassic River, had no hangars, no terminal, no tower, no people.

He started down the only road, assuming it must lead to Chow Doc. He felt completely isolated, the only person on the planet. Aside from himself, nothing moved, nothing stirred except one white egret, winging low and unhurried over the endless miles of high wild reeds.

However, the dull, lonely day could not totally erase the excitement Mark felt.

To know at last! To put an end to this charade with Janet. It was worth all of this.

He walked almost an hour before he noticed dust rising in the road ahead. Well beyond the dust, he could make out the first white buildings of a town.

Presently a Tri-Lambretta puffed up to him and stopped. The driver, a small Vietnamese with a happy grin, said, "You land in chopper?"

"Yes."

"Any more peoples?" He pointed in the direction of the air strip.

"No, I'm the only passenger."

"I take you to Chow Doc."

"How much?"

"Oh, maybe one hundred twenty P."

"That too much. I thought you my friend."

"You want be my friend?"

Not quite sure what this friendship required, Mark paused for a moment.

337

Then, throwing caution to the wind, he said, "Yes, I want be your friend."

"Okay, okay! You get in. No charge!" He held out his hand and Mark shook it vigorously, and then climbed in the back of the little three-wheeled lorry after the driver turned it around.

"You my new friend!"

"Yes. Let's get going," Mark replied.

"First, how 'bout smoke for number one friend?"

He gave the driver an almost full pack of Salems.

"Now, let's go, number one friend!"

With a merry grin of thanks, the driver took the cigarettes and lit one while he coaxed the motor into loud, racing sounds. Then, with total disregard for his passenger, he released the clutch and the little lorry lurched into motion.

"Where you want go?" he called above the wind and noise of the engine.

"Best Hot Toc in town."

"You want number one massage?"

"No, I want number one haircut."

In minutes they wheeled into the center of the little delta town, typical of the farm communities of the southern part of the country. In the center was the town square that served as the marketplace. It was a hodge-podge of bamboo and canvas stalls and counters. Around the square on three sides were shops of a more permanent nature. The fourth side was the province capital building and local government administrative offices. All the French-era buildings of white stucco now wore streaks of red from years of contact with the Red Delta soil. The square was crowded with soldiers, farmers, merchants, and housewives, all going about their business. Although he was the only American soldier in town, no one seemed to notice Mark as he descended from the vehicle and entered the barbershop. Inside he saw a familiar face, Sergeant Nam, Major Ho's first sergeant.

The normally stoic Nam greeted Mark like an old friend and led him out into the square and down a crooked road to the waterway. They boarded a long narrow sampan with a woven reed cabin that

338

looked very much like a small Quonset hut located amidships. Mark entered the cabin and almost stumbled on Major Ho.

"My God, Ho, I thought we had decided that you wouldn't be mixed up in this."

"But Colonel Mark, you see I already in it."

"But you have nothing to gain and everything to lose."

Ho looked directly into Mark's eyes. "I may lose friend if I no help."

Mark didn't answer. There was no answer he could give.

As he sat there in the cabin, he could feel the motion of the boat getting underway.

"Here. Put on. I got big one," Ho directed as he handed Mark a bundle of clothes.

The American removed his fatigue blouse, T-shirt, trousers, and boots and dressed in the provided peasant's shirt and trousers. He left his .45 automatic in its shoulder holster strapped against his side. The blouse was too small and did not close across the chest, but Ho took string and laced it across the front, which concealed the pistol.

"You big man. You no look Vietnamese; you wear hat, be better."

Mark took the conical straw farmer's hat and put it on his head, although he realized the inadequacy of the gesture.

Who in hell do I think I can fool? I hope it will be dark before I have to face anyone, friendly or otherwise.

The boat picked up speed and headed toward the mainstream traffic.

"You see," said Ho, "For many years no border between Cambodia and Vietnam. Many people go back-forth, back-forth. When French came, they make border of colony, but so what? We all under French, so make no difference. Then comes time for French to leave. Bang! We have hard boundary. But people still same-same. They no like boundary. They go back-forth, back-forth, see friends, see relatives. Only now harder. Police patrol area. Too bad. Must pay.

"Today my friend pay man who pay police. We go tonight and two, three days we come back. Police stop, look at some boat, but not stop this boat. You see!"

Mark hoped that it was that simple. He would be in real trouble if Ho's payoff didn't work. He glanced out the rear of the cabin at the

little helmsman handling the small Briggs & Stratton gas engine, balanced on a swivel and attached directly to an eight-foot-long propeller
shaft. By swinging the engine to right or left, the helmsman could
steer the boat. Similarly, by moving the engine up and down, the depth
of the propeller could change. This was a distinct advantage in the Delta, as it allowed the sampan to maneuver in very shallow waterways.

Mark nodded to the helmsman, then turned to Major Ho. "He one
of your men?"

"No. He Sergeant Nam wife brother. Trai. He know country across
border very well. His brother live there many years."

Sergeant Nam grinned proudly and called to his brother-in-law in
Vietnamese. The helmsman grinned and waved.

Ho looked at his watch.

"We on time. It just be dark when we reach Trong Thoi. We land in
town and go directly to my house. There we meet all group who go.
We talk plan one time all way through. We eat, then we leave 2200
hours."

Mark listened with satisfaction. He had always admired Ho's precision, a trait he had not often found in the Vietnamese Army.

The narrow waterway from Chow Doc to the Mekong was teeming
with commerce, and many boat crews exchanged friendly greetings
with them as they sailed. The palm-studded banks of the canal revealed
the flat miles of farmland that seemed to extend to eternity.

Occasionally they passed a small Vietnamese farmhouse on posts or
the decaying remains of a once-proud French colonial planter's house
close to the canal.

The sun was a red ball on the horizon when they passed through a
small fishing village located at the meeting of the canal and the Mekong River. The nets, stretched between bamboo poles to dry, looked
like giant cobwebs against the gold sky. They passed into the Mekong,
and at once the water became choppy and muddy. The sun had disappeared below the flat land and now darkness, like a mist, seemed to
appear from nowhere to cover the Delta.

Mark glanced back at the village on the riverbank. Tiny lights were
appearing in the small fishing huts and on the boats, making a host of

long golden water snakes that shimmered and wriggled in the darkening water.

Suddenly Mark could see the high mud walls of the Special Forces camp, looming black and foreboding in the fading light. A distant voice shouted a sharp challenge.

Nam answered, and the little boat passed below the walls of the fortress to a little-used wharf in the village. Mark was ushered through the darkness to Major Ho's small house. The going was rough on his bare feet. He would have to wear some kind of footwear if he were to complete this operation. Thunder in the distance made him forget his problem for a moment—there was going to be a night storm.

They moved through the brightly lighted front room of Ho's house and up the stairs to a large bedroom, empty except for a desk, two chairs, and three single beds placed against different walls. A single, erratically flickering and buzzing fluorescent tube in the ceiling provided a tentative light. The smooth terrazzo floor felt good on Mark's bruised feet.

"This better here. No one look in windows."

Mark turned to answer Ho but, catching his reflection in a mirror, he gaped in wonder at the picture he presented. Ho, seeing his expression, looked Mark over critically. "You pretty big for farmer clothes. You skin stick out."

"I'll say it does. All the way down the front. If I have to draw this pistol in a hurry, I'll be in a bad way."

Mark looked at his legs. The trousers stopped about halfway between his knees and feet. His white legs stood out like road markers. He made a mental note to rub dirt on them the first chance he had.

There were voices downstairs. Sergeant Nam appeared with two men. Mark recognized one as the helmsman, now introduced as "Bin." The other new man was Troc. Ho told the men to take seats on the beds, while he and Mark sat at the desk. The men smoked quietly while the two officers went over the plan to make sure they were both in agreement.

They traced the route completely on a large-scale map that Ho produced. Only after they had carefully ironed out every uncertainty did they turn to the others. Ho, speaking in his native tongue, was halfway through the briefing when the storm broke, and a wall of water engulfed the little town. In moments, a power failure plunged the room into darkness.

The pounding noise of the rain on the roof made talking impossible, but Ho brought a candle and placed it on the map. With the men grouped about, Ho traced their route in silence, then he had each man trace it with his finger.

Finally, when the rain softened to a dull, droning sound, Ho continued the briefing. Moths and other insects, originally attracted by the fluorescent light, now descended to the candle and circled the flame in eccentric flight patterns, but neither their presence nor their large eerie shadows distracted the men from intense concentration.

"Now we rest for two hours. Please."

Ho pointed to one of the beds and Mark was happy to stretch out for a while. Ho and Nam took the other two beds, while Troc and Bin curled up on straw mats on the floor. Mark was asleep before Bin blew out the candle.

There were low voices in the room when Mark awoke. They were women's voices and there was a smell of food. Mark looked about him, but did not rise. The power was still off, but now there were two candles in the room. The women had brought up two small braziers. A large pot of soup occupied one, and atop the pot was a covered bowl of rice. On the other brazier, they were cooking fish.

"Now 2130 hours. It time to get up."

Mark glanced at his watch and rolled out of the bed. He noticed that Ho and the other men had changed to peasant clothing much like his. Soon, the whole team was seated on the floor, eating fish and rice and drinking the hot clear soup.

Mark recognized broad-faced Madame Ho as one of the women. He nodded and smiled. She shyly returned his greeting and returned to her cooking duties, leaving him to wonder how much she knew about tonight's projected madness.

Bin rose and handed his chopsticks and bowl to Madame Ho. He spoke a few words in Vietnamese, then turned and left. Ho explained to Mark that he was going out to put extra gas cans in the sampan and check the fuel tank and engine to be sure there had been no rain damage. A quarter of an hour later Mark spoke to the group: no one had to go on the trip; they could step out now if they wanted to. After translation, no one moved. All just grinned and shuffled their feet.

Mark then passed out small pen flashlights to each of them. He also gave to Major Ho and Sergeant Nam a pen-size flare gun with several red and green flares. He demonstrated the loading and firing of the flares, and made them dry run the procedure several times. He looked at his watch: 2200 hours.

"Pass out the weapons and let's go," he said.

It was good to be out of the warm house. Light rain refreshed the men as they moved toward the river. The town seemed deserted. Because of the power failure, most of the people had gone to bed. Mark's bare feet again suffered as he walked on the gravel-covered road. Finally, they made it to the river where Bin was waiting patiently by their boat. He drew their attention to the painted eyes on the bow, brightened with white, the better to see the dangers ahead and to help guide them.

In the darkness, Mark had not noticed Madame Ho walking with them. He was surprised to see her scramble aboard and enter the cabin.

"Madame Ho, is she going?"

"No, she just come bring food and water for us," Ho laughed.

Having stowed the food, Madame Ho returned to the dock. The rescue party climbed aboard and they cast off. They were on their way.

Mark looked back at the lonely figure of Madame Ho on the dock and waved, but she did not respond. Then curtains of darkness and rain came between them. He looked at Ho, who was staring forward out of the cabin. As far as Mark could tell, the two had not even said goodbye.

They worked their way up-river. It was midnight when the little sampan passed below the walls of Binh Hiep, a tiny, triangle-shaped Regional Forces camp.

Mark noticed several small flashes of light from the camp lookout station above the riverbank. He saw Ho give a similar signal with his penlight, but the boat continued upstream, its little motor sounding very loud to the occupants above the quiet of the night. Suddenly Mark could see lights ahead.

"The border," said Ho casually.

Mark watched the river patrol boats stopping several sampans for search. He knew that the Mekong was an international waterway and legal, international shipping could not be stopped. However, vessels could be searched and, if war materials were discovered, impounded.

As they neared the police boats, Ho shouted in Vietnamese. A powerful spotlight played upon the sampan. In the darkness of the cabin, Mark watched the bright light play over the bow and stern, knowing by the way the light bobbed on the water that a boat was approaching them.

In a moment, there was excited talk in Vietnamese. Then, lines were thrown to the sampan. Mark heard a thud as a policeman jumped to the smaller boat, and he sank down deeper in the shadows.

Ho entered the cabin. "He wants a smoke. You have?"

Mark groped in the pockets of his discarded fatigue uniform. He finally found the cigarettes and passed Ho a full package of Salems. Ho grinned and returned to the stern. Suddenly Mark heard the roar of the more powerful boat and, amid shouts from both crews, the police left and the sampan was underway again.

It was still several hours before daylight when the boat pulled into a small creek channel. Mark could sense high growth on each side. They followed the meandering channel for some time before they came to a stop. Ho left the cabin. There were hushed voices and activity among the crew. Ho then returned to Mark's side.

"We now at boat stop place. Boat hidden. Now we sleep."

Mark tried to shut his eyes and rest, but it was impossible. The dangerous situation, combined with the thought of the next night's activities, was too much for him to take calmly. The others also were finding it hard to sleep for, throughout the night, they fought to a stalemate a host of vicious mosquitoes, making the first streaks of dawn a welcome sight for everyone.

The sun came up on a motionless world that caught the little group of men in a special spell of silence which each feared to break. As more light infiltrated the channel, Mark could gradually make out the hidden bank to which the boat was tied, and the narrow channel they had traveled, lined with thick reeds that extended high above them.

Ho looked up and down the channel. Then, followed by Bin, he stepped onto the shore. Immediately both men disappeared into the reeds. Mark knew they had gone to inspect their hiding place and to search for possible VC in the area.

In a few minutes, they returned and Ho explained to Mark that their hiding place was even better than Bin had promised.

"Now our only worry will be the possible approach of another sampan," said Mark, after listening to Ho's description of their location.

"Never happen, Mark. This not fishing place. No one come here."

"Anyway, you will have a hell of a time explaining me to anyone that comes along, so I'll plan on hiding in the boat if we hear anyone coming."

Sergeant Nam had taken some of the food out of the containers and was preparing it on the bank. Some slanting rays of the early sunlight had found their way through the tall reeds, and had painted red lines on the quiet water. The sky above them was a light blue, bounded by the high green walls of the reed canyon. It was soon light enough to illuminate the bottom of the waterway, and Mark watched several bright fish playing in the water plants along the opposite bank.

"Do you think it's okay for me to swim?"

"Oh sure, Mark. This number one swim place."

Mark shed the peasant clothing and his pistol and eased himself into the cool, clean water. He dove deeply and slowly cruised the bottom until his breath ran out and he was forced to surface. Back on the sampan, drying himself with his peasant shirt, he felt suddenly refreshed and alive. Hope shot through him like whiskey on a cold day. He had the feeling that everything would work well that night. Now all he had to do was sweat out the next twelve hours of daylight.

Ψ   Ψ   Ψ

Colonel Uhm had loaded up again in the Brinks Hotel PX.

Kim picked him up along with an armful of PX treasure at the hotel parking lot, and was now waiting for the traffic light by the Continental Hotel. He looked across Tu Do Street, directly at the apartment building where he had last made love to Thi. Suddenly he saw her through the crowd, leaving the building, carrying a suitcase. Where was she going? While he watched, a black Mercedes pulled up and halted in the traffic while she entered the car. Kim fingered the apartment key in his pocket as he watched Thi drive off. She was obviously going away for Tet. This would be a good time to take a look at the apartment when Colonel Uhm dismissed him for lunch.

After carrying many packages to Uhm's room, Kim was free to go. He quickly left the Rex and, leaving his car parked, walked down Lam Son, past the Marine Memorial, to Thi's apartment. The hallway was empty when Kim reached the flat. Then he was inside with the door locked behind him.

There was evidence in the bedroom that Thi had packed in a hurry. A few pieces of clothing lay strewn on the bed and a dresser drawer was ajar. But this did not interest him. After checking to see that he was alone in the flat, he went directly to the hidden room and opened the door. He used his lighter to illuminate the switch panel and turned on the lights.

He went to the cupboards and inspected the wigs and costumes. The jewelry and makeup equipment next caught his eye. Then he moved over to the makeup table and mirror. There was a whole drawer of necklaces and earrings. He wondered if any of them were valuable. Thi was a woman who had always puzzled him. She had told him she was once a film actress who now was a dressmaker and English teacher. He had decided long ago that she was some sort of high-class whore, who loved him too much to make him pay.

Now, looking at the room with all of its strange paraphernalia, he thought that perhaps she was still some sort of actress—maybe on the stage. If this were true, why wouldn't she tell him about it?

Kim picked up the large hand mirror and looked at himself. Then he idly turned it over and put it face down on the table. Then he noticed that a small piece of paper had stuck to the back. He removed the paper and tried to read it, but it was in Vietnamese. Disappointed, he started to put it down, but then noticed a few of the words were in English. He studied them, sounding the syllables as he had learned to do years before. Suddenly he found himself saying Doc-tor-Jan-et-Hol-den.

Janet Holden? That was Colonel Mark's friend, the pretty girl he wanted Mark to marry!

Why would Thi have a note about her in the secret room? He folded the paper and put it in his pocket. Kam could read it and would be able to answer his questions.

Kim spent some time looking over the room and the rest of Thi's flat, but the paper seemed to burn in his pocket. He couldn't keep his mind off it. Quickly he left and headed for the studio. He knew Kam would already be there.

Ψ Ψ Ψ

Thi went through her handbag for the twelfth time, but could not find the small piece of paper with her instructions on it.

She knew the contents of the paper. Her photographic memory had imprinted the page, word for word, in her brain. It was the possibility of compromise that worried her. If someone outside of Duat's organization found the paper, she would be in trouble. Then she remembered last seeing it in the secret room, and felt it would be safe there. Plus, the thrilling contents of the paper made it hard for her to worry.

Janet Holden!

Thi knew she was selected to kill her because of their acquaintance. What a way—what a great way—to get back at Mark Buckley! She had hated Janet from the first time she had seen her at the Australian reception. Now she was about to get a chance to start evening the score with all of them.

Ψ Ψ Ψ

Kim sat on the side of the bed and listened while Kam, leaning on one elbow, smoothed out and translated the little sheet of paper he had brought:

347

"You will travel to Ban Me Thuot on 29 January, posing as a GVN official. Your travel permit and identity card are attached. You will be met and escorted to the NLF Headquarters, where you will change to peasant clothing and join the first attack group. On day number one, the first attack group will advance on the missionary school in Ban Me Thuot. Targets will be Mr. Reverend White, Madame White, and Doctor Janet Holden. It is essential that these three Americans not survive. Others in the group will recognize and dispatch the Whites. Your target is Doctor Holden. There must be no doubt that she is recognized and killed.

"This is your responsibility because you are the only one in the attack group who can positively identify her.

"You will return to Saigon on 1 February, posing as the sister of Prime Minister Loc. Identity card and travel permit are attached. Due to the probable disruption of communications and traffic in Saigon at that time, you should go immediately to your Cholon address and await instructions. Destroy this paper when contents are memorized."

Kim made Kam read the paper several times. He could not completely comprehend the fantastic story it seemed to tell.

"What you think going happen, Kam?"

"Oh, Kim! This bad stuff. This maybe mean much trouble for Madame Holden."

"You think maybe she get zapped?"

"That Thi, she pretty bad. She number ten."

"Number ten thousand."

"You think she VC?"

"You know it, baby. You so right."

"What you think we do?"

"I find Colonel Buckley. He know."

"You better find him quick. This paper say she all finished 1 February. Kim. This already 29 January."

"I go, Kam—on the double."

Kim snatched up the paper and dashed from the flat. Thi's order was of utmost importance in his mind. He ran through the heat of noon to the Rex Hotel, where his sedan was parked. He headed for the

Hangout, but in his haste, he did not notice that the all-important piece of paper he had placed on the seat beside him had blown onto the floor and finally lodged between the seat and the driver's door.

Ψ   Ψ   Ψ

Mark Buckley and the Vietnamese spent a very long day under cover in the tall reeds. While waiting for nightfall, they passed the time going over and over their plan of operation. By the time dusk came, Mark could already see the road, the large tree that was the rendezvous point, and even the small village at the edge of the jungle. He hoped he would not have to use his pistol, but knew it should be ready.

Therefore, he dispensed with the string tie on his jacket so that he could easily reach the pistol. He also put on his boots, hoping the darkness would keep them from drawing attention.

It was quite dark when Ho passed out the last of the food. After that, they sat around, smoked, and talked in muffled tones.

Finally, it was 2100 hours. After checking their penlights and their weapons once more, Mark, Ho, and Nam followed Bin through the reeds to the edge of a narrow dirt road that rose several feet above the marsh and stretched its lonely way between the high reeds. Nam remained behind and took a position in the reeds where he could observe the road.

The remaining members of the party continued north, up the road toward the village of Phu Mi. They had walked about a half mile when the road bent to the east around a large mango tree, which would be Ho's post.

"Good luck, Colonel Mark!"

Ho shook Mark's hand, and then climbed into the branches of the tree while Mark and Bin continued on.

From his position, Ho watched the two men walk toward the village. The night was clear and a quarter moon enabled him to see an outline of the small, distant village nestled between the jungle and the swampy marshland. The two men moved like specters down the road.

Mark knew that this night's effort had to be clean, straightforward, and decisive if it were to be successful. This meant that everyone in his rescue crew had to do his job with precision. He only hoped that Holden—if it really was Holden, would cooperate.

If he didn't, it would be up to Mark, for no amount of planning could cover all the possible lines of action that Holden could take if he decided not to cooperate.

He was glad Bin knew the village and the exact place where the American was staying. If all worked out as planned, the whole operation would be a piece of cake. If it didn't—well, Mark didn't like to think of the consequences.

They came to the ruin of a small hut on the outskirts of Phu Mi and Bin indicated that Mark should go inside and wait. He slowly approached the building, which was actually two walls joined at a right angle with some thatch over a few beams strung between them. He covered his penlight with his forefinger and allowed a minimum beam to escape, enough to assure him that the place was empty. Then he settled down to wait.

He looked back down the road and saw the distant outline of the large tree against the light sky. He wondered if Ho could see the place where he was. He hoped so, as Ho was to cover him and signal with his flashlight if more than two people approached his position. While he waited, he checked his .45. Carefully he pulled back the slide and checked the round in the chamber.

While Mark waited, Bin walked quietly into town. Although many people here were his relatives, it was safer to keep his presence unknown as long as possible.

The late hour and the absence of electricity were both in his favor. Bin passed his uncle's house and his wife's father's store and turned down a narrow alley to a small farmhouse on the edge of the town. He did not go to the front door, but silently went to the rear and looked in the lighted window. He had chosen correctly.

Dr. Ted Holden, a tall lanky man with a scruffy beard, was seated at a rough, homemade desk, writing by kerosene lamplight. He was absorbed in his work to the extent that he did not seem to notice the many insects swarming about him, attracted by the light. Bin looked over the room carefully. His eyes quickly discovered the young girl asleep on the bed.

She was very pretty. How could he get Holden's attention without waking the girl?

Several times he made a hissing sound, each one louder than the last, but Holden did not notice. Finally, Bin picked up a small pebble and tossed it onto the desk. It bounced over and hit Holden's hand. He turned and looked at the window, his eyes squinting into the darkness.

For an instant, Bin was afraid that the man would call out, but he quickly put his finger to his lips, and Holden, heeding the warning, rose quietly and walked to the window. When he got there, Bin slowly whispered the English words that Mark had coached him to say: "I have news of your wife, Janet. Please come with me."

"Where? How? What do you know?" Holden seemed alarmed.

Bin, however, had exhausted his English vocabulary and merely kept repeating, "Come with me," as Mark had instructed him to do.

Then, to Bin's surprise, Ted Holden broke into fair Vietnamese, "Who are you? Where have you come from? Is Janet ill? Where is she?"

For a moment, Bin considered answering Holden in Vietnamese, but he remembered his instructions and answered only in English, "Come with me."

Ted Holden returned to the desk and set on the edge of it, hesitating, thinking, wondering what he should do.

Often he had thought of Janet, but always in the sense that she was so capable, so very able to fend for herself. It never occurred to him that Janet might be in a position where she would actually need him. Now, for the first time, he had a feeling that this man was here because Janet was in some sort of trouble—perhaps ill. Ted never considered the realities or responsibilities of his personal life. Rather, he preferred to work and live wherever the situation seemed right for him or where he thought he was needed; that is how he came to find himself in his present situation in Phu Mi.

His capture had been a mistake. Ted was making a medical visit to a border village when they picked him up. The VC had really been after the USAID representative of the Ban Me Thuot district. By the time

351

they discovered their mistake, they had transported Ted many miles away.

Then, not knowing what to do with him, they had shipped him from border village to border village. It was lucky that he had his first-aid kit with him when he was captured. They thought he was a medical doctor and brought to him their people who needed medical attention; this had probably saved his life.

Ted felt after a while that they wanted him to escape—perhaps to give them an excuse to track him down and kill him, or perhaps to let him go free.

He knew, however, that his captors would lose face if they admitted that they had captured the wrong man. Consequently, they could not officially free Ted or ransom him. Whatever the case, he had not tried to escape for one very important reason: he had run across an interesting and important mixture of ethnic groups and cross-cultures among the border tribes. His capture actually turned into a one-in-a-million chance to live with these people and study them firsthand. It was an opportunity that an anthropologist could not pass up. Certainly, Janet would understand when at last he returned someday with a completed study.

At least he told himself that.

Ted looked over at the sleeping girl. It had not occurred to him before this moment that Janet might not understand Tanh. He had just never thought about it. He knew that Tanh was a member of the NLF and held some political post in the area, but that part of her life did not interest him. She was the one who helped him with his work, who obtained medicines for him to administer to the villagers, and the one who got rid of the guards and had him put under her personal charge. That had made the whole difference—freedom to do as he wished.

Janet—perhaps she was in trouble. Perhaps she needs me badly. I must find out what this is all about.

He turned to the window and nodded to the man standing there. Then quietly he crossed the room and lowered himself out of the window to the ground. Bin grinned and shook hands with Ted.

Again, he said, "Come with me."

Bin, leading Ted, started north on the street away from the village until it touched the edge of the jungle. Then, circling toward the west, the two intersected the road that Bin and Mark had used to approach Phu Mi.

Ted started to protest the long walk when Bin turned in to Mark's hiding place. Mark watched the two men coming up the road and was fairly sure that no one was following them. Nonetheless, he waited until Bin had taken a position as lookout before he spoke.

"You are Ted Holden." Mark shone a thin beam of light on Ted's face.

"Yes, I am, but who are you? This is a dangerous place for Americans."

"You are an American—or have you forgotten?"

Ted ignored Mark's question.

"Who are you?" he demanded. "And what's this about Janet?"

Mark realized that they had started off badly but there wasn't a lot of time. He wanted this meeting to be as congenial as possible. He paused and then said quietly, "I'm Lieutenant Colonel Mark Buckley. Here, have a cigarette. Let's sit down and I will tell you why I am here."

Ted accepted the cigarette and a light and sat down beside Mark. He had forgotten how good an American cigarette tasted.

"First of all, Janet is all right. But she misses you very much and wants you to come back with me. She loves you very much, Holden. Do you still love her?"

"Yes, of course."

"Then come on. It's all settled. Let's get the hell out of here."

"Wait a minute. I have ties here. I can't just leave. I am working on a very interesting project. Janet will understand once you tell her. You see, this is the opportunity of a lifetime. This area here—it's a unique mixture of Cambodian and Vietnamese cultures."

"What kind of ties do you call those? My God, man, you have a wonderful woman waiting for you, and you expect her to swallow this cross-culture shit? Come on, let's go."

"I can't just walk out of here, Colonel Buckley. At least, I have to

353

see Tanh once more. I wouldn't have followed your man out here if I had known that Janet was okay. I thought she was ill or something. I can't just walk out and leave Tanh. I have to see her again."

Although Mark couldn't understand Ted's reasoning about the study, it did not make him angry. However, the reference to another woman was something else entirely.

For a moment, he saw Janet as she said goodbye to him. It was obvious that she would always love Ted, but he wondered what her reaction would be if she were listening to this conversation now. Anger rose inside him. It would be difficult to keep his temper, but he knew he must keep control, or else blow the whole deal.

Very quietly, Mark said, "Listen, you bastard, Janet is back there waiting for you, refusing to believe you are dead. But here you are, apparently not even under surveillance, refusing to return, and living with some girl."

Ted looked at Mark closely in the dim glow of his cigarette. "You love her, don't you?"

"Of course I do, you stupid son of a bitch. Do you think I've been looking all over hell for you because I love you? I want to marry Janet, but she says not while there's a chance that you're alive. Well, now we know you are alive, so you're coming back with me, for Janet's sake."

As he finished, Mark got up and offered his hand to Ted to pull him to his feet.

"Now, wait a minute. I told you I couldn't just leave ..."

Bin entered the hut.

"Some people come. We go NOW!"

Mark had finally heard enough from Ted Holden to make him lose his temper completely. Bin's words triggered his actions. He had never hit anyone as hard as he now hit Ted. The blow landed on Ted's jaw with such force that his head snapped back and he fell, completely unconscious.

Mark reached over, gathered Ted in his arms, and began running down the road toward the mango tree. Bin ran beside him. He hoped their departure was not too late.

Major Ho also saw what appeared to be a search party moving

slowly toward Mark's hiding place and was about to give Bin a signal when he received one from Bin. He now watched Bin and Mark running toward him in the darkness. They were very hard to make out because the moon had set. He thought it wise to remain concealed in the tree, covering them, until Mark and Bin got past him.

Ho wondered why it took them so long to get to his position. When they finally got close, he could see Mark carrying someone.

The pursuing party seemed to become aware about this time that there were people ahead of them, trying to get away. They began talking excitedly in Vietnamese and were soon in hot pursuit.

As they came under the tree, Mark whispered loudly, "Come on, Ho, don't waste any time. We gotta move."

"I think they catching up, Colonel Mark. I give blast. Pin them down."

"No, don't. Come on. We shouldn't fire until we really have to. It will wake up everyone within ten miles. Keep it quiet as long as possible. Come on."

Ho scrambled out of the tree and caught up with Mark. Holden was getting heavy. Mark was happy to see that they were almost to the boat.

"Set off a flare so that Nam and Trac have the boat ready."

Suddenly there was a loud report. Mark felt a thud in his right arm, and then searing pain. The force caused him to drop Holden and fall to the ground.

"Ho, I've been hit!"

Major Ho had already taken cover in the reeds beside the road. He raked the advancing party with an automatic burst from his M-16, then released a flare, aiming it so it illuminated the enemy and kept his friends in the shadow as much as possible.

"How are you, Colonel Mark?" he called as he waited for the flare to illuminate the road. Suddenly the flare broke over the flat land, bathing the area in a swaying red light.

Bin had gone to Mark's side and pulled him to the edge of the reeds. Only Holden's still form was visible in the road, bathed in ominous shades of red.

Ho observed that one of the enemy lay still on the road about a hundred yards from where they were. The others had apparently taken cover in the reeds.

Suddenly a woman's voice broke the quiet.

She spoke in English. "Ted—now is your chance to come back. You can make it. They won't shoot you. Come on."

Mark had assisted Bin in putting a tourniquet about his upper arm. The dizziness had gone and he was ready to continue. The girl's voice brought his mind back into sharp focus. He saw Ted stir and assume a sitting position. He was coming around.

The flare sputtered out and the area was again smothered in black.

Again the girl's voice called out, "Ted! This way!"

"Tanh, Tanh, is that you? Where are you?" Holden called out, weakly.

"Come this way, Ted. They won't shoot you." She sounded very excited.

Ted got up and started back down the road toward the voice, but Mark, seeing Ted's movements, stumbled to a half crouch and, using his good arm, tackled the escaping man. The searing pain almost caused Mark to black out as both men fell into the road. Ted was still bewildered and dizzy from Mark's blow; otherwise he would have been more than Mark could handle.

In spite of the pain in his arm, Mark was able to pin him down until Bin arrived. They pulled Ted back while Ho gave the tall reeds another long burst of M-16 fire.

"Let's get going!" yelled Mark.

The party fell back farther down the road, knowing full well their pursuers were advancing in the reeds opposite them. Ho and Bin were half dragging, half carrying the semi-conscious Holden, while Mark brought up the rear with Ho's M-16.

"In here!"

It was Nam. They had made it to the boat landing and they cut into the reeds. At this moment, Ted Holden seemed to gain full control of his senses. He shook off Ho and Bin, turned, and shot past Mark onto the road. He was immediately met by a hail of bullets and dropped where he stood.

"Goddammit, he's going back—dead or alive," shouted Mark.

He reached out to grab Ted's collar and pulled him back into the reeds. Sergeant Nam sprayed the opposite side of the road with M-16 fire and then grabbed Holden, carrying him onto the boat.

Alerted by the flare and the fighting, impatient Trai had the motor running when Mark finally stumbled aboard. The sampan leapt forward as Ho, from the back of the cabin, swept the bank with long bursts of fire. Then there was silence, except for the pleasant hum of the Briggs & Stratton that was taking them home.

Mark's first concern was for Ted. With the aid of the others, he laid him on the deck in the cabin and used his penlight to examine the semi-conscious man. Ted had taken a small caliber burst across the chest. His condition was not good. After treating Holden for shock and bandaging the wounds as best he could, Mark sat down beside him. He was getting dizzy again.

That was all he remembered of the escape.

Ψ   Ψ   Ψ

Kim drove up to the Hangout just as Bill Scott was about to leave for MACV Headquarters.

In his excitement, Kim jumped out of the sedan, leaving the door open, and ran to Bill's jeep. No one saw the paper fall out of the sedan. A breeze announcing the coming of an afternoon storm blew it out of the driveway and away into the street.

"Major Bill, Major Bill, oh, it very important. Where is Colonel Mark? Inside?"

"Wait a minute, Kim. What's the hurry? Wait a minute. Mark isn't here. He's in Vung Tau."

Kim stopped in his tracks and turned. His face held such distress that Bill turned off the ignition of his jeep and went over to the big Korean.

"Now, come on. Let's go back to the porch and sit down. Then you can tell me all about it."

When they were seated, Bill learned from the excited Kim that Janet was in danger, that on the 31st of January someone was going to kill her, and that she must be warned.

"How do you know this, Kim? Who told you?"

Suddenly Kim remembered the paper. "Paper!" he yelled as he jumped from his seat and dashed for his car.

A few minutes of frantic searching brought Bill to his side.

"What's the matter, Kim? What are you looking for?"

"Paper! Paper here somewhere, tell all about it."

Kim pulled out the front seat and looked under the floor mats, but found no paper. As the search progressed, Kim became more frantic and Bill, in order to calm him down, kept assuring him that the paper wasn't important. Finally he got Kim seated again on the porch and made him repeat everything he could remember from the paper.

Bill took a small notebook from his pocket and made notes of Kim's information. He made Kim answer more questions as he read and reread his notes.

"Where did you get the paper, Kim?"

Not wanting to reveal that he had trespassed in Thi's apartment, Kim replied, "You know Cô Thi? She sometimes go with me before am married."

"Why, yes. I've known her for quite some time."

"This paper is hers."

"How do you know? Didn't she give it to you?"

"No."

"Then how did you get it?"

"She lend me magazine. This is inside magazine."

"Well, don't worry, Kim. The paper isn't important. The message you gave me is the main thing. I'll call up there today and tell Janet Holden to come to Saigon as soon as possible. Then she will be safe."

"You call Vung Tau and tell Colonel Mark?"

"Why, yes. I'll sure do that, but he may be hard to find. I'll try."

"Okay, Major Bill. Thank you. Miss Janet be okay?"

"Yes, Kim, all is okay. I think you better go now and if that paper shows up, please bring it to me, will you?"

Kim looked at his watch. He was overdue to pick up Colonel Uhm.

"Wow! I gotta scram! See ya round."

He saluted Bill and dashed to the sedan. A quarter of an hour later, he was receiving a chewing out from Colonel Uhm which put Janet's plight far from his mind.

Ψ   Ψ   Ψ

Duat looked down on Nguyen Hue Street and smiled.

Yes, the magnificent boulevard was again the Street of Flowers. For over a week, the trucks had been bringing in pots of flowering apricot, bougainvillea, chrysanthemums, rose bushes, and coxcomb. The street was a mass of colors, and the crowds of people who had come to buy one or two plants for Tet walked as if in a trance through the half-mile-long fantastic colored carpet.

Duat wondered how many of the people there were aware of the change that would come over Saigon within the short span of twenty-four hours. All over the city, firecrackers were on sale to celebrate the Lunar New Year, and many had exploded already. The sharp reports sounded like small-arms fire and could easily deceive the uninitiated.

Duat thought of Thi.

With all of her faults, she is still one of the best people in my organization. She can be trusted to do whatever is assigned to her and do it to perfection. I need her in Saigon for this offensive. However, there was no other way to handle that Ban Me Thuot job—and she will only be gone from Saigon during the initial phase of the attack. If all goes well she'll be back before the city is fully overrun.

Will the city actually fall to the VC? I don't know, but if it doesn't, a good part of it would be destroyed.

He smiled.

In either case, I'll prosper. If the VC take over, I'll be well rewarded. If the allies remain in control, I'll be compensated by the GVN and the Americans for any damage to my property. It is a good position to be in!

The crowd below and the slow-moving vehicular traffic caught his attention again. He noticed a black official American sedan moving with the traffic and idly wondered if the Americans would buy plants and celebrate Tet.

In the sedan, Newell Osborne and Bill Scott were talking in serious tones as they watched the crowds and occasionally caught glimpses of the beautiful floral display.

"Well, I'm glad I talked to Janet after you told me about the Korean's message. She wouldn't come down because she's wrapped up in a Tet celebration with Sally White in Ban Me Thuot. I spoke to Sally. She says that their mission is safer than MACV Headquarters."

"What did Janet say about the threat on her life?"

"Of course she wouldn't take it seriously, but I'm very glad that she's down there in Ban Me Thuot, rather than by herself in Buon Ho or Buon Sut Mgra."

Bill was thoughtful for a minute. "Wish I could reach Mark. I'd feel better about the whole thing if he were up there with Janet."

"I wonder where that rascal is."

"God only knows. I had the MPs turn Vung Tau inside out looking for him."

"Bill, do you think that Mark may be off following up a lead on Ted Holden?"

"God, I hope not. That's dangerous business."

"You know, I hate to have to confine Mark to Saigon, but by God, if he ends up in some kind of trouble over this, I'll have to do it."

Both men were silent for a while. Bill was reasonably sure that Mark was somewhere following a lead on Ted Holden, and he was praying that he would return on time and in good shape.

"And by the way, I have a meeting with the Vietnamese intelligence folks tomorrow concerning your friend, Cô Thi."

"Not my friend."

Newell Osborne laughed. "Well, whoever's friend she is, I remember her being one of the most beautiful Vietnamese girls I have ever met. She certainly should prove an interesting subject for investigation. Guilty or innocent!"

Ψ   Ψ   Ψ

The little sampan docked at Chow Doc at daybreak.

Major Ho directed the landing to be as smooth as possible, to make it easy on the wounded men. He was quite worried about the two Americans. Mark's wound had required a tourniquet to stop the bleeding, and before it was brought under control, he had lost a lot of blood.

Ted Holden was in worse shape. He had four small-caliber wounds around his heart and, although the heart itself did not seem to be hit, he had been bleeding internally and spitting blood. There was no one stirring along the riverfront when Bin brought the boat to the dock. Sergeant Nam quickly jumped ashore and looked in both directions for anyone who could lend assistance. He saw a Tri- Lambretta parked by a warehouse some distance away.

"Hey! You, driver, wake up! Come here; we need help!"

Nam started toward the vehicle. He was sure the driver was inside his vehicle, or else it would have been dismantled and taken away by thieves during the night. He was right. Within a minute, the sleepy driver emerged, rubbing his eyes.

"Here quickly! We need you. We have wounded Americans here."

The driver stumbled into a hurried walk and looked into the cabin of the boat. Ho spoke to him tersely, asking, "Are there American units here? Where is the hospital? Who is the ranking American? Can you take me there?"

The driver recognized Mark. "*Chieu Hoi* (Empty hands, I surrender)! What you done to my good friend? Is he badly hurt?"

"Listen to me, you idiot. Who is the top American here?"

Suddenly the driver became aware of the gravity of the situation. Instantly he was awake and alert. "You need Ông Teague. He is province advisor. You stay here and care for my friend. I will bring back Ông Teague."

He raced to his vehicle, praying to Buddha to favor him with a quick start of the engine.

Buddha smiled.

With the second kick of the starting pedal, the engine sputtered and roared, and the Tri-Lambretta disappeared around the corner in a series of backfires and a cloud of smoke.

Jim Teague was sitting on the second-story porch of his quarters, waiting for his breakfast when the rough explosive sounds of a cold Lambretta engine shattered the quiet of the morning.

"I'll bet it's that Tri again. Where in hell does he get all the information, rumors, and lies that keep him in a state of perpetual panic?"

At that moment, the Tri-Lambretta whipped around the corner on two of its three wheels and slid to a stop in front of the gate to Jim Teague's house.

"Hey, Tri! What's up?" Jim had come to the railing and called down in Vietnamese.

"Ah, Ông Teague! Good morning to you, Ông Teague. I have unfortunate news. Two Americans wounded in a fierce fight with VC. One is my good friend. Come quick! Bring doctor!"

"Wait a minute. Who told you this?"

"I see them. Major Ho, Commandant at Trong Thoi, he is there. He needs your help."

Teague detected the earnest note in Tri's voice. "Wait! I'll be right down."

In minutes the Tri-Lambretta wheeled onto the dock and Jim Teague, accompanied by Tri, jumped aboard the sampan.

"Well. Mark Buckley, where in hell have you been and ... my God, it's Ted Holden. Mark, you've brought Ted Holden back!"

Mark tried to smile and then nodded gratefully at Tri.

"Hi, Jim. See you have my good friend with you. Actually, Ho here brought Holden back, but I think he's in pretty bad shape."

Jim turned to Tri and told him to alert the small aid station and have the jeep ambulance sent over. Then he helped Ho and the others move the unconscious Ted Holden to the dockside.

Later, while the local doctor was doing his best for Mark and Ted, Jim Teague spoke to Newell Osborne in Saigon. Heeding Mark's advice, Jim suggested that Ted's physical condition, together with his lack of desire to return to government-controlled areas in South Vietnam, created a situation too delicate to relate to Janet by phone.

After the conversation was completed, Newell decided to dispatch an aircraft with a doctor to Chow Doc to transport the two wounded men to Can Tho, the nearest military hospital with complete facilities for handling Ted's wounds. Newell decided to catch a ride on the aircraft himself so that he could get firsthand from Mark the complete details of Ted's escape.

The hospital at Can Tho had been alerted to receive Ted Holden, and upon his arrival the chief surgeon operated immediately, in order to remove one slug that was lodged very close to Ted's heart.

Mark was examined by the medics who found his wound had been well taken care of by the folks in Chow Doc. After re-bandaging, Newell Osborne waited in the convalescent ward with him while Ted was undergoing surgery.

Mark finally gave him the full details of the rescue, as well as his assessment of Ted Holden's strange behavior.

"No, I don't believe Ted is a traitor in any true sense of the word. After capture, he was treated like a military prisoner at first, and then a civilian prisoner later. The fact that he didn't try to escape can't be held against him, as he does not fit under the military code of conduct."

"But Mark, what in God's name would keep him there?"

"It's like I told you, sir. His work and that ... girl ... not necessarily in that order."

"But, Janet ..."

"That's what made me mad, sir. That's the thing I can't forgive him for."

"What do you think we should do about Janet? How can we tell her?"

"This is a very personal thing between Janet and me. I think I should see Janet tonight, if possible, and give her the facts. Then I'll bring her down here to be with Ted during his convalescence."

"I wish I had insisted that she come to Saigon yesterday. She could have been here right now," said Osborne.

"Look, sir, that plane is standing by to take you back to Saigon this evening. How about letting me go with you, and after dropping you off, let them fly me up to Ban Me Thuot. I can see her late tonight and head back down with her in the morning."

Newell pondered the question for a moment. "I'm worried about you, Mark. The doctors say ..."

"Don't worry about me, sir. I've had worse than this. Look, with the sling my wounded arm is completely immobilized and the rest of me is in good shape."

Reluctantly Newell agreed, and Mark promised to return back to the hospital as soon as he returned to Can Tho.

About mid-afternoon, the chief surgeon entered the ward and went directly over to Mark's bed. It was obvious to both Mark and Newell that he had bad news.

"Doctor Holden is dead, Mr. Ambassador."

"My God, what happened? We were told that although his condition was critical, it wasn't expected to result in his death."

"That was overly optimistic on the part of someone. His wounds were far more severe than we expected and the amount of time that elapsed ... there was nothing we could do. Is there someone by the name of Pam or Tam that we should notify? He kept calling that name ..."

"Forget about the name, Doctor. You would be doing everyone a favor."

"Of course, I understand perfectly."

"And doctor, Ted Holden's wife is in Ban Me Thuot. I am sending Colonel Buckley up there tonight to break the news to her. He will bring Janet back with him tomorrow. Please arrange for his release from the hospital."

Mark, stunned by the doctor's news, wondered how he could tell Janet.

Why did the bastard have to go and die? Well, Janet doesn't ever have to know the about Tanh and Ted's reluctance to return. No. Tonight, when he saw Janet, he would tell her Ted had died—well.

Ψ Ψ Ψ

Thi looked over the men in the group.

They're real professionals, like the ones I met on my tour around the edges of Saigon. How smart I was not to talk big! In the end, it paid off. My very silence has enhanced my prestige. When that report finally came in on me, these tough soldiers sure were impressed with my record! They treated me with so much respect that the other women of the force are jealous. Well, let them be jealous. Most of them are only in this business because their men are in it. All ugly hags as well.

She checked her watch, which she wore hidden in her clothing on a long string around her neck.

A fancy watch on my wrist would make a lie of my farmer's disguise.

It was almost time to move out. She felt her trousers where she had concealed a razor-sharp knife with a six-inch blade, then her shoulder holster where she carried a small .38 automatic.

Their team was the vanguard. They would reach the mission school while the regular assault troops were still at the outskirts of the city. Then, after their job was completed, they would fall back through the attackers and she would pull out altogether. For the last time, she looked at the map, then drew a burning stick from the fire and ignited it.

"Burn, Ban Me Thuot, burn!" she said aloud as the map flared up briefly. The others smiled in approval.

"Let's move out!" said Ngo, their leader, who stood on the other side of the fire.

He smiled at Thi. She smiled back. She liked Ngo. He wasn't any General Trun Du, but he would do for this operation. She got to her feet and moved over to his side. They were on their way.

Ψ   Ψ   Ψ

The C-47 dropped Newell Osborne off and made its way on to Ban Me Thuot. Mark, resting with his eyes closed, felt weaker than he would like to admit, but it had been one hell of a long day. He hated to face Janet. After all, if he hadn't made Ted return—dragged him back literally—Ted would still be alive. Well, those were the breaks. He hoped that Janet would understand.

"Say there, Colonel. Take a look to the west."

It was the co-pilot, who had come back to talk to him about the return trip, but was now interested in pointing out some ground action to Mark. His Texas drawl was right out of a Western movie.

"That's a bunch of gunships attacking some river traffic ... Wow! See that explosion? The VC must have thirty or forty sampans in there. They must be getting ready for a big push somewhere."

Mark watched the battle with interest. The tracers of the gunships

365

cut streams of red fire through the darkness. Occasionally the flash of an explosion or a fire on one of the boats lit up several others in a manner that seemed to stop all the action and reveal like a flash photo, the stark, sharp horror of the battle in all its detail.

As the aircraft flew on, now out of sight of the ground action, the co-pilot returned to the subject at hand.

"Well, the boss will go ahead and make a night landing up there for you—although there are a lot better strips—but we're not going to RON. He doesn't like Ban Me Thuot. But don't worry; we've already set up a spook 'Pioneer' for first thing in the morning to bring you and your friend back."

"That's okay. No sweat. I'll look for it about nine."

God, how tired he was! He dropped off to sleep before the pilot was back in the cockpit. He slept for the remainder of the trip and did not wake until the aircraft pulled up in front of the terminal, engines still turning.

"Get this guy out. I don't want to spend the rest of what's left of the night in this sorry-ass place."

Mark heard the pilot and tried to move. He was weak and needed assistance. The crew chief helped him out and turned him over to the small group of Americans that met the plane. He turned and waved to the pilot, who had already turned the ship around to taxi out for takeoff.

"Say, this guy's sick!"

Mark somehow forced himself to look a lot better than he felt.

"No, I'm not. Just, tired. Got any transportation? I gotta get to the missionary school in town."

"You ain't goin' nowhere, buddy. There's some kind of an alert on due to the Tet stuff, and they slapped a 2200 hours curfew on us."

"Well, this is official business."

My God! It would be after one before I made it to the missionary school, and then what a shock all this about Ted will be for Janet ... better wait for morning.

"Yeah, I guess the official business can wait till daybreak," he added. "You guys had better drop me by the base hospital. This arm is giving me fits."

Ψ   Ψ   Ψ

Thi heard the dull, distant thud of the first mortar.

She looked at her watch and then placed it back inside her shirt. It was exactly 2:30. The attack was on schedule. She waited for the signal.

There it was—two small-arms rounds in rapid succession. She moved forward toward the ten-foot wall of the missionary school. The team's objective was the large two-story house used by the Americans for living quarters. She could see in the darkness other members of the team advancing toward the house. A mortar round landed fairly close as the team crossed the wall and formed inside the compound. Ahead of them was their objective. She saw a light come on in an upstairs window and a tall American man in striped pajamas come out on the porch. There was a shot and then he pitched forward and fell two stories to the ground below. A door opened on the ground floor and two Vietnamese women rushed out. They were cut down in the courtyard, less than twenty feet from the house.

Now more lights appeared at the upper windows. The people inside seemed to be clustering together. Thi could hear their excited voices above the rumble of mortar rounds and the distant sporadic small-arms fire.

Ngo moved forward and kicked in the front door. By this time, other team members were at each exit. Thi entered the house with Ngo and two others.

"Everyone downstairs. Now!" shouted Ngo in Vietnamese.

Thi repeated it in English. Two of the team started up the wide staircase, AK-47s at the ready.

Sally White had awakened when her husband turned on the light, and had watched him go onto the porch. She heard the shot and, horrified, saw him pitch over the railing. She knew that even if her husband had survived the shot, he would never survive the fall.

Being a capable woman who lived in a land of terrorism and war, she knew that she was in charge now and knew what she had to do. She thrust down the emotional response that was her right to experience and replaced it with common sense. The only others on the top

367

floor were Janet and the girls. Sally quickly snatched up a pair of cotton slacks, a man's shirt, a pair of heavy shoes, and a .25 caliber pistol, and ran to Janet's room.

Janet, awakened by the noise, realized that the school was under attack and had started making similar preparations before Sally arrived.

"Good! You don't mind if I dress in here. Save time. You know, I'm afraid he's dead, God rest his soul." Sally fought back a sob.

Janet could not believe what Sally White was saying.

"What do you mean?"

"Shot him on the porch. He fell ... Here, don't you have any shoes more sensible than that? Now I'm going to see to the girls. We'll all assemble in the council room–if they'll let us!"

Janet finished dressing and started down the stairs. The sight that she saw below made her gasp in horror and disbelief. Sally's two daughters, aged eleven and twelve, had been wrenched from their mother's arms and slung down the stairs by one of Ngo's men, who shouted, "Too slow!" in Vietnamese.

Sally's scream, combined with those of the two girls, filled the stairway and the hall below. As she ran down to comfort her children, another man walked up to them, crumpled and crying at the bottom of the stairs. In a swift movement, he triggered a burst of his AK-47.

They moved only when the initial bullets struck their small bodies, then they lay still. He then turned, fired, and cut Sally down. She pitched forward and landed on the bodies of the two girls.

The room became a horror of noise, flashes of fire, and the acrid smell of burning cordite. Janet froze at the top of the stairs, her hand over her mouth. There was complete silence. She looked down through the smoke-filled stairwell to the hall.

"No more shooting without my permission!" shouted Ngo in Vietnamese.

Janet's attention turned to the man shouting orders, but her interest was caught by the soldier standing next to him.

This soldier spoke. It was a woman's voice.

"There is Mrs. Holden! Come down, Mrs. Holden. Come down now!"

The woman was looking up at her and pointing as she spoke her commands in English.

Janet Holden had never really considered dying in Vietnam. Now, suddenly, such a possibility became a reality. So many things left un-done—there was Ted, there was Mark, there was her work, her relatives back home. She had left things very untidy, and somehow the total shock of this moment brought her scholar's personality to the fore. She was upset at the disorder, the interruption. She didn't yet recog-nize the numb terror that was starting to creep over her body.

Slowly she walked down the stairs. Another thought entered her mind. It did not seem right that she should bow out without a fight of some kind. Cold anger was replacing the academic's annoyance. She carefully stepped over Sally White and the two children.

"God bless you and keep you, Sally ... you and the girls."

Then she faced her captors. Her eyes blazed.

"You had better be careful what you do. I'm red haired and mean." Janet spat the words out with venom.

Surprised at herself and her silly warning, she realized she hadn't said anything like that since she was a small girl in a schoolyard fight.

Where in the hell did that come from?

Thi strode up to Janet, swaggering. This was her moment. She re-moved her straw hat. "Remember me, Madame Holden? The interpreter in Saigon? Friend—very good friend—of Mark Buckley?"

Only Janet's pupils revealed the fact of recognition. She merely stood quiet, proud, but inwardly furious and confused.

What is this girl doing up here? I can't believe that she is here in the highlands.

Thi turned to Ngo. "Do we have time for some special treatment for Madame Holden?"

Intrigued, Ngo nodded assent.

"Grab her arms and hold her!"

Two soldiers stepped behind the American woman and pinned her arms behind her.

"So far my dear, you have been a very lucky woman," Thi said evenly and quietly. "War has passed you by. You have no wounds, no ugly scars. It is easy for you to charm your men."

369

Now Thi's voice changed. It was harsh, loud, screaming. "But look! Look at me! See this!"

She held up her long dark hair, revealing the tiny scar on her left cheek.

"That is my war memento. Something to help me to remember forever the brave American soldiers, the dashing US artillery!"

Now fear had taken over from anger, but Janet was determined not to let this cheap little actress put her down. She summoned all her courage and prayed that her voice would be calm. She tried to remember all the facts that Poli De Salle had told her about this girl.

In perfect French, Janet let her have it, "Oh, come off it, Thi, or Solange, or Le Blott or whatever you used to call yourself. This is no time for cheap histrionics. Your soldiers have killed four people in cold blood, four innocent people of God. We all know you, and what you were. Don't blame your miserable life on that little scar on your cheek. I know all about you. You were a poor actress before you had that scar, and even in those days, you couldn't keep your man. But it's a nice crutch for you, isn't it? It gives the cheap little lousy actress a reason for all of her failures."

Thi could not believe Janet Holden's words. It was as if she had ripped off all of her clothing and left her there naked, exposed for all the team to see. They all knew enough French to understand all of Janet's rant. How did she know so much about her? Without thinking, she raised her hand and struck Janet hard across the face.

Ears ringing with the force of the blow, Janet reeled in pain. A small trickle of blood fell from her mouth. But she would not give Thi the satisfaction of seeing her succumb to the pain.

"You can't even do that well," spat Janet with scorn.

The men of the assault team were getting embarrassed.

"Let's get out of here. We can't stay all day," said Ngo. There was small-arms fire in the distance. "The ARVN or the RF is coming. Get it over with."

Thi reached for her knife. "Well this will give you a reason!" Quickly she raised the knife and slashed the right side of Janet's face from ear to jawbone. The soldiers gasped in disbelief as blood gushed forth and dripped over Janet's shoulder.

"That's enough! Kill her!"

But Thi would have her way. Again, she raised the knife and slashed the left side of Janet's face. Blood flowed freely from the angry wounds and she fainted with the pain. Stunned, the soldiers released her and she crumpled to the floor.

The fighting was getting closer. A full exchange of small-arms fire was taking place near the west wall of the school.

Thi reached for her pistol and fired three shots into Janet Holden. Already the men were withdrawing.

"Out! All out!" yelled Ngo. His voice revealed the disgust he felt.

"Don't worry, Ngo, she is dead," called Thi as she paused to sheath her knife.

Quickly she ran after the other members of the assault team. She knew she had lost much face in her encounter with Janet Holden. In her humiliation, she hoped that after that day, she would never have to see the other team members again.

Ψ   Ψ   Ψ

In Saigon, the last night in January had been one hell of a time for Bill Scott.

It started with a telephone alert call that woke him at about 0400 hours. The duty officer described the attack on the city in quick, terse terms. The enemy had violated the Tet truce and started the greatest general offensive of the war. He had been advised to remain where he was until daylight, to defend himself the best he could, and to stand by for additional instructions which would be given when the situation had solidified somewhat.

Bill picked up a captured VC AK-47, the only weapon in the Hangout. All other weapons had been turned in to headquarters in compliance with a recent MACV directive.

Bunch of morons. Lucky I have this thing. Glad Mark brought the ammo and that we hadn't gotten around to trying it out and using all the rounds. What a stupid idea to turn in all weapons in a war zone. If I'd been smart like Mark, I'd still have my .45.

He also picked up a helmet, flak vest, and a canteen of water. Then,

371

he made his way to the rooftop of the villa. The irregular roofline gave him plenty of cover and he was high enough to have a commanding view of the immediate area.

The sky was just beginning to lighten a bit in the east as he took his post on the roof, but there were still two hours before daylight would arrive. He looked north to Cholon. Red flames from the city were lighting the sky with ominous streaks. He worried about Mai Lei and Bu and wondered if their little house was near the trouble area.

Suddenly he became aware of small-arms fire in all directions of the compass.

"My God, they've surrounded Saigon," he said aloud as his eyes swept three hundred and sixty degrees.

The late hours of the night dissolved into a noisy, red-tinged dawn. To the east, pillars of black smoke became visible, each attesting to the fact that war had begun in earnest in the city. As the daylight progressed, he spotted many similar fires about the perimeter. The small-arms fire changed in tempo from numerous short bursts to fierce long bursts, with periods of silence in between. Helicopter gunships were airborne, firing into various targets about the outskirts.

Bill turned his attention to a closer situation.

Two blocks away, some of the VC had taken up positions in an apartment house and a combined group of American and Vietnamese military police was attacking the building, while civilian residents fled the battle. The local area was a gigantic discord of sirens as ambulances, fire engines, and police cars rushed through the city to the trouble areas.

One of the servants brought Bill some food and a small transistor radio. There were several announcements advising USAID and State Department personnel to report to their stations.

The fact that he was alone on the roof, completely out of the action, while the girl he loved was in danger, was too much for Bill.

I have to see to Mai Lei, but God, it will be impossible to reach her on my own. From the sound of the fighting, I can't get there without at least a special pass and probably an armed escort. I'll take the jeep and see if I can make it to MACV Headquarters, then see what I can do about joining a security team working in the Cholon area. I gotta get there. I gotta get her safe.

Chapter X

FEBRUARY

M ark Buckley was never sure just how he survived the wild ride that day.

Despite his immobilized right arm, Mark somehow drove the jeep he had commandeered at breakneck speed through the predawn, dark streets of Ban Me Thuot, ignoring the sounds of small-arms fire. Since darkness would linger for at least another two hours, it would be difficult to determine who was friend and who was foe. For that reason, he hoped to evade both sides in the fighting as long as possible—at least until he reached Janet.

Then, perhaps they could hole up and wait it out until daylight.

The firing was on Mark Buckley's left flank. He turned right down a crooked street to escape it. Now he was approaching the missionary school and he could see ahead of him flashes from small arms. He pulled over into a small courtyard and listened intently. He recognized the familiar sounds of M-16 fire directly in front of him; then, farther away, the unmistakable sound of the AK-47. The latter was coming from within the school grounds.

He silently cursed the VC and aloud he said, "If Janet is hurt, I'll declare my own personal war on those bastards."

Mark grabbed the M-16 he had picked up at the hospital, dismounted, and walked slowly up to an ARVN position. He threw himself down beside two young and very surprised South Vietnamese soldiers operating a walkie-talkie.

"*Dua Chi Huy Truong den day*." (Bring the commander here.) Mark ordered.

One of the soldiers spoke into the radio and shortly, a young captain crawled up to their position. Mark was relieved that he spoke some English. He learned that the main wave of the enemy was passing through the area, and most likely, the ones in the school would be pulling out soon as they retreated to the north. Mark said he would like to assist the soldiers in recapturing the school. The captain agreed and explained that there would be a minimum of shooting because of the children. He cautioned Mark to fire on only recognized enemy, even though he knew that it was an almost impossible order to follow until daylight brought better visibility.

Suddenly the firing grew more intense from inside the school. Then there was silence.

"I think that high expenditure of ammo was a feint. They must have escaped over the back wall," said Mark to the captain.

Restless with the waiting and uncertain of Janet's condition, Mark volunteered to reconnoiter the schoolyard.

"If all's clear, I'll open the gate and fire three shots with this M-16. That'll be my signal. If it isn't clear, you won't have to worry about me. Just get in as soon as you can!"

Mark approached the five-foot wall, on the double, and with difficulty scrambled over it. On the other side, he found himself in complete darkness. All was quiet, except the terrified crying of small children and moans of pain and anguish from the older Vietnamese teachers and nurses.

He stumbled forward toward the big house. The first rays of sun were illuminating the eastern sky, and the clouds above him were tinged with red.

Red sky in morning.

A bad omen, he thought, as he inspected the courtyard in the dim light. It was empty of enemy soldiers. He stepped out into the open—the visibility was much better now. Standing in the center of the compound, he raised his good arm, still holding the M-16.

"Come on and shoot me, you dirty bastards!"

Since no one took him up on his invitation, he assumed that the VC had gone. Quickly he rushed to the gate and opened it wide. He fired three shots, and then ran for the main house.

"Janet! Janet Holden! Janet, where are you? It's Mark!"

His heart sank as he saw the crumpled body of Fred White on the ground and two Vietnamese women by the door. With one bound, he cleared the porch and burst into the hall. Every detail of what he saw would be etched, forever, on his memory.

The gun smoke. The smell of the burnt powder. The woman and the girls heaped grotesquely at the bottom of the stairs. Vietnamese nurses, teachers and helpers wandering through the room in various stages of shock and disbelief.

Then he spotted Janet, her body just visible behind an overturned chaise lounge. He rushed to her side.

"Janet! My God, what have they done to you?"

There was slight movement there. The blood from the two facial wounds had dripped onto the floor and was beginning to coagulate in her hair.

The horror of the cuts kept Mark from seeing at first the three small, but far more serious bullet wounds in her chest. When he spotted those, he realized that the situation was worse than he had at first thought.

Mark took charge. From his position, he shouted at the shocked, speechless Vietnamese.

"You! Check Madame White and the children. Who's a nurse? All of you come over here. Come here right now! Now, who has had medical training? You? Fine. Get sterile bandages and hot water."

The Whites were clearly dead. The Vietnamese nurse confirmed this quickly.

At this point, the ARVN troops appeared, and Mark took the radio and called the military hospital for assistance. However, from the outset it was clear that the city had become a major battlefield and no ambulance would be coming that day.

Somehow, the Vietnamese staff quickly found Fred White's pick-up truck and, after laying a mattress on the open truck bed, they gently placed Janet onto it. Then, with a nurse and a supply of plasma, Mark started for the hospital, disappearing into the battle smoke that hung over everything, looming like a funeral shroud in the early morning.

By listening to the sounds of firing, this time he was able to take a safer, longer route away from some of the fighting. The nurse cared for Janet in the back of the lurching truck. Miraculously they avoided a firefight and made it to the hospital. The medics processed Janet along with many other wounded cases heading for surgery. Mark stayed with her, and although she was unconscious, he kept talking to her and assuring her that she would be all right.

At the last moment before she went to surgery, Janet regained consciousness. She opened her eyes and Mark was there, looking down at her.

"Oh, Mark, Mark, I knew you would come. Now everything is going to be fine." Janet spoke with stiff lips, feeling the pain of the cuts.

"Don't worry about a thing. You're going to be okay," Mark replied with false assurance.

Suddenly Janet's face contorted in terror and she tried to touch her cheek. "Did she really do it, Mark? Did she really cut me?"

Not the time to tell the truth ...

"Yes, darling. You have some cuts, but don't worry about them," Mark lied. "They're going to patch you up so well that you won't be able to find any scar to brag about."

"But why does she hate us so much? Why would she do such a thing—such a pretty girl. She was so friendly in Saigon."

Mark at first thought Janet was delirious from the morphine. Now, however, he wasn't so sure.

"What girl, Janet? What friendly girl?"

"You know, that Thi."

"Do you mean Thi was the one that did all of this?"

"She was one of the leaders. She had the knife."

Mark remembered. That wild night in Thi's apartment. She had deliberately showed him her little scar.

"Don't worry about it now, darling," Mark said softly. "I'll take care of everything. Just get through this ..."

Janet had closed her eyes and her breath came in quick gasps. Mark could tell she was in pain. At that moment, two corpsmen came to take her into surgery. Mark leaned over and gently kissed her lips.

"Goodbye for now, darling. I love you. I'll be waiting ..."

But somehow, Mark knew it was going to be a long wait.

He was right. Janet Holden did not survive surgery. He never saw her alive again.

Ψ   Ψ   Ψ

The war had come to Saigon and Brandy Masters had decided not to run from it.

She found a maintenance ladder and made the last leg of her journey to the roof of her apartment house. She carried with her a portable radio and a small .25 caliber revolver in a holster strapped about her waist. She stood on the roof, the air pungent with various smells of the city. Suddenly she realized that, war or no war, she had entered a real world and left behind a phony world of rumor, outrage, and self-pity. Brandy was not about to spend another night listening to the fear-ridden Americans of her billet wail about this offensive.

She had come to the roof where she could see and smell and listen, and try to find out what was actually going on.

The night before last, the explosions of the initial attack had awakened her, and almost immediately, the billet had become a quagmire of fear and rumor. The following day was grim; the stupid announcements on Armed Forces Radio; the long periods of silence; the comings and goings of frightened people unable to stay alone in their quarters. Then last night had been a real circus, with several hysterical women and men wailing about how they were getting the hell out, and no job over here was worth all this danger.

She reflected on her own rather bad performance. She had taken all she could stand from the half-drunk, completely unnerved American occupants of the building. Finally, she decided to sound off and let them have it.

"What's the matter with you all?" She had started out rather mildly.

"So the city is under attack? The only thing you've felt is a lack of comfort, due to the power failure. So now, you have to open the windows and have to burn candles. That's tough. Really tough.

"Oh, I realize that the open windows make you listen to some rifle fire now and then, but look at you: you are all becoming psychos just listening to each other cry.

"What if this building becomes a VC military headquarters and they all moved in here? Yes, it could happen, you know. I suppose you men would fight to the last martini in the true spirit of Saigon commandos. And how about you girls? Ready for a little roughing up? A little rape, maybe? And to think of putting up with the humidity and all those horrible smells. How unclean, how disgustingly indecent it all would be here, if the real world that you've been dodging for so long breaks in on you that way!"

Suddenly Brandy was disgusted with herself. She would rather forget it. It had been a bad performance. Her thoughts returned to the present. She could see the smoke rising from the various fires about the city. Cholon was the worst.

God, those people must be in a living hell!

The day wore on and as the sun went down and darkness fell on the city, great orange flashes lit up the sky, and tracers from the US gunships looped down like giant, gaudy strings of beads. In every direction, the VC were on the attack. The city had been penetrated on all fronts, but to the north, near Cholon and Tan Son Nhut, the penetration had been deeper. She flipped on the radio and tuned in Radio Saigon. Her experience with the language was paying off. She was able to make out most of the words.

A lot of the propaganda was as bad as the Armed Forces Radio station, but from the various announcements, she slowly began to visualize a picture of the real situation.

One announcement caught her interest: "Anyone with experience or training in nursing or first aid, please report to the nearest hospital. Volunteers are needed desperately."

Brandy had to listen to the message twice before she was able to understand it all, and when it was finally clear to her, she realized that the people of Saigon were suffering badly.

If they're still making that announcement by morning, I'll know that they are really hurting for help—maybe badly enough to need me.

It was about 2030 when she left the roof and returned to her flat. Brandy had already made up her mind. From the bottom of the cupboard, she pulled out her old USO fatigue uniform, and from the closet, she took out her boots. With a small pair of scissors, she removed the USO insignia. Her uniform was ready. There was nothing more she could do.

She decided to get some sleep. Suddenly she felt better than she had in years. Maybe now she would be able to do something useful. At least it was a start. In spite of the heat and the noise of the distant battle, Brandy Masters fell into a deep, calm, and untroubled sleep.

Ψ   Ψ   Ψ

General Trun Du paced the floor of his command post.

Occasionally he stopped and looked at a large map of Saigon tacked to the wall. He was located in a large room on the top floor of a semi-finished pagoda. It was about a quarter of a mile from the more imposing An Quang Pagoda, which his troops had taken from the Buddhist monks and made into the main support area.

In a corner of the room, his staff grouped about a small radio that crackled and hummed out the information relative to the movements of his units about the city. From time to time one of the staff would quietly cross to the map and move some of the pins denoting each unit.

The initial operations and the first advance into Saigon had been well executed. Du was happily surprised by the performance of the Viet Cong. Prior to the assault he had thought that they were only capable of fighting effectively in small guerilla units, but in this case, formed into battalions, they had done well.

"If support from the North continues, this offensive will be successful beyond our wildest dreams," he said aloud.

His intelligence sources had indicated that, due to the Tet holiday, most ARVN units were down to fifty percent strength when he attacked. With no national communications to summon their troops back, the allies were having a rough time forming their units. Du smiled as he again walked over to inspect the map.

His eyes swiftly glanced at his forty-six VC and NVA battalions grouped on the map. He had committed thirty-five of them to the initial assault. It had been a gamble and it was very close to paying off.

However, the attack on Long Binh had been a disappointment. He wondered if he would have fared better if he had committed five battalions against that camp instead of the three that had gone in.

One of his officers moved the pins designating the 267th and 269th battalions in from the northeast toward Tan Son Nhut. This operation was a coordinated two-prong attack, with the second and sixth battalions coming in from the west into Cholon. He looked at his watch with a feeling of satisfaction, knowing that the attack had been launched exactly on time.

He went to the open sides of the pagoda and looked over the city, deserted in the clear afternoon. Occasionally the smoke from a burning section of Cholon blanked out the sun, casting dark shadows across his observation post.

This city could easily be his if ... yes, if the promised troops and supplies arrived. Again, he reviewed in his mind the general plan for the nationwide offensive. He had disagreed with the basic concept. He wanted to concentrate on four cities: Hue, Dalat, Saigon, and Can Tho. There would have been much more chance of success. A concentration on four instead of twenty-seven cities would have assured a striking success. The attacks had to be complete and decisive before the people would turn against the government and join his side.

"Great eye of God! That convoy of sampans has to make it to Saigon," he said aloud. The troops and ammunition were essential. He asked for his binoculars and scanned the roofs of the buildings.

Here and there, he saw Vietnamese and Americans on rooftops, looking toward the areas under attack. He followed the flight paths of two US Army gunships as they strafed his men during the assault on Tan Son Nhut.

If only he had five or six of them on his side!

Ψ   Ψ   Ψ

Mark Buckley returned to Saigon on February 1st.

His report described in minute detail the horrors of the attack on the mission school at Ban Me Thuot. He was calm, factual, and very official. Not once did emotion enter his discourse in the many times he was required to tell it. All who listened to Mark and knew of his relationship with Janet Holden marveled at his detached coolness and iron nerve. Only Newell Osborne knew the truth that Mark's seemingly endless calm was a mask to cover some sort of drastic action that this officer was determined to take, but would not divulge.

Mark did have a plan. In order to protect himself and to assure success, Mark never once used the name of Thi or revealed Janet's remarks. When the last de-briefing was over, Mark talked to Newell about the situation in Saigon. Newell gave permission to take leave of his pacification duties for the duration of the emergency to volunteer his services to the Army.

Late that afternoon Mark, armed with his preferred weapon, the .45 automatic, along with the hard-to-come-by CAR-15, and a short M-16 with a telescoping stock, joined forces with the 716th Military Police Battalion, whose operational area was Saigon.

Step one in his plan had begun.

Ψ   Ψ   Ψ

Thi returned to Saigon.

She stepped off the C-47 at the Vietnamese Air Force terminal at Tan Son Nhut and easily melted into the group of people anxiously waiting for friends and relatives. Catching a ride with the enemy had been a masterful move. By the time she got to the main gate, she had destroyed her false identity cards that had ensured a plane ride and checked her real papers in order to prepare herself for the inevitable search by the guards.

All over the base, there was evidence of the battle. Huge armored personnel carriers carrying dirty, tired American soldiers dominated all traffic on the roads; hastily erected bunkers of sandbags were strategically located at all intersections, and large artillery pieces were dug in wherever she looked. Around each gun emplacement and bunker were barbed wire perimeters. In fact, barbed wire was everywhere.

She also noticed the difference in the attitude of the Vietnamese soldiers who, in the past, were always happy and friendly, ready to call to her the usual mild obscenities or invitations that soldiers always offered to a pretty girl. Now, they seemed all business and paid her no attention at all as she passed their positions.

The main gate of Tan Son Nhut had also undergone a serious change. There was a barricade of cement slabs placed across the roadway and in front of the guardhouse in such a way that vehicles entering the airbase had to go very slowly, turning first to the right and then to the left to pass the massive barriers.

The personnel checkpoint reminded her of a cattle loading ramp. It was a small raised runway made of wood, with wooden railings on both sides.

All people leaving the base had to walk up the runway to be searched by Vietnamese soldiers and military police standing alongside. She was motioned to the end of the runway by a captain. He was tired, unkempt, and very surly.

"Identification papers, please."

Thi handed them to the officer.

"Who are you? Where do you live?"

"Cô Dao Thi. Apartment 37, Minh Mang and Dui Streets."

"Spell your name."

An orderly copied the information down and checked it out with a large copy of official census records.

"What are you doing on Tan Son Nhut?"

"I just landed in a Vietnamese military aircraft from Ban Me Thuot."

"Are you military?"

"No."

"What were you doing on a military plane?"

Thi had been waiting for a good cue to launch into her diversionary story. This seemed to be it.

"I was lucky. The town was still under attack." She started slowly, warming to her subject. "It was awful! People were trying to escape the slaughter. The city was burning. Small children wounded, were screaming for their mothers ..."

A small crowd of interested Vietnamese civilians, soldiers, and police started to gather around her. They were hearing their first news of the attack outside of Saigon.

"Now, control yourself, Cô Thi!" The captain was not unfriendly. "There will be just a few more questions ..."

"I was at the airport. I had missed the evening plane. When the attack came that morning, I ran about trying to hide from the mortars. Some friendly soldiers let me share their dugout. An officer came and took me to the headquarters. One was a friend of a pilot. I was permitted to sit with the luggage and cargo. The mortar attack was the worst ..."

The orderly completed his check and told the captain that she was correctly registered.

"That's all, Cô Thi. Proceed between these two railings and give this pass to the guard at the gate."

He returned her papers and she proceeded down the narrow runway. It was necessary for her to stop at each pair of soldiers, stationed on opposite sides of the walkway. She felt their rough hands press and rub against every section of her body. The blood rushed to her face as they brought their hands up between her legs and even inside her brassiere. As usual, her mixed French heritage, which added Western curves to her body, brought much interest. She wondered if they were this thorough with every Vietnamese girl who passed by.

At last, she was free to go. As she gave the gate guard her red pass, he gave her in turn a curfew pass that was good for two hours.

"The city is under complete curfew. No civilians are allowed on the streets. There is heavy fighting along Plantation Road and in the vicinity of the racetrack. You will not be allowed in that area. Go to your home and stay there. Follow citizens' instructions on the loudspeaker trucks and on Radio Saigon."

She emerged into the deserted street. It would be a long walk. Perhaps the police would give her a lift if they stopped to check her curfew pass. She heard firing to her right. A column of trucks and jeeps carrying American soldiers crossed in front of her. They looked dusty and hot. Most of them had discarded their field jackets and now wore only flak jackets above their fatigue trousers. Very few bothered to whistle or wave to her.

While she waited for the convoy to pass, a civilian police jeep pulled up behind her, but the noise of the trucks kept her from noticing it.

"What are you doing out here?" The voice startled her.

The two policemen smiled at her surprise and momentary confusion. Silently she presented her identity papers and her curfew pass. She was angry with herself and with the police. She hated being caught off guard.

"Get in. After the convoy passes, we'll try to take you to your home. It may be behind the blockade. If that's the case, you must report to one of the refugee camps."

For a moment, Thi was too surprised to answer.

Refugee camps!

She hadn't thought of that. She certainly didn't want to get into one of those. It would be like a prison.

The last of the convoy passed and the jeep sped through the deserted city.

If they won't let me in my area, I must have an alternate spot.

"My uncle lives in Nguyen Hue. If I can't get to my own apartment, could you take me there?"

"Yes, if he identifies you and agrees to accept you."

Thi thought about that as they were stopped at the first roadblock. The guard spoke briefly and inspected identity cards. As he signaled them through, he explained what streets to avoid, if possible. Only military vehicles were on the streets, and these were racing through town in all directions, paying no attention to traffic signs or lights. The jeep experienced several near-collisions as they neared Thi's apartment.

"I guess your area is still safe, and we can get you home. But remember, if it becomes necessary to block off your area, listen to and obey the loudspeaker trucks that will be on the streets."

Thi thanked the policemen and ran up to her apartment. She hoped that the water main had not been cut, then she could get a bath and some sleep before Ông Duat called for her. She had much to tell.

Ψ Ψ Ψ

Bill Scott was on the move.

He had finally received permission to leave his post in Osborne's office and, as Newell's personal representative, he started on his first refugee inspection trip. Armed with special passes and markings on his jeep, he and a Vietnamese driver headed for Cholon. It had been forty-eight hours since the offensive had started, and his fears for Mai Lei and her father were very real.

Bill had no way of knowing that Mai Lei and her father were at the time very much involved with a portion of the attacking force. In fact, they were captives of three enemy soldiers who moved into their house the first day of the attack.

They awoke at three o'clock that morning with the first sounds of gunfire. It was about nine o'clock when the front door was suddenly forced open. Three very tired, very dirty, but apparently very well-trained and intelligent members of the Viet Cong walked into the living room. Their leader, the oldest of the trio, had a flesh wound in his side. Although it was painful, the bullet had struck no vital organ and he knew he was not in any danger of losing his life. A medic would have called it an "in and out."

Quietly he spoke to the two younger men.

"It is easy to tell that these people are not peasants. Treat them with respect."

Then he turned to Bu, who was more surprised than outraged at this turn of events.

"You will have to excuse us, sir, for making use of your house in this manner. However, it is only a matter of time before the whole city will fall to our hands. Take care in how you treat us. It may make a difference in how we treat you when Saigon is ours."

"Please leave immediately or I shall have to call for the police."

"My dear old man, don't be tedious. Not only would such action be futile, but also I am afraid neither you nor your daughter will be allowed to leave the house or communicate with anyone while we are here. Be glad you are not dead already."

The two younger men were looking with clear, direct interest at Mai Lei, who was both frightened and disgusted. Her cheeks were burning with embarrassment, but she lacked courage to do anything but stand where she was and stare at her feet.

"Here then, you two. Check the rest of the house, and then take up positions in the back garden. I'll cover the door while I talk to the old man and the girl."

"If any of you touch my daughter, I shall personally kill you," Bu said, quietly.

"Why, I think you mean it, old man!"

"Do not give me cause ..."

"Now look here, we aren't here to rape your daughter—or even seduce her—right, fellows?"

The others laughed. After checking the kitchen, they headed upstairs.

"Why are you here?"

"Your place seems to be a good location to cover part of the alley from your walled garden. Then we need food and a little medical attention."

The two men came down and reported the house clear. Their leader immediately dispatched one to the garden and told the other to get some sleep in the dining room. He then removed his shirt and told Mai Lei to boil water and bring clean rags.

Mai Lei ran to complete these tasks. For some reason, she trusted the older soldier, and felt that by doing what he asked she would gain his approval and his protection.

Bu watched the VC leader with interest. He was not just a regular soldier. His mission must be broader than merely to fight and kill. He remembered an early morning newscast and decided that he knew the soldier's mission.

"Well, when are you going to give us the speech?"

"What do you mean?" The soldier was surprised at Bu's question.

"Well, you are not a fighter. You strike me as somewhat of a scholar— at least from the interest you have taken in my books."

"Shakespeare! And in English!"

"Have you read him?" asked Bu.

"Only a few plays. I see you have kept all the old French ..."

"Why not? Maurois and Moliere are better reading than Marx."

"Look, why don't you join our side? We have the strength. We are the only ones who can bring true freedom to all Vietnamese. You are enslaved by the money-grasping pawns of the Americans. What kind of freedom will that be? Better to be back under the French than what Thieu and Ky are offering."

Mai Lei came from the kitchen with the water and bandages. The soldier stopped talking and moved to the center of the room, where he lay down on the floor. After removing the bandage, he arranged himself so that the wound would be in a vertical position.

"Now, girl, take a small piece of bandage and wipe the blood away so that the wound is exposed."

Mai Lei obeyed him and a small round hole appeared.

"The M-16 makes a neat hole, in and out, unless it hits something solid. In this case, it went right through. Now pour water into the wound until it flushes out the other side. You see the bullet did not enter the stomach cavity. Continue to clean the wound even though I may faint. Then bandage it."

With trembling hands, Mai Lei poured a thin stream of the hot water into the wound. In spite of himself, the soldier's body contorted in pain. Suddenly, blood and water merged from the exit hole and Mai Lei, grateful that the cleaning was over, proceeded to bandage the wound.

Bu held the man in a sitting position while she wound the bandage about his waist. When it was finished, he drank some cool water. Then, reclining on a pillow and watching Mai Lei clean up the blood and water on the floor, he continued his conversation.

"At least the French put mostly Vietnamese in administrative posts ..."

Bu was not going to let this rather extraordinary man continue further in his argument.

"What kind of government would we end up with if we allowed you to govern us? A government that is so calloused, so insensitive, as to deliberately and cold-bloodedly plan this offensive at our sacred time of the year. In place of joy and happiness, you have brought sorrow, pain, and death. Did you really believe that we here in Saigon would welcome you murderers as our liberators? You must believe all of those lies you write about us, to think we would be that stupid."

Now Bu was warming to his subject. He recalled the many conversations with Bill Scott, and was happy that he remembered some of Bill's words.

"You are right about one thing, though. We don't have much of a government—yet! But no doubt, it has never occurred to you to look at our government a little more closely. What you missed is that we have the ability to change our government whenever we have an election. This was our first try, and for a first try, it could be worse. But wait until next time, and the time after that. We can change our government to suit ourselves, to be responsive to our problems, while you up there in the North are stuck with the same static, dusty, sterile, Communist lies."

From behind came a coarse shout.

"Enough of this American talk! I'm going to kill them now."

The young soldier, awakened by Bu's spirited argument, was standing in the living room doorway, an AK-47 at his hip.

"Put that gun down," said the wounded senior soldier evenly and without emotion. "Go back to sleep. One more interruption like that from you will be your last."

The soldier glowered at the older man for a moment, and then started for the dining room. But a cry from the garden, followed by small-arms fire, alerted them to action.

The young soldier ran to join his comrade in the garden, while their leader rose with difficulty and followed shouting, "Hold your fire! Don't give our position away!"

Taking advantage of this diversion, Bu whispered to Mai Lei to go upstairs and get the pistol that lay in the bottom of the clothes chest. This old French weapon had been in Bu's possession since the Japanese invasion. He had never used it and had almost forgotten its existence.

Mai Lei ran upstairs and reached down among the layers of clothing. She shivered as her fingers touched the hard steel. Quickly she brought out the old pistol and wrapped it in a silk scarf.

She could hear more rifle fire as she raced downstairs again and handed the covered weapon to her father. There were more shots and a sharp cry of agony from the garden. In a moment the two young men, cursing and gasping, half dragged the older soldier into the room.

"He's hit again. See if you can help him. This bastard draws fire like flowers draw bees."

They left him moaning on the floor and returned to the garden. Mai Lei and Bu went to the wounded man. There was blood oozing from his chest and he was gasping for breath.

They put wet compresses on his head and tried to bandage the new wounds, but they knew it was no use. In minutes, he would be dead.

Slowly he opened his eyes and looked at Bu and the girl. For a time he tried to speak. Finally, words came in a whisper.

"Be careful of them. They are not ... not able to listen. They are young, so very young. We have taught them war very well. Not much else. They are like the wild tigers of the highlands. They will try ... to kill you ..."

Bu sadly shook his head. This strange man was their only means of protection from the other two—and now he was dead.

Ψ   Ψ   Ψ

The Tet Offensive had pushed the small investigation of Cô Thi to the bottom of the inbox at ARVN intelligence.

Newell Osborne's verbal request for an investigation arrived at the intelligence center on the eve of the Tet Offensive and was quickly lost under the mass of immediate cases directly related to the huge NVA and VC attack. No one in Saigon cared about Thi's guilt or innocence.

No one except Colonel Mark Buckley and Corporal Kim.

Mark was not able to talk to anyone about Thi or her present activities, but he expected she would return to Saigon, her mission completed. Then she would wish to be in on the battle for the city. As he traveled about with the military police, he took every chance to stop by Thi's apartment to see if she had returned.

If he found her in residence, he had plans for her—plans that did not include an arrest and due process of law.

Kim was also watching for Thi. He had a new job during the emergency, that of dispatch driver, operating between the various defense positions and the Korean troops' billets. Now he was in a position to hear all sorts of information, both true and false. From someone he heard the story that Janet was dead from terrible wounds. That Thi was responsible was an easy conclusion for him.

No matter how real the danger, Kim repeatedly drove by either one or both of Thi's apartments during his rounds.

He also had plans for Thi—plans that included a very Korean retribution.

After the second day of the offensive, it was clear that Thi's Cholon apartment was in the path of the advancing VC troops. Early that evening, Kim decided to make one last pass by the place before it was cut off, to see if she had returned.

As he approached the street, he could hear rifle fire about six blocks away. He looked up at her flat. Although there were no lights in the rooms, the windows were now open.

So, someone is there!

Quickly he pulled his jeep into the same alley where he used to park the sedan when visiting her. He reached into his pocket. He grasped the keys he had for both of her places.

Kim bounded up the stairs and stood in front of the door. The building seemed deserted. Slowly he inserted the key in the lock and the door opened quietly.

He entered and, keeping to the rugs to muffle his steps, inspected the flat in the twilight gloom. He found Thi on the bed in a deep sleep of utter exhaustion. For a moment, he looked down on her naked body. She must have come right from her bath. He was disgusted with himself when he felt the old desire for her rise within him.

How could he think of having sex with her ever again after what she had done? She was a killer of the cruelest sort. She had tortured and killed a wonderful woman, a woman who was loved by the man he loved and respected more than anyone.

He knew what he must do and quickly set about doing it. In the living room closet, he found a long silk wrap. Kim tore it into four sturdy pieces. These he took into the bedroom and quietly secured one to each corner of the bed frame, being careful to make a large slipknot in the free end of each piece.

Next, he slipped Thi's hands into two of the loops and tightened the knots. She stirred and awakened slowly. But Kim worked fast and was able to get her feet into the loops of the other knots before Thi became fully aware of what was going on.

"Kim! Is it really you? What are you doing?"

Kim didn't answer. He returned to each of the bed corners and in spite of her pleas, tightened the ropes until Thi was completely spread-eagled on the bed and could move very little in any direction. He tried the lights, but the power was off.

On the dresser, he found a candle. He snapped open his PX Zippo lighter and lit it. In the dim, eerie light, he could see the girl was wide awake and fully aware of her predicament.

"Kim, Kim," she pleaded in terror. "Please let me loose."

Kim merely went to her and stuffed an extra shred of silk into her mouth. Now quiet, her eyes were wide with fright and shock. It was only then that Kim spoke.

His voice was menacing.

"You think you some smart chick. You think you kill Madame Holden, no one care. Kim care. You not get away with it, baby. You are number ten fink. I think you kill *boo koo* people Saigon. You must go. Kim give you what you deserve."

He reached down and pulled his long, dagger-shaped combat knife from his boot.

At the sight of the long, massive blade, Thi made a muffled cry of terror and tried to twist her body in an attempt to get loose.

She was beside herself. Frantically she was trying to turn the tide of Kim's feelings. He could tell she was trying to talk. He reached down and removed the gag from her mouth.

"Kim, Kim, you know I love you. Look—I know all about the underground in this city. I know who does what around here. You understand? I know the real leaders of the VC. Let me loose and I promise to tell everything to the authorities. You will be a hero, get a great reward. They will kill me, but I won't care because I will be doing it for you! Please, Kim ... please ..."

Her voice rose as she saw him advancing. There was a grim set to his jaw. He mounted the bed and kneeled between her outstretched thighs. He placed his left hand just above the pubic hair on her quivering lower belly to steady her trembling body.

The knife was poised in his right hand.

Then he froze. Suddenly he realized that he had forgotten to do something. He removed his hand and rose from the bed. A glimmer of hope crossed the girl's startled face. Perhaps she had won after all. She glanced at the large Korean. He was removing his clothes! She had won! Her body and his memory of the sex they had shared had clouded his thinking. She smiled.

Another weak man. I've got him. Later I will kill him. Fool.

Again, Kim approached the bed, but this time he was naked. He had removed his clothes because he realized there would be a mess. But now, in spite of himself, he was aroused to the point of a full and almost painful erection. Joyfully, Thi saw Kim's condition.

Ah. Now I have him. So weak ...

Thi barely managed to conceal her smile of personal triumph.

"Untie me, darling, untie me," she purred in her best husky voice.

Suddenly she was puzzled. When she looked into his face, the same grim expression was there. The huge knife was still in his right hand.

Kim again kneeled between her legs. There was a long pause. Then Kim placed the knife carefully beside her on the bed, and leaned over the waiting girl.

Allowing as little contact as possible between their bodies, he forced himself into her, driving forward with his hips, withdrawing almost completely, then driving forward again.

"Please, Kim. Please untie me. I could be so much better for you if you would let me go."

He said nothing. His eyes were closed. The same grim expression covered his face.

The pace of his thrusts increased. His hips drove faster and faster. Kim heard a moan escape her, but he could not tell if it was of pain or pleasure. He did not care. The idea of it being both at the same time pleased him. With a terrible thrust, he reached a climax. Not once did he touch her with his hands.

Now he was calm again.

He was finished.

Finished with her forever.

He withdrew from her. Only then, did he open his eyes. He glanced at her body. It was the last time anyone would see it that way. Only now, he became aware of the heavy thud of B-40 rockets and sporadic small-arms fire nearby. There wasn't much time. He would have to get going. Without changing his position, he grasped his knife and, as before, placed his left hand firmly on Thi's lower stomach. This time his fingers entwined in her now sweat-soaked pubic hair. He pressed down with force.

"My God, don't! Kim ..." She was screaming now.

"This last fuck you ever get, baby!"

Slowly he inserted the blade of the knife up into her, into the same place his stiff member had been moments before, cutting her, hurting her. When the huge, dark steel hilt guard rammed into her clitoris, he released his hand. Blood was dripping from her now; it was on his hands and on his knees. He watched her shuddering, twisting body as Thi, in delirious agony, tried to escape the excruciating pain. No longer coherent, she screamed hoarsely as she watched Kim with wild eyes.

Now, deliberately, Kim reached for the knife handle. He grasped it strongly and slowly pulled it from her.

He paused and looked down at the bloody seven-inch blade.

Not enough ...

Then, with one quick motion, he passed it to his other hand. He capped both hands about the end of the handle; then he slowly and deliberately forced the large, thick knife into the writhing belly of the screaming girl. An expression of disbelief and horror covered her face as she saw the entire huge combat knife enter her, up to the hilt.

Again, Kim pulled the knife from her body. Blood spurted from the large wound and started to cover her body. Some splattered Kim's body from chest to knees. Now from both wounds came blood, spreading across the bed.

With one final, terrifying, chilling animal scream, Thi threw her head backward and lapsed into unconsciousness.

As a final gesture, Kim drove the huge blade into the bloody mattress between her legs. The long "cat's tongue" hilt reached up above her bloody crotch acting as the marker of his vengeance.

Kim, his work done, left the bed and went immediately to the bathroom. Quickly he bathed and dressed. He heard the unconscious girl still breathing, heavily now, and wondered if she would regain consciousness before she bled to death. He hoped so. In case she did, he wanted her to see the knife sticking upright between her thighs. He left it in place.

She would have a better appreciation of what he had done.

Kim left the flat hastily, feeling there was little time to spare before the attacking aircraft would destroy the whole block. The telephone was ringing and, as he closed the door, he wondered for an instant who was calling. In his haste, he did not check the door. It was open a crack.

Ψ Ψ Ψ

Mark Buckley had finally left MP Headquarters.

It was 1900 hours and now too late to be prowling the Cholon area alone. Nevertheless, after studying the current situation map, he knew the VC were close to the street where Thi's flat was located. He wanted one more chance to find her. The ARVN and the US troops would be evacuating that area before morning.

He drove his jeep alone through the streets, dodging the permanent roadblocks by a circuitous route. The candle that Kim had left burning in Thi's bedroom spilled some of its light out of the window facing the dark street. Mark saw it and pulled the car into the alley. His heart raced as he dashed into the building and mounted the stairs. Then he stood before the door of the flat.

His plan was to knock loudly, break down the door if necessary, and enter with his .45 in hand. Then he spotted the door was ajar. Mark slowly pushed it open and entered, silently.

The living room was in semidarkness, illuminated only by the flickering light coming from the bedroom. Alert now, with his automatic at the ready, Mark quietly advanced toward the light. Cautiously he entered. He was prepared first to check all dark corners of the room.

The sight of Thi, spread-eagled and tied on the bed in a large, dark pool of blood changed that. For a moment, he froze and stared at Thi's body. Then he went forward and felt her wrist. There was a slight pulse. All of this was recent; the blood had not yet dried. He stared at the handle of the large combat knife that towered over her bloody vagina. There was a small circle forming the Korean-style yin and yang symbol crudely engraved on the blade, right next to the hilt. Mark recognized it as the same army combat knife Kim had proudly shown him several months before and had pointed out his own unique personalization.

My God. So Kim beat me to it. But what a horrible ... to think I'd planned nothing more than a .45 caliber hole on the side of her head. Well, she deserved it ... yes, even this way.

"Well, Janet, you've been avenged. I know you wouldn't want it this way ... or any way, but darling, you might as well know I would have done it if Kim hadn't."

Thi stirred slightly and opened her eyes.

"Mark? Mark, help me!" Her eyes were wide. "Mark?"

"Thi, can you hear me?"

"Yes."

"Why did you do that to Janet?"

Thi did not answer. She was in terrible pain. Suddenly Mark wanted desperately to have an answer to that question.

"Thi!" He yelled her name.

Outside he could hear loudspeaker trucks, announcing in Vietnamese and English that all non-combatants must leave the area and go five blocks south. This was the last warning. Gunships would attack the buildings in fifteen minutes.

"Thi! Can you hear me?"

She nodded. Mark was bitter and vindictive. He was glad to have these last minutes with Thi.

"Thi, Janet did not die. She told me what you did to her. Now you are dying yourself in a manner more horrible than you had planned for her. You're going to fry in hell, bitch, and from the way you've treated an unarmed, innocent woman, you deserve every painful damn moment of your agony."

Thi turned her head away from Mark. She had failed!

She couldn't believe it. There were tears in her eyes, tears of anger as well as pain.

"Mark?"

"What?"

"Is she really alive?"

"Right, Thi," he continued to lie. "You failed. She's still in critical condition, but she's alive and she'll recover."

Someplace in all her pain, the fury of her failure crept over Thi. She cursed herself for her stupidity in not following orders, for allowing her emotions to dictate the cutting of Janet's face when she should have used her pistol at close range.

Her whole body trembled violently. Mark grasped her wrist. The pulse was weak and very unsteady. She turned her head toward him and he looked down at her tear-stained face. Suddenly he was ashamed of what he had said about her deserving her agony, but he could not change his feelings.

"God may forgive you, Thi, but I never will. I'm glad you're getting yours this way."

She cursed him and, although her lips moved, there was no sound. The pulse was gone. The curse was still on her lips. As he rose, he noticed the faded, tiny, jagged scar below her left ear.

Moving carefully to avoid the blood, Mark reached down and removed the knife that stood like a sentinel, standing erect between her thighs, planted in the mattress, surrounded by a pool of blood. He wiped it clean on the bed sheet and took it with him as he left the apartment.

There was mortar fire to his left. The VC had not yet advanced to this street. He hopped into his jeep and raced toward the south. Looking at his watch, not ten minutes had passed since he entered the flat. Suddenly he realized that he was covered with sweat. He wiped a tear from his eye.

Now he could settle down and fight this war.

Ten minutes later, Thi's flat became her funeral pyre as a Huey gunship rolled in on her block and the blast of 2.75-inch rockets set the building aflame.

Ψ   Ψ   Ψ

General Trun Du had taken the capture of the An Quang Pagoda by ARVN troops very badly.

At first.

Without his supplies, Du could not continue. His first impulse was to try to regroup and withdraw his troops from Saigon. These orders were followed, and during the night, the allies thought they had actually stopped Du's southward thrust. Almost simultaneously, a large convoy of sampans arrived with supplies for Du's troops. This convoy came under fire from helicopter gunships that sank one-third of the boats. Forty boats got through, however; these were well hidden along the riverbank near Gia Dinh. All night long, a work force provided by Duat's black-market organization unloaded them by hand and stashed the cargo in various buildings under NLF control.

In the early hours of morning, enough of the necessary supplies were in the hands of his troops for Du to launch a two-battalion attack on the Thu Due District Police Station. This was a diversion to draw attention away from his main body while he re-deployed them for a new general offensive.

Du was happy with this turn of events. Now he had troops and supplies east and west of the city. His plan was to link his forces just south of the airport, cutting the city in half. The morale of his troops soared with the word of a quick renewal of the assault. Daylight, however, brought aircraft and gunships against his forces at the police station, and Du reluctantly terminated this attack at that spot, secure in the knowledge that his ruse had worked and that he had gained the initiative again, elsewhere.

He studied the map of the city carefully. If his troops on the west and east could push forward until they joined, Tan Son Nhut and Cholon would be his. Then the rest of the city south of his pincers would be starved into submission.

An aide drew his attention to the arrival of a messenger disguised as a Saigon fireman. Du took and opened an envelope. The message was from Duat:

> The girl you requested has not reported in from special assignment in Ban Me Thuot, although there is evidence that someone of her description did return to Saigon as scheduled. Yesterday the block in which she lived in Cholon received the full brunt of American bombs and rockets. Therefore, it was not possible to question her neighbors to find out if she returned to the city at all. I am therefore recommending ...

Du closed the note.

So the little girl with all the charm and dedication was among the missing. Too bad. I hope she died still believing, still dedicated.

Ψ Ψ Ψ

Brandy Masters was exhausted, and she leaned against the outside wall of the hospital.

When things slacked off between waves of casualties, she came out here for a quick cigarette. Today, for the first time, she let herself reflect on what had happened to her since that morning four days ago when she stepped out on the street in her old USO fatigues and started to walk toward Cholon.

It was ten minutes later when a Saigon police vehicle had stopped and picked her up. In Vietnamese, she said that she was a first aid assistant and wanted transportation to a hospital. Which hospital? Why, any Vietnamese hospital most needing her services, of course.

It took her some time to convince the two policemen that she truly wanted to go to a Vietnamese hospital, but finally they understood that Brandy meant what she was saying. They took her to a building lately struck by rockets and mortars. The last of the victims were loaded in ambulances. In moments, she was in the back of one of the vehicles speeding through the city. She worked with a young medical student applying tourniquets and bandages, and administering plasma.

This time she did not have time to worry about getting ill at the sight of blood. It was all around her and she was too busy to think about it.

At the hospital, the need was so great that no one stopped to ask her who she was or what her qualifications were. The first day she worked around the clock. She did everything she was told to do: mopped floors, carried a full-grown Vietnamese woman into surgery, assisted in an amputation. Someone had given her a white armband with a red cross.

She wore it proudly.

It became a pass into any room in the hospital, including the doctors' private lounge.

By the second day, her confidence in the use of the language improved, as did her faith in her long-dormant first-aid skills. Her old fear of sickness at the sight of blood vanished, long lost in the urgency of the situation. There just wasn't time to worry about it.

Now she was treated as a bona fide nurse, in spite of her many protestations. Doctor Luh asked her to assist him in surgery. This elegant man, who moved with a natural grace, a graduate of medical school in the States, spoke creditable English. She tried to tell him that she had not completed her nursing course and had no practical experience.

"That makes no difference here."

"I know you need all of the assistance you can get, but I just don't want to lie to you."

"Look, all of these girls have had much less training than you have."

"But they have had years of experience."

"So will you. You'll get it in the next three days!"

Brandy mashed out the stub of her cigarette.

"Time to go in," she said aloud. "Hope I don't screw up the works while I'm getting all this experience."

As she entered the hospital, she looked with concern at the confusion and chaos. It would be impossible to explain, but somehow, she was happy. In the midst of all the pain and suffering, she felt an odd contentment. Then she was in the main stream of the hospital routine. She could not be bothered with the problems of Brandy Masters. The problems of the many wounded were much more important to her now.

Ψ   Ψ   Ψ

Bu had finished thinking and now was waiting for his moment.

It had to be when one of the VC was in the garden on duty and the other was inside asleep or eating. There hadn't been a chance to open the pistol to see if it had bullets in it. However, even if the chance presented itself, Bu had forgotten how to open it. Then, after all these years, the bullets might not work anyway.

He would have to trust to luck—and to Buddha.

The first night of their capture after the death of the VC leader had been very bad. Bu and Mai Lei had curled up to sleep on a quilt on the living room floor. The two remaining soldiers were to take turns on guard—one as lookout in the garden while the other was resting inside.

The two captives huddled together on the floor, but sleep was not possible. Mai Lei was thankful for her father's protection, although she realized that in reality it was minimal. She felt that if it ever came to a showdown, Bu would be killed, no matter if he tried to use the pistol or not.

Bu also was clear about their desperate situation, and knew that whatever happened, his best chance of success would be when the initiative was with him. He only hoped the proper moment would present itself before one of their captors decided to act against them.

They lay huddled together on the quilt in the darkness, too terrified to talk. Bu unwrapped the pistol and placed it between them. Flashes of light from flares and explosions occasionally lit up the room.

The soldier on guard in the room with them suddenly left Bu's chair and came over to them. He knelt beside Mai Lei and put his hands on her back. The young girl screamed in surprise and terror and the soldier froze.

Bu, surprised and frightened, luckily forgot about the gun.

He sat up and yelled, "What are you doing here? Get away or you will pay dearly."

Before the man could further molest her, the soldier in the garden called for his comrade. He left the girl, grabbed his AK-47, and quickly went outside. For a moment Bu thought of the two of them, fleeing the house and trying to run to safety, but the sound of increased firing outside made him realize that the house was their only chance for survival.

The soldier did not return for some time. When he did, he did not bother them again.

Morning had come and Bu had been able to hide the pistol on his person while the soldiers washed and Mai Lei made breakfast. The day was much the same as the one before, but they could hear airplanes and helicopters overhead. They were bombing and strafing an area several blocks from their house.

"What are we to do?" Bu asked one of the guards. "Stay here until the Americans kill us with their bombs? Or will you let us leave?"

"You can leave anytime you want, old man, but the girl stays here with us." He grinned and then laughed, as he looked Mai Lei up and down.

Later in the afternoon while Mai Lei was preparing supper in the kitchen, the soldier in the house, instead of staying with Bu, decided to go into the kitchen with the girl. Bu, who had been pretending to doze, suddenly realized that the proper moment had come—but not for the soldier in the house. His quarry was to be the one in the garden.

Mai Lei would have to defend herself as best she could for several minutes. She would become the bait for one while Bu stalked the other.

The scholar soldier, before he had died, had called them wild tigers; well, what better way to kill a tiger?

Bu slipped across the room and cautiously peered into the garden. It had become a miniature battlefield. Most of the shrubs had been cut down by gunfire and the two soldiers had trampled the flowers. He saw the dead VC leader lying where the other two had dragged him. The soldier was crouching behind the wall, about to fire his AK-47. At that moment, from inside the house, Mai Lei screamed. Without thinking, he raised his pistol, steadied it with both hands, aimed at the soldier's back, and fired.

There was a crashing explosion. The gun kicked out of his hands while the man in his sights spun around and fell.

Bu noted the look of astonishment on the VC's face as he died.

Bu picked up the gun and dashed into the kitchen expecting to find Mai Lei fighting off the advances of the other soldier. Instead, he found her against the wall, staring at the soldier in shocked disbelief. There was blood on the front of her *ao dai*; a short chef's knife was in her hand. The soldier, standing on the other side of the table, was holding his right arm, trying to stop the blood that ran from a deep gash across the inside of his wrist. Without waiting, Bu advanced and fired point-blank at the soldier's head. The little room filled with a sound so loud and overpowering that Bu thought his eardrums had burst. The soldier fell to the floor without a murmur and Mai Lei, overcome with the struggle and its final climax, slowly sank to the floor. The knife clattered to the ground beside her.

Their personal little war was over.

While Bu dragged the dead soldier from his kitchen, Bill Scott was at the end of the street, stopped by a roadblock.

"I can't let you go down there, sir. I don't care what kind of passes you have!"

The sergeant was polite, but adamant.

"You see that garden wall? Well, there's VC holed up in there and they control this street."

"But that's the house I want to get to. My ... my girl lives there. What happened to the people on this street? Did they get out?"

"No, sir. You see, these VC are not part of the main force. We think they were part of some unit that was to get the locals to come over to their side. The main body is still about five hundred yards west of here; we think that most of the local people are still in their homes."

Bill had made up his mind to get to Mai Lei's house.

"What kind of fire have you been receiving from the garden?"

"Sounds like AK-47."

"There hasn't been any since I have been standing here. How long has it been since you've heard a shot?"

"Well, let's see—about ten or fifteen minutes."

"There's a chance they can be reached from the other side. Look, I'm going around the block to the front door of that house. How about some of your men covering me?"

"Okay, Major, I can give you two men."

Bill retreated from the roadblock with two men riding in the back of his jeep. He circled around to the east and came out on the street that passed Bu's front door. He could see the frightened faces of civilians peering at him from the windows of some of the houses as he drove up the street. About four doors down from Bu's house, Bill stopped the jeep and the three Americans proceeded on foot.

The two soldiers covered Bill as he went up to the front courtyard. He noted with mounting apprehension the broken front door. Overcome with fear for the safety of his loved ones, Bill dispensed with all caution and raced through the doorway.

When he burst into the living room, he startled Bu, who had removed the dead soldier and was sitting quietly reading in his favorite chair. He instinctively reached for the pistol that had served him so well that day. Then, recognizing Bill, he replaced the gun and picked up the book again.

"Ah, good afternoon, Bill, we are happy to see you."

Mai Lei, who still had not recovered, was lying on some pillows close to her father. Seeing Bill, she struggled to her feet and ran into his arms.

"Oh, Bill, Bill. I knew you would come! Everything will be all right now."

When the two US soldiers outside had not heard any shots or commotion, they followed cautiously into the house, their M-16s at the ready. They were not prepared to see an old man with a book in his lap and Bill with a beautiful girl in his arms. They were completely stunned.

Both men laughed. One wolf-whistled and said, "Gee, sir, if I had known this pretty girl was in here, I would have come in three days ago!"

More American troops arrived and all heard Bu's story. They removed the three dead VC. Then Bill transferred Mai Lei and Bu to the comparative safety of the Hangout. The jeep was piled high with Bu's books, with room for little else, but that was the condition that Bill was forced to agree to before the old professor would move. After a quick transfer of scholar, books, and one pretty girl, Bill returned to the war.

When he returned to the Hangout that night, he was not surprised to find Bu propped up in a large chair, reading the volume of Shakespeare that Bill had given him.

"Have you ever read *Titus Andronicus*, Bill?"

"Well, let's see ... that's a bloody one, isn't it? They never perform it any more. Too messy."

"Not as bloody as what is going on now, here in Saigon. I think it is very much like our present situation."

The plot was coming back to Bill. "Yes, yes, you are right in some respects. You know, Shakespeare had a habit of adapting ancient history to more modern times and conditions."

"When this war is all over, the drama department at the university should do *Titus Andronicus* as a modern-day Vietnamese play. Listen to these lines, but imagine Saigon instead of Rome:

> Rome is but a wilderness of tigers.
> Tigers must prey
> and Rome affords no prey but me and mine ..."

Ψ   Ψ   Ψ

General Du sat almost alone in his headquarters.

Only one officer attended the crackling radio located at the far corner of the large room. The fighting in Gia Dinh was not going well. Although the western offensive was still pushing northeast through Cholon, the eastern side of the pincers from Gia Dinh had not been so successful.

The commander's call that morning had been discouraging, and the new intelligence proved what he had suspected. Although his troops had initially ringed Saigon, the Americans had brought in elements of the First, Ninth, and Twenty-fifth Infantry Divisions, and in effect surrounded his ring. Now, most of his troops were cut off from their supply sources.

Moments ago, he had received word that the ARVN had initiated *Tran Hung Dao*, which was a "search and destroy" operation in Saigon. If five full battalions were involved in this inside operation, as he had reason to believe, and part of three American divisions were choking him from the outside, it would be impossible for him to survive.

He heard a messenger coming up the stairs, but did not rise from his desk. He took the message and read it. His troops had reached the racetrack. They were well dug in and protected with some anti-aircraft automatic weapons. These would be helpful against the helicopter gunships and fighters, but he wondered about the other force from Gia Dinh. The silence was not good.

Two surprises had occurred during this offensive. First, the refusal of the people to rise up and join his forces had been a blow to him. Second, the Vietnamese and Americans' use of heavy bombing attacks inside Saigon to stop his men was almost unbelievable.

The use of the gunships and dive-bombers showed unexpected determination on the part of the Americans. If only I had more AA equipment to use against their air power! That exercise against the 199th Infantry Brigade showed what was possible if properly equipped. The Americans lost many helicopters and planes at the hands of my anti-aircraft, and their air assault failed.

He went to the open side of the pagoda and looked across the cemetery toward the city. The F-100 fighters were bombing an area south of Tan Son Nhut. There were secondary explosions. Smoke and fire leapt up into the humid air to contribute to the dark pall over the city.

In the distance were the tall white buildings of the heart of the city. The canopy of smoke over them looked like some gigantic, dark, ominous umbrella.

Saigon. For the first time it seems out of reach to me. For the first time I feel a doubt within me, a doubt that seems to gnaw at my insides while it says, "You will never take it. The city will not be yours."

Directly below him, his security troops were well dug in and alert. Outside this small perimeter, several units were returning from patrol—but there seemed too many to be moving in daylight. He had given the commanders specific instructions only this morning. His eyes scanned the near distance.

There are troops moving on the pagoda from the east and south! They are not mine.

Suddenly there was rifle and mortar fire. The ARVN was mounting a full-scale attack against the pagoda. The noise on the stairs announced the excited return of his staff, looking for instructions. Fight or try to run for it? He smiled; there was no place to run.

They took up observation positions around the open sides of the building. The enemy was still out of small-arms range.

"Go down and occupy the prepared positions in the graveyard. You know the plan."

They looked at him to see if he would be going with them.

"I will stay up here and watch the defense."

Many of the officers came by and shook his hand as they left. Most of them realized that their situation was now impossible.

When the last officer had departed, he watched the well-disciplined, hard-fighting ARVN troops advance.

Another surprise. Why did they lie to me in Hanoi about this South Vietnamese Army?

A mortar round hit the roof and shrapnel slashed around the large room. Miraculously, he was not hit. He did not move away.

The firing outside intensified. Now almost all of his people were committed. In the distance, he saw a flight of three aircraft. They were banking toward him out of the west.

How long will it take? How long before eternity? I estimate eleven minutes.

Time enough for a last look at the city that will never be mine.

He was wrong. The first pass came seven minutes later.

General Du caught a rocket squarely. The pagoda was overrun by ARVN troops one hour later.

Ψ   Ψ   Ψ

Duat crumpled the message in his hand as he watched Cholon blaze and burn in the late twilight.

So Du is dead. I wonder if Hanoi will continue the offensive and send down another leader to replace him. Du had been aggressive, imaginative, and possessed sound leadership ability. With proper support, he might have captured Saigon, but the initiative is gone now.

Duat turned to the north and watched the strings of tracers loop down from the flight of gunships.

I wonder if the five hundred sampans now heading down the Saigon River will make it, and whether the VC effort is still organized enough to handle the cargo of rockets and mortar ammunition that's on those boats. The second wave is to start any day now, and my people are to have a large part in it. This foolish "second wave" of popular guerrillas in the city wouldn't be necessary if the initial attack had been a bigger effort.

Now the second wave can be nothing but a disorganized effort, uncoordinated and too far behind the first wave to be effective. If there is to be any success at all, the five hundred sampans are the key. The ammunition on the barges will allow us to mount the heavy artillery barrage and coordinate it with the people's revolt.

My people are spread out all over town, ready to work as guides and advisors to the VC infiltrators. Can the VC, disguised as civilians, actually convince the people that the destruction of homes and property is really being done by the Thieu government as a way of taking the land from the people? It seems most improbable to me, but peasants are so stupid, I guess there is a chance. I wonder which idiot in the North thought that would work.

Fools.

If only Thi were still available! How I need her for this second wave! However, I am sure she's dead now, one of the 564 victims officially declared dead.

Chapter XI

MARCH

Mark Buckley was clean, shined, and pressed for the first time in many days.

Newell Osborne rose from his desk to meet him. Mark was a decided contrast from the tired, mud- and sweat-stained soldier he had called back from the fighting two days before.

Mark unhooked his thumb from a button on the front of his starched fatigue jacket and extended his hand to Newell.

"How's the arm getting along, Mark? Any better today?" asked Newell as he shook hands.

"It's okay, sir, but it still gets tired when I use it a lot."

"Well, Mark, are you ready to come back to work for me again?"

"Well, sir, you see, I still have a job to do out there ..."

"Oh, come on, Mark," Newell interrupted. "You know the worst of the fighting is over. There are a lot of people around that can do the mop-up. Are you trying to tell me that you are *the* indispensable combat soldier?"

"It's not that, sir, I just feel ... well ... needed. At last I'm doing what I am paid for, at last I'm truly helping."

"Now look here, Mark, this city had 564 of its citizens killed and over 2,800 wounded; 17,886 homes have been destroyed, making 225,810 refugees. Nearly a quarter of a million people are wandering about this city, homeless and starving."

"But that's not my business."

"The hell it's not your business."

Newell was quickly becoming exasperated with Mark's narrow viewpoint. He started pacing the room in an attempt to keep his temper in check.

"That's the trouble with you military people. You think you can walk through the battleground, messing up everyone and everything, then get out and leave all the putting together to the civilians. You remind me of a little kid knocking the hell out of a room while some indulgent nanny follows behind making everything straight again."

"That's not true, sir. Nor is it fair. I think we did a great job straightening up in Japan and Europe after World War II."

Newell laughed. "Well, maybe I did overdo it. Nevertheless, I wanted to get it into your skull that your job now is the straightening up and not the tear down. Those quarter million refugees must be cared for, you know, or else we will have a quarter of a million recruits for the VC."

"Well, I guess you're right."

"I need you, Mark. You're so damned good with these people. They trust you. You can get more work out of them than all of the rest of my staff combined."

Newell smiled and crossed the room. He put his hand on Mark's good shoulder and looked him in the eye.

"Besides, it's time to help the helpless ones. More important now than running about the outskirts of the city and killing their cousins and brothers."

Mark turned away and lit a cigarette. He knew Newell was right because Newell was the boss. That should have been enough. Then he remembered Newell had tried that boss business twice before, and he had ignored him both times. He turned back and smiled at Newell.

"Okay, boss. Where do I start?"

Ψ   Ψ   Ψ

Brandy Masters expected to be in trouble when she returned to work at USAID.

This was not the case. She had been gone for thirty days, and during that time, she had contacted her office only once. It had been a very poor telephone connection, but she had managed to assure the few brave people there that she was alive, well, and working in Saigon, and would return when the emergency was over.

Poli De Salle, however, had not ventured from his flat once during the emergency, and was not even aware that Brandy had been absent.

The hospital staff had ideas about keeping Brandy. She had filled an important void in an often needed but much neglected American-Vietnamese working relationship.

This was a first in any Vietnamese hospital. Never had an American who could work side by side with the nurses and medical aides actually speak their language. Although Brandy was not a qualified nurse by official US standards, her work was outstanding. The Vietnamese authorities did not worry about as trifling a matter as a certificate of graduation.

They wanted Brandy and knew how to go about keeping her.

It was only a matter of politics. First, her work must be brought to the attention of Vietnamese and American people in high places. Then, after she was presented to these people and her efforts had been properly acknowledged, the high-ranking Vietnamese would ask the high-ranking American if the indispensable Cô Masters could not continue her most important work.

Favors are most difficult to turn down when asked under such effective circumstances, and at so high a level.

This was a perfect strategy from the Vietnamese point of view.

So, in due course, Brandy Masters was awarded the National Order of Vietnam (Citizen's Class) at an impressive ceremony attended by General Phong, Chief of Staff of the ARVN, Newell Osborne, Hiram Green, Special Assistant for USAID, Poli De Salle, and many other Vietnamese and Americans of various ranks and stations.

The effect of Brandy's award upon the American community in Saigon varied, according to the people involved and their knowledge of her background.

Newell Osborne had forgotten about the girl after she had been placed in USAID. He was both surprised and pleased. On the other hand, Poli De Salle, who was looking for glory for himself, was jealous of a stupid girl who somehow managed to pull off a coup worthy of a Diem or a Minh.

Remembering the phone call, Poli cattily observed, "She seems to have been working during the offensive all right. Wonder what man she was working under?"

Mark Buckley remembered the night of the art exhibit, when he had tried to apologize for his stupid and unkind remark to Brandy. "I should have known then that there might be another side to this girl. She seems to have found a real job to do here," he said to himself.

He resolved to call on Brandy, apologize for his past rudeness, and congratulate her on the fine job she had done at the Vietnamese hospital. Two days passed before Mark had a chance to call her at her office and asked if he could drop by and talk to her. Brandy, remembering her performance at Trong Thoi, had always felt guilty about its impact on Mark's career. Perhaps now she could find the courage finally to apologize.

"Why don't you drop by my place for a drink tonight?" she heard herself saying.

Oh, damn.

Quickly she added, "Please, Mark. Believe me, I won't be ... I didn't mean ..."

Embarrassed, Mark broke in, "Brandy, forget it. That was a long time ago ..."

Brandy slowly placed her phone in its cradle and wondered what she would wear and how she would act with Mark. When she realized she had started sorting out in her head which of her silk underwear to wear, she stopped herself.

Goddammit, will the old itch return when I hear his voice, or will I just get over it?

That evening, when Mark walked into Brandy's apartment, she greeted him warmly and offered him a chair. She was surprised at her own calmness.

"Martini?"

"Let me make them."

"Okay. Over there."

She stayed and watched, recalling another drink she had had with him almost a year ago.

"Mark, I heard about Mrs. Holden, and I want you to know how sorry I am."

"Thanks, Brandy. I appreciate your thought."

There was silence, except for the tinkle of the ice cubes.

Mark suddenly noticed a rogue element in Brandy's attire. As she walked about, her breasts moved waywardly inside her cotton blouse, making a lie to the crisp nature of her outfit with their beckoning murmur.

Holy shit. She's not wearing a ... they're really full ... Get a grip. I've got to keep eye contact and talking to her.

"Let's talk about Brandy Masters."

His tone was bright and cheerful.

"What's this I hear she's been doing during the Tet Offensive?"

"Mark, they're making a big deal over nothing. I just heard their need for volunteers and showed up."

"Just like that?"

He handed her a glass. Keeping eye contact.

"Well, no. You see, I had two years of nursing school–ages ago."

She turned toward the couch and sat at the far end.

"And–well, to be frank, I found I got sick at the sight of blood, so I quit. Actually, my Uncle Joe didn't want me to be a nurse at all and said he needed me in his campaign. It gave me an easy out. I never admitted to anyone but myself that the real reason for quitting was, well, I got a bit squeamish at times, and then there was this married doctor on staff getting a divorce and, well, things got complicated for me there."

Mark had a sudden vision in his head of a young Brandy in a Candy Stripers nurse assistant outfit, skirt above her waist, bent over an examination table. He forced himself to skip right over that image.

"But this time, do you feel sick at times?"

Brandy laughed. "No. That's the strange thing. I just don't have time to get sick. Now I'm thrilled. I'm even thinking of returning to the States and finishing my training."

"Great! Here's cheers to your success."

"Thanks," she said.

They sat in silence for a moment, sipping their martinis.

"You make a good one," she observed, indicating her drink.

"I have several civilized traits. Housebroken, too. Mostly."

Brandy smiled. How different this all was from Trong Thoi!

"I want to apologize for that gross remark I made at Ned Green's art show."

"My God, Mark, that seems like centuries ago. I can't even remember what you said."

"Well, it wasn't very nice, whatever I said, but frankly I've forgotten what I said, too."

They both laughed. Two drinks later, Mark rose to leave.

"I haven't enjoyed myself so much since before Tet."

"I haven't either. How about staying for some supper? I don't know what Ooogg is offering this evening, but ..."

Mark was convinced it was time to leave. The room had somehow become a little too warm and way too small.

"Please give me a rain check. I have a command performance this evening. I'll give you a call."

I sure want to stay, but I don't want to get involved with anyone right now. It's too soon—after Janet ... This gal has found herself. Speaking about her work with such pride and self-assurance. But by God, she's attractive!

Brandy was secretly glad that Mark had not stayed. She thought about her own feelings as she shut the door.

The alcohol told me what I was afraid to tell myself. I'm still crazy about him. The old ache is there. In minutes, it would have goaded me on to making a damned fool of myself again over the guy. He's lost two women he really loved—the last one such a short time ago. He's not ready for me—or any other woman yet.

In the meantime, I've got the hospital to keep my nasty little mind and body busy. It just shows how an available man can wreck my whole routine. I know that they'll be sending a jeep to pick me up in about twenty minutes, but if Mark had stayed, it would have been to hell with the hospital—just like that.

Easy, Brandy, you can't afford to get involved again. There's no place in your schedule for anything or anyone—not even Mark.

My God, what am I saying? Are those really my thoughts?

Not allowing herself further contemplation, she carried the glasses to the kitchen.

"Ooogg, please put dinner on quickly while I change," she said in Vietnamese.

"What happen to number one colonel? He look pretty okay," asked Ooogg in her pidgin English.

"Oh, so you noticed. You like him?"

"You know it, baby. So do you. He hot stuff."

In her bedroom, Brandy smiled as she changed. She looked down at the black lacy panties she had finally selected, having decided to skip the matching bra. She would need to add that item back in for the hospital staff's little celebration party coming up.

Part of me had a plan.

She laughed out loud.

Yep, my best parts. And he sure noticed!

Ψ   Ψ   Ψ

Mark stopped at Kam's apartment for the express purpose of seeing Kim.

He was welcomed with joy by both of them, and Kim insisted upon his staying for a can of beer.

Kam, following the traditional custom, left the men to themselves. While they were drinking, Mark told Kim about the fighting on the outskirts of the city, and both men had soldier's stories of action they had experienced during the Tet offensive.

Finally, Kim, who could not avoid the subject any longer, said, "Colonel Mark, I hear oh-so-sad news about Madame Holden. I am very sorry for you, Colonel Mark. Madame Holden was best person of the world ..."

"Yes, Kim. She was very special. She will be missed by many people, myself most of all, I guess. I just want you to know I ... well, I appreciate what you did."

"I do nothing." Kim looked into Mark's eyes and saw there that somehow Mark knew. He looked at the floor. Neither spoke for some time. Mark rose from his chair. It was time to go. As they walked to the door, Mark pulled a package from his fatigue pocket.

"Say, I saw this for sale on the black market along Le-Loi and recognized it as yours. You must have lost it somewhere during the fighting. I knew you would miss it, so I bought it and brought it back for you."

He handed Kim the package.

Before he opened it, Kim knew that the package contained his knife, but how did Mark get it? He could only guess.

Mark paused at the door. "Thanks again, Kim. You did a very difficult job for me. If you hadn't, I would have had to do it myself."

"I do nothing."

"That's right. You did nothing. But many thanks—for nothing."

There is a silent look that passes between soldiers, or close comrades, that means a promise has been kept or a debt paid. Sometimes it's both those things and perhaps something more. It is forever unspoken. But the connection is made and can never be broken. This is what happened between Mark Buckley and Kim, all in the space of a heartbeat.

Kim laughed. Both men smiled and shook hands, and then Mark was gone.

Ψ   Ψ   Ψ

Poli De Salle was impressed with Brandy's award ceremony.

Throughout the proceedings, he was thinking that he should be standing there accepting an award instead of Brandy. He felt sure that once his pacification plan was approved and adopted, both governments would decorate him. He closed his eyes and drunk deep of his moment yet to come.

Later, during a brief social hour that followed, Poli finally understood the full extent of Brandy's achievement. He was standing near Newell Osborne and General Phong and could easily hear their conversation.

"But, Mr. Ambassador, our doctors at the hospital tell me that Cô Masters is much more than a nurse. She taught the new girls how to handle patients, how to use American equipment, but above all, she organized the staff to handle peak periods after each wave of the enemy attack. She brought order."

"General, Miss Masters is an exceptional girl. I am happy that she was such a help during the offensive. I understand why you want her to remain at the hospital. But don't you agree that not just one hospital should benefit from her experience, but all your hospitals? That is why I feel it would be a shame to keep her there. My plan is to put her in a position where she can train many Vietnamese girls."

"You mean she would start a nurses' school?"

"No. Well, not a school as we usually think of one. You see, she is not a fully qualified nurse."

"She is a good nurse."

"Yes, but we would get in trouble back in the US if they heard she were teaching. My idea is to give her a staff of six or seven Vietnamese nurses to go with her and learn on-the-job training as she visits the hospitals. When these girls are qualified, they would join hospitals and new girls would join her staff."

Poli listened to Newell's plan and realized that Brandy had "arrived." She was truly a success in the eyes of the US officials as well as the Vietnamese. He kept listening.

"In times of emergency she would have a duty station back at the hospital, but at other times she would be on my staff, working at the refugee clinics."

Poli sighed and gulped his drink.

And here I thought all this time that she was just a lousy secretary who had a great ass and knew how to use it.

Damn.

Ψ   Ψ   Ψ

Bu and Mai Lei had moved back into their house before February was over.

This was in spite of the second wave of the offensive. During the first week in March, they spent most of their time cleaning up the little garden and setting the house to right.

As they worked, Bu realized that he had long ago made up his mind about Mai Lei and Bill Scott. He knew that in a sense he had already given his consent to the marriage. The two young people now no longer observed his rule of not seeing each other socially. The Tet Offensive had put an end to that.

One day, as he and Mai Lei were painting the living room walls, he declared, "I think we should look for a housekeeper to move in with us. There are many worthy women among the refugees."

"But Father, the work here is very simple. I have plenty of time to cook our meals, and the cleaning is easily done on the weekends."

"But, my daughter, you won't always be here. Someone will have to take over when you go to America."

"Oh Father, you have decided! Then, then it's all settled?"

"Yes, Mai Lei, it is settled. You will be my little American."

A tiny cry of joy stole from her lips as Mai Lei rushed to her father to kneel before him and receive his blessing.

Ψ Ψ Ψ

As March progressed, the second wave of the enemy offensive ground to an unsuccessful close.

MACV credited the VC failure in Saigon to *Quyet Thong* (Resolved to Win): the allied combined air and ground offensive around the city of Saigon.

There were two main objectives to *Quyet Thong*. The first was to gain the initiative from the VC and NLF forces; the second was to widen the security ring about the city. This meant that the main urban areas would be out of range of the 122 mm rockets. Meanwhile, Saigon would remain a beleaguered allied enclave until the mop-up operations outside the city were completed.

Duat sat at his desk and looked at the brief summary of the results of the Tet Offensive. It was clear to him that it almost succeeded. He had toured the devastation of Cholon and the waterfront, and realized for the first time how close the city came to being divided in half by the thrust of General Du's forces.

He decided that his final report to Hanoi should be enthusiastic in nature and optimistic on the aspects of a future effort, provided Hanoi next time would mount a more extensive attack. He wondered if Hanoi was able to try again. His people had given him a full report on the effects of air strikes on the North's logistic effort.

The damage had been incredible.

Duat pondered the situation as it now existed. He left his desk and walked about the quiet pool in the garden. His reports detailed that the North had lost between five and six thousand people in the offensive so far. Most of the supplies were gone: consumed, damaged, or captured.

This review of the total situation, in spite of the good showing the Northern troops had made, pointed to an obvious conclusion. The North, for all practical purposes, was completely beaten and no longer capable of fighting in the South in units larger than five or six men. Therefore, a new offensive seemed impossible without the importation of a completely new army from Hanoi. Such an operation would be almost impossible with the present American air force bombing operations in the North. He doubted that Hanoi could transport soldiers and supplies in meaningful numbers to the South under the present conditions.

Duat looked at the quiet pool. A new lotus bud was opening. Its dark red petals were beginning to show their promise of beauty. But beside the blossom, on a leaf of the plant, lay the remains of a beautiful dragonfly, its pale green body bent and its gossamer wings crumpled. Suddenly Duat remembered Thi, his own beautiful Chuan. A dark thought crossed his mind, and he wondered if this whole effort would someday end like Chuan. He clapped his hands to summon a servant. At Duat's command, the man removed the dead insect and dropped it over the edge of the roof. Duat watched its light body spiral slowly down into the twilight traffic below.

Ψ Ψ Ψ

Poli De Salle stood before the small group of American officials and fielded their questions.

A more alert person would have sensed the air of hostility in the room, but as Poli was so obsessed with his own new scheme for pacification that it didn't register, he smiled on at brooding faces.

"I trust that this briefing has been adequate to demonstrate the basic concept of my plan. The complete report, which you have before you, will give you the full details. I will accept any questions that you might have at this time."

There was an awkward silence. While each person in the audience fingered the thick report before him, Mark Buckley was the first to speak.

"In all fairness to you, Dr. De Salle, I must say I have not read your report completely, but from your briefing I cannot help but feel that your new plan for pacification is really nothing but a scheme to use geography to conceal the truth, and falsely represent the true facts about our total pacification effort."

"Sometimes it is necessary to give false information to the enemy," replied De Salle. "Think how he will feel when he sees our ... ah ... revised reports. He would be convinced that he has lost."

Bill Scott could not believe that anyone advertised to be as intelligent as Dr. De Salle could seriously present such a dishonest scheme.

He followed Mark's lead.

"In order to make the enemy believe these figures, they must be presented as the official position of both the US and South Vietnamese governments. Yet we would know they would be false figures. Are you implying that our governments should pass this nonsense off as the truth?"

"They wouldn't be actually false. It's all in the way you slice the salami. I'm saying that by gathering the more favorable geographic areas together, our figures will result in far more 'plus' areas and far fewer 'minus' areas."

Poli pointed to the map.

420

"Notice this very definitely VC-controlled spot. Now notice these definitely pacified areas. By combining them geographically, the pacified areas swallow the enemy area."

"But it's still VC ..."

"But it won't stay VC. They'll move out when they see they have been weakened by the strongly pacified areas around them."

Mark could no longer control his feelings.

"How many people do you think will die because they may come to believe this crap you are putting out?"

Newell Osborne was angry.

"That's enough, Mark. I'll take over now."

He couldn't stand De Salle anyway, but had consented to listen to the briefing because he remembered De Salle as Janet's friend. Now he wanted to put an end to this cheap attempt to make the war situation look good by a juggling of boundaries.

Newell continued, "I cannot believe that one of our supposedly top social scientists would present such a flagrantly dishonest scheme. You say it will benefit our side by making the enemy think we are better off than we are. Who do you think the enemy is—a bunch of illiterate idiots?"

Poli De Salle was ready to play his trump card now.

"Ambassador Osborne, this offensive has hurt us. Hurt us badly. However, mostly, gentlemen, it has hurt you. There are many areas, as a result of this offensive, that are far less pacified than before. This is a reflection upon all of you personally. When the facts, as presented by your present counting methods, are fully understood back in Washington, I suspect that some of you will be in a bad way, politically. Now, what better time could there be, gentlemen, to change the signals, the counting system. You will all come out far better off."

Newell's eyes were suddenly frosty cold.

Slowly he said, "I will stand on my reputation for integrity. So will these gentlemen. We don't need any sort of cheap, lying gimmick ..."

"This offensive has hurt you ... hurt you more than you want to admit ..."

"Not hurt me, Dr. De Salle, hurt us. We are all on the same team, or have you forgotten? Furthermore, this offensive may hurt us for the present, but we are recovering fast. The enemy, however, can't recover—he has broken his back on this offensive. He cannot gather enough VC in South Vietnam to mount another effective operation. Do you know what this means? It means that we have the VC beaten. It means that in spite of the restrictions we have placed upon our armed forces, we are finally in a position to have a significant victory. By continuous bombing of supply routes in the north, we can control their reinforcements of North Vietnamese men and equipment. At last there is a chance to win this war."

"You seem always to make a distinction between the VC and the North Vietnamese. That is a mistake," said De Salle.

"Don't get me wrong. I realize that there is only one enemy, but I also know that the VC, being South Vietnamese, have a better chance for survival here. The North Vietnamese soldiers won't find it so friendly. In any event, we aren't interested in your plan, Dr. De Salle. What's more, I think it is dangerous—especially if made available to the South Vietnamese government. Please see to it that all copies are restricted, so that they cannot fall into the hands of the uninitiated."

Newell Osborne rose and left the room. The other members followed, leaving Poli alone with his charts and copies of his plan. In spite of this official rebuff, Poli couldn't help smiling. He had neglected to tell Ambassador Osborne that he had already delivered ten copies of the report to several high-ranking Vietnamese government officials.

Ψ Ψ Ψ

The beer was cold and the evening was pleasant.

Kim sat on the terrace of the flat with Dave and Red. The two Americans had stopped by to see if they could talk Kim into joining them for an evening at "The 92."

"Ba Thoa always asks, 'Where is my boyfriend, Kim?'"

Kam smiled. She had left the men on the terrace and was sewing a new American-style dress. Of course, she was listening to the men's conversation. Kam knew that Kim would decline the invitation. Ever since their marriage, he had seldom left her in the evening. She also knew that Colonel Uhm was still Ba Thoa's boyfriend, and Kim wasn't in danger of falling into her clutches.

"Kim stay here with Kam tonight. Maybe sometime later he go with Red and Dave."

"What you going to do around here?" asked Dave. He had noticed Kam listening in the doorway and was teasing her.

"Kim work on plan with Kam. Big plan. Make lotsa dough."

"You got lotsa dough. What you need more for?"

"Well, you know bombing stop today. LBJ say, 'Thasall, flyboy, stoppit.'"

"Yeah, he sure did."

"Well, we think this bad, but before today Kam and I think maybe war over soon. VC all killed. Then lotsa building start in South Vietnam. Much more US money come in. We want be ready, get some."

"What you gonna do, buy the docks and take half the cargo?"

"That's a good idea, but can't do it. We take all our money and buy good fleet of dump trucks. We train drivers, then we rent out to builders. My driver, my truck. Need civilian trucks here. Like Korea in 1956. Then when we get lotsa truck, we get cement mixer, bulldozer, cranes, flatbed. Pretty good idea, you think?"

"Say, you're talking like an American businessman."

Kim smiled, pleased. He swigged on the can of beer.

"But you're a South Korean. How are you going to stay here?"

"No problem. I finish my year, then I become civilian. I come back here as civilian technician, equipment operator. I moonlight with own company. We register company in Kam's name, but I really the boss."

"Okay, but with this bombing halt, this war may not end soon."

"That's okay. We look around. Lotsa construction being done even now. Might as well start getting trucks right now. Get in on the gravy."

"Well, I'll be damned." Red turned to Dave.

"This guy's a real Yankee businessman." They looked at Kim with awe.

Suddenly Dave jumped to his feet and held his beer can high.

"Here's to the smartest gook in the Far East!"

"Wait a minute. Kam, where are you? Come here," Red called.

Red jumped to his feet. He called again before Kam entered, wide-eyed.

"Here she is. Here's to Madame President Kam. Madame President of the ... the ... Ajax Heavy Equipment Company!"

"Say, that's a classy name," said Kim. "We use that one, eh Kam?"

Chapter XII

APRIL

March ended, and so ended the "Resolved to Win" campaign around the city of Saigon.

It had been a great success. The allies swept Gia Dinh, Long An, Bien Hoa, Binh Long, and Hau Nghia Provinces. They wrested the initiative from the enemy, and over three thousand enemy had been killed or captured. In addition, great caches of equipment and weapons had been destroyed.

Now the combined forces of American and ARVN troops again were hurled at the enemy, already staggering from the blows of this campaign. The new operation was dubbed *Toan Thang* or "Complete Victory" and, despite the bombing pause, the allied forces were resolved to make this campaign just that.

The allied forces in Saigon and all across South Vietnam included the American First, Twenty-fifth, and Ninth Divisions, the 196th Light Infantry Brigade, the Eleventh Armored Cavalry Regiment, the Third Brigade of the 101st Airborne Division, the 199th Light Infantry Brigade; the ARVN's Fifth and Twenty-fifth Divisions, Fifth Ranger Group, and the Australian First Task Force. These were organized into coordinated sweep, search, and destroy units with air support available for all operations.

Hanoi, enjoying the bombing pause, and hearing the loud, savage outcries of the American press against the war, decided to gamble on one more offensive. They wrote off their few remaining troops in the south, the remnants of the Tet Offensive, and started mounting a completely new army. They used the numerical designations of old units in order to make the allied intelligence believe these units were still in fighting shape. The unexpected bombing halt made their task much easier and allowed them to start their offensive months earlier ...

Ψ   Ψ   Ψ

Dr. Poli De Salle looked at the face of the Vietnamese officer and realized that he had a live one.

Disciple Number One ...

Now it was up to the young man to convince the other members of the Vietnamese General Staff. The young man was the interpreter and his attitude, be it enthusiastic or dull, would go a long way in swaying the others, one way or the other.

"Now take for an example the Le Thanh district of Pleiku Province."

De Salle pointed to a large map.

"These areas are definitely VC-controlled at the present. Now let's put a hypothetical boundary around the parts that are under South Vietnamese control. By closing this line, we also encompass several VC-controlled villages. Nevertheless, considering the total area inside the line, they are but a small part and thus are insignificant. Considering the percentage pacified, those VC villages only lower the figure to thirty-five percent pacified, which is well above the percentage considered safe."

The young officer's eyes were still wide with wonder. He was thrilled that an eminent American political scientist was giving them a method for liberating most of their country from the VC with the stroke of a pen. Hurriedly he translated De Salle's words. There was a short silence.

"Who will we fool with this system?" an old general asked.

"By using this method, the VC will be confounded into believing that we are in control of much more of the land. They should fill the ranks of the Chieu-Hoi and come over in great numbers."

After several more questions, the officers rose.

The old general came forward.

"Thank you, Dr. De Salle. We are very impressed. We have studied your report thoroughly. Now we are ready to put it into effect. We will need your help, of course. You will be hearing from us soon."

Poli De Salle left the Joint General Staff Headquarters with a light heart and a light step. At last. At last, he was finding his place. He was gaining recognition. His plan would be a success in spite of the Americans.

The ARVN General Staff can handle that fool Osborne and his friends.

Ψ   Ψ   Ψ

Duat was very pleased with the Americans' blunder.

Duat looked at the new plan he had received from the North. Updated after the last day of March, when President Johnson had announced the bombing cessation, it reflected the factors and options now open to them as a result of the American halt. Now, the North could form large truck convoys without danger and move them south using the roads in Laos and Cambodia feeding the Trail. They could empty Hai Phong harbor of the many tons of waiting supplies. The bombed railroads into China could be repaired.

"How accommodating the Americans are," he said aloud.

"Did you say something, sir?" Ahn was with Duat and had heard his remark.

"I was thinking that it is kind of the Americans to halt the bombing at the right moment so that we may build up again."

"We must have people of influence secretly located in their government."

"No, Ahn, they do these things without our help."

Ahn, sensing that his master wanted to expand his thesis, took the liberty of asking a question: "But why, Ông Duat?"

"The silly things are like small puppy dogs. They want to be loved. They are the only people in the world who will sacrifice the lives of their own troops in order to save those of their enemy."

"That seems to be a stupid thing to do. I do not understand."

"That is why you do not understand. It is too stupid for us to comprehend."

Duat turned again to the plan of operation.

"Most of the men and supplies will reach the Saigon area by boat from Cambodia this time. This supply route has now been fully exploited. During Tet it was only partially used."

"Will it make our job easier, Ông Duat?"

"This will be purely a military operation. We are only required to create unrest by spreading rumors among the people. Of course we should be alert to assist or protect elements of the attacking force if called upon."

Ahn was disappointed in their cadre's low level of involvement. He wondered if Hanoi had lost faith in Duat's ability to assist their effort. The Tet Offensive was a case in point.

At that time Ahn heard talk that Duat had risked his people just short of compromise and, as things worked out, the Tet failure had not hurt the organization. Now he wondered how Duat looked from Hanoi's point of view.

Timid? Cautious? Unreliable? Who can say?

Duat concluded his thoughts.

"They say General Tra has already come down from Hanoi and is at the VC headquarters in the Iron Triangle. Our regiments are already there being reactivated, and replacements from the North are being trained to fill the vacancies. Tra will be in charge of the offensive. I wish him better luck than General Du found."

Ψ   Ψ   Ψ

Bu was pleased.

Bill and Mai Lei set the day of their wedding for May 6th. Bu was particularly pleased with the manner of Mai Lei's engagement announcement. Bill had suggested that Bu make the initial announcement in Vietnamese style, and Bu arranged a small dinner party at his house. As was custom, only the immediate family was present. Newell Osborne and Mark Buckley represented Bill's family and were the only Americans. The other guests were Bu's distant relatives who had catered his Christmas party.

The dinner was simple, staying to Vietnamese standards, with a clear soup, Chả giò, fowl, and rice. The traditional fruit and cake came to the table wrapped in red paper packages. These were opened and then passed among the guests.

Bu had found through his relatives a bottle of real French champagne. Bollinger NV Brut, no less. After dessert, he poured the wine and, eyes brimming with happiness, proposed a toast to the bride and groom. It was a lovely party.

Bill's later party at the Hangout was more typically American, and Bu was at first upset at the gaiety of the guests. Bill and Mark both explained to him that in the United States this was a joyous occasion, where guests expressed their happiness by singing, laughing, dancing, and loud talk.

As the party progressed, and after Bu had consumed a glass of American "champagne," Great Western NV, he entered into the spirit of the affair and volunteered to sing a slightly risqué song that he suddenly remembered from his student days in Paris. It was a great success. So was Bu.

After this, the guests would not let Bu alone. He became their favorite and, although he had only one more glass of wine, he was included in every joke told and every song sung.

"You might think it was his own engagement party," said Bill as he stood with Mai Lei.

"I'm afraid he will get too tired. He isn't used to so much excitement."

"Let's ask him to tell about shooting the VC one more time, and then I will take him home."

It was later when Bill was driving Bu and Mai Lei home through the dark streets of Saigon that Bu said, "I like American parties. If I visit in America, will we have a party?"

"You bet we will, Dad. A big one, just for you."

"What is 'Dad'?"

"Oh, that is what men call their fathers in America. It means 'Father.'"

Bu turned to Bill. He was smiling. "I like 'Dad.' It sounds good. What should I call you? 'Son'?"

"Son will be just fine, Dad," said Bill as he patted the old man's knee.

Suddenly Bu felt that this marriage, in spite of his early misgivings, would be all right after all. It was obvious to him that even though he had been reluctant to include Bill in his Vietnamese family, Bill had readily included Bu in his American family. It gave him a warm, happy feeling he had never known before. One which he eagerly accepted.

Ψ   Ψ   Ψ

Mark snuck a look at Brandy and was amazed.

The two walked down the street of a huge refugee camp. It was one of the largest in Gia Dinh, several thousand people crammed into its confines. All the buildings were of simple wood-frame construction with canvas roofs. A city within a city, the whole complex teemed with the problems of any overcrowded urban area.

Brandy dodged a puddle of rainwater and tried to keep out of the muddy edges of a huge pool of water. Despite the hundreds of truck loads of gravel dumped in the streets, the eternal mud of Vietnam managed to fight back to the top every time it rained. Many thought there must be a message there somehow.

Mark watched Brandy and waited until she finished speaking to a small boy in Vietnamese.

"Tired?"

"When are we not tired?"

"Well, it's that moonlighting you do. All this every day, and the hospital every night."

"I know, but I'm happy." She smiled up at Mark.

"Besides, the work at the hospital is slacking off. I was there only three nights last week."

"You should have told me. We could have gotten up a game of pinochle or something."

"Neat. Really a groove."

They both laughed. Brandy was pleased with the relationship she had carefully developed with Mark. For the first time in her sexually active life, she did not rush into a situation with no holds barred. She had carefully studied Mark's emotional situation and realized that with Janet gone such a short time, he wouldn't be ready for any sort of a romantic affair. Besides that, she herself was trying to hold her own feelings back.

She knew she desired Mark physically. She had from the first time she saw him. But, she hoped that her hellish schedule would keep her occupied. To date, she had not had the time to indulge in her usual sexual fantasies and her powerful need to have every man desire her and prove it.

That's when the trouble starts ...

She hoped the situation would remain that way.

How long?

Their relationship developed on a purely professional basis, and at present was at the mutual admiration stage. It was obvious that Mark was an exceptionally well-qualified officer and liaison with the Vietnamese. He quickly got their confidence and trust. When they saw he was capable of moving mountains for them, they were always ready to grab a shovel and help.

To Mark, Brandy was a wonder. The square peg had at last found the square hole. The fit was perfect. He had never seen an American woman work with the Vietnamese with such finesse. She was sure of herself, yet never overpowering. She never professed knowledge that she didn't have. It was always, "I don't know. I will have to look it up." Then out came the small notebook, jotting down a few words to remind her to have the answer tomorrow. Somehow, in her manner or in her personality, she was able to give the Vietnamese nurses complete confidence in themselves.

Once she found a dirty dispensary at one of the camps and worked very hard helping the nurse clean it up. When it was to her liking, she showed the nurse around the room, pointing out the things they had done in order to get the dispensary up to acceptable standards.

"It is too dangerous to treat sick people in a filthy hospital. The germs stay in the dirt. I won't visit dirty clinics. Be sure to keep yours clean just like this."

Several weeks later, the nurse again had let the dispensary lapse into an unacceptable state of cleanliness. Brandy took one look at it, and remarked that she would not step inside the place until it was clean. For weeks she boycotted the clinic. The poor nurse was beside herself with grief. Each day she scoured the place, hoping for Brandy's return. Her visits were the highlight for all the dispensary personnel and no visits were a huge loss of face for all of them. Finally, Brandy returned and the nurse, overcome with happiness, dropped to her knees, buried her face against Brandy's legs, and begged forgiveness.

Brandy was sure that Mark was lonely for female companionship. She could tell by the way he treated her during their work each day, and his reluctance to leave her at night. Yet, Brandy knew that Mark had to be the one to set the pace, if in fact there was to be a pace, for the development of something more than her usual wink of an eye, bend over, take what was offered in a heated moment and then move on. Her accustomed scenario.

Some nights, naked, alone in her bed, too hot to sleep even with the air conditioner wheezing away, her thighs burned at the thought of him in her bed. She wanted more.

From this one, maybe a lot more. Maybe something I've never had. Not even once from all my men.

Oh, God, were there really that many?

As they walked along, she laughed out loud. A deep, throaty, unrestrained, lusty laugh.

Mark looked at her quizzically.

Brandy could feel her face warm. She quickly turned away from him, as she was looking at the refugees.

I think I must be blushing. So that's what it feels like. Because he's here. There is something about Mark. Different.

They had reached the jeep, now covered with about twenty small refugee children. Some of them scurried away, while others who knew Mark laughed at his feigned anger. He grabbed one of the laughing youngsters and tossed him high in the air, then swung him downward, so that the child sailed between Mark's legs, and landed gently on the ground behind him.

All the other children wanted the same treatment, but Brandy laughingly explained that it was late, the rain was about to start again, and that they would be back in two days.

The rain did start as Mark crossed the bridge into Saigon. It provided Brandy a good excuse to invite Mark in for a drink when they pulled up at her billet, but he passed and rode off into the wet evening, sadly reflecting that he should have stayed this time.

As he drove on, that full, lusty sound of her laughter stayed with him.

Ψ   Ψ   Ψ

Poli De Salle swaggered into the office.

Newell Osborne watched him strut toward his desk and then noticed a nervous smile on Poli's face. He did not get up, nor did he take Poli's proffered hand.

"Don't sit down, Dr. De Salle. You won't be here long enough for a visit."

His voice was cold, harsh, quiet. "I suppose you know why I called you here, Dr. De Salle."

The smile had left Poli's face, and the starch left his posture. He knew he should not try to fool this man.

"I imagine it's about my pacification plan."

"Yes. I thought I had made myself quite clear when I told you not to offer the plan to the Vietnamese."

"Yes, but when you told me that, I had already given them copies."

"Even before you briefed us?"

"Yes, two days before."

"Didn't it occur to you that any plan on such a controversial subject should be approved by us first before they were exposed to it?"

"Well, I thought that they had *some* say in their destiny." Poli let some sarcasm escape.

433

"Don't get smart with me, De Salle. You know damned well they have a lot to say in their destiny. They have a hell of a lot to say about their future, and we want to give them more. But we aren't helping one damned bit when we give them plans we can't support. Now why did you not tell me on the day of the briefing that you had given these plans to the Vietnamese?"

"Well ... I ..." Poli's voice trailed off into silence.

"I'll tell you why. Because you knew I would have dragged them back—then and there—while there was still time, before the damage had been done."

"You sound as if I had introduced whiskey to the Indians on the old Western frontier."

"Worse, you idiot. The damage you have done will take months, perhaps even years to repair. You leave me no choice but to ask you to leave Vietnam before the week is out."

Poli had foreseen this eventuality. "But I do not wish to leave at this time."

"I am sorry, De Salle, you have given me no choice. I am telling you. You will be gone by midnight Sunday."

"Now, Mr. Ambassador, I think that would be a foolish thing to do. Consider the havoc I could play in the States, telling how you refused to use a better system to keep from having to admit your failure when using your own."

"Do you really think anyone would believe that crap?"

"Coming from me, yes. You obviously don't read the newspapers very closely. Only the disasters and scandals of this war make head-lines. The press is against the whole US effort here in Vietnam—both civilian and military. They print the horror, not the advances. The press is always happiest when they have an authority to quote that agrees with them."

Newell Osborne was covering his temper very well. He was determined not to let this man see him blow his cool. His cobalt blue eyes were showing bitter cold, but he managed to speak in a very low, quiet voice.

"I've had enough of all this, De Salle. There is nothing I would like better than to have it out with you in the American press, because I fully intend to expose you someday for what you are—a thoroughly dishonest man. I'm sorry to say you aren't the only one that American universities have dumped on our payroll and sent over here. However, at the present, I have a war to fight and do not have time to take up this additional job—or pleasure, as it would be. You will leave by Sunday, Dr. De Salle. There will be no more talk about it."

"I warn you, Mr. Ambassador. I will call a press conference as soon as I hit American soil."

"I'm afraid you misunderstood me, De Salle. There will be no press conference."

Newell reached for a folder lying on his desk.

"Dr. De Salle, I had hoped that I would not have to stoop to use your tactics but I am too busy to spend more time on this problem, and you have given me no alternative. This is our CIA file on you. Sadly, somehow, I just knew we would have to get to exactly this spot."

Poli was genuinely surprised. "On me? What could I have done? Is this some sort of frame-up?"

"No, I am afraid not. It seems you have been dealing in the black market. Your specialty: piastres. It's all here about you and your servant, Nguyen Trach Soo. It is not one of our largest cases, but still notable. Perhaps you are not aware that there are thousands of American civilians over here that have cases against them for this activity. The military authorities have requested permission to prosecute all of them, but it has been State's position to disapprove all but a few of these requests. It would destroy the tweedy, pipe-smoking image, you know. However, we always prosecute a few creeps in order to set an example. Prison time is the usual outcome. Now, De Salle, need I go on?"

Poli thought of Stephen K. Bromfield and the Gene Winters letters. He had one month to go before his year of exile was over. Perhaps he could make a deal with Osborne.

"Look, Mr. Ambassador. I hate to leave under such a—well, such a cloud. How about my making amends? I will work with you personally to discredit my plan with the Vietnamese. I will latterly destroy it in their eyes."

Newell thought for several minutes. It would make his job of getting rid of the plan easier if its author convinced the Vietnamese that it was useless, even dangerous.

Christ, involved with drugs, prostitutes, black market, and even worse, these idiot social scientists take the cake. After their Saigon sabbaticals, they go home, bank our money, pick up a protest sign, start banging coeds, and become campus heroes. Scum. I hope this one has picked up some sort of really nasty social disease.

"All right. You must be out of here by May 31st. You will work for Major Scott. I said *for*. Clear? He will be your boss. Everything you do or write will be approved by him."

Newell Osborne reached for the buzzer button to call for Bill Scott.

Ψ   Ψ   Ψ

Bill and Mai Lei walked down Tu Do Street to the river.

They had been to supper at the Mayfair restaurant. For a moment, they lingered in the park where the statue of Tran Hung Dao, thirteenth century Vietnamese hero, still stood, although during the Tet Offensive machine gun bullets had riddled his body.

Bill looked up at the sky. To the east, it was already dark, but the western sky still had patches of red and gold. The giant statue was silhouetted against the sunset. The evening was calm, but across the river there was a spattering of small-arms fire.

"Poor General Dao. Once again, a war casualty," said Bill as he inspected the bullet holes in the statue of the heroic figure.

"Better he than you, darling."

"He probably wouldn't agree."

"Well, since he is made of metal, it probably wouldn't hurt him as much."

Several young couples rode by on Hondas, the girls behind the boys, arms tight around the boys' waists.

"I wonder if they are engaged," he remarked.

"Probably not. Just good friends. I wish we had a Honda, and then I could hug you in public like those girls."

"Well, we could sit on this bench and pretend it was a Honda."

"Silly! It's not dark enough yet," she laughed.

"It will be in a minute or two."

"No. Let's go to the bar at the Majestic Hotel."

"Why, can you hug me there?" Bill asked jokingly.

"No, no, no! My friend is playing piano there. I told you about her. She just got the job."

"Oh, that's right! Let's go and see how she's doing."

They crossed the park and entered the lobby of the hotel. The brass cage of the elevator groaned as they ascended to the highest stop. Climbing the stairs to the top floor, they heard music from the intimate piano bar.

It was a relatively small room, with one side glassed in to give a magnificent view of the river and the flat grassy land beyond. The piano was the center of the attraction and small tables radiated out from it, while around the solid walls were cozy booths.

Mai Lei's friend, Cô San, was playing Chopin as they entered. She looked up and smiled, acknowledging Mai Lei's discreet sign of greeting.

They found a booth in full view of the pianist and ordered drinks while San finished the selection.

It was early and there were very few customers in the bar, but Mai Lei and Bill became San's loud fan club and stimulated the apathetic applause into a rather enthusiastic reception. After a while, San left the piano and came over to their booth. She was very attractive with eyes that suggested a playful sense of humor and an open zest for life.

"Bill, this is my good friend, Cô San. This is Bill Scott, my fiancé."

"Happy to meet you, Bill. I hear about your engagement, Mai Lei. I so happy for you."

Bill pulled a chair to the end of their tiny table and San joined them for a few minutes.

"You know, Bill, San and I once were to be what you call sister act. I was to sing while she played."

Both girls laughed shyly.

"We were quite serious until our parents found out that we had entered a talent contest."

"Mai Lei has lovely voice. Bill, how 'bout you let Mai Lei sing to-night just once—for, what you say, old times' sake?"

"I think it would be wonderful. Would you do it, Mai Lei?" Bill asked.

"I haven't practiced! These people would all run away! They would hate it," she answered in mock panic.

"Oh come on, Mai Lei, just like old times," San said in Vietnamese. Then, turning to Bill, she added in English, "She is stubborn!"

"If she doesn't want to, I would never make her do it."

"Oh, but she want to. She love it. There little few people here now. It like singing in home. We do songs we practice *beaucoup* times."

Then switching to Vietnamese, she said, "Come, Mai Lei, I will go to the piano and announce you if you don't come with me now."

San got up and started for the piano.

"Wait, San, wait!" Mai Lei rose, followed San, and stood at the piano, smiling nervously and looking at Bill.

San made the announcement. "Ladies and gentlemen! It is good fortune tonight to have Cô Bu Mai Lei, singer of beautiful songs."

She struck a few chords and played a chorus of *Doi Toi Chi Mot Nguoi* (I have only one love to give you). It was a typical Vietnamese love song, and its poignant meaning was lost on the predominantly American audience. However, they clapped politely when Mai Lei finished.

Almost immediately, San broke into *The Wedding*, a French song that had also gained popularity in Vietnam and in the United States. Mai Lei first sang the verse in French, and then switched to English. She sang directly to Bill:

> "You by my side, I can see us,
> I close my eyes and I can see us.
> We're on our way to say 'I do,'
> My secret dreams have all come true.
> I see the church, I see the people,
> Your folks and mine happy and smiling,
> And I can hear sweet voices singing
> Ave Maria"

Bill knew that Mai Lei was singing to him from her heart and with all her heart. Her sincerity gave credence to the overly sentimental words of the song. He thought to himself that he was the luckiest man in the world to have someone love him with the depth and sincerity of Mai Lei's love.

When the song was over, the applause was enthusiastic and sincerely given. Mai Lei smiled and thanked San, then returned to the table.

Several of the Americans turned to see to whom Mai Lei had been singing.

As she neared her table, one of the Americans said loudly to Bill, "Might as well give up now, son. That Cô has you all lassoed and tied!"

"You were wonderful, darling," said Bill, ignoring the remark.

"What did he mean, 'lassoed and tied'?"

"That you have me captive to your charms." He hugged her and kissed her hair.

San was playing Chopin's E Flat Nocturne and the audience settled down and was listening quietly. Outside, the last of the sunset had flickered on the still water of the river below them and disappeared into the vast lowlands on the west bank.

Bill and Mai Lei left their table and walked to the big windows. The anti-infiltration flares were already lighting up the darkening sky. The music failed to muffle the deep boom of distant mortar shells and the sharp crack of small-arms fire. Below them and extending far to their right, around a bend in the dark river, lay the many ships, both in the channel and at the now-deserted docks.

The notes of Chopin reached Bill's ears as the tranquility of the river clashed in incongruity with the flares and sounds of the distant battle. Suddenly, an ominous feeling, spawned by the unreality of the moment, engulfed him. He reached out and drew Mai Lei close to him. His arm enclosed her as if to protect her.

For the first time since his arrival in Vietnam, he was worried about their future.

439

Chapter XIII

MAY

The southwest monsoon swept into Saigon early that year.

The grey clouds came low over the city, borne on damp winds that brought heavy, continuous rain. With the bad weather also came bad news. Rumors and speculation about a new offensive spread like a disease over the city.

Enough intelligence information was available to give credence to the stories, and most of the ARVN units in Saigon were on alert in anticipation of a full-out attack.

Mai Lei paid no attention to the war rumors. They had been part of life as far back as she could remember. Nevertheless, the early rain was very upsetting. She was to be married in accordance with the Vietnamese custom in which the wife takes the religion of the husband. Therefore, she had arranged for a Protestant chaplain to perform the ceremony at the Hangout. Two of Mai Lei's friends were to be bridesmaids and Mark Buckley was to be best man. There was to be a small reception in the garden, and the rains would surely put an end to that.

It had been difficult for Bill to obtain permission to marry on such short notice. Only the positive power of Newell Osborne, applied with skilled and relentless pressure had opened the bureaucratic doors in time. Now, on the second day of May, there was thunder, lightning, and high winds.

"Weather like this usually stays for a week or two," said Mai Lei sadly, to Bill, as they watched the sheets of rain move down the street, masking the next block.

"Don't worry. The reception can be on the porch. It will be beautiful," said Bill.

Mai Lei could tell he did not really believe it.

To everyone's surprise, the third day of May broke clear and sunny, and much of the two days' deluge had time to drain off, leaving the city soggy but clean. The greatest news to most of Saigon on that day, however, was not the end of the rainstorm, but the announcement that Paris had been selected as the site for peace talks.

Bu, however, was skeptical about the announcement. It did not seem to him that the North and the NLF were sincerely seeking peace. To attain peace would require a compromise on both sides and the North Vietnamese were demanding that all concessions be from the South Vietnamese.

Ψ   Ψ   Ψ

Duat sat in a reclining rattan chair in the garden at Xa Bui and looked toward the northeast.

It was the early morning of May 5th. His watch read 3:30 a.m. In one half hour, if all went well, the May Offensive against Saigon would begin.

Duat was focused on the opening attack because his people had been directly concerned with this operation. The Second VC Mobile Force Battalion, which would lead the initial attack on the Newport Bridge, would wear South Vietnamese Marine uniforms. Duat's people had the task of obtaining these uniforms and delivering them to the VC battalion without suspicion, capture, or compromise. The job was completed with a week to spare and there had been no tip-off to the South Vietnamese. He wondered if all the other units were ready. He had not communicated with General Tra for over ten days now, and Duat did not know the state of the general's readiness.

Suddenly, there was a great flash of light to the northeast. The sluggish sound waves working their way across the sleepy city finally delivered a tardy, dull explosion. Duat looked at his watch. It was exactly 4:00 a.m.

The May Offensive had begun.

Ψ   Ψ   Ψ

Brandy Masters was not pleased.

She leaned her back against her front door. She heard the sound of Mark's jeep driving away.

Again.

Damn. Why didn't he come in? The moment felt right. Okay, this is the end of day one of the damned attack. But really, what do I have to do to get him to make a move? Some move? Any move …

Her thoughts fixed on the picture she had found in Mark's footlocker back in the Special Forces camp that seemed to be so long ago. Then they turned to Janet.

"Goddamn ghosts!" she said aloud.

Her quarters were empty. Ooogg had the night off and, with the start of the offensive, would probably not be back for days.

With all that in his head, he's not going to move forward. It's up to me.

Brandy had doubts. Not in Mark's attraction to her as a woman. There had been enough signs in the past, and men were always attracted to Brandy. She was the one who made the choice and selected the man.

No, for the first time in her adult life, she had mixed feelings about a man. Her female side wanted Mark Buckley as a man. That was clear from the first moment she met him.

Interest him. Possess his waking thoughts. Create that look of almost worship mixed with desire in his eyes. Use him, on her terms of course, and then when she was bored with him, move on and not look back.

Poli De Salle had been the last in a long line of these.

Wore his skinny ass out, didn't I? Little jerk couldn't believe it when I dropped him. He actually thought he was in control somehow.

She started to laugh out loud. Then caught herself.

But there's this something with Mark that makes me want more than just his tight body.

Her lips curled with a passing flash of amused desire that ran up and down her and then was gone.

Nope, maybe I want more from a man than ever before. Can I really want that? Could he be the one that would make me stay? Surrender enough? Trust enough? Wow.

One thing's sure. I'm never going to find out if he stays stuck where he is.

"Well, little girl, one thing you know how to do is to move a man." She laughed out loud.

Brandy Masters was now in motion. The idea of a man she wanted was now clear.

As she walked across the living room toward her bedroom, the noisy rattle of the air-conditioner was the only sound in her quarters. She started to unbutton her blouse. She reached her bed and dropped it. Then the skirt.

She turned and looked at herself in the small wall mirror. Her black lace bra accented her large, full breasts. Unconsciously, Brandy took her hands and cupped them with a slight upward thrust. She smiled.

Reaching behind her, she popped open the bra hook. Again, she smiled when she remembered the first time she took a small set of pliers and pried a bra hook slightly so that it would be easier for a man to release it.

Nothing like a stuck bra to ruin the mood!

She checked the mirror again.

Thank God they still don't sag. Use 'em or lose 'em!

Brandy's face in the mirror reflected a wide grin. She ran her hands slowly over her slim stomach, and stopped over the low front of her matching black lace panties. She could feel herself beneath the thin silk. Then she moved her hands over her heart-shaped hips and then behind up to her full, round, rear.

Damn, this is going to be fun. Maybe, just maybe, I can move that man off his tight little ...

Her deep, low, lusty laugh filled the room. She headed for the bathroom. A shower, a subtle hint of makeup, and one of her softest perfumes were directly ahead in her plan. Ooogg had made up her bedroom before leaving and everything looked perfect.

The phone rang in the Hangout. Mark was alone, about to head out the door on his way over to MACV to check in for the latest word on the offensive. In a war, nothing good comes with a phone call.

Especially in Saigon. Especially in the midst of a large enemy attack.

He grabbed the phone.

"Colonel Buckley," he said in his low, even, army phone voice.

"Mark, it's Brandy ... I'm ... I ..."

"Brandy, what's wrong?"

"Oh, maybe I'm just ... I'm alone. Ooogg is not here tonight. There's a lot of noise outside and I've heard the front door knob rattle twice now. Do you know if the VC have made it this far yet?"

"The door's locked? Right? How about the windows?"

"I'm sure they are. I don't know. Ooogg takes care of most of that. The door's locked now. I checked it. I just don't know what ... I think I just heard something outside again. The blinds are slightly open. Do you think I should go look through the windows?"

"Brandy, stay away from the windows and turn the lights out."

"Ok, Mark," she interrupted, breathlessly.

"There's no hope of getting the MPs or the Saigon Police to go over there now. They've got too much on their hands. I'm coming over."

"Oh, Mark. I feel like such a child calling you like this when I know you have so much to do and so much on your mind."

"Forget it. I'm on my way. I will knock three times on the door when I get there. Don't open it until you hear my voice after that."

"Hurry, Mark. I think I heard them again."

"Right. See you shortly," Mark said.

Mark Buckley headed for the door. He picked up his CAR-15, grabbed his web belt with the holstered .45 and magazine pouches, and swung it over his shoulder. In a moment, he was tearing across Saigon in his jeep, hoping to avoid roadblocks and the fighting.

Damn. I hope I'm not too late. A pretty blond American girl would make an easy and eager target for VC infiltrators or any remaining neighborhood VC.

Christ, even some ARVN or VN police lowlifes who had seen her coming and going. One look at that babe and anyone would ...

"Shit," he said out loud and tore around a corner, just keeping the four wheels of his jeep on the ground.

He could hear small-arms fire in the distance and the sporadic rumble of heavy explosions. The horizon was lit with flares dancing in the night sky.

Am I going to lose another one? Another *one? Damn it. Where did that come from?*

In the back of the house, Brandy heard three quick, loud knocks on the door. Then Mark's loud voice:

"Brandy? It's me. Mark. Mark Buckley."

Brandy silently counted to five and then ran flat out to the door and whipped it open.

"Mark. You came!" she said, with a more than a hint of breathlessness and her hair in disarray, both from her run across the house. She hoped she wasn't overdoing it.

Mark Buckley looked at the blond girl in the doorway. She was wearing a short, red silk Asian bathrobe tied at the waist showing a fair amount of generous, creamy white cleavage. Her long blond hair was tussled and she looked scared.

Mark moved quickly into the quarters and shut the door behind him, snapping the lock on. He brought his index finger to his lips motioning Brandy to be quiet. Then like a large cat, he first swept his eyes around her living room and then silently slid into the darkness of the other rooms, the automatic rifle at the ready, safety off. For a big man, he moved with a smooth grace.

Brandy waited with some quiet impatience while Mark checked out the house. She was eager for her plan to proceed. She had to hold a balance and not over act.

Eventually Mark returned, snapped the safety on his weapon, smiled, and spoke.

"Looks all clear. The windows are locked and secure."

"I heard them just a minute before you knocked. Do you think they ran off when they saw you drive up?"

"Could be."

"Do you think they're watching the house, waiting for you to leave?"

"Well ..."

"Oh, Mark, it's a long time to dawn. If they come back, I don't know what to do ..."

Mark Buckley checked his watch. She was right. Far too many hours before sunrise.

"Okay. How about I stay until first light?"

"Oh," she sighed. "Would you? I would feel so much safer."

"No sweat. Always happy to save a damsel in distress!" he joked.

"Now you're making me feel silly," Brandy giggled.

"Not silly at all. This is a dangerous moment. You would make quite a trophy to the enemy."

"Trophy? Whatever do you mean, Mark?" A bare hint of slyness crept into her voice.

It went unnoticed.

"A gal that looks like you and ... well, a trusted, terrific nurse for one thing!"

"The way I look right now? All flustered. No makeup on and in this old thing?" she said, eyes demurely downcast, all the while running her hands down the sides of her red silk robe.

Even in the staccato light coming in through the slightly open venetian blinds Mark could see her well enough to disagree with that.

"Honey, you look great. You always do. Like a ... a movie star or something."

Brandy gave a grateful shy, little girl smile. This was her moment.

There was a small rattan couch against the living room wall opposite the door. The flickering light of a small candle in an empty glass jar revealed a small teak table in front. Brandy casually, slowly, led Mark over, continuing to speak with just a hint of fear in her voice.

"Would you sit with me for a bit? Maybe they'll go away with you here."

Mark put his rifle on the floor next to the couch and sat down. His web belt and pistol holster were awkward on the cushions.

Brandy giggled. "It can't be too comfortable with all that gear on. Why don't you take it off for a moment?"

Mark, after giving her a surprised look, stood up, did so, and sat back down.

The couch was barely big enough for two, so Brandy easily managed to sit close to Mark, her bare thigh, revealed by her short silk robe and the candlelight, brushing up against his green uniform trousers.

Easy does it, girl. Don't scare him off.

Brandy gently touched his arm and said, "I didn't think the fighting would get this far into Saigon."

"They must have placed infiltration teams around the city to coordinate with the NLF's major thrust."

Brandy slowly and gently leaned her head against his shoulder. Her long blond hair spilled down across the front of his uniform. She gave just the hint of a sniffle and a tiny, stifled cry.

Mark instinctively patted her bare leg and said, "It will be okay."

Brandy moved even closer. Mark reached around and put his arm around her.

Count to four. One. Two. Three. Four.

Brandy looked up and Mark looked down into her blue eyes, just visible in the candlelight. She kissed his cheek and then put her head back on his shoulder.

Let's see what happens now. Maybe adding this.

With a subtle move of her free shoulder and tiny arch of her back, she felt the low front of her robe slide open just a bit more. More than half of her right breast was now revealed.

Inside his cool exterior, Mark Buckley was on fire. His throat was suddenly very dry. He tried not to look past the honey-haired head on his shoulder, down to the most amazing cleavage and even farther beyond that to the nearly revealed hips that Brandy's crossed, bare legs had now angled toward him.

He tried. He looked away. Tried to breathe slowly. Then he looked back. He had to.

Brandy became even softer against him. A subtle yielding that to Mark's deeply male brain signaled surrender.

448

Brandy's head moved off his shoulder and their eyes met. She had a small smile with just a hint of challenge. She raised her head just a bit, angling her lips toward Mark's, and paused. Her eyes drew him on. He was lost.

Their lips met. Brandy kissed him gently. Pulled away an inch. Paused and returned again. This time with more commitment.

Mark felt his body respond to hers. He kissed back. He took her upper lip gently between his. Then the lower. Then he was back full upon both of hers. He felt her lips open so slightly to him. He gently took the invitation.

Brandy was on fire, too. But she was too focused on her plan to lose control this early.

Keep it together, girl. Just a bit longer.

She gently pulled away from Mark, keeping eye contact and that little smile that she used to practice in the mirror when she was younger. The one that men reacted to. Every time.

Mark looked with some concern. No, she was not angry or put off.

Not with a kiss like that. Jesus Christ ...

Brandy stood up, still making eye contact. Still with her purring cat smile. She silently turned and walked toward the door to her bedroom. Her bed was just visible with the light of another candle on the bedside table. As she left the circle of candlelight, she could feel Mark's eyes on her back. She reached in front of her and took the ends of her robe tie in her hands.

Right about ... now.

Unseen by Mark, she untied her robe and, with a small shrug, let it slide off her shoulders and fall to the floor as she continued to walk into her bedroom. She had practiced her walk in the mirror as well.

This should look amazing.

In the low light, Mark could see that Brandy was wearing only a pair of black silk bikini panties and her high-heeled sandals. As she walked away, her long blond hair hung down her back and pointed his eyes lower to take in the full spectacle of her round, firm rear moving hypnotically as she walked away from him.

Mark's body took control. Suddenly he was on his feet moving across the room. He caught up with Brandy as she reached the bed. Taking her shoulders in his hands, he turned her around toward him. Without thinking, he looked down.

Holy shit. Just look at those ...

He forced himself to look up. Brandy's smile had broadened. There was now more than a bit of a challenge in her eyes. He took her in his arms and kissed her deeply. Even through his army greens, he could feel the large, solid, firmness of her bare breasts against him. He felt her tongue move though his lips and find his. There was much heat and a welcome, old familiar, tingling, tightening feeling in his loins. Brandy pressed her thigh between his legs, against him. His body responded even more.

He pulled back a moment. Then he felt Brandy start to unbutton his uniform shirt. He waved her away and did it himself. As he was reaching the final button, he felt her unfasten his belt and trousers, ease them over his lean hips, and let them drop to the floor. Mark tossed the shirt away, leaving his GI tee. She took his firm erection, poorly concealed under his boxers, in one hand and with her other, pushed him onto the edge of the bed.

Kneeling in front of him, she unlaced his black combat boots and pulled them off, one after another. Then the GI socks. As Brandy pulled off his trousers, she looked up. Through her tussled hair, she could see his eyes, large and burning.

One more little move coming up, now.

She tossed Mark's trousers across the room. Reaching up, she slowly pulled down his shorts. He was ready.

Well hello there, big fella. Now we're talkin', sugar! I'm going to love this ride! And you still have no idea.

Moving closer between his legs, she took him into her mouth. Mark gave a loud groan, almost a shout. She pulled away, watched him for a moment, and then returned with all her skills.

Mark felt a bolt of electric flame running up and down, deep inside him. He had never felt this before with any woman. Ever.

Ah ... ah ... oh ... Christ!

He would wait no more. He pushed Brandy's head away, stood up, and pulled her up from her knees. In one swift move, he pivoted and placed her down on the bed. He could see her eyes flashing in the candlelight, her blond hair all aglow. And that smile. With slightly opened lips and just the tip of her tongue visible, giving a taunting flick.

He slipped her panties down her legs and off into the darkness in one sweeping motion. Brandy opened her legs wide and Mark was between them. He slid inside in one quick, easy movement. He leaned over her. His upper body was suspended by both his extended arms, like stout columns above her shoulders, keeping his upper body weight off her breasts. As he started to move his hips in a controlled rhythm, he looked down and saw her closed eyes. Her smile was now broader. Her breathing was faster.

He thrust harder. Fascinated, he watched her pink nipples grow larger, erect, and harder.

Jesus, they're as big as thumbs.

He lowered his head to her chest and took her left nipple between his lips. Then he gently stroked it with his front teeth. Then he applied suction. Her reaction was loud and instant:

"My God! Don't stop. God, don't stop!"

She took her hands and held his head to her chest. Mark alternated with a slight sucking and slight touch of his teeth to each nipple. Back and forth in a slow easy rhythm that matched the thrusts of his hips.

With each of his moves, he felt Brandy respond. She arched her pelvis and matched her motions with his. Mark rose up over the girl by extending his arms again. Her breasts, thrusting up at him from below, echoed his movements against her hips with a pulsing motion of their own.

He closed his eyes to concentrate. To delay. He changed the angle of his attack. He went deeper. Then upward. He could feel her response immediately. He pressed on.

He's hitting it. Oh my God. He's hitting it. He's holding off. For me. Oh my God.

Brandy felt the contractions starting deep within. In a moment, her primal female writhing would start. She would lose control. She knew this. Still, she wanted to prolong this moment. As always, she wanted this to go on forever. Her arms lay outstretched from her sides. Her hands gripped the sheets and twisted them, hard.

Mark felt Brandy's body move to another level of passion. He opened his eyes. Now, there was a subtle rosy blush on her chest that began in the deep valley between her breasts. It meandered up to her neck and faded as it reached her cheeks. Her closed eyelids were dark. Brandy was somewhere deep inside herself. Her body was now in charge: automatically pulsing, moving, thrusting, pulling at him, and then stroking him deep inside.

Then Brandy screamed loudly with passion, pleasure, and everything a woman can feel, all at once:

"Fuck me! Fuck me now! Fuck me! Dammit fuck me harder! Never stop. Now. Fuck me!"

Mark felt her hips rock and gyrate against him in ways he had never felt before. Brandy's body gripped him inside her like a vise, and pulled and stroked him. He could feel her fighting her climax. Somehow, he held on.

How does she do that? Let it go, woman, before you kill both of us. Oh my God ... Oh my God.

With one huge, powerful, strong rocking of her hips and a deep contraction, Brandy let it all go. Loudly.

"Ah ... ahh ... ahh ... ahh ... Yes! Yes! Don't ... Don't stop! Fuck me!"

Her body continued to pulse in her long, long aftershock. It wouldn't stop. With that, Mark let go.

He went deep. He went hard. Up to the hilt. It was thunder, lightning, explosions, fireworks, all at once. And, for him, it seemed to go on forever.

"Yes! Yes! Ah. Yes! Don't stop now!" he yelled.

Brandy, eyes closed, still in a very deep place of her own pleasure, felt him release. She could hear his words. Her body responded. She took care of him.

Then, her familiar old feeling of power over men washed over her. It was almost a second climax. It felt luxurious and comfortable as if she had put a long, cool mink coat on over her naked body.

Wore your little ass out, didn't I? You think that's all? Just wait and see.
She wanted more. Right now. And she knew how to get it.

Ψ   Ψ   Ψ

Mark Buckley awoke to the sound of distant explosions and small-arms fire.
Not close. But not that far. The damn offensive. Damn VC.
He looked over at the shape in the bed next to him. Brandy Masters
was dead asleep. The sounds of war were too far away to disturb her.
There was still a flickering light of the failing candle at the bedside. Mark
was fascinated by the glow of her long, blond, honey hair on the pillow.
On her lovely, sleeping face, he could just make out what looked to
be a very satisfied smile on her very attractive lips.
Damn. I thought she was never going to tire out. Wow. God, she's beautiful.
Mark heard more small-arms fire in the distance.
Time to go.
He slipped out his side of the bed and felt around for his clothes. Silently, he dressed himself, leaving his boots off for the moment. He made
his way over to Brandy's side of the bed. For a moment, he stood and lis-
tened to her soft breathing and watched, fixated, her bare breasts moving
up and down in a slow, easy rhythm. Her creamy, pale skin was striking in
the candlelight. His thoughts returned to a few hours before and the
amazing series of lovemaking bouts that had taken place. He shook himself
loose from the strong, powerful memories that began to capture him.
No time. No time.
Mark leaned over and brushed his lips against her cheek.
"Bye, baby," he whispered.
The warm, soft scent of her perfume almost overwhelmed his
sense of purpose, but he turned and moved away, taking his boots and
heading for the living room.
What did she say that perfume was? Ah, right. Unforgettable. *That's an
understatement!*
He gave a low laugh and smiled to himself.
Then his boots were on. His web belt with pistol was on his hips.
His rifle was in his hand. He was out the door and gone.

453

Ψ   Ψ   Ψ

It was 0545 hours when Brandy Masters awoke to the sound of mortar fire.

Obviously, the new offensive had geared up in earnest. She looked over and saw that Mark was gone.

God damn this war. God damn him for being a good little soldier.

Then she laughed.

"Damn good is right!" she said aloud.

Then she remembered the hospital.

It must be hell there right now.

How would she get there? Brandy knew a big, tall, take-charge man who could make that happen. She hoped she would be able to get through to Mark. She reached for the phone and dialed the Hangout.

"Mark? This is almost a miracle."

"Miracle, hell. It's the offensive. I've just washed up, changed, and I'm off to MACV."

"I know you are. It's amazing that I merely dialed and somehow got you!"

"Look, we'll be cut off any moment. Sorry I had to leave. I didn't want to wake you. You're off to the hospital, I suppose."

"Right. How to get there. That's the reason for my call. That and wanting to hear your voice."

"I'll come and get you and drive you over. It's not far out of my way to MACV Headquarters."

"When will you be by?"

"In about ten minutes."

"Thanks. I'll be ready."

Then the line went dead.

Ψ   Ψ   Ψ

There was daylight in the sky as they made their way to the hospital. Mark, trying to stay focused on driving and avoiding any firefights, explained to Brandy that there was a lot of intelligence on this offensive and everyone had been ready for it since May 1st.

454

"It shouldn't last as long as the last one. We only hope that we can keep them out of the city."

To the right was the sound of heavy mortar fire, mingled with loud, deep thuds of 122 mm rockets.

"From the sound of all that, I wonder if you should trust your intelligence."

"Sounds bad for the moment, but that's because we haven't started a counter-attack. We'll locate those positions and things will quiet down around here," Mark answered.

"Mark, are you ... well, are you still unhappy about not being in a combat unit?"

"Not like I was. I'm convinced now that this refugee mess is Vietnam's biggest potential problem."

There were more mortar blasts, this time closer to Mark's jeep.

"God, those were close," murmured Brandy.

"Want to pull up?"

"No. You wouldn't stop if I weren't with you."

"Brandy, you're quite a ... wonderful girl. I wish ... I wish we hadn't started out the way we did."

"Mark ... I don't know how long this offensive will last, but ... maybe we can somehow start all over again."

She glanced up at him and he turned and smiled.

"Brandy, I'm pretty sure we did a few hours ago. At least I did."

I know I did, too.

They turned onto Troung Min Cang and immediately came to a roadblock. Ahead they could see the rubble of a damaged and partially demolished building. There was a fire on the second floor and some people were organizing to put it out. Others were carrying out the wounded and the dead.

"Mark, drop me off here. This is where I'm needed now."

"Okay, I'll stop, and help until the fire trucks come, but I can't leave you here, Brandy."

They hopped out of the jeep and stood next to each other watching the fire.

"Don't worry. The ambulances will arrive any minute and I'll go on to the hospital with them."

They could hear the distant sounds of two sirens, the high tone of the ambulance, and the deeper tone of the fire engines.

Brandy reached over and touched Mark's hand. She was fighting back an impulse to take him in her arms and not let go.

"See you after the battle." She smiled, trying to be cheerful.

Suddenly Mark's hands were on her shoulders. He pulled her toward him and kissed her hard on the mouth. Long and deep. Brandy felt her legs start to tremble and her body automatically moved closer into his. She did not care about the war around her, the sounds and the smells. She felt his hand gently move down her back to her waist, hesitate, and then go lower, much lower, and lightly brush and then cup her firm, round behind. She could feel her thighs automatically start to open to him. Instinctively, one of his firm, muscular legs moved slightly between hers.

It was hard for Brandy to stop from starting to move herself against his leg. Somehow she did.

No, not just another one-time lay. What? What did I say? Oh my God. Oh my God. He is the ... He ...

"That's for luck, baby," he said as he eased her away. His eyes looked straight and long into hers.

He knows it too.

There were tears in Brandy's eyes as she turned and reached back into the jeep for her first-aid kit. She walked to the line of wounded women and children. Only once, she looked back and saw Mark working with the Vietnamese policemen and soldiers, pulling combustibles away from the fire. Then she went back to her work.

There was much to do and she pushed the lingering memory of that kiss, his touch, his eyes, out of her mind.

Ψ   Ψ   Ψ

Bill Scott was going to get married, war or no war.

Bill had not seen much of Mai Lei since the offensive started, but today was his wedding day and by God, he was going to get married.

456

He talked it over with Newell Osborne and decided that although the guests would be few, they would go ahead with their plans.

Early that morning, it became obvious that Cholon would again receive the brunt of the Communist attack, and Bill decided that his new family-to-be should again move into the Hangout. While the enemy troops drove a wedge into the city westward from the eastern boundary, Bill gathered up Mai Lei and a grumbling Bu into his jeep and drove them back to his billet.

"It'll keep your mind off the wedding! No jitters now!"

"Oh, Bill. We get married in less than five hours, and I spend the time moving!"

"Don't worry, darling. At least you know where you will sleep tonight—in my bed!"

Mai Lei looked at the floor of the jeep and smiled bashfully.

Will I ever get used to the so direct, so crude American ways?

At one o'clock, San arrived by taxi with the orchestra: a small, portable organ. She had promised to supply the music, but no one had expected her to brave the storm of small-arms fire to make the wedding.

"I borrow this from friend in the Methodist mission. I never play before. Now go away. I practice."

Bu had taken over sovereignty of an easy chair in one corner of the living room. Now buried in a book, he was oblivious to the bustle and confusion going on around him and the war going on beyond the walls.

Bill, Mai Lei, and the servants were frantically decorating the living room, heedless of the ominous rumbles of distant mortars and the louder sounds of the American and VNAF air attacks on VC-held areas of the city.

"Now, if we only had some guests."

"Now, if we only had a *preacher*."

"You mean ... oh, I forgot. We do need one."

"It won't be legal without one. Let's give him thirty minutes, and then I'll go out and round up another one."

"Thirty minutes? You mean it's that late? I haven't changed!"

Mai Lei dropped the garland of paper flowers she was putting on the table and ran giggling up the stairs. Bu raised his eyes from the book and smiled as he watched his daughter's hasty exit.

It was three o'clock when Mai Lei came down the stairs. She was dressed, fitting in with the American theme, in a beautiful white-and-silver brocade *ao dai*, and carried some white blossoms from a tree flowering in the garden. Her black hair was brushed back over her shoulders and hung loose down her back. Her smile betrayed her happiness.

Bill had never seen her look lovelier.

Bu looked up at his daughter. He was proud of her. In his heart, he knew he would miss her badly, but in his mind, he knew he had no right to interfere with her search for happiness.

"No chaplain yet, Bill?"

"No, darling. I think I'll take off and see if I can find one out at MACV."

They walked into the dining room where the beautiful cake the cook had made awaited the reception.

In a low voice Mai Lei said, "Don't be gone long, Bill. It is not very important to be married today. Maybe tomorrow. Cake will keep." She tried to smile.

"I'll be right back with a real live preacher. You wait and see, Mai Lei."

He headed for the door.

Bill drove the jeep down the driveway, but at the street, the Vietnamese police stopped him. While he was trying to find out what was happening, Mark and the chaplain drove up in Mark's jeep.

"Boy, you guys are a sight for sore eyes. Come on in, Padre. You're late."

Mark filled him in, "There was a matter of a firefight. The cops want to use our front yard with its high wall to shelter civilians while they rout out the VC. It's liable to get lively around here."

A sharp crack of a pistol shot up the street served to emphasize Mark's remark.

The three Americans entered the house: the chaplain, carrying his

Bible, Mark, carrying a short-barrel assault rifle, and Bill, relief clearly on his face.

"You want a preacher, beautiful, I bring you a preacher!" said Mark proudly.

"Mark, Bill! Oh how do you do, Chaplain?"

In a matter of moments, the small crowd was properly placed: San played the Bridal Chorus from *Lohengrin*; Bu escorted Mai Lei to the makeshift altar, and Mark in his battle fatigues stood up for Bill. His CAR-15 was discreetly placed in a nearby corner.

The chaplain, a captain who had jumped with airborne troops and seen much combat, declined to notice Mark's .45, still in the holster on his web belt.

During the ceremony, small-arms fire could be heard down the block, but the principals of the wedding hardly heard it. After the "I do's," they noticed for the first time the many faces pressed against the windows. The police had brought in locals to shield them from the firefight, and they had heard the Western organ music inside the house.

"Oh look, Bill, we have guests!"

Mark and Bill sensed her thoughts and it took very little doing to have the cake and champagne carried out to the side garden, as originally planned. The astonished refugees from the firefight found themselves guests at a wedding reception.

Mai Lei was radiant. As she and Bill moved among the cyclo drivers, students, shopkeepers, a truck driver or two, and a few soldiers, they asked them all to be welcome and help themselves to the food. Most of these people were shy and reluctant to participate, but with more urging from the Americans, they finally joined in.

The cake was cut and champagne poured for everyone. Mark proposed a toast and all drank to the bride and groom.

"Oh, Bill, I am so happy! What a beautiful day—what wonderful guests—what a beautiful wedding!"

Mark smiled down at her and kissed her on the cheek.

"You are a beautiful girl and a brave one. You're getting exactly what you deserve."

Bill leaned over and kissed Mai Lei on the lips, and then he stared into her eyes. In the distance, they heard the low-pitched sound of a fire truck siren and heavy thud of 250-pound bombs.

"Wish they were church bells."

Ψ   Ψ   Ψ

The initial VC and NVA attack on the city was successfully executed, and refugees by the thousands streamed through Cholon into the relative safety of eastern Saigon.

Once more, the South Vietnamese government called on the RVNAF and the US Air Force to stop the advance. The southwest corner of Cholon was the point where the enemy would be stopped. The surrounding area at that spot was declared a target area if air action was necessary.

Within the next two days, fifty city blocks were flattened and civilian casualties mounted.

Doctor Luh watched Brandy closely as she cleaned up around the sutured stomach wound of a Vietnamese girl.

What would we possibly do without her?

He wondered if what he had to tell her would make her happy or sad.

Perhaps this change will be only temporary.

After Brandy bandaged the wound, he asked her to come with him. They washed up and then went to the doctors' lounge. Brandy collapsed into a welcome chair while Dr. Luh sat down, looking at her steadily. He took a pack of Salems out of his pocket.

"Cigarette?"

"Love one, thanks. That's great."

"Cô Brandy, I have some news for you."

Instantly alert, Brandy sat up in attention in spite of her aching body.

"Good or bad?"

"Bad for us. I don't know how you will feel."

"Please tell me, Doctor."

"Well, they have asked us to release you—that is, if you approve."

"Release me? For what purpose? Don't we need everyone we can get?"

"Yes. That's the trouble. There has been a great battle south of the city at the south end of "Y" Bridge. We have two of our battalions trapped, with many wounded. It's a matter of time until the Americans fighting in Saigon will control the bridge again and push into our area to free our troops. But until they do, we must evacuate our wounded by helicopter. The first-aid station is surrounded. It is defended by our troops, but the wounded must be cared for until the choppers can get in and remove them.

"Plenty of supplies have been dropped, but our medical corpsmen and doctors cannot read the American box labels. They also cannot tell the American chopper crews the condition of the men they are removing. They need someone who can. Right now."

"What will you do here?"

"Get along as best we can until you return."

"You make me feel like Clara Barton or something."

"You are better nurse—and twice as pretty."

"Okay, Doc. Flattery wins every time. Where do I catch the bird?"

Ψ   Ψ   Ψ

Massive bombing and the relentless fighting of the allied ground forces contained the attacking enemy regiments within the northern part of Saigon.

Along the southern boundary of the contested area, US and ARVN tanks, placed nearly tread by tread, formed a steel ring that stopped the enemy.

As their advance slowed, the Communist units fought harder than ever. Their ground forces increased the pressure of their attack and simultaneously unleashed a massive barrage of rockets and mortars against the city. The word spread about the streets of Saigon was that the new battle cry of the NLF was "What we can't take, we destroy."

Civilian families used whatever they could find to make shelters in their homes. A flourishing business began in stolen sandbags, bricks, loads of sand, or even plain mud. Many of the wealthier people made complete shelters out of large sacks of rice and boxes of canned goods that they had hoarded.

Duat had decided against the construction of a shelter at Xa Bui. His residence, standing high upon the skyline, could be seen from almost every direction. He had received assurance from General Tra that all the

VC and NVA gunners were aware of his residence and that it would be spared.

What Duat did not realize was that no matter how honest the promise, the inaccuracy of the VC and NVA weapons made such an assurance impossible. So, when the 122-mm rocket hit the office complex at Xa Bui, the lack of any preparation made the damage much greater than would be expected.

The rocket struck his office at 5:20 p.m. Duat, still asleep, was blown out of bed. For the first few seconds he was convinced that he must be wounded. As the shock wore off, he rose and inspected himself carefully.

Once assured of his own well-being, he put on a robe and inspected the wreckage. The heavy blackout drapes, which covered the glass walls of his room, had saved Duat from certain death from flying glass fragments.

He threw open the drapes and at once saw the garden in a shambles and the office complex in flames. Most of the roof was collapsed. Many of the walls were missing or partially destroyed. The servants' quarters were totally destroyed.

Suddenly he realized that Ahn and the two servants were in the wreckage. For almost a split second, he thought that he should try to rescue them. Then he weighed their importance against his own and dismissed the thought. The sound of the approaching fire trucks focused him on other problems. He would have to open up the stairwells that originally connected his private floor with the floor below him.

With the regular elevator undoubtedly wrecked, he knew that the firemen would ascend via the stairway to the top of the building. He hurried to the heavy door that blocked final access to his private domain and threw open the bolt. A rush of stale air greeted him as he descended the unused stairs and unlatched a lower door at the next landing. Then Duat hurried upstairs again to check if any of his files would be in danger of compromise.

He had anticipated just such a contingency and all the sensitive material dealing with his war activities was written in code on the stationery of his import-export company. Still, it did not seem smart to tempt fate by leaving any of his papers lying about.

It was a needless worry. Compromise was not a possibility; the raging fire had already destroyed the records.

Twenty minutes later the first fireman reached the top of the building. It took another fifteen minutes to get water onto the blaze. The bodies of Ahn and the others were discovered in the rubble after the fire was out.

Duat thanked the fire fighters and police who had fought the fire.

"Can you identify the three dead?"

"They were my servants."

"Do you have names and addresses?"

"I have names, but I do not know where they lived."

"Of course. Did they have family?"

"Not that I know. Perhaps the official records will show."

After the bodies were removed and everyone had gone, Duat closed and bolted the door. For a while, he poked about the ashes, but when he saw how dirty he was getting, he returned to his own quarters, washed thoroughly, and changed to clean clothing. His other rooms were intact, as the bedroom had shielded them from the blast.

With time to think, it was now clear to him what this unfortunate incident would mean. His whole operation was shut down and would not be effective again for some time. He would have to promote one of his other agents to Ahn's position.

The training, the rebuilding ...

As these thoughts came to him, he sat down heavily in a rattan chair and placed his head in his hands.

Suddenly his thoughts turned to General Tra.

Was the hit really an accident? Tra was no fool, after all. Perhaps ... Well, perhaps it would be best to let them think they had been successful.

It was now obvious to Duat that the North had little chance of winning an all-out war against the Americans. It seemed prudent to go underground for a time in order to see how things would progress.

It might be necessary to change sides for a time.Who do I know?

Ψ Ψ Ψ

The dark smoke of battle rose in the humid air and spread over the southern section of Cholon like an ominous shroud.

Through this thick cloud the US F-100 fighters dove to release their bombs at targets in the city, while below the cloud the choppers, like angry hornets, struck at the VC and NVA units whenever they could find them.

The enemy had mounted the final phase of its attack on Saigon from the south. They had chosen to thrust directly into the city via the Y Bridge, which linked Saigon with the swampy flatlands south of the river.

The Y Bridge, a wide concrete structure, lay with its stem running east and west along an island, bordered by the Ben Nghe River on the north and the Doi Canal on the south. Both of these were fed by the Saigon River which coiled along the lower boundary of the city. Thus, one arm of the "Y" stretched north across the river and the other south across the canal. The northern arm terminated in Cholon, and the southern ended in a jumble of shacks and shanties that had sprung up along the southern edge of the canal.

A small band of South Vietnamese troops had formed a defense perimeter one kilometer south of the bridge, but the enemy had infiltrated the rice paddies and the shanties near the canal and now held the foot of the bridge behind them, cutting off the ARVN positions.

To the north, NLF infiltrators had occupied most of the buildings along the Cholon waterfront where the northern end of the Y terminated. Thus, the enemy held the bridge but couldn't use it to move troops because of the dogged defense of that small group of ARVN forces.

MACV knew that, although the small South Vietnamese force was fighting valiantly, it could not hold its blocking position another night. Plans were in effect to pull them out by helicopter. The wounded were already in the process of being air-evaced.

The North Vietnamese were having none of this and quickly set up an effective fire screen. Each time the choppers made a trip, it became more difficult for them to land within the perimeter of the ARVN position. The hail of small-arms fire greeting the crews, with or without large Red Cross markings on their birds, resulted in the missions being named "Flying the gauntlet."

One Huey was shot down as it landed in the defended area. The crew, somehow unhurt, joined the defenders until other aircraft evacuated them. After that, gunships with M-61 mini-guns came in to fly the perimeter continuously to suppress enemy fire.

Brandy had arrived the day before and had been working almost continually. She was so tired she had no sense of time or of feeling. She didn't even hear the sound of the guns anymore. She went about her duties mechanically, working alongside one of the exhausted Vietnamese *bác sĩ*. Brandy heard two American soldiers talking.

"I wonder how the battle is going on the Saigon side?"

"God knows. Heard a radio announcer this morning say that the RVNAF was using bombs and napalm on the area."

"That should discourage the bastards a little."

"Wish they would use some of that stuff on the enemy on this side of the bridge."

"Can't. They would hit us. Those enemy bunkers are too close to our position."

"How much longer do you think these guys can hold out?"

"Not another night. They gotta clear out by nightfall or they'll be overrun. It'll be hard to keep up continual air support when there's no moonlight. Be hard as hell to see this place without a lot of night illumination."

Brandy glanced around her. It looked like about four more "dustoff" flights would do it. She checked her watch.

About 5:30 in the afternoon.

She might even be back in Saigon by seven and maybe in a hot bath by 7:30.

God, what a wonderful thought!

She heard the doctor calling and she returned to the job.

It was about 6:30 when the last two Hueys came in. They were to take the final group of troops and all the medics out. The doctor got into one and told Brandy to get into the other. Brandy helped load some of the wounded troops. It was not until she was standing alone on the ground that she realized they were one seat short. The port gunner grabbed Brandy and pulled her up next to him.

"Come on honey, if you miss this bus, you'll be hitch-hiking home."

He spoke into his intercom and told the pilot that they were all set. The gunships circling overhead were giving superb cover fire.

The first chopper rose and circled right. A few seconds later, Brandy's took off and circled left. Suddenly, a burst of machine-gun fire raked the aircraft, catching the two pilots across the chest. For a moment, the chopper shuddered. Then it spiraled out of control, landing hard in a hollow between the VC bunkers and the bank of the canal.

When the chopper hit the ground, Brandy blacked out.

Ψ   Ψ   Ψ

Hours later, slowly regaining consciousness, Brandy felt great pain in her legs. She tried to move, but found it impossible. Somehow, the hot turbine engine had missed her, but the radio equipment and part of the heavy undercarriage had pinned her down.

All was quiet except for sounds of small-arms fire somewhere behind her. Then she realized that the orbiting gunships had come to see if there were any survivors. They flew low over the broken helicopter, while she waved frantically, but the elephant grass was too high. They did not see her.

She called out in Vietnamese, "Is anyone alive? Can anyone hear me?"

There was no reply.

She tried it again and again, both in English and in Vietnamese. No one answered. Suddenly she realized that her cries might bring the enemy so she lay very quietly after that, listening for the sounds of approaching soldiers.

She struggled trying to free herself. She could move only the upper part of her body. It looked like there was a lot of weight above her, but somehow, something was holding most of it away. The pain in her leg was getting worse. She managed to reach her first-aid bag and gave herself a shot of morphine.

Brandy waited for the drug to take effect. She thought calmly about her situation and what she would do next. First, there was no fire. That had been a lucky break. Second, there seemed to be no other survivors. Third, the enemy was either pinned down or not nearby. If not, they certainly would have heard her calling.

Brandy noticed a small red light above her. The setting sun seemed to catch in the little red bubble and make it look like it was on. The red light belonged to some sort of a small auxiliary radio. She could see the on-off toggle switch.

Maybe it has its own batteries.

She managed to move to a sitting position and raised her arm. She could just reach the switch. She put it in "on" position. Instantly she heard the sound of transmitted voices, but they came from a location closer to her than the radio. It was then she noticed the wire leading from the equipment. On the other end was a telephone handset. The sound was coming from that. She grabbed the cord out and dragged the instrument to her. She pushed the button and the sound stopped.

Quietly she said, "This is Brandy Masters. Our medevac chopper is down at the south end of the Y Bridge. Can anyone hear me?"

Ψ   Ψ   Ψ

Newell Osborne was very upset and worried.

He had called Mark in from the site of the new refugee camp. The two men now faced each other across Osborne's desk.

"Did you know that Brandy Masters was working on a Vietnamese air evac mission south of the Y Bridge?"

"Air evac? The Y Bridge? God, no, sir!"

"Well she is, and what's worse, her chopper was shot down. The first report—a visual by the gunships—no survivors."

Mark was stunned. "Good Christ! That poor kid."

"Yes, it looks pretty bad. I haven't the slightest clue what I'm going to tell the senator, her Uncle Joe ... Mark? What's the matter?"

"Well sir, you see ... lately I have seen quite a lot of Brandy. I have gotten to know her very well. She is ... was ... a really fine person. She was a girl who finally found herself in life, had at last found that niche that was really made for her."

Then it finally hit him hard. "My God! Poor Brandy."

"Had you become, very ... close?"

By Mark's anguished look, Osborne knew that the two had, against all the odds of their history, become more than just friends.

Damn it. This guy can't catch a break. And somehow, that young woman had finally settled on the right guy for once ...

The phone rang. Newell picked it up.

"Yes?"

There was a pause while he listened.

"Repeat that," Osborne said into the phone. Still on the line, he turned to Mark.

"She's alive! They have her on a survival radio of some kind."

"Where is she?" Mark rushed to the telephone extension by the couch at the other side of the room.

When he was sure of all the facts, both of the girl's situation and the prospects of rescue, he said, "Tell her to hang on. Tell her Mark says to hang on. We'll come and get her."

When both men had hung up, Newell said, "Mark, don't be a fool. They said they can't risk choppers in there. It's not just a pickup, you know. She has to be extracted from that wreckage. If it were just a pickup, we could do the whole operation with flares, but to cut away the chopper under enemy fire, it's just too hazardous."

"Sir, I realize that an aerial rescue is out of the question, but how about the armored column that is planning to assault from our side of the bridge? The last I heard they had wiped out the VC on the north side and were ready to go."

468

"But she is not that easy to get to. Remember that the VC complex seems to be between the bridge and Brandy Masters."

"Sir, can I go?"

Newell looked at Mark, whose face was focused, hard, and dark.

Quietly he said, "The official answer has to be no. But since I don't expect to see you around here for the next few days ..."

Mark headed for the door.

"Take care of yourself, Colonel."

"Yes, sir. Thank you." Then, he was gone.

Before leaving the building, he stopped at J-2 to pick up a copy of the latest aerial photo of the Y Bridge area. With a grease pencil, he marked the original defense perimeter that Brandy had helped evacuate, and the probable location of the dug-in enemy troops. They had well camouflaged their positions and the bunkers were not visible on the photo.

Next, he took Newell's sedan and driver. His plan was to study the map as they headed for the north end of the Y Bridge. Looking at the photo, he noticed a depression that was a probable location of the downed helicopter and noted that it was at the edge of a swampy area that led to a winding inlet of the canal. Perhaps he could work his way up the inlet. It looked relatively free of activity.

They approached the Y Bridge through the burning debris of several blocks of the city. Finally, the street became impassable because of the column of M113 armored personnel carriers and M48 tanks of the US Ninth Infantry Division that was making ready to assault the bridge.

My tanker friends disagreed with Westmoreland's splitting up the tanks and attaching them to infantry units. Right now, this looks like it was a great idea.

Mark, realizing that the sedan was useless now, left the car and ordered the driver to return to headquarters.

He ran along the side of the tank column toward its head, hoping to reach the command vehicle before it started moving forward. It was hard going along the narrow streets. Many of the buildings were still burning and crowds of civilians and military personnel blocked the narrow area between the vehicles and the buildings. A thin covering of ash was falling from the great black cloud overhead and covering the streets.

Coated with sweat and grime, Mark finally broke out of the crowded area onto the riverbank. He spotted the column, led by a tank, starting forward over the bridge. The second vehicle was an open-top M3 half-track with several soldiers aboard. He raced along the side of the column and swung up on the vehicle.

"Observer from MACV," he yelled to the sergeant above the roar of the engines.

The whole column was moving now, slowly advancing across the bridge in the final hour of daylight. Mark figured that they wouldn't do much fighting before dark. Perhaps they could *debouch* and encircle most of the enemy troops if the ground were solid enough. It would be pretty tricky to do all this at night. Perhaps the whole operation was a diversion in order to make it easier to evacuate the perimeter, but that didn't seem to make sense. The perimeter was already evacuated, except for Brandy. He wished he had time to talk to the commander.

They were past the intersection at the stem of the "Y" now and were well on their way along its southern arm. Mark noticed that the second half of the column had turned right at the stem of the "Y" and had taken up positions on the island.

Suddenly the column ground to a halt. Several of the tanks opened fire. Then, after a short pause, they began to move again.

The half-track had almost made it across the canal, when there was a loud explosion and concussion. The vehicle shuddered and ground to a stop.

"Shit, they got our left tread. Those dirty sons of bitches!"

Mark looked over the situation. He had to move, and move right now.

"Sorry I can't stay and help you folks. It's been a real nice ride."

He jumped off the vehicle, his CAR-15 firmly in hand, and then dropped off the right edge of the bridge into the slimy water of the canal. When he surfaced, he struck out westward along the southern bank. Mark was counting on the firefight to divert attention from him and, from the sounds of the battle above, felt he had been successful.

He paddled slowly along the muddy bank, every now and then looking back at the bridge, using it to estimate the remaining distance before he would reach the inlet he had seen on the photo. In addition to the short, lightweight rifle, his boots, .45 and fatigue, and the web belt with canteen and ammo clips made headway difficult and he found it easier to use his free hand to pull himself along by using low branches of trees and exposed roots.

Several times, he thought of dropping the rifle and letting the web belt and his canteen go, but changed his mind when he realized he did not know what the situation would be when he got to Brandy. Suddenly the bank turned sharply left. He had reached the inlet.

Now the going was harder. The water was shallow and the bottom soft and muddy. His boots sank deeply into the muck making each step almost impossible. Finally, Mark lay prone in the water and managed to go forward, half swimming, half pulling himself forward, using the reeds and bushes that grew close to the bank.

The sun was setting in a bath of violent red and gold as Mark reached more solid ground. He was able to leave the stream and keep hidden in the high elephant grass. He found a narrow path. It went off in the direction he wished to travel. He moved cautiously forward on it, crouching to keep in the shelter of the high grass and reeds. There was a little red left in the sky as Mark spotted his goal, the depression, and struck out away from the path. Moments later, he came upon the wrecked chopper. He remained hidden in the reeds, watching closely for signs of the enemy. Then he moved slowly toward the wreck, keeping as quiet as possible. The shelling sounded muffled and distant in the twilight.

"Brandy?" He almost whispered the name.

"Yes! It's me. Who is it? Mark! Here. Oh, thank God."

Now he saw her pinned under what must have been one of the landing skids of the Huey. He also saw the other bodies, lifeless, in and around the wreckage.

There was so little time. The sun was gone now. Only the dusk remained. He lay down beside her and gently kissed her parched lips.

"Here's water."

She drank greedily, until he pulled the canteen away. They spoke in whispers.

"It's too dark to see how you're pinned down. I hate to chance prying up anything. The whole damned engine might fall. I can't see well enough. How much pain are you in?"

"It's not bad. I gave myself some morphine a while ago. The important thing is that you are here. I prayed that somehow you would come. Are there others?"

"No. I took a chance as to where you were. I lucked out and found you, but there won't be help until daylight, now."

"I don't care. Just lie here with me. Hold me close. With you here, everything will be all right."

Mark lay down beside Brandy and slipped one arm behind her to hold her close.

"Hope you don't mind a little river mud."

"River mud is just fine, thanks—as long as you come with it."

In the final gloom of the twilight, Mark found the radio handset.

"This is Lieutenant Colonel Mark Buckley. I am with Miss Masters. She is pinned under the chopper wreckage. I cannot remove her. I will remain with her. Do you read me? Over."

"This is Rescue Five. We read you loud and clear, Colonel. Where did you come from? Over."

"I came across the Y Bridge. It's dark here now and we are going silent for security reasons. Please monitor. We will come on if we need you. Over."

"Rescue Five. We read. Will monitor. Out."

Mark reached up and turned off the radio. The red power light faded into the darkness. He brought his hand down to feel Brandy's dirty face in the darkness, then leaned over and kissed her again.

"More water?"

"No, we have to ration it. How about a cigarette?"

"Not a chance. We're drenched in fuel. We'd go up like a torch. I think you should try to sleep."

"No, darling. I'm ... not quite comfortable enough for that." She laughed nervously. "Besides, I've wanted to talk with you like this for a long time. You know, with no hidden thoughts. Just saying what we mean plainly, honestly ..."

A new thought crossed her mind. "It's all right to talk softly, isn't it, Mark?"

"It's okay if we keep it down low, whispering like we are."

"Mark, how could I mess up my life so much that it takes a helicopter crash before I'm able to get sense enough to talk to you like this?"

"Join the club. My life's been one big foul-up ever since the accident with Jane and Bill. After that, it was Janet, and now ... now this."

"Don't talk that way, Mark."

"Brandy, it's obvious to me that you were in no danger until you got involved with me. Once we got involved ..."

"Are you trying to tell me that I am somehow cursed because I have become a serious part of your life?"

"I hate to believe in this kind of stuff, Brandy, but here we are. Together, trapped, and surrounded."

"Well I don't feel that way. Didn't you ever hear about the third time breaking the spell? I've found happiness for the first time in my life, Lieutenant Colonel Mark Buckley, US Army, and I'm not going to leave you—ever."

Mark was silent for a long time. Then he kissed her tenderly.

Brandy, more than a little dopey from the shot, imagined looking into Mark's eyes, hidden somewhere in the darkness, and said, "Here I am totally alone with you, in love with you, wanting you, you wanting me, and I can't even get my pants down to do something about it."

They both choked down their laughter trying to keep quiet. Both silently remembered their moments together, the night before.

Slowly, the morphine began to wear off and the pain started returning. Try as she might, Brandy could not keep from showing the agony.

Mark tried to comfort her, but he could feel in her trembling and tears that she was in pain beyond any words she could say. Without asking, he reached into her medical kit and felt for the familiar tubes of field-issue morphine. Quickly he prepared one and administered it. In a few minutes, she calmed down and a quiet sigh escaped her lips. She had fallen asleep.

Mark lay beside her, trying to collect his thoughts. He knew that in the morning there would be a really first-class rescue attempt. He was sure that Osborne and MACV would see to that.

473

Probably a squad or two of engineers, some medics, infantry. Whole nine yards.

All would land by chopper, make a swift pick-up and get the hell out. He noticed that the Huey and Cobra gunships were scrupulously avoiding their area in order to keep attention away from them. He wondered if some of the air units that were flying over had them covered with starlight scopes or the new low-light-level TV gear he had first heard about in a briefing by the ARPA folks a few months ago. Now and then, he could hear sporadic action in the direction of the Y Bridge, and flares were prevalent in that area.

But there was nothing he could do about that fight.

He was anchored here with Brandy. Where he belonged. Their lives were tied together from now on out. Slowly his eyes closed and his tired body gave in to sleep.

It was about an hour later that he awoke with a start. His trained ears had caught the sound of moving troops. Instantly he was alert. It took only a moment to realize that the enemy was moving in a major force for an all-out assault on Y Bridge at dawn. They were taking advantage of the fighting by the bridge, using that fight as a diversion while they organized for the major attack. There was the sound of men dragging heavy artillery pieces, and the endless shuffle of marching troops. The muffled commands changed the order of the sounds, and the chomp of shovels in dirt revealed that the troops were digging in.

At first, Mark was worried that the VC would try to utilize the wrecked Huey as a troop area or a gun position. Even if they passed close by, a spark from a sneaked cigarette could set off the fuel. As time passed, however, Mark finally decided that the area was too low and swampy to be a good position.

He listened to the enemy's preparations all through the night. By dawn, they would be very cleverly camouflaged. This would prevent effective air attack against their positions until the artillery barrage against Y Bridge was over and the assault was well under way.

As the eastern sky grew red and gold, Mark quietly awakened Brandy.

He immediately put his hand over her mouth and whispered, "Listen to me carefully. In the night, enemy troops have moved in—a lot of them. They are all around us, dug in and hidden. I don't know if they will be able to see us or not when it gets light."

He released his hand and kissed her. "Good morning, darling."

Mark fed her some water while he let her fully digest their situation.

"What do you plan to do?" Brandy whispered.

"As far as I can figure it, we have just been dealt the Joker. With all these troops around us—and I mean that they are really close—we cannot expect to be rescued. In fact, our chances of survival are pretty poor."

"Mark. That's it. Leave. Go right now! You have to."

"Look, I will never leave you, no matter what happens. Just put that out of your head."

"If you don't, I'll … I'll scream!"

Despite the seriousness of their situation, Mark smiled and suppressed a chuckle and kissed her.

"You just want me shot, don't you? That's what would happen if I moved from this spot. I wouldn't have a chance. Now look—in minutes it's going to be light. We don't know if we will be seen or not, but how do you feel about my getting on the radio and calling in an air strike?"

She was silent for a few moments.

"Would it do some good … before … we …"

"It will probably save the bridge, certainly the lives of a lot of our guys and maybe even the whole damn city."

"I'm with you, Mark, all the way. Just promise to hold me and kiss me again before it starts."

Now the red sky was turning to gold and Mark opened the radio link. When he described the numbers of troops in the area and the hopelessness of his own situation, MACV decided to reconnoiter the area with helicopters. In minutes, two Hueys were circling the area. Almost instantly, they were met with a furious wall of small-arms fire that came from hidden positions. Command was quick to appreciate Mark's estimate of the situation and, after ruling out all other alternatives, reluctantly agreed to Mark's plan.

The first F-100s, guided by Mark's direction, came in with a combination of 250-pound bombs and napalm. They reported that targets were not visible, but it was obvious that their munitions had found targets on the left flank of the enemy area.

Mark, on the radio, called in a correction to the strike point. He put down the handset and turned off the power to the radio. The little red light faded out.

Then he said to Brandy, "If it's napalm, suck in as much air as you can. If it's H.E. it won't make any difference."

Above her, shining in the sunlight, Brandy could see the aircraft.

Brandy Masters looked in his eyes and said, "Hold me. Hold me tight."

Mark Buckley thought about this beautiful woman who loved him. Then he hugged her and covered her lips with his.

It was napalm.

Epilogue

T he enemy attack failed at the Y Bridge.
  Then, the whole offensive slowly died. Saigon, the old whore,
had again withstood another assault on her decaying body and, though
she was scarred and bleeding, she was still alive and free.

As the Viet Cong and the NVA withdrew, they left behind hidden
caches of murderous 122 mm rockets. So, each night for weeks following the assault, the remaining VC assembled and fired these
weapons into the unfortunate city.

The aftermath of the ground offensive was devastating to the popu-
lace. In spite of a superhuman effort on the part of both Vietnamese
and American officials, the facilities dealing with the 100,000 new refugees were woefully inadequate. Over ten thousand more homes had
been destroyed. The camps, already bulging with victims of the Tet
Offensive, became overcrowded pestholes. The people, quiet in their
misery, still looked to the Americans for help.

Newell Osborne sat at his desk. He was emotionally and physically
exhausted.

*God almighty. I would like a rest. Get out of this place for a while. Stand off
and look at the whole mess from a distance. Get some kind of perspective. There's
that little place on Maui—beautiful beach. Let Grace and the boys meet me there.
Not possible now with Mark Buckley dead and Bill going stateside. I just can't leave.*

*I miss Mark more than I can say. He was a magnificent worker, but he was
also a loyal friend that I really counted on. His loss is a real tragedy to all of*

477

us. And that blond gal. At least Senator Masters took it well. Passed a Senate resolution declaring Brandy an American hero. Who would have thought that?

"Excuse me sir, will you be able to see us off?"

Bill Scott had entered the office. He knew that Newell Osborne was taking Mark's loss keenly. Bill had wanted to postpone his own rotation until both his and Mark's replacements were on board and well briefed, but Osborne would not have it. They had discussed this to the point of argument before Bill agreed to go ahead with the original plan.

"Of course I am going out to the plane. Actually, it's Mai Lei I'm going out to see off. How she gets along with that no-account, worthless GI husband of hers, I'll never understand."

"She is really long-suffering."

Bill smiled at Osborne's poor joke. It was good to see him at least try to shake his sadness.

"Bill, why don't you take my car and driver? It will be easier for you, what with all the luggage and Ông Bu."

"Great, sir, thanks very much. That would be a big help. But how about you? Shall I set up Sergeant Finletter with the small sedan?"

"Yes, why don't you? Then Finletter can take Bu home after you've gone."

"Terrific, sir. If it's okay with you, I think I'll head home. As you know, I have to be out at Tan Son Nhut two hours before departure."

"Right, Bill, I'll see you out there about three this afternoon. That will give us plenty of time to say goodbye."

Ψ   Ψ   Ψ

Dave and Red were the first in the long line of troops waiting to leave Vietnam at Tan Son Nhut.

Although they were still standing up, they were almost beyond fatigue. They had been celebrating their departure for the most of three days. Privately, each was looking forward to the long sleep flying home. It would be a good drying-out process. Right about then this seemed essential to them both.

Red looked up at the ceiling of the large terminal for the sixth time.

"God, they sure clobbered this place yesterday."

"Yeah, three GIs standin' right where we are now, their year over … They had made it and were processin' to go home when whammo! Your orders have been changed, dogface!"

The large gaping hole in the ceiling, the dormer windows all blown out, the shrapnel holes in the walls, were all mute evidence that Tan Son Nhut was still very much at war.

Red leaned over and spoke confidentially to Dave.

"You see, if they process you, and take your stuff and get it all inspected and all, you can go through that gate and go up in the restaurant and drink and eat and stuff."

"What kind of stuff?"

"Shut up and listen. If you're already processed, if the plane is late, you stay up there with all the comforts of home."

"Whose home?"

"Shut up and listen, you big-mouthed swabbie. But if you're still in line and the plane is late, they stop processin', and brother, you stay in line and no going upstairs."

There was a flurry of excitement at the end of the large terminal building. Both men followed the stares of the 200 men in the line.

"Well I'll be screwed! If it ain't Ba Thoa and three of her girls."

"Look! She brought Ta. Remember? She's the one lackin' in morals."

"It was your idea."

"No, it wasn't. It was hers. She called it 'in a sandwich,' only in French."

"It musta been the French that taught her. Hey, they're wavin' at us!"

They could hear the girls calling their names.

"I'll keep your place, Dave. Go over and tell Ba Thoa to go upstairs and get a table and order drinks. Got any money left?"

"No, and I ain't going over there. Every one of these guys knows those girls, real well."

479

"What do you care? They came out to see us off. It's the gentleman-ly thing to do. Here. Give Ba Thoa this 300 P and tell her I got more."

"That's what I been waiting for, your dough. But wait a minute. What about Kim and his bride? Think they will join us with those Côs?"

"Hell, yes. Kim knows 'em all and Kam does most everything he says."

Dave took off and headed for the girls, who were on the other side of the barrier. As he neared them, they all squealed and crowded around him.

There was whistling and shouts of approval from all the men in the processing line. Dave was embarrassed. Each girl kissed him with great fervor. Somehow, he managed to pass the money to Ba Thoa and give her Red's message before a Vietnamese policeman warned the girls that they could not talk to the Yankees while they were processing.

As Dave got back in line, the window opened and processing start-ed. MPs inspected their luggage for firearms, explosives, and even dirty pictures. Travel orders were stamped, shot records checked, tickets and gate passes issued. It was all over in ten minutes.

Now, revived by the girls' arrival, the large soldier and the small sailor bounded up the stairs to the restaurant.

Watching the two from farther back in the processing line was Poli De Salle. He had finished his year in Vietnam and was now returning to face Stephen K. Bromfield, President of Kingston University. The last month's work in Newell Osborne's office, from Poli's point of view, could, if cleverly handled, be passed off to the uninitiated as that of an advisor to the assistant ambassador.

He smiled at the thought of the informal notes with Osborne's sig-nature that he had pocketed. Osborne had the habit of writing short notes on a small notepad which had pages imprinted "From the Desk of Ambassador Newell Osborne." He attached the notes to studies and memoranda submitted to him.

During the month he had been in the office, Poli had acquired five of these personal notes. They were marked "Return to Sender" and clipped to original work. Usually the message was *Good work, let's get on this* or *I like this. See me and we will discuss.*

480

They were all signed, *Newell*.

Poli had never received any of these notes on his own work. However, the first one he found in a wastebasket gave him the idea that these could be valuable and took the others off old work papers he found in the files.

Poli's plan for these notes ranged from using them as prestige symbols for his desk to actually attaching them to papers he had yet to write. At this stage of the game, he was not worried about Stephen K. Bromfield.

Not at all.

He felt the sweat rolling down his back. The day was very warm and his white shirt was completely soaked. Every drop of sweat felt like it was an insect, and every time he thought of insects, he thought of those damned flesh-colored lizards. And his public humiliation.

Well, at least now I'll be away from those things forever.

He gazed out on the open front of the building and saw Newell's black sedan arrive.

Hey, that's Osborne's car. If I can see him for a second he might get me out of this line and over with the VIPs.

He watched Mai Lei, Bu, and Bill get out of the car and was very disappointed.

That damned stupid major with his slant-eyed wife isn't high ranking enough to get a free cup of coffee from the Salvation Army. How did he rate that car?

From behind him a deep voice yelled, "Get going up there in the line!"

Poli, watching Bill, had lagged behind.

"Whatsa matter civilian? You like it here and don't wanta go home?"

Poli grabbed his heavy bags and moved forward. He didn't see the pretty Air Force WAF who came up to Bill and offered a snappy salute.

"We have been expecting you, sir. The ambassador's office called and said you were to get the VIP treatment. How many bags do you have?"

Bu had already taken charge of the luggage. He had quelled the onrush of Vietnamese porters with a few well-chosen words. Now he selected two men and told them in no uncertain terms that they were each going to carry an honest load for once that day, and there would be no double charging. The chosen two grumbled, but managed to carry the bags over to the VIP staging area.

"As you know, we were shelled yesterday, sir. Consequently, our VIP lounge is completely out. The best I can offer you is the upstairs restaurant. Why don't you go on up while I take your papers and process you both out. Please leave the keys for your luggage."

"Thanks very much, miss. When the ambassador comes, will you direct him upstairs?"

Bill, Mai Lei, and Bu crossed the large, battered terminal, passed through the gates, and ascended the stairs to the restaurant. Bu, his little triumph over the porters completed, was pleased with himself. He was ready to sit in the cool restaurant and watch the big planes take off, heading to the four corners of the world.

As Bill and his family entered the restaurant, Kim and his wife arrived at the terminal in a taxi. The big Korean was carrying two packages, one each for Red and Dave. Kam led the way upstairs to the restaurant, where they spotted Red and Dave surrounded by Ba Thoa and her girls. At the sight of Kim, the girls stopped talking and looked first at Kam and back at the Korean. Kam had dressed carefully for this visit. Her choice was a peach-colored *ao dai* and white trousers. Her long hair was piled on top of her head, with several long strands of curls cascading down her back.

Red made the introductions and immediately all of the girls exercised their party manners and their talk became quiet and demure. Kim, on the other hand, became noisy and demonstrative with Red and Dave to hide his sadness over their departure.

He slapped Red on the back and said, "In twenty hours you'll be in land of Big PX. I guess you be lookin' for some big round-eye to sleep with!"

All the girls laughed and some hid their faces in their hands.

"You know it, Kim." Red was pulling up two chairs to the table for the new arrivals.

"Hey waiter, come on over here."

Dave was standing up in the crowded room, trying to catch the waiter's eye. Suddenly, Ba Thoa grabbed him by his white Navy jumper and pulled him down into his seat.

"Hey, what you doin'? How would you like it if I did it to you?"

"I would like!"

As the girls laughed, a waiter appeared and took the order.

"Colonel Uhm wouldn't like."

"Oh, he number ten. He go back to Korea. I never see again."

"How come you got to stay?" Red had turned to Kim. The mysteries of the Korean Army were beyond him.

"I got released from army and now in technical assistance group."

"How in hell you do that?"

"Don't worry, GI, it cost me plenty."

"Leave you enough to buy any trucks?"

"Oh, yes. Two big Dodge. Now come by boat. I already order them. Soon we really in business!"

"Say, that's great. Let's all drink to the new trucks."

Dave was on his feet and made all the men rise.

"To the trucks!"

Kim quickly poured the beer that the waiter had brought and joined Red and Dave.

"Isn't that the ambassador over there?"

Dave had noticed Newell Osborne arrive and quickly scan the room. They all followed his progress to the table where Bill, Mai Lei, and Bu were sitting.

Kim recognized Bill and Mai Lei.

"Look! That's Colonel Mark's friend."

"Mai Lei," murmured Kam. "We go see my friend. Come, Kim."

She turned to the girls. "We be back."

Newell was seated when Kim and Kam arrived at the table. The friends were glad to meet again, but seeing each other brought back the sadness of Mark's death, which hung like a dark cloud over their happiness.

Kim especially was eager for more details of Mark.

"Major Bill, when I read the paper about Colonel Mark I feel again like my own father died. Why he go there, Major Bill?"

"Kim, I know how you feel. Mark was close to all of us sitting here. But you must always remember that there are people in this world who like to help others. They get their happiness this way. Mark was one of those people. He was helping another person when he died. Therefore he died doing what he wanted."

"Maybe Saigon now be Ho Chi Minhsville if not Colonel Mark bring in airplane."

Kam, normally shy among a group of Americans, was proud of Mark. She was quoting Kim.

Newell was glad that someone like Kam thought that way of Mark. He hoped many Vietnamese felt the same way. He smiled at Kam and said, "Madame Kim, you just may be right about that. He was a very brave man."

Newell thought back to his impulse to get Mark Buckley a medal for his sacrifice at the bridge. But Mark hadn't been part of any combat command at the end. Only a staff officer. And one relieved from a combat command under cloudy circumstances. That made things tricky. Bill Scott finally convinced him that Mark wouldn't have wanted a medal in any case. Newell dropped the matter with some regret. Making his story known as widely as possible seemed the best tribute.

In the years to come, some staff officers would routinely recommend each other for Bronze Stars and other decorations for much lesser things, but not then.

While Kam and Mai Lei spoke of their own plans, Kim explained to the men about his trucking business, which he had organized in Kam's name. He also spoke of his new status of technical advisor to the South Korean Army Command.

"You wait and see, Koreans will help Vietnam become strong like US helped Korea become strong."

"Well, it looks as if you have gotten off to a good start," said Newell, privately hoping for the best for this young couple, as Kim and his wife said goodbye.

After the two had returned to Dave and Red, Newell turned to Bu and said in French, "There goes your new Vietnam."

Bu was happy to discover that Ông Osborne was fluent in French, as he had long wished to talk to him, but was reluctant about speaking English. Eagerly he broke into French.

"Perhaps you are right. We sometimes forget that with all the horror, some good things have come out of all this."

"That's right. It's not all bad. You have a new prime minister. Perhaps ..."

"Perhaps, perhaps, perhaps. Americans feel that by feeding us the right combination of American ingredients, you can make into little Americans. You forget that Asia was Asia long before there was even one savage on the whole continent of America. It is too bad that you can't sometimes think there must be another way to do things besides the American way. Over here your methods are as foreign to us as our ways would be in some place such as Chicago."

Newell suddenly thought of Janet.

That's what she used to say in her gentle way, and Mark used to say that everything in Vietnam that was done with American help had to be done in the American way.

"The problem, Ông Bu, is that we only know our own way of doing things. We couldn't help you very much if we tried to switch."

"You have been here over eleven years. By proper schooling, you could have learned our way and we could have learned yours. Our six-year-olds are now seventeen. Our young *lycée* graduates could, by this time, know your methods and be able to help us to help ourselves. But no. You would not teach our young people. Instead, we are expected immediately to take up your equipment and use it—your way. Then, we are unable to perform efficiently. So you shove us out of the way and say, 'You don't know what you're doing. Here, let me do it.' After this, my people are merely inclined to sit back.

"We are Asian. We must use Asian ways to make our place in the world. It's not that we don't appreciate what you have tried to do for us. You have, so far, saved us from the darkness of Communism which, I might say, is another product of your Western culture, not ours.

"But even you must admit that in the overall business of winning the war you have failed. You failed when winning would have been so easy."

Bu paused and sipped his hot tea. He wanted to make sure Newell Osborne would get his major point, and to make sure of this, he was going to make him ask for it.

Bill looked at his watch. About twenty minutes to go, twenty minutes to sweat out. He held Mai Lei's hand. His thoughts were 9,000 miles away in his homeland with his new bride. Away from the seemingly impossible political and military situation that entangled South Vietnam. He was glad Bu was having this chance to talk with Newell. He had wanted the ambassador to hear Bu's position—his thoughts and ideas—because they seemed to be coming from the hearts of all Vietnamese, a place where Americans rarely had a glimpse or ever gained entrance.

The distant public-address loudspeaker announced another aircraft departure. The sound triggered the restlessness of most of the Americans in the restaurant because they were all waiting for one special flight, the one that would take them back home.

Finally, Newell Osborne said, "Well, Ông Bu, after making a statement like that, it isn't fair not to elaborate."

He was careful to conceal the edge of sarcasm in his voice because he knew the old man was sincere.

Bu looked Newell Osborne directly in the eye. There was a faint smile on his face.

"Only once in modern times have the Western people handled a vanquished Asian nation properly. That was at the end of World War II. Now, from twenty-five years away, we feel that the westerners must have acted properly in that case only by accident. At least they have never again used such good insight and judgment.

"The secret of winning over here is that we Asians understand nothing as well as we understand force. To use kindness against one's enemies is, to us, a sign of weakness. In our culture, the loser must be brought to his knees and then trampled. He expects that. He is contemptuous of any show of compassion or kindness. If he has been beaten, he expects to be killed—or at least placed in servitude. To do anything else with him is an insult to his honor. He has fought hard with all his will, with all his abilities. Can you understand the face that he loses when you, as the victor, only offer kindness?

"Each time you back away from the war the enemy thinks he has had another victory. The Tet Offensive is a very good example. The individual VC or North Vietnamese soldier thinks he has won a great victory because you paused the bombing right after crushing them in battle.

"Now you are doing the same thing in Paris. You are going to the bargaining table weak—weaker each time you make another concession. Yet you wonder why the Northern enemy does not make similar concessions! Why should he? He wins more and more just by sitting there and sneering at you every time you offer your latest manifestation of weakness."

"You are saying that our cultural traits are not compatible with your more ... ah ..."

"Realistic may be a good word here," interjected Bu.

"All right, your realistic point of view."

"Yes. You Americans try to fool yourselves into thinking that you are, perhaps, more civilized than we Asians, and therefore can fight a more civilized war. How naive you are! All races are human, but humans are but animals with the animal tendencies and traits. The veneer of civilization is thinly stretched over all of us, no matter what color."

"Well, Ông Bu," Newell smiled, "Your views certainly differ from ours about everything we've done so far. But tell me, how do things look for us now? Have we broken the back of the NLF and the VC?"

Bu smiled briefly but it was obvious to Newell that the answer would not be to his liking.

"As I tell the so few Americans that I am able to talk to, this is a people's war. In your country, the leaders don't seem to understand this and they are making a big mistake. In America, it is only a politicians' war. The difference is very large. Your leaders turn the war on and off like a water faucet for their own reasons without regard to the situation over here. Hanoi on the other hand, has organized the people of the North and many here in the South to fight as long as victory requires. Your people in the US have never been convinced that this war was worth the deaths of their finest young people. Therefore, to win you should have performed a quick, complete war with victory before your people became hostile to it. Now it's too late. Now, your people have at last stepped in—but not on our side—not to help us. Those wild demonstrations in your country are aiding the North. How can you win now?

"The sad part is that although, as the young woman has said, Colonel Mark kept Saigon from becoming Ho Chi Minh's city, it will probably come to that, someday, after you Americans leave."

The loudspeaker boomed with the boarding announcement for Bill and Mai Lei's stateside flight, negating any chance Newell had to answer Bu's thesis. The whoop of joy from Red and Dave was heard all over the restaurant, and brought smiles even to the faces of those who were to be left behind.

Bu grasped his daughter's hand. He spoke in Vietnamese, "Be a good American, daughter."

Tears came to Mai Lei's eyes, but she smiled.

"Now, Father, please don't be too hard on your new housekeeper."

"Don't worry, Mai Lei. She's a young, pretty woman." He laughed, "Maybe I will marry and start a new family!"

Per the ambassador's request, Bill and Mai Lei were loaded with the VIP crowd, and Bu was allowed to go aboard the long, "stretched" Douglas DC-8 jet.

The lines of soldiers and sailors slowly ascended the loading stairs. Red and Dave turned at the top and waved to Kim and Kam, then gave a special wave to Ba Thoa and her girls. They were all crying.

"It is very sad," said Kim. "All at once, I find father and two brothers, then father and two brothers go away."

"You also find wife."

"Good wife. Number one." He smiled down at her.

Bu again said goodbye to Bill and Mai Lei. Then he and Newell left the plane. The doors were closed and the jet taxied into position for takeoff. There was one last flurry of waves and goodbyes. Newell noticed tears in Bu's eyes.

He said, "Come with me. I will take you home."

"Thank you, Ông Osborne. Perhaps you will honor me by staying for some lotus blossom tea?"

Newell knew he could ill afford the time, but out of consideration for the old man's loneliness, he accepted the invitation.

"It would be my pleasure."

As the aircraft gained altitude, Mai Lei watched her country slip away under the wing. Her thoughts were of her father, her friends, and her mother, long gone, long ago.

Bill was also thinking of friends–dead friends–Mark, and in the end, Brandy. He wondered if the cost of their lives had been worth it. Behind him, he heard a soldier's voice. It was Red.

"Damn. We made it. We're on our way home. A whole damn year."

"Hell, I know, it was a year out of my life."

"What yer going to tell anyone back in the world about all of this?" Red asked, suddenly becoming quite serious.

Dave looked at his friend with questioning eyes. This was a new role for Red, talking seriously to him for the first time. He thought about his answer for a moment.

"Red, you 'n me, we're just regulars and we go where they tell us and do what they tell us. No one's ever going to ask us what we think about it. When we weren't scared, we played everything for laughs 'cause we knew we were stuck. Stuck for a year in a place we shouldn't be in, fightin' a war we sure can't win the way we're fightin' it.

"So what the hell! We worked our asses off as we figured out that the whole thing was nuts, and partied our asses off every chance we got to keep from blowin' our stacks. How could you explain all that and every fuckin' thing we saw to some dumb asshole drinkin' next to you at a bar, who's never been here, doesn't care, and wishes it would go away? Even if he asked in the first place."

"Well ... we could tell about the girls," Dave replied.

"Yes, yes ... that we could."

The End

AFTERWORD

The day I turned seventeen, my father was aboard a C-130 gunship on a mission over Laos and South Vietnam.

The story of *Wilderness of Tigers* began a year earlier, in the summer of 1967.

I got my driver's license. My father was forty-nine, and a professional soldier. He went off to war. His third.

When he came home, over a year later, he wrote this book. He had changed, I had changed, and the America he had travelled so far away from, again, to fight for, again, had changed forever.

Context counts. Those were serious and dangerous times and everyone knew it. A very short list of current events includes the Six-Day Arab-Israeli War, race riots in American cities, nuclear war always minutes away, the USS Pueblo seized, assassinations, and the Vietnam War.

A more complete timeline of this amazing period is in **Appendix One**.

This era had its own soundtrack. Some of the top tunes played on the radio were brand new cuts (not tracks then) by Lulu, the Doors, the Association, the Monkees, the Beatles, the Rascals, Frankie Valli, Cream, Aretha Franklin, Sam and Dave, the Rolling Stones, Van Morrison, Janis Joplin, and so many more.

See **Appendix Two** for the complete Top Fifty for 1967-68. A rich variety of sounds that still play today, over forty-five years later.

National news magazines such as Time and Newsweek were thick and had extensive world reporting. People read newspapers, which had large reporting staffs with only a very few "pundits" who were actually older reporters who had seen a few things in their time and been places. There were only three TV networks and a scruffy, nascent thing called PBS.

491

A new media, called cable TV, had a channel that featured an automated camera panning back and forth among a clock, a thermometer, and a barometer. Occasionally some soul, off screen, would place a card in a slot that had an advertising pitch written on it. Some *Weather Channel*.

There was really only one phone company. AT&T controlled it all. Most everyone hated them. Okay, they left a few tiny spots here and there to some others to show to the Feds that they really weren't a monopoly. Didn't work out.

Premium gas, 100 octane, was thirty-three cents per gallon. A pack of top-brand cigarettes cost the same. And everyone smoked. Everywhere. All the time. Airlines gave out free cigarettes and chewing gum to passengers.

The world of 1967-68 must seem like an ancient and primitive civilization to anyone under thirty.

When my father returned from Vietnam, it was a difficult time in our house. I had been driving and actively dating for over a year. My hair was a tiny bit longer, but to him it was hugely long, as he would remind me often. This became a frequent cause of loud conflict. Many, many years later, I showed him period pictures of me. He publically apologized, emotionally and immediately. It was a big moment for the two of us. So much unsaid had been wrapped up in that. Only now, I realize it was a symbol of so many larger things for him.

But back in 1968, he was withdrawn and suspicious of the country to which he had returned. He felt that he and his comrades and their allies had been betrayed. He was suspicious of me, too.

I remember buying a two-inch-wide belt that had an open, simple, circular metal belt buckle. Looked pretty good with my black Levi jeans.

Pop took one look at it and demanded to know "What does that stand for? What does that mean?"

It was only a belt.

There was anger just below the surface that had never been there before. Today we would use the term Post Traumatic Stress Disorder, or PTSD. Unknown then.

Then he started writing this book.

When Pop would return home at night from his new post at the Pentagon, he would head upstairs to his home office and work on *The Book*. He did not discuss it with my mother or me. We knew better than to ask. I would not enter his now-private space unless bidden.

Sometimes I got glimpses of maps taped to the walls. *Saigon*. There were stacks of DOD-published materials.

Slowly over about a year, the man my father was started to return. The humor, laughter, and warmth I loved so much came back. Then *The Book* was done. He put it away. We never directly spoke of it.

Years later, in the late 1970s, he revisited it and spent many hours doing a rewrite with the idea of publishing it. Sadly, this never came to pass.

At that time, we had several conversations that I knew were really about *The Book*. He asked me for titles of contemporary popular fiction that had effective writing in certain areas. I offered a list. We later discussed several of them over drinks on occasions when he and I would be on a guys' trip to the old family ranch in Sonoma, California.

These memories came in handy, decades later, when I worked on his manuscript. I felt I had a good idea where and what he wanted to add, amplify, and expand, but could not find his way.

Pop passed away in 1992. My mom, four years later.

A poor photocopy of *The Book* surfaced when I cleaned out their house. Some years later, I decided to read it. Took a bit of nerve, given the history it had with me.

I found it an exciting tale with unusual characters in compelling circumstances. My Pop had written a terrific, even epic, adventure novel. He meant this book to be an entertaining and lively read. I found it so. I was intrigued.

I decided to use a bit of the expensive education that my folks had provided for me to add those things Pop had left hanging years before. In addition, I created and expanded the backstories of the major characters and of the 1967-68 time period.

Pop was an avid reader with a large personal library that followed us wherever his career took him. He had a particular affection for the *Alexandria Quartet* novels of Laurence Durrell. Perhaps he saw his Saigon in that way, full of an exciting blend of cultures, intrigues, and passions.

Before she died, my mom shared stories about Pop's time in Vietnam. As I read the manuscript, I realized that at least one of his adventures and the risks he had taken had become scenes in the story.

In **Appendix Three,** a summary of his career will contain recounts of some of these.

My father was a soldier. He was a wonderful storyteller. He had a deep and wonderful sense of humor. He was fiercely loyal to his friends and allies. He was a patriot. He was a realist. His life experience had taken him from small to large places and the widest possible range of people and circumstances. Top to bottom.

For my part, I have tried to bring all of my life's experiences to the characters in the story, where appropriate. To all those over the years who, unknowingly, provided me colorful, rich, and *boo koo* source material, I say thank you.

A special thanks to my wife, Kathleen Guild Arnold, who spent many, many days editing my draft of the manuscript. Her advice, as always, was flawless and indispensable. Her son, Ambrose Stevens, high on the short list for the title of *World's Greatest EMT,* and the one you want with you when your life is on the line, provided key medical knowledge.

My oldest friend, Bill Depuy, spent many hours of his time, which is in much demand in matters of the Nation's business, reading and providing extensive notes, pinpoint analysis, and annotations. He has his own family story intertwined with the history of the Vietnam War and takes the subject seriously. Thanks, Bill. *Cheers!*

However, this is a work of fiction, not a documentary.

Any errors here are all my own, not Kathy's, not Ambrose's, not Bill's, and not my father's.

Fate did not allow Pop to be here with me for the final draft, but I felt he was always somewhere close by, keeping a friendly eye on me and showing me the way.

Thanks, Pop. You are, as always, the hero of my life.

Robert Bruce Arnold
Sonoma, CA
June, 2014

APPENDIX ONE

Return now to the thrilling days of yesteryear ...

1967–1968

Super Bowl I
JFK conspiracy theories ramp up
Boeing 737 takes its first flight
Large demonstrations against the Vietnam War start in major cities
Greece ruled by military junta after a coup
Expo '67 opens in Montreal
Elvis Presley is married
Arab-Israeli Six-Day War happens
Biafra–Nigeria civil war begins in Africa
Beatles release their *Sgt. Pepper's Lonely Hearts Club Band* album
Monterey Pop Festival takes place in California
Red China tests first hydrogen bomb
John Coltrane dies
Pope Paul VI ordains cardinals, including the future John Paul II
Summer of Love in San Francisco
Race riots begin in one American city after another, including Washington,
    D.C.
Father of the atomic bomb, Dr. Robert Oppenheimer dies
Coup in the Congo
The Doors defy censors on the *Ed Sullivan* TV show by using the word
    "higher"
Che Guevara captured and killed
John McCain is shot down over North Vietnam
British troops clash with Red Chinese over the future of Hong Kong

Rhodesia passes apartheid laws

Eugene McCarthy runs for president

First heart transplant

Term "black hole" used by science for the first time

USS Pueblo seized by North Korea

Winter Olympics in Grenoble

LBJ mandates that all computers purchased by the US government
    support ASCII character coding

Robert Kennedy enters race for president

LBJ announces he won't run for reelection

2001: A Space Odyssey premieres in Washington, D.C. (My mom and I
    see it first run in that theater)

Planet of the Apes movie is released

Martin Luther King, Jr. is assassinated

Black Panther shootout in Oakland

Musical *Hair* opens on Broadway

Robert Kennedy is assassinated

Beatles create Apple Records

US Navy nuclear submarine *Scorpion* sinks

Intel Corporation is founded

US explodes its largest hydrogen bomb to date

Pope Paul VI condemns birth control

France explodes its first hydrogen bomb

60 Minutes debuts on CBS

Olympics held in Mexico City features Black Power demonstration by
    US athletes

Jackie Kennedy marries Aristotle Onassis

Richard Nixon is elected president

Yale admits women

The Zodiac killer active in the San Francisco Bay area

Apollo 8 orbits the moon—takes the most amazing photo in history, up
    to then

The Khmer Rouge forms in Cambodia

and the Vietnam War ...

APPENDIX TWO

The Soundtrack of the Period

This is a compilation from various sources.
See where the tunes you remember, or the ones played frequently today, placed back then.

Top 50, 1967

1. *To Sir with Love*, Lulu
2. *Light My Fire*, The Doors
3. *Windy*, The Association
4. *The Letter*, The Box Tops
5. *Ode to Billie Joe*, Bobbie Gentry
6. *Daydream Believer*, The Monkees
7. *Happy Together*, The Turtles
8. *Somethin' Stupid*, Nancy Sinatra and Frank Sinatra
9. *I Heard It through the Grapevine*, Gladys Knight & The Pips
10. *Incense and Peppermints*, Strawberry Alarm Clock
11. *Groovin'*, The Young Rascals
12. *Can't Take My Eyes off You*, Frankie Valli
13. *Respect*, Aretha Franklin
14. *Little Bit o' Soul*, The Music Explosion
15. *The Rain, the Park & Other Things*, The Cowsills
16. *Never My Love*, The Association
17. *Hello Goodbye*, The Beatles
18. *Tell It Like It Is*, Aaron Neville
19. *Come Back When You Grow Up*, Bobby Vee
20. *I Was Made to Love Her*, Stevie Wonder
21. *I Second That Emotion*, Smokey Robinson & The Miracles

22. *Sweet Soul Music*, Arthur Conley

23. *I Think We're Alone Now*, Tommy James & The Shondells

24. *Expressway to Your Heart*, Soul Survivors

25. *Apples, Peaches, Pumpkin Pie*, Jay & The Techniques

26. *Love Is Here and Now You're Gone*, The Supremes

27. *Kind of a Drag*, The Buckinghams

28. *Boogaloo Down Broadway*, The Fantastic Johnny C

29. *Soul Man*, Sam and Dave

30. *Georgy Girl*, The Seekers

31. *A Whiter Shade of Pale*, Procol Harum

32. *Ruby Tuesday*, The Rolling Stones

33. *I Say a Little Prayer*, Dionne Warwick

34. *All You Need Is Love*, The Beatles

35. *The Happening*, The Supremes

36. *Come On Down to My Boat*, Every Mother's Son

37. *Please Love Me Forever*, Bobby Vinton

38. *For What It's Worth (Stop, Hey What's That Sound)*, Buffalo Springfield

39. *Reflections*, Diana Ross & The Supremes

40. *Dedicated to the One I Love*, The Mamas and the Papas

41. *Release Me (And Let Me Love Again)*, Engelbert Humperdinck

42. *San Francisco (Be Sure to Wear Flowers in Your Hair)*, Scott McKenzie

43. *It Must Be Him*, Vikki Carr

44. *I Got Rhythm*, The Happenings

45. *Good Thing*, Paul Revere & The Raiders

46. *This Is My Song*, Petula Clark

47. *Up-Up and Away*, 5th Dimension

48. *There's a Kind of Hush*, Herman's Hermits

49. *Then You Can Tell Me Goodbye*, The Casinos

50. *Penny Lane*, The Beatles

Top 50, 1968

1. *Hey Jude*, The Beatles

2. *I Heard It through the Grapevine*, Marvin Gaye

3. *Love Child*, Diana Ross & The Supremes

4. *Love Is Blue*, Paul Mauriat

5. *Honey*, Bobby Goldsboro

6. *Sittin' on the Dock of the Bay*, Otis Redding

7. *People Got To Be Free*, The Rascals

8. *This Guy's in Love with You*, Herb Alpert

9. *Judy in Disguise (With Glasses)*, John Fred & His Playboy Band

10. *Woman, Woman*, Gary Puckett & The Union Gap

11. *Mrs. Robinson*, Simon & Garfunkel

12. *Who's Making Love*, Johnnie Taylor

13. *Hello, I Love You*, The Doors

14. *Tighten Up*, Archie Bell & The Drells

15. *Harper Valley PTA*, Jeannie C. Riley

16. *Young Girl*, Gary Puckett & The Union Gap

17. *Those Were the Days*, Mary Hopkin

18. *Little Green Apples*, O.C. Smith

19. *The Good, the Bad and the Ugly*, Hugo Montenegro

20. *Bend Me, Shape Me*, American Breed

21. *Cry Like a Baby*, The Box Tops

22. *Magic Carpet Ride*, Steppenwolf

23. *Green Tambourine*, The Lemon Pipers

24. *Midnight Confessions*, The Grass Roots

25. *For Once in My Life*, Stevie Wonder

26. *It's a Beautiful Morning*, The Rascals

27. *Spooky*, Classics IV

28. *Abraham, Martin and John*, Dion

29. *Stoned Soul Picnic*, 5th Dimension

30. *Chain of Fools*, Aretha Franklin

31. *Mony Mony*, Tommy James & The Shondells

32. *Cowboys to Girls*, The Intruders

33. *Classical Gas*, Mason Williams

34. *I Love How You Love Me*, Bobby Vinton

35. *The Ballad of Bonnie and Clyde*, Georgie Fame

36. *I've Gotta Get a Message to You*, Bee Gees

37. *Grazing in the Grass*, Hugh Masekela

38. *Angel of the Morning*, Merrilee Rush & The Turnabouts

39. *Fire*, Crazy World of Arthur Brown

40. *(Theme From) Valley of the Dolls*, Dionne Warwick
41. *Born to Be Wild*, Steppenwolf
42. *The Horse*, Cliff Nobles & Co.
43. *Lady Willpower*, Gary Puckett & The Union Gap
44. *Slip Away*, Clarence Carter
45. *I Wish It Would Rain*, The Temptations
46. *Jumpin' Jack Flash*, The Rolling Stones
47. *Light My Fire*, Jose Feliciano
48. *(Sweet, Sweet Baby) Since You've Been Gone*, Aretha Franklin
49. *La-La Means I Love You*, The Delfonics
50. *Girl Watcher*, The O'Kaysions

APPENDIX THREE

The singular career of W. Bruce Arnold, Colonel, USAF.

My father was the descendent of many soldiers. One of our ancestors served at Valley Forge with George Washington. Another, a Union soldier, survived the Battle of Gettysburg. Two relatives died in the Civil War's notorious Andersonville Prison.

Pop's grandfather served as a US Army doctor during the Spanish-American War. His father, my grandfather, was a West Point graduate and ended his career as one of only nine ever to wear the Five Star rank in the US Armed Forces. But that is a tale for the next book.

Colonel Arnold attended both the Naval Academy and the Military Academy at West Point. Not as a visiting cadet at either, but fully admitted student at each.

Between the two academy periods, he was an enlisted trooper in the US Cavalry. George Patton's horse cavalry. That would be the *Brave Rifles*, the Army's Third Cavalry Regiment.

He graduated from West Point in the class of 1943. In those war years, the academy graduated two classes per year.

He trained with the US Coastal Artillery Corps, now long defunct, and qualified on the huge "disappearing guns" at Fortress Monroe, Virginia. That's not a typo. This historic installation is known today as Fort Monroe.

Colonel Arnold qualified Expert with the .45 Colt, the .50 machine gun, and field artillery, and wore those badges.

For a time in World War II, he wore a US Marine uniform during the brutal Okinawa campaign.

So far, that's Navy Midshipman, Army Trooper, West Point Cadet, regular Army, and US Marine uniforms.

501

Colonel Arnold ended World War II in Army artillery and quickly moved into the world of missiles, including the fabled JB-2 American buzz bomb. He transitioned to the newly formed US Air Force following his father's wishes and joined the early ballistic missile program at its beginning in Englewood, California as one of the "Schoolhouse Gang" under old Arnold family friend and Air Force legend, General Bernard Schriever.

Add a blue US Air Force uniform. That takes the total to six.

He retired in 1973 from the United States Air Force proudly wearing a Command Missileman's Badge.

My father spent his career in high tech. Considering his early days riding horses for Colonel George Patton's cavalry, that was quite a leap.

Along the way, his love of music led him to learning to play the concertina. One of these always traveled with him across the globe. He easily made friends both in the drawing rooms of power and in taverns by breaking it out and playing a tune or two.

During 1967-68, the period of this novel, Colonel Arnold was DARPA's man in South Vietnam. He was the head of its Research and Development Field Unit (RDFU-V) based in Saigon. His program responsibilities ranged far and wide: social science studies, psyops, weapons testing, technology for the POW search, support for certain intelligence operations, and much more. He was in the thick of the search for a cure to the M-16's early problems.

He knew and managed many Dr. Poli De Salles as well.

I met one of these "characters," years later. He told me of my father's "silly insistence" of accounting for and controlling top secret documents entrusted to his Saigon unit. During a war, of course, in a war zone. Silly? Sorry, Pop took such things very seriously.

Pop told me stories about the USAID folks in Saigon. These became part of the *Tigers* saga. My father was a soldier at war. A lot of the others in Saigon he met and worked with were doing something else.

Colonel Arnold operated on both high and low levels, participating in meetings with General Westmoreland (these often did not go well), as well as flying fire support missions for first-hand weapons testing.

Two of these stand out, though he did not speak of them often or in any detail, but his log survives, as do some of the letters he wrote my mother.

Mission: June 7, 1968 – Korat. 7.5 Hours. EC-121. North Vietnam and back. Combat.

Late in life, my father told me about this entry. DARPA stuffed an EC-121 (that was a vintage, four-engine, slow-flying, propeller-driven aircraft) with technical equipment and sent it off into the night over North Vietnam. Manned by technicians and my father, they orbited and tried to draw the North Vietnamese into firing surface-to-air missiles at them.

Then, as the SAMs homed in on the EC-121, the crew would tinker with the equipment, trying out various jamming scenarios. One person called out the range as the SAM neared and whether it began to veer off. Must have been a bit exciting. All this was in aid of developing new EW for US strike aircraft that were not doing well against NVN's air defenses.

Pop's log shows that the next day, he hopped into a new C-130 gunship (a successor to the original C-47 "Spooky" that appears in the prologue of this book) and headed off for a 4.5-hour mission over Laos and the Ho Chi Minh Trail. These gunships continue to serve today, in more sophisticated models, supporting US Special Operations Forces in faraway places. *Don't go sneaking around without one on call* ...

Also during this period, he flew numerous fire support missions in Hueys. First-hand testing of rockets and guns in actual combat.

My father was a soldier. There was a war going on.

The other event, and one that is reflected in this novel, is somewhat different and one that I would learn about only after he passed away. My mother told the story to me.

Part of Colonel Arnold's portfolio was support to the search for and possible rescue of US POWs. This and certain other activities led him into the circle of one Father Hoc, a shadowy figure, a Vietnamese Jesuit priest, educated at Boston College and from a "well-connected" Vietnamese family.

I know of several Father Hoc adventures, but this one stands out.

Father Hoc came to my father in Saigon and told him this story. A rogue VC unit had an American prisoner and would turn him over to a US officer for cash. But, that officer must be alone and come to a certain spot up a certain river at a certain hour, in the dark. Father Hoc's friends, who lived in the shadows of both sides, would hold the money until the transaction had taken place. Black-market friends? Like Qui in *Tigers*? Perhaps.

Colonel Arnold trusted Father Hoc, so off he went. He obtained a small boat from his ARVN friends and, armed with only his personal World War II vintage Colt .45 automatic, went off into the night. Before going, he wrote my mother a goodbye letter to be posted if he did not return.

Much like Lieutenant Colonel Mark Buckley, he journeyed small rivers and canals and finally came to the appointed spot, tied up, and got out onto the riverbank and waited. Hours went by. To his disappointment, no one appeared, and finally as dawn started to break, he left. When I first read this section of the manuscript, I knew that some of the Ted Holden rescue attempt had to be from that adventure. The swimming scene was all Pop. Must be true.

He never spoke of it, though his efforts in the search for missing POWs continued for much of the remainder of his life. The relationship with Father Hoc lasted through a final chapter during the fall of Saigon in 1975.

Colonel Arnold worked well with his Vietnamese allies. He earned their respect in a way similar to Mark Buckley in the novel. At the end of his tour in 1968, he received from the government of South Vietnam the National Order (Knight) of Vietnam. You don't see a lot of those.

The character of Kim, the Korean corporal, must come directly from his experience in the occupation of Korea from 1945-47. This was prior to the official Korean War, but as he often mentioned, this did not stop the "bandits from the North" coming south to shoot at him and his men. Mom remembered riding in a Jeep to go shopping along with a GI escort carrying a Thompson submachine gun.

The first of many undeclared wars, post WWII, for the US? Probably. But no one was paying attention.

In 1969, Pop witnessed the takeoff of Apollo 11's fight to the moon at the Cape, where he had launched missiles so many years before. Brought me home a mission patch.

Colonel Arnold, after retiring from the USAF, spent many years as the Washington representative for a high-tech company. During this time, he and my mother traveled widely and enjoyed their years together.

No longer did he leave alone before dawn for faraway places and then return weeks later, late in the night, as he had so often done in his Air Force days. Many new friends knew him as the man who played the concertina.

His volunteer role as a key player in the securing of long-delayed Veterans' rights for the Women Airforce Service Pilots (WASPs) of World War II brought him much satisfaction, even at the risk of his private-sector career.

Finally, in 1986, Pop, Mom, and I started Chandelle Winery in Sonoma, California.

In 1992, he passed away in the city of his birth, Washington, D.C., and was buried near his parents and two of his brothers in Arlington National Cemetery. My mother, Barbara, joined him there in 1996.

At the standing-room-only funeral service at Fort Meyer, Virginia, where he had once ridden army horses so long ago, Bruce Arnold was celebrated as a wonderful man, full of life and great humor. He was a fiercely loyal friend, self-sacrificing, and a true professional soldier.

Horses, missiles, Navy, Army, Marines, Air Force, author, traveling musician, winery owner.

A singular life and career.